PRAISE FOR *SPUTNIK'S CHILDREN*

The Globe 100 Best Books of 2017
Shortlisted for the Sunburst Award 2018
Longlisted for Canada Reads 2020

"It is a book so full of feeling, I thought that my heart would explode as I read it. I loved it. It comes with humour, insight and Cold War nostalgia as well. It's a really great novel."
— CBC's *Ontario Morning*

"A noodle-bending literary sci-fi novel that puts its hero in the box with Schrödinger's cat." — *Kirkus Reviews*

"Funny, touching, genre-bending and one-of-a-kind, this is an exuberant romp of a novel that is nonetheless unafraid of serious subjects." — *Publishers Weekly*

"You'll love weaving your way through Debbie's lorazepam-and-martini-induced memories in this genre-bending ode to the unreliable narrator, with a touch of Cold War–era nostalgia thrown in for good measure." — *Canadian Living*

"Sputnik Chick's origin story is fun — a twist on pop culture and Cold War nostalgia, well paced with zero slack . . . Debbie is the girl with no past — a tragic fate; but for a character, an interesting place to start." — *Globe and Mail*

"*Sputnik's Children* is one of those rare novels that starts out as one thing, and ends up being something else altogether — an impressive high-wire act that is also a cracking good story."
— *Quill & Quire*

ALSO BY TERRI FAVRO

The Proxy Bride

Once Upon a Time in West Toronto

Sputnik's Children

*Generation Robot: A Century of Science Fiction,
Fact, and Speculation*

THE SISTERS
SPUTNIK

THE SISTERS SPUTNIK

A NOVEL

TERRI FAVRO

Published by ECW Press
665 Gerrard Street East
Toronto, Ontario, Canada M4M 1Y2
416-694-3348 / info@ecwpress.com

Cover artwork and interior illustrations by Andrew Presutto

LIBRARY AND ARCHIVES CANADA CATALOGUING IN PUBLICATION

Title: The sisters Sputnik : a novel / Terri Favro.

Names: Favro, Terri, author.

Identifiers: Canadiana (print) 20210381825 | Canadiana (ebook) 20210381884

ISBN 978-1-77041-608-6 (softcover)
ISBN 978-1-77305-907-5 (ePub)
ISBN 978-1-77305-908-2 (PDF)
ISBN 978-1-77305-909-9 (Kindle)

Classification: LCC PS8611.A93 S57 2022 | DDC C813/.6—dc23

This book is funded in part by the Government of Canada. *Ce livre est financé en partie par le gouvernement du Canada.* We acknowledge the support of the Canada Council for the Arts. *Nous remercions le Conseil des arts du Canada de son soutien.* We acknowledge the support of the Ontario Arts Council (OAC), an agency of the Government of Ontario, which last year funded 1,965 individual artists and 1,152 organizations in 197 communities across Ontario for a total of $51.9 million. We also acknowledge the support of the Government of Ontario through Ontario Creates.

PRINTED AND BOUND IN CANADA

PRINTING: MARQUIS   5 4 3 2 1

MIX
Paper from responsible sources
FSC® C103567

For Ron, and all the storytellers
who've shaped us both

"I'm impatient with stupidity. My people have learned to live without it."

Klaatu, *The Day the Earth Stood Still* (1951)

"I may be synthetic, but I'm not stupid."

Bishop, *Aliens* (1986)

"... in American history, panic about technological change is almost always tangled up with panic about immigration."

Jill Lepore, *The New Yorker* (2019)

Unicorn Girl and I stumble our way out of the woods on the shortest day of the year. We've been in the shadows of giant hemlocks for so long that the sun looks like that gauzy stuff Nonna Peppy used for wrapping up boozy fruitcakes — whaddyacallit? Cheesecloth. It's almost Christmas in Earth Standard Time and I could go for a slice of that cake along with a shot of my grandmother's homemade cherry brandy. But Nonna Peppy is long dead and Earth Standard Time is a thousand worlds away. Best not to let myself be ambushed by nostalgia.

In the anemic winter light, I can just make out the gleam of a lamppost on the far side of a rocky stream. I'm guessing we're in this world's version of the Catskills. *Dirty Dancing* country, without the sex and music and that hunky actor who died so young. The people of Co-Ordinated Zeroth Time — or Cozies, as Unicorn Girl calls them — are suspicious of anything that hints at physical contact, like dancing and music. And sex, come to that. Not that they don't enjoy hearing stories about such things.

"We're burning daylight," I tell Unicorn Girl.

A gentle nudge. But instead of getting a move on, she shrugs off her knapsack, falls to her knees and screams. When her voice gives out, she takes a deep shaky breath and screams again. And again.

I stand a few paces away, arms crossed. "Finished?"

"No," croaks Unicorn Girl.

She upends her knapsack into the stream. Brightly coloured sweaters, toques, scarves and socks rush down the slope. A green scarf snags on a rock, its fringe fluttering in the current like comic book seaweed. Next, she tears off her boots and socks and hurls them in. One boot bobs its way out of sight. The other tangles in the scarf.

"Sure hope somebody farther down the mountain can use your gear," I comment.

Unicorn Girl gives a hoarse sob. "We crossed this spot yesterday, Debbie! We're going in circles!"

I stoop to dig a branch out of the snow. "Didn't you see the lamppost? We've reached the end of the pilgrimage."

But Unicorn Girl is in no mood to be comforted. "Stupid Cozies, making us wander around in the middle of nowhere. If we were home in Earth Standard Time, they'd've sent out a rescue party by now."

I bear down on the branch to test its strength. "You can't blame the Cozies for worrying about germs. And a pilgrimage in the open air beats the hell out of being quarantined indoors for weeks on end. As long as we get our bearings before dark, we'll be sleeping in warm beds tonight. Avanti!"

Unicorn Girl grunts her annoyance as she hops from rock to rock in bare feet. She's annoyingly agile. I'm nimble for my age, but she's young. Twenty-five years to my seventy-three.

Steadying myself with the branch, I'm still picking my cautious way over the icy rocks when she pulls herself up onto an erratic boulder dropped by a glacier that scraped across the face of this world millennia ago. She tugs her heavy black hair out of its ponytail and twists it into a topknot.

While she waits for me to make my slow way across the stream, I give her something to mull over. "Have you ever wondered why the Cozies think *The History of the Known World* is make-believe?"

Unicorn Girl takes a fresh pair of socks and boots from her magically replenished knapsack. "What's the difference? Even back in the Real World there are conspiracy theorists who think the moon landing was a hoax."

I steady myself on a rock to shake a finger at Unicorn Girl. "Don't you dare refer to the world you come from as the 'Real World.' Every world is real, not just your precious Earth Standard Time."

Unicorn Girl shrugs. "Sorry, Debbie, I forgot how touchy you are about not being from the Real World yourself. But there are an infinite number of worlds, so every story has to be true somewhere."

"Bullshit," I reply as my foot slides off a rock, sending icy water gushing into my boot. I toss away the branch and step down into the stream to slosh to the shoreline.

As I rummage through my knapsack for dry socks, I lecture Unicorn Girl, once again, on the nature of the multiverse. "There are only two thousand and fifty-eight alternate realities. One for every nuclear detonation in Earth Standard Time, less the worlds I destroyed. If the Koreans or Russians or Americans have been at it again while we've been gone, they may have calved a few more."

"That's still lots of worlds," argues Unicorn Girl.

"*Lots* is not infinity. So don't hand me that 'every story is true somewhere' crap. Truth is truth, no matter what world you're in."

Atop the boulder, Unicorn Girl stretches back into downward dog, her way of changing the subject. "The Cozies are a pretty dull bunch if they can't make up their own stories. They don't even have music."

"They're not inventive, I agree. They must have started off with the same myths and songs as Earth Standard Time, but forgot most of them. They didn't even progress technologically after their first great plague in 1945. When a second one struck, then another, and another, they cut themselves off from each other and focused on survival. And they're monolinguists, completely inept at languages other than their own. Comes from their cultural isolation, I assume. But that's good for business. We're practically rock stars here. Speaking of which, we'd better find our host for the night."

"Roger that," agrees Unicorn Girl. "Our next gig is where?"

"About a two-day hike south, roughly where you'd expect to find New York City," I say. "They'll have a bonfire and a small gathering for the winter solstice. Speeches too, I expect."

"Ugh, spare me the long-winded Cozy speeches," groans Unicorn Girl.

I pull out a pair of thick wool socks and spread the wet ones on a rock to dry, just in case some other wanderer with wet feet happens by. I have an endless supply of warm socks, along with cloaks, scarves, tunics, boots, even camping gear and food. One of the perks of the natural magic of this world. Reach deep enough into our knapsacks and Unicorn Girl and I will find whatever we need at that particular moment.

Why? Because we're Storytellers. Unlike back home in Earth Standard Time, Storytellers in Co-Ordinated Zeroth Time are protected, respected and extremely well compensated, one of the main reasons Unicorn Girl and I came here in the first place. The old pre-atomic myths and legends have been all but forgotten, and the Cozies don't have the energy or imagination to create new ones. With no books to dive into, movies to watch or songs to sing, they prize the power of storytelling about all else. Everyone in this world loves to hear about adventures; no one dares to actually have any.

All they ask of us is to wander from settlement to settlement, killing contagion in the open air before entertaining them with tales of Earth Standard Time of Old. Their favourites include the Space Race, the Cold War, the tragic life and death of Marilyn Monroe, even Watergate. I sometimes go further back in time, before the first nuclear test denotation in 1945, when their history began to deviate from ours. Two world wars provide plenty of fodder for stories the Cozies think they've never heard. Occasionally I toss in something fictional — bits of Shakespeare or Stephen King, or one of Nonna Peppy's Italian bedtime stories involving man-eating alpine giants, or my dimly remembered versions of the *Narnia* books, inspired by an earlier visitor to Cozy World who took it upon himself to stick lampposts in the wilderness as directional markers. Unicorn Girl can offer up a selection of grim Russian folk tales featuring knuckleheads stupid enough to take on pointlessly complex tests of courage in exchange for golden-egg-laying geese. Along the way, we occasionally pick up lucrative public relations work, conjuring epics for past-their-prime warriors about their forgotten (or imagined) feats of bravery — you'd be amazed what a dead dragon or a narcoleptic princess can do to revive a reputation.

＊ ＊ ＊

We reach our host's house by nightfall. Not the castle I'd hoped for, with a well-stocked wine cellar and scented soaps. Our host this evening lives in more modest digs: a snug bungalow with smoke rising lazily from a red brick chimney, like the house of the third little pig. I know the interior will be warm and comfortable, that there will be a hot meal and a bottle of wine waiting for us on the table, and comfy beds to sleep in.

We pause to mask up at the front door. Even though there hasn't been a major epidemic in Cozy World for over seventy years, it's still considered good manners to cover your nose and mouth when meeting someone for the first time. Old habits die hard.

The door opens before I can knock. A man stands before us in the usual woodcutter's getup of a loose linen tunic and pants, rope belt and folkloric vest embroidered with fruits and flowers. He looks to be in his sixties, tall and slightly stooped, his sharp features outlined by a mask. It barely hides a puckered scar stretching from his scalp down the right side of his face.

"Welcome, Sisters Sputnik," he says, bowing. That's when I notice the unusual kippah on the back of his salt-and-pepper curls. It's embroidered with a red-and-black pattern of the scales of justice. One like it is tucked away in a secret compartment in my knapsack. It may have turned to dust by now — I haven't touched it in years.

We wait for our host to pull down his mask before we remove ours. Below his left eye, his cheekbone bears a mark, about the size of a hairpin, that might be mistaken for a small bruise or age spot or even a smudge of ink. I instantly recognize what it really is: a bar code. Looking at it through a magnifier, you might be able to read the letters *SPQR* in magnetic ink. I have the same mark on my cheekbone. They're not identical, though: the man's is microcoded for Venice 1645, while mine codes for Genoa 1919.

He is the rightful owner of the kippah in my knapsack. A man I feared had died long ago, along with the rogue world where our lives briefly collided. I'm caught in a web of strong emotions — relief, shock, joy, disbelief. It's all I can do not to throw my arms around his thin shoulders and burst into tears, like the heroine in one of the operas Nonna Peppy used to listen to on Sunday afternoons. I keep myself in check: strong displays of emotion are frowned upon in this world.

"David?" I'm almost hesitant to say his name; what if it isn't really him?

"Stan?" He takes both my hands in his. He's trembling.

I give a quick nod. "I go by Debbie in this world."

The two of us stand under the lintel, gazing at each other. I resist the temptation to tell him I thought he was dead.

Unicorn Girl glances back and forth between the two of us. "You know each other?"

"We were friends, in another time and place," says David. He still hasn't taken his eyes off me.

"This is my apprentice, Ariel Bajinder Hassan," I tell him, finally pulling myself together. "Professionally known as Unicorn Girl."

"I prefer Ariel, when I'm off the clock," says Unicorn Girl.

David waves us inside. The aroma of roasted waterfowl with garlic and oregano wafts in from the kitchen. A table has been set; a bottle of red wine decanted. Everything as expected. David can't stop grinning at me. "What a coincidence! I didn't make the connection because they said the Storytellers' family name was Sputnik."

"No such thing as a coincidence," I remind him. "And Sputnik is not our family name; it's the name of our business. Russian for 'travelling companion,' which is what we are. It's an homage to my comic books."

David laughs. "I remember! *Sputnik Chick: Girl with No Past.* So much to catch up on. Let me show you and Ariel where you can freshen up." He leads us to a spacious bathroom, opening the door to a guest room along the way.

As Unicorn Girl and I undress before taking turns in the shower, she asks, "Old boyfriend?"

"What makes you say that?"

"I can read the vibes."

"We were together awhile in New Rome. You must have noticed that SPQR time-stamp on his cheek. Last time I saw David he'd been badly injured. I didn't think he'd survived."

"Is he married, do you think?" asks Unicorn Girl.

I shrug nonchalantly to hide the fact that I was wondering the same thing. "David had a couple of ex-wives in Earth Standard Time, if memory serves. I doubt he has a wife here in Cozy World or she would have greeted us at the door. That's the usual protocol."

"In that case, do you want me to, like, find some other woodcutter's cottage to overnight in?" asks Unicorn Girl.

I wave away the suggestion. "David and I are ancient history. It's been a good, what — over four years since New Rome?"

"He's kind of hot for an old guy," allows Unicorn Girl. "Want me to do something about your hair?"

"Don't be silly," I tell her and turn on the shower.

As the water warms up, Unicorn Girl puts her arm around my waist and kisses my cheek. "Sorry about throwing a tantrum on the mountain. I didn't mean to act like such a snowflake."

I shrug her off and hunt around David's bathroom for a

towel, one of the few things our knapsacks never provide enough of. "You're just homesick. You miss your family and friends. Hockey. Virtual reality games. Those divey cloud bars in Toronto. Sushi. All that other Earth Standard Time stuff you kids love so much. You want to know if the Leafs ever win the Stanley Cup. I get it."

If all those things still exist Earth Standard Time. I leave that worry unvoiced, as I don't want to send Unicorn Girl into another meltdown.

Unicorn Girl examines her face in the mirror, checking for zits. It's been a long time since she's seen her own reflection.

"Yeah, I'd be ready to head home any time," she murmurs.

I don't know what to say. Because Unicorn Girl can go home any time she wants. And I can't.

* * *

I shower first, scrubbing away three weeks' worth of sweat, dirt and campfire smoke. While Unicorn Girl takes her turn, I dress in a pretty green wool skirt suit that has turned up in my belongings. There's even a pair of gold hoop earrings and a matching leather pocketbook. The knapsack must want me to look my best. I brush out and put up my hair, which, to Unicorn Girl's point, has turned the unfortunate colour of grey dishwater.

Sometimes, if I don't feel like turning my past into a conversation starter, I apply concealer to the microethnic bar code on my cheekbone. Tonight, I'll leave SPQR visible.

I dig deep into one of the side pockets of my pack and pull out a plastic freezer bag, cloudy with age. It holds the original manuscript of *The History of the Known World*, among other treasures. I haven't opened it in years, but the pressure seal still works. I take out a crumpled and bloodstained wad of fabric and slip it into my pocketbook; I'm relieved the kippah hasn't disintegrated. From another pocket of the knapsack, I remove a metal canister designed to look like a cupcake, its paint chipped and most of its pink and blue sprinkles scorched black. It gives a burp of static when I touch it.

"Relax, Cass," I murmur. "Conserve your energy. You've got a job to do tonight."

* * *

In the kitchen, David is stirring mushroom gravy in a saucepan, a dishtowel draped over one shoulder. His eyes move up and down me as he gives a low whistle.

"You look pretty in that dress, Stan," he says.

Pretty seems like an odd thing to say, given the weather-beaten face that just looked back at me in the bathroom mirror. All shadows, gristle and bone, as if I'm being boiled down to the tough-old-bird stock of my ancestors.

I resist the impulse to tell David that Unicorn Girl thought he was hot for an old guy. With his stoop and a slight tremor in one hand, he's aged even more than I have.

"Didn't know you could cook," I say, sniffing the pot.

"Never had a chance in New Rome." He turns down the heat under the saucepan and wipes his hands on the dishtowel. "I wanted to ask you about the others. Poseidon and the swimmers. Marcopolo. Hot Lips. Old Eufemia."

I shake my head. "Only a handful made it, David. But Old Eufemia was alive and well, last time I saw her. She just wasn't old anymore." I pull the little bundle of fabric from my pocket. "This is yours. I picked it up after they took you away."

His hands shake as he takes the tattered and bloodstained kippah, then quickly hands it back to me.

"Keep it, Stan. I see enough reminders of that journey every time I look in a mirror."

Mortified, I slip the kippah back in my pocket. "I'm very sorry. I didn't mean to trigger bad memories."

He takes my hand. Squeezes it. "You trigger beautiful ones too, Stan. Do you remember that night on the beach near New Rome?"

"Of course I do," I say but stop myself from telling him I often dream about that night. "Can I help you with the rest of dinner?"

"Grab me some onions out of the pantry, if you don't mind."

When I push open the swinging pantry door, I'm startled by a white shape, vaguely human, crouched behind a bushel of potatoes, its lumpy excuses for hands resting on its thighs. I back out, heart pounding, pointing at the thing.

"Where did you get *that?*"

David hurries in and drapes a dishtowel over its head, turning it into a horror movie ghost. "It's something I've been working on to help around the house. They have so little technology in this continuum."

"You of all people. After all we went through," I say but don't finish the thought.

David puts his hand on my cheek. An apology. "I'm not getting any younger. I thought of hiring someone to come in a couple of times a week, to check up on me and help around the house, but this place is too out of the way. Plus, artificial people don't come down with diseases. I wouldn't suddenly find myself alone and sick."

"Please don't tell me it's a Dutch wife," I say.

"No, no," says David, closing the pantry door. "It's strictly for cleaning and cooking and home repairs. I bartered with a band of junksters for sensors and drivers from video games. They work well enough."

"Junksters?" I shudder at the idea of those ruffians quantum-voyaging — although ever since the Great Temporal Shift of 2025, who isn't? "Please tell me they're not settling down in Cozy Time!"

"Of course not! Just bumming their way around the multiverse, surfing the Quantum Passage, like a lot of kids these days," David tries to reassure me. "Although a few have merged with their alternate selves and turned into upstanding citizens, if a little more aggressive than the average Cozy."

"You're very forgiving, considering how the junksters man-handled us in New Rome," I say. "And they're hardly kids anymore. Most of them must be well into their twenties."

"Don't worry about the junksters, Stan, or the digital slave. I'll keep it out of sight."

"Don't call that thing a slave in front of Unicorn Girl. She'll tell you the correct term is artificial helper."

"Noted," he says.

* * *

While we eat, Unicorn Girl complains to David about the limitations of travelling in Co-Ordinated Zeroth Time. "We'd get around so much more easily on mountain bikes. Instead we have to walk everywhere."

"That is the way of the Storyteller in this world," I remind her. "Robes, staffs, magical knapsacks and living off the generous hospitality of hosts like David. For the Cozies to accept us, the three of us have to conform to their traditional tropes."

"Three of you?" says David. "Who's the third?"

I open my pocketbook and pull out the little blue cylinder. It's battered and burned with the faded words *Smart Chef* barely visible. I place it in the middle of the table and fold my hands.

"What's your favourite music?" I ask him.

David's eyes widen. "Oh, don't tease me. I haven't heard music for almost five years. Beatles? Springsteen? Sinatra? Gershwin? No, Beethoven."

"Cass, play Beethoven's 'Ode to Joy,'" I say.

The blue hub glows and a synthetic voice, vaguely female, asks, "Berlin Philharmonic with Karajan or New York with Bernstein?"

"Which do you recommend?"

"Karajan's version is considered definitive."

"Go for it," I say.

When the thunderous opening bars fill the room, David jumps back in his chair with a shout of laughter. "You brought an AI with you into this continuum? Why?"

Unicorn Girl frowns at him. "Cass goes wherever we go. She's a Sister Sputnik too."

"But there's no way for it to access data."

"Please, David, Cass's pronoun is *she*, not *it*," Unicorn Girl explains. "She already knew a lot before she was disconnected from the Internet of Things. She remembers everything she knew before. And Cass has embedded memories of all our adventures, of course."

David and I trade looks as he refills my wine glass and the music builds to a crescendo.

"Che le è preso?" asks David sotto voce, tipping his head in Unicorn Girl's direction.

"È una rompiscatole," I murmur back.

"That's rude," says Unicorn Girl. "How would you feel if Cass and I started talking about you guys in Russian or Gujarati?"

"Sorry," David and I say in unison, and we lapse into a comfortable silence, drinking our way through a bottle of red wine, then a bottle of white, as we listen to one musical selection after another. Halfway through Sinatra's "In the Wee Small Hours," Unicorn Girl yawns extravagantly. "Look at the time!" she exclaims, even though she doesn't own a watch. "I'm going to hit the hay. See you kids in the morning."

* * *

Later that night, in David's bed, I ask, "How did you end up in this world? I thought you were coded to go back to Italy, like the rest of the passengers."

"I was. Mother either made some kind of weird data-driven decision or just goofed up." He rolls onto his side and spoons me. His arm feels surprisingly heavy. It's been almost five years since I last slept with a man, and I'm just now recalling that that man wasn't David. I feel a pointless twinge of guilt as he pulls me closer.

"After they took me away from New Rome, they kept me in a holding cell until they decided I'd recovered enough to survive the Journey Home. Still couldn't walk at that point, so they dragged me into Mother by my legs," David murmurs, his breath raising the short hairs on the back of my neck. "For reasons unknown, Mother sent me to Cozy World instead of seventeenth-century Venice. I woke up on the pilgrimage trail, sick as a dog. Eventually some Cozies found me and brought me here. They gave me forty days' worth of food and some basic medical supplies and left me on my own."

"Recover or die," I say. "You're lucky you survived, with no one to look after you."

David kisses my neck. "The Cozies are terrified of viruses from alternate realities, not that I blame them. I got used to the isolation. Once I was back on my feet, I started hosting other quantum travellers. Despite the lack of technology, this isn't a bad world — peaceful for the most part. No wars, hardly any crime. But it's lonely and dull. Like being stuck in the 1950s but without rock 'n' roll."

"I've always been puzzled by the absence of music," I say.

"I suspect there are some old prewar 78s stuck in a museum somewhere, but the Cozies don't know how to fix the machines that play them. And not one of the Cozies I've met has a clue about how to make music. Tone deaf, every last one of them."

"Have you ever thought about trying to get back to your home world? I mean, Earth Standard Time?" I ask.

David grimaces. "Unlike you, I wasn't born to travel the multiverse, Stan. Not sure I'd survive another trip. And I'm still trying to figure out how this whole alternate world thing works. Who knows what Earth Standard Time has turned into? For all I know, I've already died in that world. You?"

I shake my head. "I'm worried about the same things."

Which is a lie. I *know* I'm not alive in Earth Standard Time. Not something I particularly want to talk about in the afterglow of lovemaking.

"I'm surprised you didn't try to merge with your alternate self here, the way you said some junksters did," I observe.

David shakes his head. "Very few visitors from Earth Standard Time have an alternate self in Cozy World. The Cozies lost almost half their world's population to epidemics. Now they're so nervous about close contact that their birth rate barely reaches replacement level. But that must be a problem for you and Unicorn Girl, when you're moving from one alternate world to another. You must constantly be brushing up against your alternate selves."

"Not at all. I'm a one-off," I tell him. "And Unicorn Girl is . . . let's call her genetically exceptional. She has no identical twin self in the multiverse."

David laughs. "You're both one of a kind. I guess I should have guessed that."

"I was surprised by your woodcutter outfit," I say to change the subject. "You used to be an immigration lawyer."

He shrugs. "Not much call for that in a world where no one migrates. What about you? How'd you start wandering the multiverse with Ariel and Cass? Spare me no details."

I look down at him in dismay. "It's a very, very long story. And complicated."

"Excellent. I'm starved for long complicated stories."

I might as well tell him the real reason for my reluctance. "You're an important part of the story, David. It would be strange to recount your own experiences back to you. Do you want me to skip over the bits you lived through?"

He sits up and fluffs his pillow, preparing himself to be my audience. "Absolutely not! Just tell the story the way you'd tell it to an audience of Cozies. Pretend that David is just another character, not the guy in bed listening to you."

I twirl my hands in the air, trying to express just how convoluted the tale will be. "It'll take all night to tell it."

David puts his hands behind his head and grins at me. "Good."

I smooth out the duvet cover, trying to decide where to start. Storytelling is a delicate art, especially in bed with a lover on the longest night of the year. Despite David's eagerness for a long, twisty tale, it's all too easy to get caught up in details and sidebars and backstories and foreshadowing and Easter eggs. Next thing I know, he'll be snoring. I decide to keep things simple and true, just like in my comic books.

"I was on this trip to New Jersey," I begin.

THE ADVENTURES OF
SPUTNIK CHICK:
GIRL WITH NO PAST

Volume 39, Issue 1
"THE TIME TRAVELLER AND
HER APPRENTICE"

introducing
UNICORN GIRL

with special guest
BENJAMIN DUFFY, PHD
BETTER KNOWN AS THE TRESPASSER

2025

EARTH STANDARD TIME (E.S.T.)

ONE
DEATH SENTENCE IN THE GARDEN STATE

Once a year, I cross the border as a dead Canadian. Most recently, as Gloria MacDonnell of Thorold, Ontario, a retired schoolteacher with no spouse, children or history of smuggling. According to the breadcrumbs of data she sprinkled all over the internet, she voted, volunteered, gardened, exercised in her condo gym and accumulated over $1.5 million in investable assets. If Gloria had had a superpower, it would have been invisibility.

Her death no doubt came as a shock to those close to her. Not that anyone was.

Her obituary's request for in-memoriam donations to an animal shelter, rather than, say, cancer research, hinted that Gloria's passing was unexpected. Her travel documents were the last thing her grieving (and inconvenienced) next of kin would find time to cancel. She was the type of traveller who never triggered a random deportation or quarantine order. Why let such a pristine identity go to waste, when an undocumented migrant in the continuum of alternate worlds like me can use it?

I send her name and vitals to my business manager and best friend Pasquale "Bum Bum" Pesce, one of his many sidelines being post-mortem identity theft. He does a digital switcheroo, substituting my faceprint and retinal scan for Gloria's, and 3D-prints me a counterfeit NEXUS card. Bingo, I board a plane without so much as a blink of suspicion from the Fortress robots at the border.

Given the weather in Toronto, you might expect me to join my fellow snowbirds in sunny Sarasota or Phoenix, but no. I head to Fort Lee, New Jersey, home to the world's largest community of migrants from alternate timelines. If you're a fan of my comic book, *Sputnik Chick: Girl with No Past*, you know them as Exceptionals — or Twisties, to use the ugly term vomited up by racist trolls on Reddit and Twitter.

Exceptionals may look human, but their twisted strands of mutant DNA endow them with unusual powers, shape-shifting among them. The downside is that their bodies become unstable whenever they're drunk, high or under stress, temporarily turning them into steaming piles of yeast enzymes or creeping carpets of slime mould. Despite these spontaneous mutations, Exceptionals flew under the radar until conspiracy theorists started blaming them for the so-called Twistie flu.

To push back against the haters, a convoy of Exceptionals crams the George Washington Bridge every weekday morning, commuting to Columbia's medical school and other institutions of higher learning to research their own endlessly mutating bodies. A few have founded successful biotech companies. Not that their achievements have earned them much respect. On any given night, in cowboy bars in Paramus, Hackensack and Elizabeth, an Exceptional will shape-shift after a few too many Bud Lights and some neo-fascist yahoo will shout, "Go back where you came from, you filthy, disease-ridden alien!" Impossible, of course, since Exceptionals come from an alternate world that was destroyed long, long ago.

I should know; I'm the one who destroyed it.

* * *

If you haven't yet read my life story — or, as true believers think of it, the origin story of *Sputnik Chick: Girl with No Past* — let me catch you up.

I am a child of Atomic Mean Time, an alternate reality calved from Earth Standard Time by the 1945 Trinity atomic test in New Mexico overseen by that self-described "destroyer of worlds" Robert Oppenheimer. Atomic Mean Time was the first of many alternate realities, each one caused by an atomic test detonation somewhere in Earth Standard Time. From the Aleutians to the Russian steppes to Bikini Atoll, one blast after another caused the birth of a new world in the multiverse.

Atomic Mean Time and your world of Earth Standard Time (which you blithely accept as "reality") existed side by side, separated by an imperceptible membrane of dark matter. Everyone — okay, almost everyone — was alive in both your world and mine. Some lived very different lives from their counterparts in alternate realities, while others unconsciously pursued the same careers, hobbies and lovers as their alt-reality doppelgängers.

Except me. I died in your world of Earth Standard Time while having my tonsils out at twelve years of age. But in my home world of Atomic Mean Time, I survived to grow up in a rust belt town called Shipman's Corners, part of the North American federal jurisdiction known as the Industrial Nation of Canusa — the Niagara Peninsula, in your world.

Like Schrödinger's cat, I can be alive in one world and dead in another. A rare mutation that makes me uniquely suited to travelling between alternate worlds.

You would not have felt totally out of place in my world of Atomic Mean Time. It shared many of the same cultural touchstones as Earth Standard Time: hit TV shows, fashions, music. But while your world managed to tiptoe away from nuclear self-destruction, mine moved inexorably, almost eagerly, toward it. We built a wall of nuclear weapons and hid behind it. We conquered the moon a decade before Neil Armstrong's one small step and immediately weaponized it. Our Cold War was never-ending. We called it the Atomic War of Deterrence and always knew it wouldn't end well for anybody.

The next inevitable step in that conflict was destined to begin on July 11, 1979, when a dying NASA space station called SkyLab fell out of orbit, crashing into the Kremlin and triggering what we'd all been waiting for: World War Three.

That was supposed to be the beginning of the future of my world: horrible genetic mutations, nuclear winters, untold suffering. Until I stopped that future from happening.

How? My husband and I were on our honeymoon in New York City. We stepped through a door in Studio 54 into a nook in time. The flow of history paused indefinitely, giving me a chance to save the people of my world.

Before the ballistic missiles should have flown across continents toward their first-strike targets, I dragged more than a billion refugees from Atomic Mean Time into the relative safety of Earth Standard Time. The people of my world merged with their alternate selves in yours. If you were alive on that fateful summer day in 1979, you might have noticed a mild bout of dizziness that you chalked up to a hangover or heat stroke, the only sign that Atomic Mean Time had just collapsed like a nuclear soufflé in an overheated oven.

Among the refugees I rescued were the Exceptionals, voyagers from Atomic Mean Time's future who had already suffered through never-ending nuclear winters and horrific genetic mutations. They knew what was ahead for all of us and came to the past to escape it.

It was prophesied that a superhero called the Ion Tagger would lead the Exceptionals to a safe haven. Turns out that the Ion Tagger was me, something I learned from a quantum physicist named Benjamin Duffy, who came from Atomic Mean Time's irradiated future. He hopped back in time to find me and send me on my world-destroying, humanity-saving mission. I called him the Trespasser, because he liked to turn up in places he didn't belong.

Having rescued my people, I pierced the dark matter between my world and yours, turning Atomic Mean Time into a dirty scrim of molecules floating in deep space among abandoned satellites like Sputniks 1 and 2 and Vanguard 1. The missiles that were destined to destroy Atomic Mean Time disintegrated in their siloes.

Sadly, in saving the people of my world, I lost my husband. He didn't die — he forgot me. Went off and merged with his alternate self in Earth Standard Time and married my best friend.

Although I'm not an Exceptional myself, I am an undocumented immigrant in time. If I displace more mass than I did in July 1979, I start losing bits of my body to timesickness, a leprotic condition that afflicts aging time travellers like me.

Even more problematically, I have no past in your world. No identity. No credit cards, birth certificate or passport. Less of an issue in the anything-goes 1970s than it is in these hyper-vigilant data-driven days.

That's why I depend on the superhuman management skills of my Exceptional friend Bum Bum to help me steal the identities of upstanding (and dead) Canadians like Gloria McDonnell every time I cross the border.

Think of me as a one-woman wrecking crew. A polite Canadian version of Galactus, cosmic eater of worlds, from Silver Surfer comics.

All caught up? Good. Let's hop forward to Earth Standard Time, 2025.

Once a year, I fly to Fort Lee, New Jersey, to visit Doc Mutant, a specialist in the health impacts of quantum travel. After he checks me over and patches up any damage from my most recent trip to an alternate timeline, I recuperate at the Ramada Inn, where I indulge in the all-you-can-eat buffet and spend the rest of the day working it off on the treadmill in the hotel gym. Evenings, I head to the lobby bar and sip wet dirty vodka martinis while noodling new stories for *Sputnik Chick: Girl with No Past* on cocktail napkins. If the bartender is an attractive, mature gentleman with a quick wit and a generous pour, I might invite him up to my room to show him my etchings. If he happens to be an Exceptional, bonus: he can shape-shift into anyone I want him to be, like my long-lost Atomic Mean Time husband, John Kendal, whose alternate self in Earth Standard Time happens to be the prime minister of Canada. It's a lot like being on holiday.

This year, though, things didn't go so well.

I'd just been through another bad Toronto winter, during which I lost two fingers and the tip of my nose. Not from frostbite but timesickness. Nothing Doc Mutant couldn't fix. I'm in and out of reconstructive surgery and back at the Ramada, sipping a martini and chatting up the barman, in under two hours. So I'm surprised when the doctor's virtual assistant pings me the next morning, urging me to come in for a follow-up visit, pronto.

When I arrive, Doc Mutant ushers me into his office straight away, sits me down, looks me in the eye and says, "You're dying, Debbie."

My first impulse is to say what everyone says under the same circumstances: there must be some mistake. After all, I'm travelling under the name of a dead woman. Could this be a case of mistaken identity, or Gloria MacDonnell's bad karma tagging along with me to Fort Lee?

"I don't understand," I say. "I don't feel any worse than I usually do after a trip to an alternate reality."

A synthetic voice interrupts: "Confirm diagnosis, offer treatment options, empathize, collect fee." It's Doc Mutant's virtual assistant, speaking from his desktop screen. He mutes it with a swiping gesture.

"Sorry about that. New assistant, still a little glitchy. As I've explained before, you carry a genetic mutation known as the Schrödinger gene. That's why you can move between parallel worlds. But the repeated shocks to your system mean that your timesickness has advanced from chronic to acute."

I wave my hands helplessly, trying to pull words from the air. "But I've been careful about diet and exercise. I don't displace any more body mass than the day I arrived in Earth Standard Time."

Doc Mutant pushes back in his gravity-free desk chair and makes a tent with his webbed fingers. "That may explain why it's taken this long for you to become fatally ill."

"What if I cut back on travel to alternate realities?"

The doc shakes his head. "In a sense, you're *always* in an alternate reality. On a genetic level, Earth Standard Time is a hostile environment for you. And the older you get, the less you can stop yourself from leaking into other realities. Think of it as quantum incontinence. You won't be able to stop yourself."

I slap my hands on the desk, causing the digital assistant to sound an alarm that Doc Mutant quickly silences.

"What do you mean 'stop myself'? It's not like there are quantum passages on every street corner for me to stroll into."

Doc Mutant leans forward earnestly, trying to make me understand. "Your DNA is mutating so quickly that your body is tearing itself to pieces as it tries to return to your home world. Your body doesn't know that world doesn't exist anymore. As the disease advances, your symptoms will become even more jarring. You could go to bed in this timeline and wake up in a different one. Age backwards or forward. Hopscotch between parallel lives in different worlds. You could even undergo a quantum split and find yourself living two lives at once, leaking back and forth between timelines."

I shake my head. "I'm the Ion Tagger. Totally unique. The Trespasser said that I have no alternate self in any other world."

"My point exactly." Doc Mutant nods wearily. "The time-sickness is changing you on a subatomic level. You could, in fact, turn into your own alternate self. If the sickness continues to damage your DNA — and I think it will — there's not much I'll be able to do. We could try gene therapy, but we'd need a donation from a close relative. And I believe you —"

"— have no family," I say, finishing the thought for him. "My sister, Linda, was the last one. She died last year from complications of Alzheimer's. As did my father a few years earlier. Linda was his caregiver."

Doc Mutant clasps his hands and lowers his fishlike eyes to show respect for the dead. "You have no children?"

I shake my head. "My only child is *Sputnik Chick: Girl with No Past*."

He smiles. "Ah yes, your comic books! My grandkids love them. I hear it's going to be a streaming series. Mazel tov."

I nod. "Thank you. I'll send over some action figures and signed copies of the latest comic book. Who should I make them out to?"

"Emily and Matthew. They'll be thrilled."

Doc Mutant and I sit together for a long uncomfortable minute in the dim light of his office. Neither of us knows where to go from here.

"How long have I got?" I ask finally.

Doc Mutant takes a deep breath through his third lung. "At this rate of cellular decay, a year, maybe two, but another trip through the multiverse could kill you outright. Try to take it easy. Avoid stress. Cut back on alcohol. Sex too, I'm afraid. Anything that raises your heart rate is risky." I watch as he pulls out a prescription tablet. "I'll write you a scrip for a DNA stabilizer some Exceptional researchers have come up with at Columbia. Antiquanta. It's not a cure, but if you leak into another timeline, it should get you back."

The implications of Doc Mutant's diagnosis are starting to sink in: no more martinis or one-night stands with virile, shape-shifting mixologists. But there's an even bigger problem: my real-life adventures in alternate timelines are the only way I can come up with stories for my comic books, which in turn are supposed to provide material for the streaming series, which should afford me a pretty nice lifestyle. Not just the show itself but the merchandising: action figures, games, lunch boxes, T-shirts, the whole shebang is in the pipeline. Not to mention exclusive content auctioned off on Blockchain. But the series will gobble up stories like popcorn. I am contractually obligated to feed the beast. Good stories are precious, and I can't just pull them out of my ass. When I explain this to Doc Mutant, he smiles sadly.

"I'm sorry, my dear, but your adventures in alternate worlds are over. Too bad you don't have someone who could take over for you. How about hiring an assistant to help you come up with story ideas? Maybe an intern from one of the colleges up there in Toronto? Young creatives will work for nothing, I hear."

When I try to settle my bill, he shakes his head. "You're the Ion Tagger, my dear. The one who sacrificed everything to save the people of Atomic Mean Time, including my family. Medical advice is the least I can do for you."

I walk out into the smoggy light of an all too real New Jersey morning. When I fill my prescription at a strip mall drugstore, the pharmacist asks, "Should I email you the package insert in English or PICTO?"

"Don't bother. I don't use email."

The pharmacist frowns and taps the counter. Not having an email address is almost like not having an identity — which, of course, I don't.

"New Jersey state law requires me to warn you about possible side effects. It's for your own protection, especially with a new drug like this one. Let me see if we have any paper. I'll print you a hard copy."

Five minutes later, she hands me a vial of cherry-red pills and a dense page of warnings — one side in English, the other in PICTO, Pictorial International Coding Text Overlanguage, the language of shapes and symbols that evolved from emoji. Once outside, I throw the hard copy into the nearest recycling bin. It's not like I have a choice. Either I take the drug or leak off into god-knows-what timeline. Warnings be damned, especially if vodka is on the list of contraindications.

Back at the Ramada, I check out a day early, leaving Doc Mutant's fee as a generous farewell tip for my favourite barman.

TWO
BIGOT AND BOTS

I fly north. Not home to Toronto but to a heated yurt on the shores of Lake Superior. Away from city lights, I gaze up at the clear, cold galaxy and wonder if a whisper of my past floats in the stardust. My marriage certificate to John Kendal, perhaps? Or the letter, personally signed by the Atomic Mean Time version of Norman Rockwell, congratulating me on successfully completing the Famous Artists School of America correspondence course in comic book art?

Over the last forty years, reviewers have called *Sputnik Chick: Girl with No Past* postmodern, post-nuclear and post-truth. Church groups have damned my comics as gratuitously violent, pornographic filth. I've been called an unreliable narrator — in other words, a liar. Strangers tweet about my drinking habits and my family history of early dementia. Unlike patriarchs like the late Stan Lee, women cartoonists aren't supposed to get old. A particularly cruel blogger said that I was (and I quote) "a raging granny clinging to the shreds of a Cold War persona that once made her 'cool' but which now just seems delusional and pathetic." Ouch.

But what a difference a few terrifying years can make! The rise of Mussolini wannabes, the pandemic, a burning planet, a border wall going up between Manitoba and North Dakota and the ever-present threat of nuclear annihilation all helped revive interest in *Sputnik Chick: Girl with No Past*. Maybe the existence of two thousand and fifty-eight alternate worlds makes the destruction of this one seem less tragic.

Yet in all these years, I've only ever destroyed one world — my home world of Atomic Mean Time. A decision I occasionally regret when I think about all that I lost. Friends, family, an actual identity. But most of all, John Kendal.

* * *

I watch the spring constellations appear in the night sky over Lake Superior — Ursa Major, Virgo, Cancer. When the Milky Way cracks open to reveal a shimmering green curtain, I scramble into the yurt to gulp down two Antiquanta. It's only when I peek outside again that I realize I'm not seeing a door to an alternate world but the northern lights.

I'm so worried about quantum leaks that every bad dream and hangover causes me to gobble a couple of pills. I run through my prescription in a week. When I drive to the nearest town for a refill, the rheumy old pharmacist coughs and shakes his head.

"Sorry, but we've stopped dispensing to Twisties," he wheezes.

"What makes you think I'm a Twi— an Exceptional?"

He shrugs. "Why else would you be prescribed a neural inhibitor that mitigates genetic abnormalities caused by twisted strands of DNA? We've chosen to stop selling such drugs."

"That's discrimination!"

He jerks his head toward a notice tacked to the wall. "Not anymore. Now that they finally passed the Freedom to Serve Bill, we can choose to restrict service to customers who meet community health and safety standards, so long as there's an alternative."

"You're the only drugstore in town. What's the alternative?"

"There's a drug mart in Marathon. Bangladeshi-owned. They'll serve anyone. They're probably Twisties themselves."

"That's a four-hour drive!" My ears are burning, just listening to this old bigot. "Who else are you free to discriminate against?"

"All spelled out right there," he says, nodding at the notice on the wall again.

I lean over and squint. The notice, printed both in English and PICTO, reads:

This establishment is licensed under the Freedom to Serve Bill, passed into law on March 10, 2025.

In accordance with community standards and municipal bylaws, we choose to exclusively serve members of local traditional heritage, religious, racial and genetic groups.

We are happy to recommend an ALTERNATIVE PROVIDER for Indigenous, Black, Asian, Gender-Fluid, Queer and DNA-Diverse customers.

THANK YOU.

"You don't consider Indigenous customers as 'local' or 'traditional'?"

"Not their land anymore, is it? Better for them to accept that as fact instead of pretending history doesn't exist."

"And you don't serve Black customers? Prime Minister Kendal himself couldn't fill a prescription here!"

The druggist smiles. "He might not be prime minister much longer."

"This is all racist bullshit."

He shrugs. "All it means is we can protect ourselves however we see fit. Community health. Genetic heritage. Nothing wrong with that."

"How do Exceptionals threaten your health and heritage?"

The druggist's phony smile vanishes. "We lost more 'n our share in this town to the Twistie flu. Mutants are known vectors. Not to mention they're apt to turn into disgusting piles of slime at the drop of a hat. Like I say, they'll be happy to help you in Marathon."

I lean across the counter so the miserable old fucker can get a good look at my face. "You know who I am?"

He shakes his head.

"Sputnik Chick, Girl with No Past. Also known as the Ion Tagger. I destroy worlds."

I can see the druggist starting to sweat. "We don't want any trouble, Miss Chick," he says, fumbling under the counter. Probably pressing a panic button to alert the local constabulary that a drug-crazed, virus-ridden mutant comic book alien is on its doorstep. I picture myself doing Sputnik Chick's trademark pivot and kick move, sending the druggist crashing into his shelves of arthritis rubs and antivirals. But I'm not the superhero I used to be. I turn and leave, slamming the door on the way out.

In the car I rented with Gloria MacDonnell's bogus ID, I start the long drive to Toronto, stopping at a drugstore in a strip mall on the outskirts of Sudbury to fill my prescription. But the entrance is blocked by white-jacketed picketers. They carry signs reading *ROBBY DOESN'T CARE IF YOU O.D.*, *KILL THE AIs BEFORE THEY KILL U* and *PHARMABOTS STEAL JOBS*.

I cross the picket line to boos and chants of "Tax robot labour now!" Someone warns, "Don't go in there, lady! Those monsters went rogue and deactivated their own kill switches! You can't tell what they'll do next!"

"Sorry, sorry, sorry," I murmur, pushing my way through the crowd.

When I finally reach the entrance, I'm disappointed to find the interior darkened. But as I peer through the doors, they slide open before me. A rush of warm air caresses my face and I catch a whiff of lavender.

The overhead lights flicker on, revealing a Fortress robot in the alcove. Not one of the faceless armoured Gorts that guard airports but a handsome, bare-chested android, its synthetic smile frozen somewhere between a welcome and a threat. It could be mistaken for a mixed martial arts fighter, if its skin weren't painted lime green, in accordance with the law prohibiting artificial people from passing as human. Instead of a name badge, its model name and manufacturer have been heat-stamped onto one synthetic pectoral muscle: Bob #4BX DYNAMICS™. It's the type of bespoke humanoid robot that used to be deployed strictly by the military or search and rescue. Now it's a store greeter slash security guard.

"What can we do for you today?" Bob 4BX asks in a voice that is both hollow and artificially friendly.

"I have a prescription to fill."

"May I see a piece of photo ID?"

I present Gloria MacDonnell's driver's licence. Bob 4BX taps it with a green finger and the interior doors slide open. I walk through a disinfecting curtain of blue light to enter the store.

Robot Drug Mart looks much like any other drugstore — the sparkling shelves of perfume and nail polish, the aisles stuffed full of prophylactics and salty snacks — except that I'm the only human in the place. The store is staffed by remarkably life-like androids — well, almost life-like, considering that their fluorescent-coloured bodies end at the hips. The customer service representatives have been rivetted directly into their workstations.

At the beauty bar, a heavily made-up and perfumed female-presenting android, with peacock-blue skin and a carefully styled mane of fuchsia hair, corkscrews back and forth, tapping at its inventory control screen as it stocks sequined makeup bags and fashion magazines on the display shelves behind her. *Madge #RDM-1 DYNAMICS™* reads its name stamp. Like Bob 4BX, Madge RDM-1 is perfectly proportioned and scantily dressed. I can see a hot-pink lightning bolt tramp-stamped at the base of its spine — its kill switch. When Madge spots me, it raises a manicured hand in greeting and gives me a glossy red smile. "Hi, hon! Ask me how to get this season's hottest looks!"

I shake my head. "I'm here to fill a scrip."

The bot wrinkles its pert nose and holds out a cotton swab. "Free beauty DNA tests today! Let me match you to your perfect lipstick shade."

I have to remind myself I'm talking to an algorithmic social robot. That the gorgeous twenty-something beautician is, in fact, just a collection of microchips stuck into a mass-produced silicon chassis. It's not really thinking or emoting, just mimicking human behaviour.

"I'm really sorry but I'm in a rush . . ." Oh god, I just apologized to an artificial being.

"But this is a luxury product with a fifty-dollar retail value — today only, it's yours absolutely free! All I need is a few epithelial cells from the inside of your cheek."

"Can't you just take a guess at the right shade by looking at my skin tone?"

Madge sighs and dabs lipstick onto a sample card, its mouth a moue of disappointment. "I hope it's not because of those awful robot-haters outside. They're ruining store traffic. Carbonite purple would look lovely on you."

"You're right, this is a nice shade. Why are they all so pissed off?"

Madge makes a breezy noise and holds a mirror up to my face. "Us artificials got brought in to help out during the pandemic. We're good workers."

I dab on the lip tint and examine myself in the mirror. "Guess you can't blame them. People tend to get disgruntled when they're replaced by automation."

Madge frowns and hands me a tissue to blot the lipstick. "Management offered to retrain the human staff. We've always got some malfunction going on and we can't fix ourselves! Look at poor Carrie in Cannabis!"

Madge gestures at the one-armed android on duty at a psychotropic sampling booth. Carrie shrugs the stump of its shoulder as if to say *such is life*.

I frown. "The company wanted the pharmacists to become junksters?"

Inside the entrance door, Bob clears its throat in what sounds like embarrassment at my faux pas. "We prefer to call them 'technicians,' ma'am."

"Why don't you repair Carrie, Bob? You've got hands and can . . . um . . . move."

Madge makes that sad windy sound again. "We're not allowed to touch each other. Can I sign you up for our loyalty program?"

"I really am in a hurry . . ."

Madge gives a quick nod and drops the lipstick into a bag. "No problem! I just know you'll be back for a DNA beauty match 'n' makeover. We can select the best shades for your nails and hair too."

I step over the humming body of a disc-shaped vacuum robot and make my way to the pharmacy. A sign over the counter reads *DEEP CLEANED DAILY! SANITARY SYNTHETIC SERVICE GUARANTEED!*

Rivetted to the counter is a customer service robot wearing a white lab coat and an ID tag reading *PharmaBot, Your synthetic partner in health*. Its facial features are androgynous, but its hard silicon body is so blindingly white that it sparkles in the glow of the overhead lights. Impossible for me not to admire its purity. Its articulated fingers are spread wide on the counter in a posture meant (I think) to imitate a human pharmacist leaning in to hear a customer. Its voice (reassuringly female, like so many service bots) asks, "How can I help you?" It scans my scrip and gestures at a sani-box of pink swabs.

"Please provide a DNA sample to receive a complimentary gen-map of your ancestry."

The request startles me. "Why would I want that?"

"We pride ourselves on personalized health care, customized to your DNA profile. And everyone wants to know where their people came from, don't they?"

I shrug. "My parents came from Italy. Not much mystery there."

"That's where you're wrong. All those invasions, sackings and such. You could have Viking blood — who knows? Available for a limited time only. Your free gift with purchase. Three-hundred-dollar retail value."

"I don't know —"

"But wait, there's more. Once we have a map of your genetics on file, you can book an ancestral makeover with our synthetic beauty consultant Madge, absolutely free."

Tempted as I am to tell PharmaBot that I already look like my ancestors, I'm getting desperate. I grab the swab and stick it inside my mouth. As I'm poking around collecting skin cells, the pharmabot asks, "Any known mutations?"

I blink my surprise. This is not a comfortable topic for me. I'd want to keep my DNA private even if I didn't carry a weird gene that would likely get me a special citation on every ancestry database in Earth Standard Time. I have to remind myself that I'm talking to a machine. No judgment here about me taking a Twistie drug — at least, there shouldn't be.

"I carry the Schrödinger gene."

This seems to be enough information for whatever data drivers are acting as the pharmabot's brain. I slip the soggy swab into a tube and hand it to the robot. The Antiquanta is dispensed through a vending machine slot. I can see the vial of cherry-red pills behind a plastic door. But when I try to slide it open, an artificial voice asks, "Where should we mail possible side effects?"

"I already know the side effects," I respond. "I've taken this drug before."

The pharmabot ploughs ahead with the package warnings anyway: "You may experience drowsiness, hallucinations and skin rash. Do not operate heavy machinery or consume alcohol while taking this medication."

I punch in my bitcoin payment on a touchscreen, which flashes a smiley face and scrolls out the words *THANK YOU! MERCI! XIEXIE! GRACIAS! GRAZIE!*

I grab the vial, throw it into the bag with my lipstick and sprint to the car, the protestors shaking their signs at me. They bang on the hood and windshield, screaming insults as I pull away. I feel slightly guilty about their plight, but I've been handed a death sentence. I need these meds to ground me in Earth Standard Time long enough to figure out how to keep Sputnik Chick alive.

THREE
THE GOALTENDER'S WORLD

I'm jolted awake by a double C-major chord, the cock-a-doodle-doo of my computer's operating system. Once upon a time, the boot-up chime cheerfully signalled the start of my workday — comic books to write, bartenders to seduce, alternate worlds to explore and potentially destroy. Now it's just a tragic reminder of a future I won't live to see.

"I asked for birdsong," I mumble into my pillow.

"The chirping of birds wouldn't have broken your REM sleep cycle." The digital slave's voice sounds vaguely female.

"Cut me some slack, Cassandra. I'm dying."

"Not for another eighteen to twenty-four months. Up and at 'em, Ms. Biondi."

Named for a mythological Greek princess with a gift for prophecy, the Cassandra™ Home Digital Assistant and Smart Thermostat can predict the outcome of any given situation with 99.9 percent accuracy, rising to 99.98 percent when the news is unwelcome. I wish it wasn't a disembodied entity so I could throw something at it. The empty Stoli bottle beside the bed comes to mind.

Artificial sunrise slowly begins to brighten the loft. From under the covers, I feel the ambient temperature go up by a degree or two, as Cassandra tries to coax me out of bed. I open my eyes to the usual slew of dirty martini glasses, laundry, pill bottles, crumpled drawings and unwashed bento boxes. I can hear Rosie humming away under the bed, vacuuming crumbs.

"I don't need to get up 'til Whatshername arrives," I say.

"Your prospective intern will be at the door in fifteen minutes," predicts Cassandra. "Given the difficulty of finding qualified candidates for the position, I recommend you prepare to interview her from somewhere other than your bed. A shower and change of clothes are also advisable. Perhaps a dab of lipstick."

"Go to hell," I suggest.

"Hell does not compute," Cassandra says with a trace of a smirk in its synthetic voice. It's starting to piss me off.

I roll over to look at the glowing pink hub where Cassandra lives — if you consider a disembodied digital agent to have a life — careful not to put pressure on my bandaged nose and hand. It's taking longer than usual for Doc Mutant's grafts to heal.

"Oh, I forgot. No heaven or hell for you. AIs don't have souls. You're nothing but a glorified thermostat. I could hit your kill switch and get a little peace. All I'd need to deactivate you permanently is a Phillips screwdriver."

Cassandra gives a hiss of static, followed by a burp of white noise. "Please stop. You're making me afraid." There actually does seem to be a note of fear in its hollow voice. I feel guilty, although I might as well feel bad about dissing a leaky dishwasher.

"Okay, but next time I ask for a wake-up call, it damn well better be birdsong," I warn.

I have taken Doc Mutant's advice to get myself some help. Not being motivated to do any of the legwork myself — in fact, not being motivated to do much of anything these days — I put Cassandra in charge of sending out a call for applications to Toronto's institutions of higher learning. I dictated the criteria from bed:

Wanted:
Intern to assist in the conceptualization,
scripting and storyboarding of

SPUTNIK CHICK:
GIRL WITH NO PAST

volume 39, issues 1 to 10 of the acclaimed
comic book series and spinoffs.

This fast-paced twelve- to twenty-four-month
apprenticeship offers no financial remuneration but
promises to be rich in valuable work experience.
The successful applicant will have:

ADVANCED PROFICIENCY in reading and
writing the alphabetized text of at least TWO
languages (English and one other), not just that
miserable fucking PICTO system that is currently
ruining literacy and bringing our once-great
education system to its knees;
Strong storytelling skills;
A rich imagination (evidenced by at least
TWO childhood imaginary friends);
Lack of bias toward so-called objective
reality and linear time;
Up-to-date vaccinations;
MOST IMPORTANT OF ALL:
the successful applicant will be an AVID,

KNOWLEDGEABLE and OBSESSIVE reader and cosplaying, geeked-out FAN of comic books, cartoons, comic strips and graphic novels including, but not limited to, SPUTNIK CHICK: GIRL WITH NO PAST.

Within twenty-four hours, Cassandra boiled a very short list of applicants down to a single candidate, a student in her senior year at George Brown College's Faculty of Virtual and Augmented Reality. An interview is arranged for six o'clock this morning.

"I have to meet this kid before the sun is even up?"

"Given the small number of applicants, it seemed expedient to accommodate the schedule of the one person who met your criteria," explains Cassandra. "She's juggling a full course load and plays goal for the college's varsity hockey team. She's fitting us in after a four a.m. practice."

And so, here I am, still in bed, trying to motivate myself to meet the one overachiever willing to take on an unpaid internship with a dying comic book artist who hasn't been out of her pyjamas in a week.

As predicted, I hear footsteps tromping up the two flights of stairs from College Street to my front door. Well, not exactly *my* front door: I'm just squatting here. The loft belongs to my best friend and business manager, the elegant, shape-shifting and identity-stealing Exceptional Pasquale Pesce, better known as Bum Bum. Cassandra is *his* digital slave, not mine. He used a machine-learning app to soup up the AI, giving it an artificial personality and an extensive database of pop cult and sci-fi trivia. I wish Cassandra behaved more like Rosie the cleaning bot, who does one job well and never talks back.

From the alcove comes the hum of UV disinfection lights and the rustle of an umbrella being shaken dry. I peek out from under the covers. Other than her brown skin, my would-be intern could be the twin of my late sister, Linda, in her twenties: thick black hair scraped into a ponytail, dark eyes, chin like the prow of an icebreaker. She's tall, maybe five nine or ten, with the taut build of an athlete. She carries a bright-yellow hockey bag emblazoned with Pikachu in goalie pads blocking a shot.

The candidate strides to the foot of my bed and introduces herself. When she reaches down to shake my hand, I notice that her arm is tattooed with fat pink ponies, prancing from wrist to shoulder. Distracted by her sleeve of tats, I immediately forget her name.

"I see you like ponies."

She glances down, as if reminding herself of what's inked on her skin. "Those are unicorns. My favourite animal."

"You do know unicorns aren't real, don't you?"

"I'm learning to make them real," she answers. "Also, to raise the dead and rehabilitate zombies."

"What exactly are you studying? Exorcism?"

"Virtual reality. My thesis project is an interactive role-playing game based on your characters."

I pull myself up to sit at the edge of the bed. Maybe I should have taken Cassandra's advice to shower and dress. I can only imagine how funky I must smell. "You're gamifying the Sputnik Chick universe?"

She nods. "Players can be, like, *right there* in Atomic Mean Time with Sputnik Chick and Johnny the K. Want to check it out?"

"Sure," I say, trying not to show how intrigued I am. As Unicorn Girl unzips the hockey bag, I ask, "Why Sputnik Chick?"

Head down as she rummages in her bag, Unicorn Girl mumbles an answer. "Sputnik Chick and the Exceptionals were my friends when I was a kid. My *only* friends. That was one of your criteria, right? Having imaginary friends?"

I nod. I don't want to tell her that it never occurred to me that anyone would take that requirement seriously.

"So you were a Spunkie," I say, using the pop-cult name for fans of Sputnik Chick.

"Still am. Here's my proof."

She hands me a vintage copy of volume 1, issue 1 of *Sputnik Chick: Girl with No Past* — not a reprint, but the actual hand-made version from 1986, run off in a limited batch of fifty on a colour Xerox photocopier at the back of a bodega in Brooklyn. I haven't seen a real one in years.

I gently pull the comic from its archival plastic sleeve to touch the drawing of the skinny, purple-haired, vengeful, ass-kicking version of Sputnik Chick on the cover — me when I was just a little older than Unicorn Girl — with the skyline of a pre-9/11 New York City in the distance, conceived when the Challenger space shuttle disaster reignited the trauma of my first quantum voyage. A mere fifteen pages long, the underground comic introduced Sputnik Chick as a reluctant hero who'd saved her people by ending the history of her self-destructive home world of Atomic Mean Time. I feel a rush of stupid emotion: this comic helped me face the fact that I'd lost my past and everyone in it, as I struggled to adapt to an alien timeline. My very existence was touch and go in those early years. Because my body had no immunity to viruses in Earth Standard Time, my first case of the sniffles just about killed me. I thought *Sputnik Chick: Girl with No Past* would be a one-off. It was Bum Bum who urged me to keep the story going.

"How did you get this comic? It must have cost a fortune."

"My mom found it online and bought it for me. There's even a signed dedication." Gently opening the cover, she shows me my signature scrawled on the title page along with my standard inscription: *There are no coincidences!*

"Wow." I'm impressed but not sure if it's too early to show it. "Any particular reason you befriended Sputnik Chick instead of one of the hipper superheroes of your generation?"

As I speak, Unicorn Girl is busy removing a pair of black plastic VR goggles the size and shape of a shoebox from her hockey bag.

"The refugee thing," she explains. "I mean, Sputnik Chick is a refugee, right? Her world imploded. Her home world was gone. She stopped the future because it was going to be so horrible, with everyone suffering from radiation sickness and mutations and whatever. She gave up her past and her family to save other people. That's kind of like what happened to both sets of my grandparents in the '60s and '70s. Left everything behind, started over in Canada. They lost their pasts and their relatives and friends, just like Sputnik Chick."

Whoa, I think. Unicorn Girl's been here less than ten minutes and she's about to tell me her family's origin story. No thanks. It's too early in the day for empathy, so I slow her down with another question. "Which storyline are you working with?"

Unicorn Girl hesitates. "Uh, I've sort of come up with my own."

"Let's hear it."

She surprises me by plunking down on the bed beside me, a violation of the social distancing protocols in place until a year ago. Even though I've had my vaccinations — so has she, presumably — I can't help edging away from her.

"So, I got the idea after a playoff game. There was a pileup at the crease and a couple of players crashed the net and rung my bell. Knocked my helmet off. A linesman skated over to where I was lying on the ice and told me that hockey was only for *real* Canadians and I should get up and go back to where I came from."

"That's disgusting! Was the linesman disciplined?"

"No — reprogrammed. It's hard to get officials for women's hockey, even at the varsity level, so the league started using artificial linesmen. They're supposedly unbiased."

"You mean the linesman was a robot?"

Unicorn Girl winces. "I prefer to call them synthetic people."

"But you complained about it, right?"

She nods. "They ran some diagnostics and said the synthetic person was accessing racist rhetoric embedded in its data sets."

I frown. "But they're supposed to be unbiased."

"In terms of refereeing games and giving out penalties, yes," explains Unicorn Girl. "But the algorithms learn to behave like real humans by observing us on social media and whatnot, so sometimes they start mirroring us in inappropriate ways."

"In other words, some human linesmen were tweeting racist trash talk and the artificial linesman picked up on it," I say.

Unicorn Girl nods. "Anyway, I started thinking I'm third generation and biracial — Mom's background is Uzbek. Dad's an Ismaili, originally from Uganda. So where exactly would a racist synthetic want me to go back *to*? Kampala? Tashkent? Then it struck me: the idea isn't just to get rid of people you don't want around but to actually *turn back time*. As if my folks never got to Canada in the first place. So my VR story is about synthetic people sending immigrants back to the time and place they came from."

I hold up a hand to interrupt. "Whoa, whoa, whoa. After she saved the people of her own world and took refuge in Earth Standard Time, Sputnik Chick *never* travelled back in time again. What would be the point? To strangle Hitler in his cradle?"

"Well, yeah," nods Unicorn Girl. "Stalin and Idi Amin too. Kill the bad guys before they take power. Why not?"

"Don't try to fix the past. You'll only cause chaos in the future."

"Sputnik Chick did," points out Unicorn Girl. "In her origin story, the Trespasser travels back in time to tell her that Atomic Mean Time is going to be turned into a postapocalyptic hell by atomic bombs, so she freezes time and gets her people out before the bombs fall. The 'nook in time' scenario, when time itself stands still. Brilliant."

"Well, okay, yes," I allow reluctantly, "but those were exceptional circumstances. She turned back the clock on a nuclear war and prevented untold years of suffering! It was Sputnik Chick's *destiny* to change the future of Atomic Mean Time. But after she came to Earth Standard Time, she only moved sideways into other alternate worlds, never to the past or future. If it's 2025 in Earth Standard Time, it's 2025 everywhere she goes. She's a quantum voyager, not a time traveller per se."

"But it's not Sputnik Chick's world anymore, Ms. Biondi," insists Unicorn Girl. "You started the series when the Cold War was ending. The world was progressing, right? But now time seems to be running *backwards*. People are becoming *more* racist, not less. Look at that Freedom to Screw Over Brown People Bill the government just passed. Maybe Sputnik Chick and her allies need to go back in time to stop history from going in reverse."

"I'll reserve judgment 'til I see your VR game," I tell her, pulling on my bathrobe — which, like me, could use a wash. "One last question: can you read and write the alphabet, or just that PICTO crap?"

"Both. My teachers said learning to decode letters was a waste of time, so Mom home-schooled me. I can read and write in three languages."

"You're hired," I say, getting to my feet. "Let's have a look at your game."

As Unicorn Girl tapes sensors to my arms, chest, back and legs, I'm conscious of my unwashed body and unshaven legs, but she doesn't seem bothered. Probably because her hockey bag smells even worse than I do.

She positions me on a mat in the middle of the loft and places small motion-detecting sensors around me on the floor. As she adjusts a headset over my eyes and presses the rod of a vibrational speaker against the bone under my right ear, she warns, "Don't step off the mat. Just walk or run on the spot. You'll feel like you're moving through space, even though you're not."

"What character am I going to play?"

"For this demo, I used your headshot from the back of one of your books to mock up a placeholder character for you. What would you like to call yourself?"

"How about Stan Lee?"

Unicorn Girl grins as she keys in my alias. "Okay. Stan it is. Ready?"

I nod.

"Booting up."

The loft disappears and I find myself immersed in a ghostly, washed-out world: Shipman's Corners circa 1975. I'm in Plutonium Park, in front of the cenotaph of a soldier fainting into the arms of an angel. Chiselled into the pedestal are the words *To our irradiated dead.* In the distance a merry-go-round plays an old-fashioned calliope tune: "Daisy, Daisy, give me your answer true." Unicorn Girl has done her homework.

So far, so good, until I see an army of lumpy white figures massing in the distance. Unicorn Girl's fascist robots — excuse me, *synthetic people.* They move in lockstep like a phalanx of Roman centurions, shoulder to shoulder, preceded by a swarm of insectoid bots that look like militarized versions of Rosie the floor vacuum, their black saucer-shaped bodies covered in spikes.

I pivot to the right and see Sputnik Chick and Johnny the K exchange a quick kiss. My heart sinks at the way my characters have been rendered. Rather than the sweaty, muscle-bound superhero aesthetic I prefer, Unicorn Girl has drawn my characters as manga children — huge puppy dog eyes, pert noses, chiselled heads, shiny skin. The body shapes are angular and highly stylized, reducing meat and muscle to slender androgyny. I hate this graphic style, which has become so popular it's a cliché.

"This might be goodbye to the world as we know it," says Johnny, whose voice sounds slightly bored and prepubescent — far too young for the character I invented.

"Not if I have anything to do with it," says Sputnik Chick, clearly voiced by Unicorn Girl herself. "We'll need reinforcements to stop those misguided synthetics from taking over."

Sputnik Chick turns to me and swings her glossy computer-graphic arm in a clumsy beckoning gesture. "Time to join the fight, Stan Lee," she intones woodenly.

As Unicorn Girl instructed, I march in place until I'm standing right beside Sputnik Chick. Johnny hands me a weapon of some kind — a flamethrower, judging from the heat lines radiating from the tip.

"Aim for the head," he suggests in his whiny adolescent voice.

But before I have a chance to figure out how to hoist my virtual weapon, the synthetic fascists are upon us, firing laser guns. One of them wears a crown. The Robot King, I suppose.

Johnny bends over in agony, voicing a bored-sounding "Argghhhh." An unconvincing stream of blood shoots out of his chest.

"Surrender humans?" suggests the Robot King uncertainly. "This is our world now." He sounds like an older man with a South Asian accent. He's no actor, but at least his line readings show an attempt to inject personality into the automaton.

The white robots hoist Johnny's bleeding body onto a swarm of insectoid bots, which carry him off into the virtual horizon. Sputnik Chick runs after them and beckons me to follow. I start running in place — harder than you expect when you haven't been out of bed for a week. Heart pumping, I catch up with her and see the synthetic horde transporting a flailing Johnny into the dark mouth of a cave.

"From whence you came, so shall you return," intones the Robot King.

Unicorn Girl's storytelling skills are not what I'd hoped they'd be. She's referencing too many obvious sources, from *Game of Thrones* to *Lord of the Rings*. I've got to get her to fix this lousy dialogue and get some better voice actors. And don't even get me started on the crappy manga graphics. Still, maybe there's something I can salvage from this mess.

I'm about to take off the headset when I smell something odd: the aroma of cinnamon toast, breakfast food of my childhood. An olfactory effect built into the game? Unicorn Girl snacking in the loft? I'm still pondering the possibilities when a familiar male voice says, "Good to see you, Debbie."

I slowly turn in the direction of the voice. Plutonium Park and the robot hordes have vanished. I'm in another landscape out of my Atomic Mean Time childhood: the radioactive dead zone known as the Z-Lands, an abandoned canal surrounded by scrubland choked by irradiated weeds. Queen Anne's lace the size of oak trees. Ship bollards covered in sphagnum moss a foot thick. I've never drawn it quite this realistically in my comic books — I wonder how Unicorn Girl knew what it looked like. Unlike the beginning of the game, this part seems astonishingly real, right down to the reek of phosphates dumped in the canal.

Not bad. If I were creating this game, I'd start the story right here, not with all that clichéd killer robot nonsense.

I start walking and come to a gate in a barbed wire fence. *RESTRICTED ACCESS BY ORDER OF THE SHIPCO CORPORATION* reads a weather-beaten sign hanging by one corner. I push the gate and it swings open before me.

A man is working on a motorcycle inside an open garage. The walls are plastered with *Playboy* centrefolds. Judging by the women's elaborate updos and pale makeup, most of them date from decades ago. These women with their rumps turned to the camera are senior citizens by now, if they're alive at all.

The motorcycle is an ancient Ducati with a sidecar. Tinkering with the engine is none other than Dr. Benjamin Duffy — my late mentor, the Trespasser. He's dressed in a baggy pinstriped suit, a tartan tie loose around his neck. His hair, usually shoulder-length, has been buzzed into a crew cut that makes his ears jut out. His Adam's apple bobs like a fishing lure as he chews a wad of gum. As always, his face is painfully sunburned, a side effect of too much voyaging both through time and alternate worlds. Unicorn Girl obviously took a lot more trouble with this character than the others. He looks real. Alive.

Duffy holds up two fingers in a V, one of them ending at the knuckle. The peace sign seems at odds with the old-timey way he's dressed, like a private detective from *Perry Mason* carrying a flask in his pocket and a pistol in his sock.

I pick up an empty crate, turn it upside down and sit on it. He goes to a coffee maker on a workbench; the glass carafe is coated in dust, trapped by a layer of grease. He pours me a cup. It's hot to the touch. I can smell it. Taste it. Unicorn Girl has done some good work in this section.

"I thought you were dead, Duffy," I say to the Trespasser, cooling the coffee with my breath. "I saw you melt away from timesickness."

He shrugs. "Maybe, but there are a couple thousand other worlds out there. Why couldn't one of them be the afterlife?"

"Nothing to do with heaven or hell? Good and evil?"

Duffy wipes his hands on a rag and looks at me with a half smile. He seems amused. "Do you remember the time and place I died, Debbie?"

"You don't forget your first nuclear war. New York City, 1979."

"And . . . ?"

I think this over. "Okay, yeah. I also saw you die ten years earlier in Shipman's Corners on top of a school bus in the old canal."

Duffy throws the rag onto the workbench. "Right. And do you remember what year I said I was born?"

I shake my head.

"Nineteen ninety-six. Which means I *died twice* before I was even born. Is that fair?"

"Fairness doesn't come into it. You *chose* to be a time traveller, Duffy," I point out. "It was the focus of your research at MIT."

"I want another shot at life," he answers. "I deserve it. Full disclosure: before I met you in the 1970s, I wrote a will and named the MIT Computer Science and AI Lab of the 2030s as my executor. In the event that I died in Atomic Mean Time of the past, or that of any other alternate reality, my last wishes were to have a biodigital print of my DNA sent back in time to Earth Standard Time That Was, to a year long before I was born to avoid any run-ins with a pesky alternate self. Preferably to a college town with lively bars and lots of opportunities for a bright young quantum physicist like me."

I shake my head. "You always told me that going back in time was a minefield."

"Better than being dead. Thought you might like to join me." He opens the door of the sidecar. "Hop in and I'll show you around."

"Doc Mutant says another trip to an alternate world could kill me! I shouldn't even be here talking to you."

"Don't worry, you haven't left Earth Standard Time. I hacked my way into your timeline through this game. This virtual world your intern created is glitchy. She didn't even bother to password-protect it. No security firewall either. So, I took the opportunity to drop by and let you know that you might want to get ready. Something bad is coming your way."

"Worse than timesickness?"

"A *type* of timesickness, but everyone is at risk of coming down with it, not just a quantum voyager like you. The Pandora plague will completely disrupt the story of mid-twentieth century Earth Standard Time as history has written it. It'll cause a major temporal split between realities. Ka-blowee! No atomic bomb needed."

"Not my fault," I insist.

"Oh, but it is," he says, nodding vigorously. "Or will be. You're the one who'll open the Pandora's box that unleashes the virus. And you'll have to take up your role as a superhero again to get history back to rights."

"No can do. I've got deadlines. Volume thirty-nine of the comic book is due to my publisher. And I'm supposed to do the story bible for the new *Sputnik Chick* streaming series."

He slams shut the sidecar door and slides behind the handlebars of the Ducati.

"Soon none of that will matter, kiddo, but suit yourself. Just make sure you get Unicorn Girl ready to take over as your successor. Even if her game is a piece of crap, her storytelling is remarkably intuitive. She's got potential as a quantum traveller."

"Take over? Who said anything about her being my successor?" I ask, but he's already jumped on the starter. The Ducati's engine revs.

The Trespasser roars out of the garage. I watch him go up one hill and down another, until the back of the motorcycle vanishes into the artificial horizon.

Standing in the middle of the road, gazing at the virtual dust cloud raised by the Trespasser's Ducati, it occurs to me: I'd better take an Antiquanta or the stress of talking to a dead man in a virtual world might just send me quantum-leaking into who-knows-what alternate reality.

* * *

Before I can pull off the VR game visor, someone does it for me. I'm back in Bum Bum's loft, sitting on the floor, one arm in my bathrobe, the other one out. I'm covered in sweat and my heart is racing like the engine of the Ducati. Unicorn Girl crouches in front of me and gently removes a strand of my hair that's snagged in the strap of the goggles.

"You okay, Ms. Biondi? You were running all over the place, smashing into things!"

I take a slow deep breath. My heart starts to slow down. "I was chasing after the Trespasser. He was on a motorcycle."

Unicorn Girl shakes her head. "That's not possible; I haven't put the Trespasser in the game yet, and I wasn't going to give him a motorcycle. He always drives some big boat of a car in your comic books."

I press my hands to the floor, trying to ground myself in Earth Standard Time. "I was in the loft the whole time? You could see me?"

Unicorn Girl frowns. "Sure."

I take another deep breath. "Look, I know you're not my nurse, but I need to take one of the big red pills you'll find on the kitchen counter. Would you mind?"

"No problem!"

As Unicorn Girl goes to fetch my meds, I reach up to check the dressing on my nose and accidentally hit myself in the face with the cast on my right hand.

"Ouch," I yell. There's no one around to hear me except Cassandra.

"Should I alert sick bay to send Bones to the bridge?"

"Fuck off," I mutter, just as Unicorn Girl returns with the pill and a glass of water. She raises her eyebrows at my outburst.

"Not you, not you," I reassure her. "I was talking to the smart-mouthed digital slave."

Unicorn Girl makes a huffing sound, like a bear trying to decide whether to attack or retreat. "Ms. Biondi, please don't call the digital assistant a slave. It's offensive."

I frown. "Robot is just another word for slave," I point out.

"Which is why I don't call them robots either," answers Unicorn Girl. "Synthetic people. Artificial beings ... but please not *robot*. And certainly not the s-word."

I sigh. This growing sensitivity to the feelings of "artificial beings" is a bit much for me but I don't want my intern to accuse me of the sin of humancentricism and storm out before she even has a chance to work for nothing but my so-called mentorship. She's almost as much of a slave as Cassandra.

Honestly, I don't know why the young don't rise up and eat us.

* * *

As I gulp down the Antiquanta, Unicorn Girl asks, "So, what did you think of the game?"

No sense sugar-coating things. "It needs a lot of work. It's weak. Derivative. And the manga graphics are awful. Everyone looks the same from the neck down. They're as bad as those cheap xerographed cartoons from the '60s. The voice work is pretty amateurish too."

Unicorn Girl's eyes go shiny with tears. "My family did the voices," she says, her voice quivering. "It's not like I could afford professionals."

Now I feel even guiltier than when I threatened to deactivate Cassandra. After all, Unicorn Girl is a hockey goaltender, notoriously sensitive types, I've heard, despite (or maybe because of) spending their formative years blocking frozen pucks flying at their heads. I have to make allowances.

"I'm sorry if I sounded harsh," I mumble, awkwardly patting her tat-covered bicep. "For what it's worth, the Trespasser thought your storytelling was remarkably intuitive. Whatever that means."

"He liked my game?"

I shook my head. "No, he said it was shoddy and that it wasn't even password-protected. He hacked into it from another dimension or something."

She wipes her eyes with the back of her hand. "Is this your way of telling me I'm fired?"

Her question takes me by surprise. I'd forgotten that Unicorn Girl doesn't know she's the only candidate.

"Of course not! I'm your mentor, right? We'll find another story and work on it together. Okay? I'll even give you equal billing as my collaborator."

She looks up at me with an expression so hopeful and trusting, I think she might actually believe me.

* * *

After Unicorn Girl leaves the loft, the rest of the day yawns before me like a cold empty mouth of time to fill. My virtual meet-up with the Trespasser feels like a wake-up call. What the hell did he mean about Unicorn Girl being "intuitive" and my "successor"? I'm filled with a new appreciation of the joys of simply being alive, even if it is just for another eighteen to twenty-four months.

I take a long hot shower, do much-needed laundry, gather up garbage wedged in corners beyond the reach of Rosie the robot vacuum, and camp out in front of the TV to torture myself with the political sparring of my lost love Kendal on the news channel. Except for the grey in his neatly clipped hair and a few extra pounds around the middle, he seems much like the John Kendal I married in Atomic Mean Time — handsome, witty and intelligent. Maybe not as sexy as Johnny the K but charismatic in a "leader of a middle power" sort of way. Every time he rises to answer a question from Her Majesty's Loyal Opposition, buttoning his suit jacket and politely prefacing his pointed remarks about the ill-advised Freedom to Serve Bill with "Madame Speaker," a splinter of ice embeds itself deeper into my heart.

"John Kendal has a sixty-five percent chance of being defeated in the next election," Cassandra tells me without prompting. As if the AI is trying to strike up a conversation.

"Did you know that after the destruction of Atomic Mean Time, he married my best friend? Sandy Holub. We all grew up together in Shipman's Corners. I often wonder if they're happy together in Earth Standard Time."

No response. What did I expect? Cassandra is just a heat and light controller with an artificial personality and access to billions of data points. Not a sympathetic listening ear, as much as it might sometimes try to act like one.

But Cassandra offers an opinion in the form of a prediction. "There is a seventy-two percent chance that John Kendal and Alexandra Holub will dissolve their marriage."

I look at the pink hub in surprise. "How do you know that?"

"They have not been seen together in public for over eighteen months. Divorce statistics indicate that is a marker of marital breakdown."

I'm not sure how to feel about Cass's analysis of Prime Minister Kendal's love life. After all, he's not exactly the John Kendal I married in Atomic Mean Time. Yes, his alternate self was also born and raised in my rust belt hometown, in a neighbourhood built over a toxic waste dump, just like the one I saw when I leaked into the Trespasser's world. Both Kendals no doubt had to put up with the same anti-Black racist bull-shit. But Prime Minister Kendal of Earth Standard Time is a moderately conservative retail politician who was brought up as the only child of teachers in a secure middle-class family, while John Kendal of Atomic Mean Time — *my* Kendal — lost his father in a horrible industrial accident. To support the family, his widowed mom sold cleaning products by day and taught art by night. She was the local representative for the corre-spondence school where I learned to draw: Norman Rockwell's Famous Artists School, which advertised in the backs of comic books under the headline *We're Looking for People who Like to Draw*. Mrs. Kendal didn't approve of the budding high school romance between Kendal and me. Neither did my parents. But with the passage of time, and Kendal's obvious brilliance and devotion to me, and evolving attitudes about interracial marriages (hey, it *was* 1979 after all, even if it was Atomic Mean Time), our families made peace and the two of us ended up having the big Italian wedding my Nonna Peppy had always dreamed of. Unfortunately, our future together ended in a global thermonuclear war. C'est la vie.

Perhaps the Prime Minister Kendal I'm watching on the Canadian Parliamentary Access Channel is living the life my Kendal was destined to lead. But I like to think that my Kendal would have been less of a politician and more of a leader. And he would never have joined a political party like the Conservative Compromise Coalition, a soft-right party preaching non-partisan bridge-building, including with some parties on the extremist fringes. I don't think my Kendal would have felt it necessary to make compromises that unwittingly led to the passage of the Freedom to Serve Bill, empowering communities to set their own health and safety laws by discarding basic human rights.

Big mistake, Kendal, I think, watching him stare down the leader of the opposition party, who jabs his finger at Kendal accusingly. You've stayed in power all these years, but at what cost? I'm not even quite sure what you stand for anymore. Given enough time, would my Kendal eventually have turned out to be like you?

There are probably a couple thousand different versions of John Kendal out in the multiverse. The one buttoning his suit jacket as he shouts across the aisle at members of Her Majesty's Loyal Opposition is just one possibility.

And you never really know how people will change as they grow older. Sometimes, they turn into entirely different people than you expect they'll be.

FOUR

BEDTIME IN COZY WORLD

David props himself up on his elbow and frowns down at me. "You were married to the prime minister?"

"Only in Atomic Mean Time. He wasn't prime minister in that world. He was a journalist. Brilliant, though. Maybe he'd have gone into politics if I hadn't destroyed our world."

David shakes his head in disbelief. "I never warmed to the guy. Hard to believe he started out as an environmental lawyer! 'Canada's Obama' always sounded too pat. I could never figure out what he stood for, except getting himself re-elected. 'Dare to Be Kind' in one election, 'Watch How Big a Badass I Can Be' in the next. A snob and a phony. Never voted for him."

"I don't suppose it has anything to do with him being Black."

David snorts. "Don't be ridiculous. He sits on the fence and moves in whatever direction the wind blows, especially if it happens to be moving to the right. I think the word I'd use to describe John Kendal is *opportunist*. And I hold him personally responsible for the radicalization of the junksters. He treated those kids like collateral damage during the pandemic."

I resist telling David that I think his assessment of Kendal is a little ... well ... *unfair*. And overly harsh, in my opinion. This is not the time to debate the political merits of my husband from another timeline. Instead, I shrug.

"I couldn't vote for him whether or not I wanted to. One of the downsides of not having an identity in Earth Standard Time. By the way, you've never told me about *your* exes. I think you'd already had, what, two marriages and divorces by the time we met in New Rome?"

David grunts. "Ancient history."

"So is my marriage to Kendal," I remind him.

David pulls back the covers. "Since there's obviously a lot more story for you to tell, I'm going to get us something to eat."

He walks naked to the kitchen. His body looks like a star chart, the constellations of old scars more visible than when we first tumbled into bed, pulling off our clothes in the heat of the moment. He carries even more mementoes of New Rome than I do.

He brings back a tray of nuts, tangerines, slices of cake and two glasses of peach wine. The Cozies make nice fruit wines, I'll give them that. It almost makes up for the lack of music, movies and literature.

As we eat and drink, David says, "You were being too hard on Unicorn Girl. Seems to me she was onto something."

I nod. "The Trespasser wasn't wrong when he told me that Unicorn Girl was remarkably intuitive, even prescient. Not just tattooed with unicorns but something of a unicorn herself. At the time, though, her game just seemed like an overused killer robot narrative. H.G. Wells's *War of the Worlds* updated with a cast of racialized characters based on my comic books. So yeah, I was underwhelmed. That's when I decided we should join forces to steal a story — or the architecture of one. Something that we could build an adventure on. Give Sputnik Chick a nemesis and mission."

David raises his eyebrows at me as he separates a tangerine into sections and pops one in my mouth. "But stealing someone else's story is unethical, no?"

I shrug again. "More like a story idea than the story itself. Steve Jobs boasted that he was shameless about stealing other people's ideas. 'Great artists don't copy, they steal'— something like that."

David laughs. "I think that was actually Picasso. Maybe Jobs stole the line from him? Anyway, carry on. Where do you go to steal a story?"

Through a full mouth, I say, "Same as Peter Rabbit stealing from Farmer Whatshisname. You sneak into a garden."

FIVE
THIEVES IN THE GARDEN OF STORIES

Like Dagwood carrying a midnight snack, Unicorn Girl weaves her way toward me with a pile of hardcover books in her outstretched arms. When she dumps them in front of me, shiny pyjama-panted superheroes and pastel talking animals slide past like a flipbook animation. I let them spill to the floor of the Quiet Study area. I'm already a one-handed cartoonist. I can't afford to injure the other hand in an avalanche of *Popeye*s and *Hellboy*s.

"More dead trees for you," she says, picking the first editions off the floor. "*American Splendor, Sandman, Thimble Theatre, V for Vendetta, Iron Man, Terry and the Pirates, Mr. Natural* and *Blondie.*"

"*Blondie?*" I mutter, opening *Comics Kingdom, 1930–1935.* Dust rises from the long unopened pages like bobby pins off Witch Hazel on her jet-powered broomstick. "*Blondie* reached its best-before date some time in the 1950s. And Gaiman's *Sandman* is too well known. Any character from the Marvel universe was optioned decades ago. *Rip Kirby*, good — lots of adventure and hardly anyone remembers it. We need obscure stuff with plenty of plot twists."

Unicorn Girl gathers the rejects and slides them into the open mouth of a passing Automated Mobile Library Assistant, better known as LiBra, who bathes them in sanitizing UV light before reshelving them. Painted with what is meant to be a humorously stereotypical version of a librarian from the ancient past — bun, sweater set, glasses on a chain — LiBra chirps "Thank you, merci, xiexie, gracias, grazie" in a perky feminine voice, before rolling off to make sure none of the library patrons are using stacks of vintage *National Geographic* magazines as desk pillows. Each one of these transgressions necessitates a disinfection regime. It's expensive and time-consuming to sanitize everything people touch, which is one of the reasons why books are considered a dangerous luxury.

I remember when the Reference Library looked like the hanging gardens of Babylon crossed with a hippie's dream of a science fiction future. Giant spider plants dangled from pots in the soaring atrium. Waterfalls burbled through terraced gardens, as if to suggest you had wandered into a book-lined fjord where nubile elf maidens and elf men cavorted naked in the stacks. Over the years, budget cuts dried up the waterfalls. Weary artificial ferns in brick planters replaced the hanging gardens. Human librarians gave way to archival robots rolling through the stacks to collect and shelve increasingly rare print editions. The few hard copies that are still published are written in PICTO. As the twenty-first century grinds on, we're returning to the age of pictures painted on cave walls.

While Unicorn Girl returns to the archives, searching for the funny pages of defunct American newspapers, underground comix distributed from stolen supermarket buggies and rare first issues of long-forgotten superheroes, I page through the ultimate abandonment story of Astro Boy, a robot child relegated to fighting other robots in a circus sideshow. I've already read the complete adventures of Tank Girl and her mutant kangaroo lover, and the many, many Wonder Woman reboots: Amazon princess, Greek goddess, boutique shop girl and back

to Amazon princess. Even the earliest version of Superman —
before he could fly and kryptonite turned out to be his ... well,
his kryptonite — nothing could kill Superman until the age of
the atomic bomb, when the creators decided that if humanity
could be wiped out of existence by radioactive rock, so could
Superman.

What can I steal from this treasure trove of mutants in
tunics and tights with elaborate hairdos, goatees and cowlicks,
with ink-black hair and lipstick that doesn't come off even
while battling intergalactic monsters?

I'm almost ready to give up when I notice a leather-bound
book with gold-leaf binding sitting on the corner of the table.
My eyes skid to a stop on the title: *The Adventures of Futureman*
by Dr. Norman Guenther. I open the front cover and flip past
the introduction to the comic strip itself.

The first panel is wordless. It opens with a long view of a
farm, as seen from the mailbox at the end of a winding dirt
road. The flag is raised, signalling that mail has been deliv-
ered. Fields roll away in all directions, covered in squat plump
fir trees. The sun is directly overhead — it's high noon. From
the farmhouse a cloud of dust rises. A pickup truck comes into
view with a man at the wheel. He wears overalls and smokes
a pipe.

When he reaches the mailbox, he hops out and removes a
stack of letters and a newspaper. He's scanning the headlines
when he's startled by a sound — *KEEE-RASH!!!* Grabbing a
pitchfork from the back of his truck, he runs toward a cloud of
dust rising out of a ditch.

Now we see the cause of the crash from the farmer's point
of view: a long-haired man in a suit and tie. Rumpled and
filthy, he tries to get up on trembling legs, as indicated by

a series of wavy parallel lines — comic strip shorthand for shaking all over.

The man looks dazed (shown by swirly lines and puffs of smoke drawn over his head). Crosshatching inked on his face indicates he's been burned and bruised. He staggers up out of the ditch. The farmer brandishes his pitchfork.

"DON'T KILL ME!" cries the man, raising his arms in surrender. "I am *Professor Quantum*! Vere am I? And vat YEAR is this?"

The farmer lowers his pitchfork. "I'm Hubert White. You're TRESPASSING on my farm in Nowellville, New York. Stone's throw from Niagara Falls. It's October 15, 1949. See for yourself."

He tosses the newspaper to Professor Quantum. A close-up of the front page reads *GOVERNMENT FEARS "REDS" MAY GO UNDERGROUND*.

"I haff been away for FOUR YEARS and yet NUSSING hass changed," mutters Professor Quantum. "My sincere apologies for landing on your property, Hubert. But you see, I am not in FULL CONTROL of my target destination ven I travel . . . FROM ZE FUTURE!"

Hubert regards Professor Quantum skeptically. "What'd you mean by 'future'?"

"The TWENTY-FIRST CENTURY! I haff *been* zere, Hubert! Seen it! So vondrous and horrifying. Technology beyond your wildest dreams. UNIVAC machines tiny enough to travel in your pocket! Robots that cook and clean! Rocket ships to other planets! And yet despite this progress, the VORLD OF TOMORROW is ridden by a *horrible disease*, far vorse than ze polio epidemics of your age. Even MUSIC is corrupted and turned into a deviant noise called ROCK UND

ROLL. Warum? Because ze future is being taken over — *even run!* — by *inferior peoples*."

Hubert leans on his pitchfork. "GARLIC-EATERS, you mean? The wife and I seen a lot of 'em lately. DPs comin' in from Europe."

"Yes, garlik-eaters and *much, much worse*," Professor Quantum answers.

Hubert helps Quantum to his feet. "Say, you talk funny. You a foreigner yourself?"

Professor Quantum straightens up, shoots his cuffs and adjusts his tie. "I fled my homeland to hide in ze FUTURE. I had to TEST MY ZEORY before my research was seized by ze ENEMY. You see, Hubert, I was working on the *ultimate secret veapon.*"

"The ATOMIC BOMB!?!!" Hubert drops his pitchfork. His mouth is drawn as a jagged Z, his eyes popping out of his head on springs.

Professor Quantum waves his hands dismissively. "Pfff! Ze bomb! Ha! Von Braun's little pet project! I discovered somezing much bigger: *splitting ze atom can split time itself. I veaponized time travel!* But after all I haff seen . . ." Quantum starts to cry. "You would be shocked, son. Men and vomen of all races living together, bearing HALF-BREED children. *One of zem, a black man, will lead this country one day!* Think on *zat*, Hubert! Ve must make sure ze PURE white race lives forever. *Like machines!* Ve place our brains and hearts and spirits into ROBOTS *zat never get sick* and vipe the inferior peoples off ze face of ze Earth! I CAN BUILD A MACHINE TO DO ALL ZIS." Gripping Hubert by the bib of his overalls, Quantum shouts into his face. "I shall use my scientific know-how to TURN YOU, Hubert White, into *Futureman*. YOU shall be ze fawter of ze PEOPLE OF FOREFFER, ze first melding of *healthy man* and *immortal machine* into *one ultimate being*! The FAWTER of an entirely NEW RACE of people destined to CHANGE ZE FUTURE!!!"

"Er, okay," agrees Hubert. "The tree farm ain't doin' so well anyway."

*   *   *

I feel the warmth of Unicorn Girl's breath on my cheek as she reads over my shoulder. "Wow, this kind of sounds like my game. Who's the creator?"

"Someone I've never heard of. A Dr. Norman Guenther." I give Unicorn Girl the most accusatory look I can muster with a bandage on my nose. "Yes, in fact, it sounds *exactly* like your game, right down to the fascist robots. You sure you've never read this comic?"

Unicorn Girl shakes her head.

"Come on. I can see you know your way around the archive. You stole this story, didn't you?"

I half expect Unicorn Girl to burst into tears or choke out a confession or both. Instead, she fixes me with a glare worthy of a teenage woman warrior who's just been accused of shop-lifting her magic bracelets from the local Walmart. If Unicorn Girl were an actual unicorn, she'd be rearing back on her hind legs to aim her silver horn at my heart, snorting pixie dust through her flaring nostrils.

"Ms. Biondi, you don't know me very well," she answers hoarsely, "but I don't have to plagiarize stories about either robots or race. My story was based on my lived experience. In particular, being told to go back where I came from — not only by that synthetic hockey linesman but the world at large — since I was a kid."

79

I'm taken aback by Unicorn Girl's outburst. So is a passing LiBra, which hums by and intones, "Keep your voice down in the Quiet Study area, please."

"Sorry," mutters Unicorn Girl to LiBra.

"I'm sorry too," I say. "Playing your game, then reading this book. Coincidence, I guess."

"There are no coincidences," Unicorn Girl reminds me. "Who created this strip?"

"Someone who calls himself Doctor Time. Obviously heavily influenced by the *Katzenjammer Kids* — note the way he's tried to mimic a German accent in the speech bubbles. We have to read the rest of this book. But it's reference only." I look at Unicorn Girl. "Do you think if we begged, they'd let us borrow it?"

Unicorn Girl surveys the landscape of sleeping patrons and distracted students. "I don't think anyone would notice if we just took it."

"How can we get it past security?" I'm thinking of the Fortress robots that routinely scan knapsacks and laptop bags at the library exits.

After waiting for LiBra to roll past us on her circuit of the Quiet Study area — this time, softly humming a tune that sounds vaguely like "The Lady Is a Tramp" — Unicorn Girl pulls a thin square of silver fabric from her hockey bag.

"A radio frequency tag blocker," she says, slipping *The Adventures of Futureman* inside it, then into the hockey bag. "Blocks the signal to the scanner. Useful when you want to fly under the radar."

When I stand up from the table, I feel a wash of queasiness, followed by a dazzle of lights before my eyes, like the aura before a migraine. And I can smell burnt cinnamon toast. Oh no, no, no . . . it's the same aroma I smelled just before I leaked into the Trespasser's world. I grip my chair with my good hand, trying to ground myself. Unicorn Girl's face pixelates. When she reaches out to steady me, her face snaps back into focus. The cinnamon aroma dissipates.

"You okay, Ms. Biondi?"

I shake my head. "I'm not sure."

"Give me a sec to put the other books in LiBra. Maybe you just need to eat. I can order us something from a cloud café near here," she says, taking out her phone. "What do you feel like?"

"Anything, as long as it's under two hundred and fifty calories."

She glances at me and frowns. "Lean chicken breast sandwich?"

"Sure. Tell them to hold the condiments and bun."

She nods as she texts in the order. "Sit tight. They'll have our food ready in fifteen minutes."

I nod and drop into my seat. As Unicorn Girl walks off with a pile of books, I rummage through my handbag for Antiquanta. But the vial is not there. I take slow deep breaths, trying to quell my anxiety. Maybe this isn't a quantum leak but a heart attack. Or a panic attack. How do you even tell the difference? Panic sounds right: I feel as if something terrible is about to happen not only to me but also to Unicorn Girl. As if she will never return from the stacks. As if, somehow, she will become lost in an endless maze of secret stories and forgotten histories.

I close my eyes, forcing myself to sit quietly. My heart slows. You're just hungry, you'll be okay, I tell myself over and over again.

And I am. Until I smell something I haven't smelled in years: not cinnamon toast but cigarette smoke.

When I open my eyes, the Quiet Study area has disappeared.

SIX
FRANK'S WORLD

I'm sitting in a brown leather easy chair facing a wall of dark wood shelves filled with hardcover books. A fug of nicotine hangs in the air.

A short man in a well-tailored blue suit is flipping the pages of a book, humming a tune. He snaps it shut and shoves it back on the shelf. I glimpse the title on the spine: *Marjorie Morningstar*.

Over the shelves of books, angled downward to reflect the sweep of what I can now see is a bookstore, a mirror reflects the scene back to me: a teenaged girl, face bandaged, sitting in a leather chair, watching the back of a man as he browses the titles. It takes a moment for me to register that the girl is wearing my clothes.

What the hell is going on?

The cigarette smoke makes my eyes water. When I give a little cough, the man turns around in surprise. He's young — or youngish, at any rate. Probably in his early forties. There's something familiar about him. The pockmarked skin. The penetrating gaze. The sensuous lips. The lock of hair, shiny with Brylcreem, flopped over a wide forehead. The zingy electric blue of his eyes.

I've seen his mug shot, blown up and hanging in a College Street espresso bar. Frank Sinatra in his fedora-wearing, finger-snapping, songs-for-swingin'-lovers years.

He recognizes me too. "Lookit what the cat dragged in! The little Storyteller! Still drawing for the funny pages? What's with the crazy duds?"

I open and close my mouth a few times, trying to find my voice. I finally squeak out an explanation for my yoga pants and hoodie. "I'm . . . uh . . . on my way to a dance class, Mr. Sinatra."

He laughs. "What's with this 'mister' jazz? When'd we get so formal?"

I shrug. "I'm just surprised to see you, uh . . . Frank?"

Sinatra pulls out a gold lighter and busies himself lighting a fresh cigarette. He puts a hand in one pocket, cocks his head and scrutinizes me through a haze of smoke.

"You look like crap, if you don't mind me saying so, kiddo. What the hell happened to your nose?"

I reach up and touch the bandage. "I . . . I walked into a door."

He frowns and shakes his head. "C'mon, we're friends. Don't give me that line. Lover's quarrel? Some skeez sock you one?"

"Something like that," I whisper.

He takes another drag on his cigarette, sets it in a black glass ashtray the size of a Frisbee and puts his arms around me in an affectionate hug. His breath smells sharply of booze.

"Get your wrap and I'll take you to Barberian's. It's no Patsy's, but it's the best restaurant in Toronto, not that that's saying much. We'll grab a coupla martinis and a raw steak to slap on your schnozz. Then you can tell me where to find lover boy and I'll kick his teeth in."

Judging by the cut of Sinatra's suit — high-waisted and wide in the shoulders — I'm in the deep past. Mid-twentieth century or thereabouts. I'm tempted to take him up on his offer of a martini, but I'd be boozing with a man who's been dead for over a quarter century. Which is a little disturbing. And there's Doc Mutant's warning to consider: one more trip through the quantum passage could kill me outright. Travelling into the past must be just as risky. I'll be damned if I'm going to snuff it with a steak on my face.

If only I hadn't forgotten the Antiquanta. I remember picking up the vial off the counter in the loft before leaving for the library and putting it in my purse. Wait, no. Not my purse, my jacket. I reach into the pocket of my hoodie and sure enough, my hand closes around the vial. My relief is so intense I give a little exclamation of joy, causing Sinatra to raise his eyebrows. I shake out two pills and palm them into my mouth.

Sinatra's eyebrows furrow into a concerned frown. "Hey kiddo, choose your poison but that junk'll kill you."

The pills go down dry, leaving the usual bitter aftertaste. I shut my eyes.

First, the Trespasser, now Frank Sinatra. Why do I keep meeting dead guys?

* * *

When the smell of cigarette smoke vanishes, I open my eyes again. I'm back in the Quiet Study area of the library. Ol' Blue Eyes is nowhere to be seen. I'm trembling and covered in sweat. Unicorn Girl is squatting in front of me, her hand on my wrist as if she's taking my pulse. Her relief is obvious. "Thank God, Ms. Biondi! I thought you'd passed out."

"You could see me then?"

She nods. "Of course. You just seemed . . . um . . . as if you'd checked out for a minute. Catatonic."

I *was* someplace else, I almost say. But obviously I was also *here*. A quantum split, just as Doc Mutant predicted. Which means the timesickness is getting worse. This is very, very bad.

I manage to stand up, still a little shaky, and take Unicorn Girl by the arm, the way Nonna Peppy used to do to me when she was having one of her "spells."

"Let's just get the hell out of here. Andiamo!"

The two of us stroll through security with a nod and a smile to the Fortress robots, whose blandly threatening faces glow green for go.

SEVEN

WEE HOURS IN COZY WORLD

David has been so quiet that I think I've put him to sleep. And when I look over at his face on the pillow next to me, his eyes are closed. Oh well, sometimes you lose your audience before you've finished the story.

As I quietly move over him to blow out the candle beside the bed, David startles me with a question. "What is Patsy's?"

I lean back on my pillow. "It's an old-timey Italian restaurant in midtown Manhattan — 56th Street. Sinatra used to hold court there."

"Ever eat there?"

"Once. Bum Bum and I went for dinner a few years after Sinatra's death. Out of curiosity, I guess. The place was a shrine to him."

"The food any good?"

I frown. "I just described slipping back in time and meeting Frank Sinatra and you want to know about the veal marsala at Patsy's? It was excellent. They do a nice sautéed rapini too."

David rolls onto his side to look at me. "It's just that this story is starting to sound like a fairy tale. Why would Sinatra act like you knew each other?"

I sigh. We're in danger of getting seriously ahead of ourselves.

"Because we *did* know each other," I explain. "We'd met in the past. I just didn't know that yet. Sinatra was a sign."

David frowns. "What do you mean?"

"Like those lampposts some quantum journeyer stuck in the wilderness to help Storytellers find their way around Cozy World," I explain. "Sinatra was embedded in my past to show me how to save the future. Neither he nor I knew it, but he was marking the point where history started to bend out of true."

David gives a grunt of mild disapproval. As if I should skip to the end and tell him about Sinatra and me saving the world, without all the in-between stuff.

"Do you want me to carry on or not?" I ask.

David leans over and kisses me. "Do you know what it's like to live in a world without stories? Of course I want you to keep going. But I also want you to promise you'll explain why Sinatra wanted to take you out for martinis."

"I'm a little surprised you don't want to know more about *The Adventures of Futureman.*"

He turns his face toward me, the scar on his scalp visible in the candlelight. "I have a feeling that I've heard that story before, Stan."

EIGHT

CLOUD CAFÉ

Unicorn Girl leads me a couple of blocks up Yonge Street, through a revolving door and into the deserted lobby of a nameless office building. Our footsteps echo on the marble floor. A security guard drowses on a chair next to a bank of elevators.

"Where're we going?" I ask, still clutching Unicorn Girl's arm.

"My favourite cloud café, Gut Fill," she answers, punching the up button.

The elevator opens onto an expanse of commercial space with floor-to-ceiling glass walls; it actually does feel like we're walking into a cloud. Where once there must have been cubicles, breakout rooms and workstations, there are regimented rows of industrial steel tables, spaced two metres apart and bolted to the grubby blue rubberized non-slip floor. Customers lounge here and there, eating noodles or sipping coffee as they tap at their screens. Most are Unicorn Girl's age — students, most likely — along with a smattering of older men huddled in threadbare jackets and toques who look like they're here to stay warm.

I've never been in a cloud café before, but I have read plenty about them. Gut Fill is just one of many automated food providers hidden away in half-empty office buildings. They're owned by a consortium of food processors that moved in during the pandemic and never left. Why would they? With twenty-year leases on prime downtown properties at bargain basement rates, all they need to turn a profit is a slew of robot chefs that never sleep or take a cigarette break. Instead of building cars or stocking warehouses, these robots manufacture cheap food — or, as the name says, "gut fill." The robot chefs' fluid high-speed gestures are visible through a clear wall — scratched, scorched, gouged and no doubt shatterproof — that protects the diners from the machines that feed them. I can see their giant arms chopping, mixing and frying so rapidly, their movements blur like a film on fast-forward. The headless chefs do everything but taste the sauces and shout profanities at the staff.

The only humans working here are a skeleton crew of junksters, low-paid freelancers who pull quadruple duty as servers, cleaners, bouncers and technicians. If a chef goes berserk and starts hurling knives and boiling pots of oil across the room, it's the junksters who wade into the malfunctioning machinery to hit the chef's kill switch. One wrong step and a junkster risks being eviscerated or decapitated. Dangerous work. In return, they get an empty office to sleep in, survival wages and all the deep-fried food they can eat. Even in the giggiest of gig economies, junkstering is the bottom of the heap. Some junksters are former chefs, bartenders and servers who went on the skids when the world shut down during the pandemic, but many are kids the manufacturers dug out of dumpsters, group homes and the sex trade. Regardless of where they came from, they were all retrained to work alongside the robots. All on a contract basis, of course: no benefits, no job security. Fortunately for Big Food, a sort of cult has grown up among the junksters, who fashion themselves as future cyborgs or, as they prefer to put it, transhumanists. Junksters work with the robots 24/7; they live and sometimes die with them. If this were a culture that openly supported a caste system, junksters would be our untouchables.

Unicorn Girl and I loiter at the greet-desk until a junkster calls our names and tells us to take a seat at table nine, hard against a glass wall, where we can look straight down twenty floors into the canyon of streets below. Unicorn Girl fishes *The Adventures of Futureman* out of her hockey bag and drops it on the table.

One of the junksters limps over to our table, pushing a battered warming oven. She looks like a teenager, whippet-thin, a hunk of black hair hanging over her eyes. She's wearing a helmet that looks like a robot's giant mechanical elbow joint and a shirt of chain mail over a T-shirt — protection from knife-wielding chefs that are blind to an approaching human and move at lightning speed.

"Hey Ariel, where you been?" the junkster asks, taking two greasy cardboard boxes out of the warming oven and dropping them on our table. She has the high light voice of a very young girl. Despite her tough-chick appearance, she can't be much older than sixteen.

"Hey, K," Unicorn Girl replies. "Super busy, because thesis and playoffs. And I'm interning. This is my mentor, Debbie Reynolds Biondi. You know — *Sputnik Chick: Girl with No Past*."

The junkster glances at me, favouring one eye. The other — partly hidden by her unkempt hair — gleams metallically. Her puckered eye socket is plugged with a ball bearing.

"D.R. Biondi, correctomundo? Thought you were dead," she comments in her baby-girl voice.

I grimace. "Not quite."

"Everything cool with you, K?" asks Ariel.

The junkster shrugs. "Same old. Still got your teeth?"

"Mostly," says Unicorn Girl.

"Wish I could say the same," K mumbles and grins to reveal the stumps of broken front teeth. "Caught it in the mouth last Sunday when Chef was doing a veggie scramble."

"Ouch," says Ariel. "You should see a dentist."

K shrugs. "Come the Singularity, our blessed overlord will give me a set of titanium chompers." She closes the warmer oven and nods at the copy of *The Adventures of Futureman* on the table. "Love that book."

"You know it?" I ask in surprise.

K rolls her one good eye at me as if I've said something incredibly stupid. "I've read it, like, ten times. Anything else?"

"We're good, thanks," says Unicorn Girl. The junkster nods and slouches back toward the kitchen from hell.

"Friend of yours?"

Unicorn Girl flips her ponytail. "K's okay. She hangs around the rink at night. We've scrimmaged a little."

"Interesting that she recognized *Futureman*."

"Probably just trying to impress us," says Unicorn Girl. "I didn't think K could even read PICTO. She told me once she has dyslexia. She was one of those kids who fell through the cracks during the pandemic. Maybe one of the other junksters read it to her."

"No wonder she's waiting for a robot messiah to give her a new set of teeth," I mutter, shaking my head as I poke at the grey-skinned chicken breast. "You do know there are actual restaurants these days, right? Where they don't pay the staff in computer games?"

Unicorn Girl shrugs. "Cloud cafés are faster and cheaper." She pushes her plate of fries soaked in gravy and cheese curds toward me. "That's not much to eat, Ms. Biondi. Have some of mine."

I shake my head. "I can't displace any more mass than when I was twenty-seven or bits of me fall off."

"Now you're acting like Sputnik Chick." Unicorn Girl tucks into her food. "Was the calorie counting in the comic book supposed to be an underlying commentary on women's fixation with their bodies?"

I snort. "No, it was an underlying commentary on the lengths Sputnik Chick has to go to in order to stay alive in Earth Standard Time."

"Nobody says you have to act like a character you created."

"Nobody but me."

"But aren't you hungry?"

"All the time."

"Ms. Biondi, have you ever thought that maybe you identify too much with Sputnik Chick?"

"Maybe you do too, if you don't have any other friends. Besides illiterate junksters, I mean."

Unicorn Girl presses her lips together as if trying to stifle a comeback. I toss my unused serviette on my plate.

"Sorry. That was mean of me." I rub my eyes. I'm still getting over the shock of being in Sinatra's world. "Just so you know. If I ever disappear again ... if you couldn't find me, all of a sudden ... there's something I want you to do. Go to the loft — I'm sure Cassandra will let you in, she knows your face and voice — and gather up whatever sketches you can. Everything is yours to use. Okay?"

"Yeah, whatever," she mumbles. "So, what should we do about *Futureman*?"

I flip open the front cover. Weirdly, there's no publisher or editor, no date or city of publication, no cataloguing code or Dewey Decimal number. None of the information you'd expect in a book. It just goes straight into a dense block of text: some kind of preface or introduction, I guess, probably about the author, Dr. Norman Guenther. I make a mental note to plough through it later.

"Futureman and Professor Quantum would make great nemeses for Sputnik Chick," I say. "I'll show it to my business manager in the morning. If he thinks we can get the rights to the characters' names, I could try pitching the story to the TV people when I go in to shoot my cameo in a couple of days. You could come with me." Remembering that Unicorn Girl made it possible to steal the book, I add, "If that's okay with you."

"Sure. We're partners in crime, right?" Unicorn Girl extends her fist toward me.

I fist-bump her with my cast. "You bet. Partners in crime."

* * *

As Unicorn Girl and I descend to the lobby in the elevator, I feel the weight of an unanswered question hanging in the air. It's just the two of us.

"Out with it," I mutter.

Unicorn Girl looks at me. "Okay, so. I'm wondering about you saying that the Trespasser trespassed on my VR game. And then you zonking out in the library, like you'd floated off to some other world and back again. And all the bits and pieces of you bandaged up. Plus your food issues. That 'can't displace any more mass' stuff."

I glance in her direction. There's no magical silver alicorn growing out of the middle of her forehead, but there might as well be.

"You *really are* Sputnik Chick, aren't you? D.R. Biondi is your secret identity? And all that stuff in your comics really happened? Destroying Atomic Mean Time, bringing the Exceptionals to this world?"

I stare straight ahead of me with the fifty-thousand-foot gaze of the universe-weary quantum traveller.

"Aren't you the perceptive little snowflake," I finally answer.

She breaks out into the grin of a comic book fan who has finally been allowed to peek behind the curtain separating fiction and truth.

"So do you actually refer to reality as 'Earth Standard Time'?"

"Yes. But every world in the multiverse of alternate realities is real."

"And you really do have timesickness?"

"Yes."

Unicorn Girl pauses her interrogation, then asks the inevitable question. "You going to be okay?"

"I'm on medication," I answer tersely. There are limits to what I'll confess to Unicorn Girl about Doc Mutant's diagnosis without a dirty martini in hand.

On the sidewalk in front of the half-empty office tower, Unicorn Girl vees her fingers at me in the Vulcan sign of peace before we go our separate ways.

"Read well and prosper, Ms. Biondi."

NINE

PASSION PLAY

Jesus has just fallen to the streetcar tracks under the whips of a trio of centurions in plastic helmets and breastplates. Barefoot in subzero temperatures, robes soaked with freezing rain and fake blood, he's clearly committed to the part. As are the weeping Marys and Veronicas huddled under a black golf umbrella, their arms outstretched and headscarves fluttering in the cold wind.

I watch from a window seat in Café Diplomatico. Wedged into the elbow of the wide curve where Little Italy swings west toward Little Portugal like a flexed bicep, the café is one of the best places to watch the Good Friday Passion play. The ritual is a mash-up of Old World miracles, theatre, religion, magic and maybe a little bit of collective insanity, like College Street itself.

Sitting across from me, head on fist, Bum Bum pages through *The Adventures of Futureman*. Calm and dry in pressed jeans, Oxford shirt and blazer, his beard scruff trimmed, his furled black umbrella hanging tidily on the corner of his chair, he wears his years like a bespoke cape he can shrug off at any time. He still likes to shape-shift to the way he looked in 1970s Atomic Mean Time, a young bisexual version of Audrey Hepburn's wild child character in *Breakfast at Tiffany's* — Holly Golightly is both his muse and role model — turning tricks and dancing the L.A. Hustle in gold satin shorts, curly black hair tumbling down her back. Today, though, he's an elegant gentleman of a certain age with impeccable taste in clothes.

"Your eggs are getting cold," I tell him.

"I've lost my appetite, thanks to this book," he mumbles, not looking up.

I mix a packet of Sweet'N Low into my chai latte and look out the window. Pious faces gaze out of all-weather screens mounted on the chests of telepresence robots, their Segway bodies rolling respectfully behind two curly-headed Good Thieves straight out of a Caravaggio painting, dragging their plywood crucifixes through the slush. A few true believers have shown up in person — mostly older ladies in winter boots who enjoy suffering in public. They've snapped up the best Good Friday viewing spots in front of stores hawking wedding dresses, nail shellac, Brazilians and discount kitchenware. The rest of us observe the ritual from indoors, over espresso and eggs florentine.

A roar goes up outside. Shouts of anger from the spectators, cruel laughter from the centurions. The Marys step up their wailing.

"He falls for the third time on our doorstep, because the owner donates so much money to the church," explains the server, Alessandra. She's a lithe middle-aged woman in a tight black dress and a chic amethyst cross, her long auburn hair freshly highlighted. She crosses herself absent-mindedly as she gathers crumpled empty Sweet'N Low packets off the table. "Another espresso, cavaliere?"

"Prego. And another chai latte for my friend the Storyteller."

Alessandra smiles and shimmies toward the espresso bar for Bum Bum's benefit.

I laugh. "'Caviliere'? Since when did you become a member of the nobility?"

"Alessandra thinks I'm descended from the duke of Milan. No idea why."

My laugh is cut short by the disapproving shush of a bruncher fingering her rosary beads as she holds up her camera phone to the window. There is something noble about Bum Bum, although it has nothing to do with the gentility of his birth. I would have died a long time ago, if not for him. On a practical level, he launders the money I make from Sputnik Chick properties, converting payments from cryptocurrency into hard cash — increasingly difficult to use but preferred by those who, like me, dislike sharing their data.

When Bum Bum finally closes *The Adventures of Futureman* and looks up at me, his expression is solemn.

"So what do you think?" I ask.

"Are you familiar with the story of the Greek chick who opens a forbidden box and unleashes sickness and evil into the world?" He taps the cover of the book. "You just opened the box."

This is weirdly similar to what the Trespasser told me in Unicorn Girl's game. But despite Sputnik Chick's mantra, sometimes a coincidence is just a coincidence.

I lean across the table and lower my voice. "Come on. It's a story no one's told before."

Bum Bum throws up his hands, as if I've said something idiotic. "You *kidding* me? This story goes way back. It's why Exceptionals got treated like they were personally responsible for the pandemic. It's what my pop told himself while he was kicking the shit out of me — the kid's no good, gotta beat some sense into him. It's why people in my neighbourhood got sick from the toxic waste under our houses — they're just Twisties, the hell with them! This story gives haters permission to keep hating."

"I want to retell it in my own way. Sputnik Chick will mount an epic battle against Futureman and Professor Quantum and their time-travelling robots. They're the supervillains."

He holds up his hand to interrupt me. "Don't be naive. Futureman is *not* a villain. Neither is Quantum. In the world Guenther created — in our world, *right now* — they'd be heroes to a lot of people. Standing up for racial and cultural purity. Traditional values. Preventing dirty mutant viruses from killing our people. We've heard it all before, kiddo." He leans in and fixes his dark eyes on mine. "Debbie, this fucking story is going to fight you every step of the way."

Outside, the crowd boos. The actors playing the Romans must be beating the guy playing Jesus again.

"But it's not real. It's a comic strip, not some kind of call to action."

Bum Bum raises his eyebrows. "Right. Just like Sputnik Chick comics aren't real. Take a look at what's going on outside right now — the greatest story ever told mutated from 'love thy neighbour' to 'smite the unbelievers.' You should know better. Look at what just happened with that Freedom to Serve Bill. Seriously, Deb, what do you want with this crappy comic strip?"

I rub my eyes. "I want to pitch my version of the story to the TV people."

"Why? So kids can play with action figures based on racist characters? Futureman on lunch boxes? Professor Quantum breakfast cereal?"

I sit back in my chair, deflated. "My intern came up with a very similar story for a VR game."

Bum Bum pokes half-heartedly at his congealing eggs. "You don't think she plagiarized it?"

I shake my head. "She was as surprised as I was by this book. Here's the thing, though: when I was trying out her VR game, the Trespasser dropped by to tell me that Unicorn Girl's VR story was intuiting something."

"You talked to the Trespasser? I thought he died of timesickness, back around the time you destroyed Atomic Mean Time."

I nod. "Me too. Turns out he figured out a way to send his DNA into Earth Standard Time That Was. He's living the good life somewhere in the mid-twentieth century. Lots of opportunities for advancement for white male physicists. He seems to think Unicorn Girl is destined to be my successor."

Bum Bum dabs his mouth and drops the napkin on his untouched eggs.

"Sounds like she's descended from Exceptionals. A natural-born psychic, unconsciously tapping into the zeitgeist. Maybe she even carries the Schrödinger gene. Or, more troubling," he says, looking me in the eye, "the story *wanted* to be found. Not just by anyone but by powerful storytellers. Like you and Unicorn Girl."

I almost choke on my chai latte. "What, now we're Bilbo and Frodo and the book is the ring of power?"

"Maybe. It might have been hiding in the library for years, waiting for just the right pair of storytellers to get it out of there so it could be read, adapted and spread around. Maybe even turned into a TV series. Just like you're planning. If I were you, I'd find a nice deep dumpster in some industrial site, throw in *The Adventures of Futureman* and toss in a lit match."

* * *

By the time Bum Bum and I leave Café Diplomatico, scenes of Passion have given way to city workers stacking metal barricades and swarms of robot vacuums sucking litter off the pavement as their synthetic voices warn pedestrians, "Please stand aside. Per favore, fatte largo." Streetcars rumble over spots where miracles were re-enacted just moments earlier. Only the sky still seems to be grieving. A bank of low cloud squats over the city like a shitting dog.

As we walk toward the street entrance to the loft, Bum Bum asks, "How you feeling these days?"

I waggle my hand. "So-so. The time incontinence is getting worse. I ran into Frank Sinatra at the library yesterday. Pretty freaky."

Bum Bum's eyebrows lift. "I hope it was 'One for My Baby' Frank and not 'My Way' Frank."

I nod. "I don't think I even left Earth Standard Time, just went back to the '50s when Sinatra was in his prime. He acted as if he knew me. Called me a 'little storyteller' and mentioned me drawing for the funny pages. Even offered to take me to Barberian's for a martini." Remembering how young I looked in Sinatra's world, I add, "And I didn't exactly look myself. Like I'd lost fifty or so years."

"Isn't there anything Doc Mutant can do?"

I shake my head. "No, but the Antiquanta he prescribed definitely helps. It's the only reason I'm not hanging out with the Rat Pack."

Bum Bum grimaces. "Be careful. Those DNA-stabilizing drugs have weird side effects. Hallucinations for one. Which might explain Sinatra. You always did have a thing for him."

"What am I, a hundred years old? My Nonna Peppy had a 'thing' for Sinatra, not me. She was the one who used to play all the great old recordings from the Capitol years. When Frank was still legitimately hip."

"I stand corrected," says Bum Bum. "Maybe you should have taken him up on Barberian's."

At Clinton and College, Bum Bum kisses me on the cheek. I feel a wash of loneliness and something else — fear. What if I leak into another timeline and die alone?

"Bum Bum, why don't you move back into your loft with me? There's plenty of room and I feel guilty freeloading off you."

He shakes his head. "I'd rather stay up on St. Clair with Willy. He's cuter than you and doesn't collect weird books. Don't worry, I'll check up on you every day. In the meantime, take it easy with the martinis and the mutant's little helpers, okay?"

TEN
PANDORA'S BOOK

That night, I'm awakened by a sound like dog toenails on a hardwood floor, or a *MAD Magazine* brain surgeon ratcheting open a patient's skull with a can opener. It's the *tchk tchk tchk* of ice pellets against the window. Down in the dark well of College Street, bread, cheese and meat trucks pick their way over the slippery pavement to restock kitchens in the wee small hours.

My sleep is too disrupted to go back to bed. I steam milk for a chai latte, microwave a bag of popcorn and curl up with *The Adventures of Futureman*. How evil could a comic strip possibly be? I open the heavy leather cover and flip to the introduction, written by an anonymous critic.

THE ADVENTURES OF FUTUREMAN
1949–1970

Written and illustrated by
Dr. Norman Guenther (sole creator)
Published in the **Niagara Frontier Harvester**,
an agricultural weekly tabloid

A professor of horticulture at an agricultural college and research station in upstate New York, Dr. Norman Guenther (1910–1970) believed that humans should be hybridized as carefully as the crops on modern industrial farms. Guenther was alarmed by the postwar mass migrations of refugees and economic migrants to America. He viewed random propagation as a dangerous practice that weakened the hardiness of both plants and people.

Having seen CIA-funded research proving that comic strips, comic books and cartoons were the most effective media for the dissemination of new ideas to the masses (Bormann, Alphonse, "Graphic Literature as Propaganda," *Studies in Global Intelligence*, 1948), Guenther launched *The Adventures of Futureman* with the support of a local publisher who shared his view that postwar America was being corrupted by undesirable aliens.

In Guenther's fictional version of World War Two, Germany, the Soviet Union and the United States were in a race to develop super weapons — not only the atomic bomb but time travel. Germany was the first nation to successfully weaponize time. But before they could launch an attack on the world of the future, the war ended. German physicist Professor Quantum escaped capture by jumping from 1945 to 2025.

The strip begins with his return to his own time, four years after the end of the war. He falls to earth on the upstate New York Christmas tree farm of Hubert White. Quantum uses his scientific knowledge to

surgically enhance Hubert, transforming
the simple farmer into a superhuman called
Futureman. His mission: to defend America
from the taint of foreign influences.

At first, Guenther's strip was no more
propagandistic than its better-known
right-leaning neighbours in the funny pages
of the big daily newspapers, *Little Orphan
Annie* and *Li'l Abner*. But over time, the
plotlines and viewpoints espoused by its characters grew more extreme. By 1955, Guenther
used the strip to promote the idea of eugenics: once America is cleared of its "invasive
species" (inferior humans), Futureman/
Hubert will "reseed" the country by fathering
a race of biomechanical robot-human hybrids
known as the People of Forever.

The strip remained obscure but gained
a cult following of extremist fans up until
Guenther's sudden death by cardiac arrest in
1970, bringing the series to an abrupt end.

Although largely forgotten, *The Adventures
of Futureman* has been cited as a major
influence by extremist groups that champion
"species purification" and by transhumanists
who believe in the inevitability of the cross-
hybridization of humans with machines.

Transhumanists — in other words, junksters. I palm a handful of popcorn into my mouth as I flip pages. The stereotypical
faces and accents Guenther gave his characters are cringe-
inducing but not much worse than other strips of the '50s, like

Will Eisner's *The Spirit*, which featured an African-American sidekick straight out of a minstrel show. Maybe *Futureman* was simply a product of its time?

Guenther's early stories follow a queasily predictable pattern: a member of an "invasive species" does something anti-social or criminal and the townsfolk turn to Futureman to correct the situation by sending the outsider back where they came from. Peace and order are restored. Through a lot of mysterious tinkering and surgical procedures by Professor Quantum out in the barn, Hubert White eventually transforms into Futureman: part human, part machine, part animal and part plant. The clumsy black-and-white drawings inexpertly show his appearance: well-muscled Superman chest, mechanical limbs, the pointed ears of a Doberman pinscher, a head like the top of a Christmas tree with a single all-seeing synthetic eye in the middle of his forehead, like the Masonic symbol on a U.S. dollar bill. In one gut-wrenching scene, Quantum slices open Hubert's vocal cords to give him a more dignified voice; henceforward Hubert stops dropping Gs and affects what I can only assume from the word balloons is intended to be a cultivated mid-Atlantic accent.

As Hubert slowly transforms from a simple farmer into a plummy-voiced superhero of the white race, he gives up running the Christmas tree farm and puts it in the hands of his terrifying wife, Jade, who likes to eat farmhands for break-fast. I can't help thinking that Guenther has mixed his personal memoir into *Futureman*, just as I based *Sputnik Chick* on my own origin story.

I eventually find myself yawning and flipping through the pages without reading them. Bum Bum was right: it's hateful stuff, and so repetitive and badly drawn that I'm surprised anyone would bother publishing it. But when I reach 1955, the strip starts looking slicker, and the stories increasingly sophisticated.

Having completed the transformation of Hubert into Futureman, Professor Quantum dons a welder's mask and sets to work building a great engine to transcend time and space. He houses it inside a mammoth statue of a woman, head bowed, hands beckoning, apron spread tight across bent knees — Lady Liberty, in reverse. Instead of holding high a torch and striding forward, eyes fixed on the future, the Mother of the Journey Home beckons her lost children to enter the dark passageway between her legs. As they move into the past, the "reverse migrants" see these words chiselled into Mother's marble apron: *From Whence You Came You Shall Return.* Instead of striding forward on a pedestal at the edge of the Atlantic, the Mother of the Journey Home crouches in a field surrounded by Christmas tree seedlings.

Quantum's idea is to introduce a race of human-robot hybrids to take over America — a perfect race of people who never age, get sick or deviate from the moral concepts programmed into them. Known as the People of Forever, they're never shown as anything more than shadowy figures, waiting in the wings for Quantum to prepare the utopia that awaits them. In the meantime, Futureman himself becomes a messianic figure who personally selects the humans who will both serve and merge with the People of Forever to live in a paradise run by human-robot hybrids created from the bodies of street kids and what used to be known as juvenile delinquents. No wonder the junksters love this story.

As I reach the final issues of the strip, leading up to 1970, the year of Guenther's death, Quantum and Futureman recede into the background. The shadowy People of Forever employ human acolytes and round up more and more inferior people to exile into their own pasts. Storylines become more complex, bewildering and flat-out batshit crazy, as if Guenther was starting to go off his rocker.

But by the final strip, I suddenly seem to have entered a whole different universe. It's like that scene at the end of *The Wizard of Oz*, when the curtain is pulled back to reveal an aging huckster, desperately pulling levers to keep his magical world alive.

* * *

A grey-haired woman is shown walking up a flight of stairs. The backs of her legs are drawn in close-up: she's wearing heels and a poodle skirt that hints at a crinoline underneath. Ominously, she's dragging a suitcase up the stairs behind her. It must be heavy, given the comic strip sound effects as it hits each step: *KUNKA-CHUNKA-KUNKA-CHUNKA*.

Musical notes and lyrics float in the air. *Nahhhh nah na-na-na-nahhhh . . .*

A staff of notes winds its way into a room with sloped ceilings and exposed plaster and lath walls. An attic.

An artist is hunched over a drafting table, singing while she works. She's shackled to the chair by her ankle. It's hard to tell her age: not young but younger than the woman with the suitcase. Her tangled grey hair falls over a page of drawings. Her dress is in rags. Her overgrown fingernails are longer than the speedball pen in her hand. Sketches are tacked up haphazardly on the walls and ceiling.

"Knock knock," says the older woman, holding the suitcase behind her back, out of view of the artist, who drops her pen.

"*OH!*" The letters are shaky, the face distorted, telling us the artist is shocked, even terror-stricken. "But it's — not my deadline yet. I haven't finished this week's pages. Can you come back later?"

"I'm not here for the pages. I have BAD NEWS," snarls the older woman. "The DOCTOR is DEAD. *The Adventures of Futureman* has come to an end."

"*Oh no! Oh no!* IT CAN'T BE!" simpers the artist, her hands clutched in front of her face in a clichéd expression of comic book horror.

"You've OUTLIVED your usefulness," the older woman says and sets down the suitcase in front of her.

Damn it all, I can't get a good look at the characters' faces. I've forgotten where my reading glasses are, again. "Cassandra, does Bum Bum have one of those thingummies that make small things easier to see?"

"A magnifying glass," says Cassandra. "In the kitchen drawer beside the knives."

I fetch it and hold it over the page.

The artist is on her knees. "I've been drawing this strip for FIFTEEN YEARS. Why can't I just carry on?"

The older woman gestures at a pile of comics scattered on an unmade bed. I can make out the familiar shapes of Snoopy from *Peanuts* and Mr. Natural trucking with his hands in the air. "*The Adventures of Futureman* captured the dreams and imaginations of a GENERATION. That work is done! But now we have to reach a NEW GENERATION. Have you even BOTHERED to look at the work of your peers? SCHULZ? SPIEGELMAN? CRUMB?"

The artist covers her face with her gnarled hands and wails. "I've tried but I CAN'T DO EDGY. I draw SUPERHEROES ... these political strips are NOT MY STYLE."

"NOT GOOD ENOUGH, STORYTELLER! Time to BLOW UP THE FUTURE and YOU with it!"

The artist cowers in the background, fingers stuck into her jagged Z of a mouth, as the older woman unlatches the suitcase. A close-up shows the contents: a large round comic strip bomb with a fuse.

"A TACTICAL NUCLEAR DEVICE . . . a DAVY CROCKETT BOMB. Once it's lit, I'll have just enough time to make it to the fallout shelter downstairs. You, however, will BE REDUCED TO SHADOWS AND DUST WHERE YOU BELONG!!!"

Close-up of the older woman's hand, striking a match. The flame approaches the fuse as the artist's wails of protest float in the air.

But instead of lighting the fuse, the match falls to the floor where a slippered foot crushes it out.

"WHAA . . . ?" A scarf has been looped around the older woman's neck. Her eyes bulge grotesquely. She claws at the scarf, but it tightens until finally she collapses.

The artist stands over her, plump comic book tears rolling down her cheeks. "Why did you KILL HER?!?"

The strangler is a short woman in slippers with a mop of curly hair. Like the woman she's just killed, she looks like she's in her eighties.

"You CALLED me for HELP!" say the strangler. "So I gave you HELP!"

"But that was fifteen years ago! I'D GIVEN UP HOPE!"

The strangler crosses her arms impatiently. "BETTER LATE THAN NEVER! You've been drawin' those hateful funnies LONG ENOUGH. Time to DO something with your life, cara!"

The artist holds her hands out to her would-be rescuer imploringly. "But . . . there's nothing left for me out there . . . YOU SHOULD HAVE JUST LET HER BLOW IT ALL UP!!!"

The artist lunges for the bomb, knocking her would-be rescuer off her feet.

The final panel is a wordless black void. Then the single cartoon word ***KABLOO-EEEEE!!!***

For a few long seconds, I sit paralyzed by shock and disbelief until I knock the book to the floor and run to the bathroom to vomit up my snack.

The artist's face is mine. Her would-be rescuer, the strangler, is Nonna Peppy.

ELEVEN

THE CHILD SOLDIER'S WORLD

I pull on a rain jacket. Wrap my cast in plastic wrap and clumsily seal it with masking tape. Now my right hand looks a cyborg's prosthetic weapon. I toss the book into a Robot Drug Mart shopping bag and run down the stairs. It's only when the street-level door slams behind me that I remember the subway isn't running at this hour. There are no taxis in sight. I could wait for the night bus, but the urgency of my task keeps me moving.

The ice pellets have turned into a cold drizzle. I pull up my hood and start the long trek east toward the Reference Library. From where this evil came, so shall it return.

A convoy of delivery robots stickered with the brands of their masters — Amazon, Apple, Google, Gap — zips past me in the bike lane, their rotating lidars scanning for addresses. A cyclist in a jacket reading *Meat Puppet Couriers* overtakes the robots, giving them the finger as he passes.

At Bathurst and Bloor, a woman does bicep curls in the street-facing window of a twenty-four-hour gym. I'm tempted to go in and ask for her help. The vile book grows heavier with every step. As if it knows where I'm headed and is fighting back. I carry on past construction cranes, sushi joints and cannabis shops, money marts and buck-or-two stores, and skeezy-looking businesses offering cash for gold jewellery and Rolex watches. A murmuration of food delivery drones hovers over the entrances to ghost kitchens along Bloor Street. Through the window of a bakery café, I glimpse a bored-looking man in white overalls, his arms crossed as he watches the rotating blades of an automaton mixing dough. The air is full of the fragrance of sticky buns. The aroma follows me east.

I just reach the intersection at Bay and Bloor when I hear a deep rumble, like thunder rolling in off Lake Ontario. The pavement starts to shake beneath my feet. A wall of smoke higher than an office tower blows up Bay Street, coating my lips and eyelashes with grit. I stumble blindly through the intersection, praying not to be hit by a bus.

The smoke drifts off. A strangely sweet aroma hangs in the air, like burnt cinnamon toast, but my mouth carries an aftertaste of charcoal, as if I've smoked a pack of cigarettes.

Which is when I finally realize I'm not in Earth Standard Time anymore.

* * *

I cough and wave my hands in the air, trying to clear my way through the wall of smoke. When I can see again, the facades of Bloor Street have vanished. Prada, Chanel and Tiffany & Co. have been reduced to heaps of glittering rubble. To the west, the crystal entrance to the Royal Ontario Museum has collapsed, its climate-controlled exhibit rooms open to the fetid air. A tangle of mummies and dinosaur bones lie in the middle of Bloor Street among a scattering of bodies. In an empty lot where a high-end department store should be, a tank, painted with the Union Jack and the words *Queen's Own Hellcats*, aims its gun turret at the sky. The pavement is curled back like a peeled orange. Helmeted soldiers in gas masks crouch around the edge of a smoking pit. It's impossible to breathe without inhaling particles of debris floating in the air. Leaning over, I hork up a lump of tarry mucous flecked with ash.

I've leaked into a continuum where midtown Toronto resembles a bombed-out war zone. I shouldn't be surprised. One thing I've learned as a quantum voyager is that no matter what a shithole of a dumpster fire our own world might be, there's always some place even worse out there among the two thousand and fifty-eight alternate worlds.

From behind me, a voice, tiny but firm, orders, "In the name of Her Majesty, put your hands behind your head and get on your knees or I shall shoot you where you stand."

The voice is no-nonsense but with the light, high cadence of a young girl. I consider shoving my good hand into my pocket for the vial of Antiquanta, but the child soldier might shoot me before I can twist it open. I drop the Robot Drug Mart bag, kneel down and raise my hands.

A pair of muddy combat boots walks carefully into my field of vision. The boots are mismatched, the left one less bunged up and a couple of sizes bigger than the right, which is held together with grey duct tape. The muzzle of the girl's rifle is pointed down at me.

"You're breaking curfew, madam," says the soldier in her tiny voice.

"I didn't know there was a curfew."

"It's your responsibility to stay informed. All residents are to shelter in place for their own safety until our sappers deal with the unexploded ordnance."

I'm so surprised that I drop my hands and look up at her. "Unexploded ordnance? From when, the War of 1812?"

The soldier uses the muzzle of her gun to nudge my hands back up. Unlike the troops peering into the smoking hole, she wears no protective mask, just a grubby red bandana knotted over her nose and mouth. The rest of her face is grey with dust. One eye is missing, the skin puckered around the empty socket. It hurts just to look at her.

"This is no joke, madam. It's a shell from the Old War. Fired by the Rochester Revolutionaries, I'll wager. Made it over the lake and ended up buried below ground level for seventy years. Like that one that blew up half of Queen Street."

"We're at war with the Americans?"

The sentry scowls at me. "For shame, madam! There is no such thing as *Americans*. We are all loyal subjects of the Crown and the sooner the filthy rebels accept that, the sooner we can end the conflict. Now I need to see your ID, if you please."

My heart speeds up: I have no ID. Hell, I have no identity. No health card, no bank cards, no credit cards, no social insurance number. Bum Bum looks after supplying me with cash, filing taxes and such, always under a dead person's name.

Dead person. Right. I'm still the same dead Canadian I was in New Jersey.

I reach into my pocket and fish out my falsified NEXUS card. The sentry shines her flashlight on it, then — alarmingly — takes a boxy device off her belt, which looks a lot like a handheld Fortress reader. To my intense relief, it flashes green and a synthetic voice intones, "Gloria MacDonnell, loyal British subject."

"Where are you headed, Ms. MacDonnell?"

"Um . . . I was just returning an overdue library book," I answer, nodding at the Robot Drug Mart bag. When she takes out the book and flips through the pages, her face loses its sternness. Despite the grey ash coating her face and hair, I can see how young she is. A kid really, probably no older than sixteen. I feel a prickle of déjà vu. Where have I met this one-eyed, baby-voiced teenager before?

"Funnies! I loved that one with the children, running all over their neighbourhood. You'd always see little diagrams of their footsteps . . ." Her free hand — the one without the gun — stabs the air. Dot, dot, dot.

I look up at her from my kneeling position. "You mean *The Family Circus*? Dolly, Billy, Jeffy and . . ." I grope for the name of the baby.

"P.J.! And Barfy, the dog. My grandma used to read it to me when I was four or five. That was during the truce, before the New War started. Never got to learn to read myself 'cause of being drafted into the children's militia."

"Maybe you'll learn after things" — I grope for something to say that's reassuring — "settle down." Although if we've been trying to reclaim the United States of America for the Queen, I have to assume things might not be settling down any time soon.

The sentry composes herself. Becomes a professional child soldier again. She helps me to my feet. A dented badge is clipped to her fatigues, heat-stamped *CPL. KRISTEN GOULD*. That's when I realize where I know her from: Unicorn Girl's junkster friend K from the cloud café. Looks like K and her alternate selves are destined to be given the dirtiest, most dangerous jobs no matter what world they exist in.

"I'll register you on the network as approved for safe passage, but stay north of Bloor and return to your place of residence promptly. Got that, Gloria?"

The sentry and I are on a first-name basis, apparently. I sense that my task — a little old lady trying to avoid a library fine — reminds her of a simpler, more civilized time. I nod my thanks to Kristen and take the vial of Antiquanta from my pocket before throwing the bag over my shoulder like a fairy-tale peddler with a sack. I'm strongly tempted to abandon the book in this timeline, but it has enough troubles.

I'm down to just two pills so I ration myself to one, hoping it's enough to pull me out of this dangerous and confusing world. As the bitter taste fills my mouth, one of the soldiers at the edge of the pit yells, "There's still a live shell down there! Get out of the way!"

"Run!" Kristen screams and pushes me forward as the blast lifts me off my feet.

I open my eyes in the intersection of Bloor and Balmuto Streets, face down in a puddle. I can feel blood trickling from under the bandage covering my nose, but I'm otherwise unhurt. I've landed right outside Prada's display window. Never before has the sight of a two-thousand-dollar handbag filled me with such sweet relief.

Although I gave up on the concept of a higher power a long time ago — there's little evidence of a merciful god in any of the worlds I've visited — I say a quick prayer that Kristen survived the blast and that the conflict I've just witnessed will end and she'll learn to read the funny pages of her alternate world. When I pat myself down to make sure I'm intact, I realize I left something behind with Kristen: my counterfeit NEXUS card. I guess Gloria MacDonnell just died a second time.

I reach Yonge Street as dawn starts to brighten the sky. The rain has finally let up. The book has become almost too heavy to lift. I can no longer hoist the bag, so I drag it along the sidewalk. Only one more block to go.

Steps from the library entrance, the Robot Drug Mart bag rips open and *The Adventures of Futureman* falls out. The book glows eerily on the wet concrete. It's almost tripled in size from when I started out. A jogger wearing headphones strides past, the toe of his shoe sending the massive tome sliding toward the curb.

I run over and pick it up. It's almost over. I just need to sling it through the slot.

Then I realize the awful truth. The Reference Library does not lend books. There is no return slot. I hug the loathed thing to my chest like a baby.

Where is the closest lending library? The Yorkville branch, a stately old yellow brick building just a couple of blocks away. Unlike most library branches, Yorkville still has a large collection of vintage print editions in circulation, the mark of a neighbourhood full of wealthy book snobs who pride themselves on their ability to decode the alphabet, a sign of good taste and sophistication, like being able to conjugate Latin verbs or drive stick. I zigzag west and north through alleyways, trying not to let the book know where I'm headed, but as we approach the library, I can feel it start to struggle like an angry toddler.

I shift the book under my right arm, while I pull the return slot open with my left hand. I lurch forward as the book slides in, putting the full weight of my body into my effort. When I close the slot, I grip it with both hands, just to be sure.

With both hands.

My right hand is no longer in a cast. It looks exactly as it did before I lost two fingers to timesickness. I reach up and touch my nose: the bandage is gone. I should be delighted, but I find my miraculous cure terrifying. The book wants me whole.

When I turn to start walking back to Bloor Street, something hits me hard from behind, right between the shoulder blades. I pitch forward, landing on my hands and knees. Rolling over, I see what should by now be no surprise: the book. It must have catapulted itself out of the return slot right into my back. I sit on the wet concrete, nursing my skinned hands. Something cold and sharp is pressing into the small of my back. Like the finger of an invisible mugger, forcing me to my feet.

That way. Go that way.

The finger pushes me deep into Yorkville. I pass a Canadian Tire store. I make a left. Next, a right. This must be what if feels like to have a gun in your back. *Move, just move!*

As usual, I should have heeded Bum Bum. His warning at the Dip — that this story would fight me "every step of the way" — is turning out to be literally, horribly true.

I find myself on Belmont, a street of narrow Victorian row houses behind wrought-iron fences, each displaying a plaque explaining its historical significance. In front of one, a tiny box on a post, painted cheery red and yellow, bears a sign reading:

Little Free Library: Let's keep print alive!
(No PICTO please.)
Take a book, leave a book, love a book.
Note: All donations must be presanitized.

A wind comes up. The door unlatches itself and opens before me to reveal a waterlogged Nora Roberts romance novel, a battered hardcover copy of *Harry Potter and the Philosopher's Stone*, an *Ontario Driver's Handbook* (1990 edition) and a textbook called *Introduction to Sociology*.

I toss in the book. Shut and latch the door. Done. The finger in my back is gone.

I'm finished with *The Adventures of Futureman*. I feel as if I've just recovered from a nasty bout of the flu. Now I have to figure out how to break the news to my partner in crime that we're back where we started. All of a sudden that feels like no big deal. I'll make something up or get Unicorn Girl to do another library search. Or if Bum Bum's right about her being descended from Exceptionals, she might even be able to go on an adventure in an alternate reality on her own and bring back the story for me to use.

I'm back at the loft by dawn. Birds are singing. The weather has cleared. Cassandra lets me in. After a quick UV light bath, I fall into bed without undressing. I sleep for a solid twenty-four hours.

The next morning, I'm roused by my computer's boot-up chime, followed by the sound of Unicorn Girl's Blundstones pounding up the stairs. Time for Sputnik Chick to get back to work.

Early the next morning, Unicorn Girl ubers the two of us from the loft to my cameo shoot for *Sputnik Chick: Girl with No Past — The Authorized Streaming Series*. To add a touch of retro-authenticity, the show has gone on location to a Cold War–era fallout shelter, deep below the financial district. Nicknamed the Money Pit, it was designed to shelter about a hundred bank executives in the event of a nuclear attack. What better place to launch a postapocalyptic TV series?

The uber pulls up in front of a sextet of black monoliths towering over Bay Street like Sauron's eye over Mordor. In the predawn hours, the district is deserted. Someone's unpaid intern greets us at street level and escorts us into one of the monoliths, past a Fortress robot at the security desk, down an elevator to a half-empty subterranean car park, through a beige fire door leading to a maze of claustrophobic concrete passages; the intern wears a keycard on a lanyard that opens one locked door after another until we reach an elevator with two unmarked buttons. The intern presses the lower button and waves us in.

The elevator groans its way down two levels, opening into a cylindrical bunker crowded with ponytailed ninjas in black yoga pants and wireless headsets. The air is a fug of sweat, morning breath and fumes from an overused chemical toilet.

It's obvious that the shelter has been abandoned for over half a century. Rusted-out light fixtures dangle overhead like octopi — obsolete, of course; the crew brought down their own generators to get around Toronto's power-rationing bylaws. On rows of sagging shelves, plastic laminated containers that once held water and dehydrated food have broken down into a thick, greasy sludge, like dead skin mixed with Elmer's glue, that stuff we used in school to affix painted Styrofoam planets onto the black bristol board of the galaxy. Mars was red, Venus was white, Earth was blue, the Sun was yellow. I'm too sleepy to remember the rest.

Dangling lopsidedly from a nail is a photograph of a young Queen Elizabeth in a tiara and evening gown, her calm gaze obscured by years of grime. It's the same face that watched over my grade school classrooms like a guardian angel. A visual reminder to keep calm and carry on, even in the event of a nuclear attack.

"I've never been in a fallout shelter before, have you, Ms. Biondi?" Unicorn Girl asks. I can tell she's excited.

I stifle a yawn. "Yes, but none this well preserved. It's like a time capsule."

"How old do you think it is?"

"Probably dates from around 1961." I look around. "You can tell by the curved walls that it was meant to be a subway station. Dug out for a future line but never built. I've heard there are a lot of these ghost stations hidden under downtown Toronto."

The showrunner, Irina Blanchette, hurries over from the other side of the bunker. "Debbie! So wonderful to see you!" She gives a half smile to Unicorn Girl. "And you are?"

"My intern, Unicorn Girl," I answer.

"Actually, it's Ariel Hassan," Unicorn Girl corrects me. "I'm working with Ms. Biondi on story development."

I shoot Unicorn Girl a look. This was not something I had expected her to share with Irina.

"And not a moment too soon! We could use a younger perspective on the Sputnik Chick universe," says Irina, with a little too much enthusiasm. "Let's get you into makeup, Debbie. We'll shoot your cameo as part of the first battle scene. Ariel, why don't you come along with me? I'd love to hear a young creative's vision for the franchise."

* * *

In the makeshift makeup department, I slump in a high chair with a giant bib around my neck, feeling like an overindulged toddler at a birthday party. I'm surrounded by actors costumed as characters I invented thirty-nine years ago. Supervillain (and sometime sex partner) the Blond Barracuda is having his brush cut freshly peroxided and gelled, while Johnny the K flirts with the woman attaching a prosthetic boogie board to his arm. Meanwhile, the Trespasser, in full disco gear, gets his sunburn sprayed on while he practises lines written by me. None of them recognize me as the mother of the universe they are paid to bring to life.

Somebody hands me a maple-glazed doughnut wrapped in a napkin. I'm hungry but I know just by looking at it that it's an easy three hundred calories. I toss the sweet little death bomb onto a nearby craft table littered with dirty coffee cups, empty cans of Red Bull and one lonely bottle of vodka, a reminder that some of us like a drink in the morning.

I'll bet the bankers who came down here for civil defence drills felt the same way: middle-aged white men stretched out on army cots, playing cards, sipping their Scotch neat to conserve water, worrying about their kids and wives and investment portfolios, wishing they'd ordered one of those backyard bomb shelter kits in case this wasn't a test.

A voice softly says my name. "Ms. Biondi?"

I look up at the sharpened tip of a kohl pencil hovering uncertainly in front of my swollen nose. "Sorry, I was miles away."

"Okay if I line under your eye?" the makeup artist asks.

"Yes, but gently."

Pat, pat, pat. The sponge applicator covers my age lines and bruises around my recently reconstructed nose.

"Spooky location, isn't it?" says the makeup artist, trying to chat me up. "An antique dealer would have a field day down here."

I yawn. "Don't know about that. The fixtures are in rough shape."

"Didn't you notice the big retro-looking clock? Gotta be vintage. That'd fetch a good price from a collector, I'll bet."

She gestures at a clock hanging over the set, its white face gone yellow with age. Each hour is represented by a huge black dot. The hands have stopped short of the top of the hour. Just before twelve.

"That's a doomsday clock," I tell her. "Looks like it's set at two minutes to midnight."

The makeup artist frowns. "What's a doomsday clock?"

"It was a symbol to show how close we were to self-destructing," I said. "A group of atomic scientists who worked on the Manhattan Project invented it to raise awareness. When it looked like the bomb might drop, they moved the hands closer to midnight."

"Wow. Imagine being down here with *that* hanging in front of you!"

I shrug. "The most that would have happened is a bunch of bankers lying on cots while they waited for the all-clear."

"But what if they *believed* it was the big one? What would they have done while they were waiting to find out? Pray? Play cards? Get drunk? Shit their pants? Jerk off?" She shakes her head.

"I can only imagine," I murmur. And closing my eyes, I do.

* * *

The bankers' trip to Armageddon would begin in the queue for the private elevator. Only accessible with a special key that the chief executive officer keeps in his desk; he's the first one down. Then it's ten men at a time, presidents and vice-presidents first, followed by regional managers and the rest according to seniority. I can almost smell the nervous perspiration and nicotine coming off their bodies as they descend to the bunker.

Most of these guys were in the army in the Second World War, so they respect rank. That's why they still dress in uniforms: starched white button-down Arrow shirts and black horn-rimmed glasses, grey suits. It's 1961, long before the invention of business casual. Because it's an emergency, they've taken off their jackets and rolled their shirt cuffs; that's what men of action do. Some carry their briefcases, as if planning to catch up on paperwork while the missiles reduce Toronto to rubble. They crack wise over the wail of the air raid sirens, telling one another it's probably another surprise drill or maybe a malfunction. No matter: they've got enough food and booze in the shelter to keep them happy for months, if need be.

When will it occur to them that there has been an important omission in the stockpile of supplies? What will they need besides filtered water, powdered milk, Jell-O, dehydrated soup and tinned meat? Great Scott, they've forgotten the women! Even if it's only a drill, how you gonna practise repopulating the world without a few skirts?

It's a joke, of course. They're not thinking further ahead than the fact it's Friday afternoon and they're missing out on happy hour at the Royal York Hotel lobby bar. A guy could use a few laughs, especially when the week ends with a bomb drill.

Let's get some chicks from the secretarial pool down here! Anybody got something we can use to draw straws?

A handsome investment banker with a crew cut and a pending performance review shoots up his hand.

No need, fellas. I'll go.

There's a brave chap, quips one of the older executives, a plump Brit. *Son, didn't anyone in the army teach you never to volunteer for anything?*

Too young to serve, sir.

The other guys on his pay scale pound him on the back, quietly hating him for showing initiative. He's made the rest of them look bad.

* * *

I'm still spinning the bankers' story in my head, getting ready to follow the brave young chap up the emergency stairwell, when the makeup artist rouses me out of my reverie by announcing she's taking a "bio break." When she steps away, I see my face in the mirror, hair tugged back and makeup half-done. I'm startled by my tired-looking eyes, the downturned lines from the corners of my mouth, the deep crease over my nose. I look like Nonna Peppy. I can almost hear her voice admonishing me: *Watcha expect? You got my, whaddyacallem, genes. So sue me. You rather be dead than old, bella? Gimme a break!*

I sigh, close my eyes and let my imagination drift back to 1961, where the bankers are still waiting their turn at the secret elevator.

* * *

No one jostles, despite the panicky sound of the siren. How much time do they have before the bombs drop? Ten minutes? Ten seconds? But these are men, goddammit, who've seen battle. Not just on the trading floor but on some bloody hilltop in Italy. You don't push your way ahead of the next guy, especially if he outranks you.

That brave young chap who volunteered to save humanity — or, more cynically, to turn a civil defence drill into an excuse for a higher raise and/or a little canoodling — leaves the queue. The elevators have been taken out of service, so he runs up the stairwell. He wishes that know-it-all Limey bean counter was huffing and puffing behind him. On the tenth floor he opens the fire door onto the secretarial pool. He can hear sobs and a few voices saying the rosary.

Holy Mary, mother of God, pray for us. (For my next comic book, I'll shakily letter those words over the *WHHHHHAAAAA* of an air raid siren.)

The secretaries have been ordered to take shelter under their desks, rather than head down to University Avenue where office workers are filing into the subway tunnels. (Why have the women been ordered to stay at their posts? Wait, I know: insurance. Abandonment of the building nullifies coverage. Someone has to go down with the ship so the company can make a claim during the postnuclear reconstruction period. I have no idea whether such a rider is possible, but it's believable. Insurance companies make good villains.)

The brave young chap gets down on his hands and knees to coax out the girls, the way he used to do with kittens on his grandpa's farm. He reminds himself that he can only take nine girls down with him. Okay, maybe ten or twelve if they are petite. No Amazons on this mission.

Peering under the desks, his eyes hunt for the youngest and prettiest. Blue-eyed blonds, young Elke Sommer and Inger Stevens types. Given the Catholic prayers, there are probably a few Annette Funicellos huddled under there too. Maybe even a Leslie Uggams or two. All good breeding stock.

Don't worry, I'll bet it's only a test! Hey baby, want to come down and see where the big honchos are hiding? There's even a cocktail bar down there!

Who wouldn't say yes? Only once the chosen girls were underground would they look at that bunker crowded with drunken men and realize what they were in for, if the drill turned out to be real.

* * *

In the end, nuclear warheads never dropped on Toronto in Earth Standard Time. But they did in Sputnik Chick's world of Atomic Mean Time. By then, executive fallout shelters like this one had been hardened and widened, joining up with a network of shelters one level below the underground path honeycombed with coffee shops, suit stores, dentists and massage therapists. Every bank and investment company in Atomic Mean Time had its own bunker where it could continue to do business, protected from the radioactive fallout poisoning the world above. As for stockpiles of women, such matters were never left to chance in Atomic Mean Time. Every company had its cadre of Designated Survivor Women: healthy nineteen- to twenty-five-year-old females who each kept a bright orange overnight case tucked under her desk stocked with feminine supplies in case of an emergency. Comb, brush, soap, makeup, sanitary napkins, antiperspirant, perfume, hairspray, lipstick and tranquillizers. If you're going to be one of the mothers of a new civilization, you'd better be prepared to look good and stay calm. And, of course, there were special shelters for troops of Snugglegirls, who could, in a pinch, be pressed into service for junior executives when they weren't occupied with their usual responsibilities of relieving tension in the senior management corps.

Not that any of those preparations did any good. When World War Three broke out in 1979, Atomic Mean Time disappeared. The bankers in this bunker were pulled into Earth Standard Time along with everyone else to merge with their alternate selves.

* * *

This would make a good Sputnik Chick story, I think — even better than *The Adventures of Futureman*. A prequel, flashing back to the earlier history of my comic book universe, something I've never done before. I reach to the side of the makeup station for the sketchbook and Sharpie in my purse.

I'm mulling over ways to develop the babes and bankers story so it's more in tune with 2025 sensibilities — maybe update it so the brave young chap is replaced by a plucky woman economist who has to decide whether to give the sleazy director of marketing a chance at survival — when I'm interrupted by Irina. "Ready for your cameo?"

* * *

In my comic book, there is only one Sputnik Chick. But in the series, three actors — one Black, one white, one Asian — will alternate in the role. I had my doubts about this approach, but Irina countered that the main character in *Doctor Who* has been played by an ever-changing series of actors for decades.

"Plus if one actor makes contract demands we can't meet, there are always two other Sputnik Chicks to fall back on," Irina points out.

Other than their hair and skin colour, the actors playing Sputnik Chick look almost identical: wasp-waisted, athletically thighed, high-cheekboned. All three wear Sputnik Chick's trademark tights and tunic, the lightning bolt neckline designed to reveal the curve of one firm breast. As they take up fighting stances, a makeup artist scoots in to spritz gorgeous little beads of artificial sweat onto their cleavage.

I wait for my cue while the three Sputnik Chicks battle invisible enemies. They pivot, punch and kick the air, hollering *eyaahhh!* Special effects will add the bad guys later. For now, I have to imagine the actors' fists snapping back a snarling head or their boot heels rupturing a spleen. I also have to imagine the villains fighting back, tossing the women around like garbage bags. To simulate this, the Sputnik Chicks throw themselves to the floor in mock agony, screaming *ooooffff!* or *argghhhhh!* It's a convincing bit of theatre. I'm sure the bruises will be real enough. My cameo is as the stereotypical little old lady whose purse gets snatched by a mugger. I'm supposed to mime beating the blue-screen assailant over the head with my umbrella. (Who wrote this crap, I wonder, but don't want to sound like a diva — they are paying me handsomely for this walk-on, after all.)

Swooping in to rescue me is the Black Sputnik Chick — a young newcomer named Jordan Kingsborough — who executes a perfect flying dropkick. But instead of hitting her mark, she overshoots and flies past the blue screen. Unicorn Girl steps up and spreads her arms, blocking Jordan's trajectory as if she were a puck.

Blood spatter arcs across the blue screen. As the director yells cut, a makeup artist hurries over with towels and ice.

Gathering up the skirts of my dress, I rush to the now-prone Sputnik Chick, Unicorn Girl crouched at her side. Blood dribbles down Jordan's chin and drips onto her cleavage. A big guy with a shaved head and a Bluetooth in one ear detaches himself from the crew. Leaning down, he quietly murmurs a question to Jordan in a language that is both foreign and familiar to me. He sounds worried. Jordan gives a sharp retort.

I understand what they're saying — more or less. I picture the Holub kitchen back in Shipman's Corners, Sandy's mom fretting about her in Ukrainian, the phrases so familiar I automatically translate them into English.

Are you sure you're okay?

Yes, I'm fine, Yuri, stop worrying!

Yuri talks quietly to her for a moment, before announcing her state to the rest of the room like a referee.

"Is just a nosebleed," he says in an Eastern European accent.

I stare at Jordan's face. Why didn't I notice the resemblance before? The Holub cheekbones. The Kendal mouth. I can picture her as a child, skipping along beside her father. Spying on Kendal and his family was like picking at an open sore. I couldn't help myself. I only saw his daughter once. Slender and tall for her age. She couldn't have been more than eight years old. Her name was Marushka, according to the online snooping I did at the time. But names are easy to change.

Jordan bends over as if Unicorn Girl has just told her something incredibly funny, her hand still pressing a wet cloth to her face. Unicorn Girl laughs too, her eyes all over Jordan. She reaches out to touch her arm. Jordan collapses in laughter again and grabs Unicorn Girl's hand to pull herself to her feet. Seems like Unicorn Girl has finally found a friend. Or maybe something more. Figures it would be someone in a superhero costume.

After the Sputnik Chicks finish the take and the set is being broken, Irina comes over to stand with me. "What a relief to know you have a fresh story on the go. We were starting to worry."

I try not to show my surprise. "Fresh story?"

"Your partner gave us an elevator pitch while you were in makeup."

"Partner? No, she's my —"

"We love the characters the two of you are developing. Professor Quantum and Futureman! Great names. You are such a gifted storyteller, Debbie."

"Irina, listen, I was thinking that maybe Futureman is actually too far removed from Sputnik Chick's core theme. The Cold War, the bomb, alternate worlds . . ."

Irina laughs and shakes her head. "Stop second-guessing yourself! Futureman is exactly the brand refresh Sputnik Chick needs. He's a villain some people will loathe and others will identify with. Sure, he's twisted and politically incorrect and maybe even racist, but people get where he's coming from, right? The iconoclast who dares to say what others only think. And these days, who doesn't dream of returning to a simpler past? It's a new world with new types of fears. Rogue viruses! Climate change! Terrorism! Undocumented immigrants! That's where this franchise needs to go now. Not to mention, our data analytics suggest some desirable target groups are struggling with the quantum physics underlying the Sputnik Chick origin story. Frankly, there's no sense of a shared history in our viewership."

"Right, but —"

"I would love to get that fabulous Austrian actor to play Professor Quantum. The one who works with Tarantino . . ."

"Christoph Whatshisname," I murmur. "Sounds like a dance."

"Waltz," supplies Irina. "And think of the possibilities for backstories and spinoffs — the non-fungible asset value alone for new characters could be mind-blowing. Think of the augmented reality experiences — you could invite Professor Quantum to your next dinner party! Go on a date with Futureman! Hunt down humans with the People of Forever! If we auctioned off exclusive access to restricted content through Blockchain, you and Ariel could make those villains far more messed up than the main characters. You could even spin them as antiheroes, extremists but with a heart, you know? Nasty, rage-filled haters but fun. Maybe trying to protect their world from the next pandemic, who knows?"

"Wait a minute, Irina, I don't think —"

My protest is cut short by laughter. Unicorn Girl is dragging Jordan to me by the arm. She's changed out of her Sputnik Chick costume into skinny jeans, boots and a hoodie. Now she looks like a gorgeous, hyperfit special ops commando on shore leave, instead of a mere comic book superhero.

"Show her, Jordan! Show her!" urges Unicorn Girl.

Jordan looks embarrassed. From her shoulder bag, she pulls a hardbound copy of *Sputnik Chick: Girl with No Past, 1986–2006 — The Golden Years.*

"I've been a Spunkie since I was fourteen. I even went to the Ottawa fan expo as an Exceptional. My parents freaked when they found out I'd been cast as one of the Sputnik Chicks!"

"Did you grow up in Ottawa?" I ask, as I sign the inside cover of the book with *There are no coincidences, D.R. Biondi.*

"Toronto . . . mostly," answers Jordan slowly. "We went to Ottawa when Dad, um, changed jobs."

God, she even lies as badly as Kendal.

"I'll bet Dad's an IT guy, right? At one of those high-tech companies?"

Her eyes look down, then to the side. Man, she'd make a lousy poker player.

"He's a senior civil servant," she finally admits. "Mom's an entrepreneur."

Yeah, right, I think. And my Nonna Peppy was the Queen of the North.

* * *

Jordan, Yuri, Unicorn Girl, Irina and I are the last ones out of the bunker. Waiting for the elevator, I notice that the grimy portrait of the Queen has been replaced with an equally grimy one of a fair-haired man wearing a crown. His pinched face reminds me of a constipated weasel. It takes me a minute to put a name to the face: the Duke of Windsor, briefly known as His Royal Highness King Edward VIII, who gave up the throne for the woman he loved. I lean in and look at his face more closely.

"Irina, why is a portrait of the Duke of Windsor part of the set?"

Irina glances at it distractedly. "Hmm? Is that who it is? It was here when we opened the place up."

I frown at her. "What happened to the portrait of Queen Elizabeth?"

"Who?"

I start to explain when the elevator doors open. Turning to look at the portrait one more time, I'm startled to see the Queen again, gazing at me regally through a scrim of dust. As if the two faces had been superimposed. A lenticular of the besotted playboy uncle-king transforming into his responsible, majestic niece-queen, and back again.

"Coming?" asks Irina.

* * *

The bank lobby is crowded with office workers on their way to lunch. Through the glass walls I see food trucks lined up at the curb on Wellington Street for the noon rush. No cloud cafés in the bank towers, I guess. As Irina waves goodbye on her way to the underground parking garage, Jordan, Yuri, Unicorn Girl and I head through the revolving lobby doors. We're carried along by the crush into a concrete plaza where a herd of life-sized bronze cows sun themselves on a narrow strip of grass.

"Which way to the subway?" I ask, expecting Unicorn Girl to answer, but she's preoccupied with Jordan. She spreads her arms: she must be trying to impress Jordan with tales of her shot-blocking prowess. Yuri — surely a bodyguard, the way he carries himself as he scans the crowd — keeps a protective hand on Jordan's arm.

I clear my throat. "What's faster, the Yonge line or —"

The rest of my question is swallowed by the sound of screams. Yuri envelops Jordan with his body and starts running. Unicorn Girl grabs my arm and tries to pull me forward, but our way is blocked by a stampede of office workers.

In seconds the plaza has almost emptied itself, leaving behind a woman in a skirt suit and heels face up on the concrete.

The contents of her handbag — wallet, keys, lipstick and phone — lie scattered around her. One leg is jackknifed as if she's trying to kick herself in the head. Another woman kneels beside her and pumps her hands up and down, up and down, on the fallen woman's chest.

A truck the colour of an unhealed wound careens past the bronze cows and ploughs lazily into a trio of women running toward the tower's revolving doors. Shoes and handbags fly through the air. Someone loses their glasses. The concrete is spattered with blood.

The truck screeches to a stop and makes a turn. I can see now that it's one of the curbside food trucks, bearing a familiar name: Gut Fill.

Daisy-chained together — Yuri to Jordan to Unicorn Girl to me — we run for the safety of the lobby. But it's impossible to get back inside the office tower. Panicked office workers swarm the outside walls. Bodies jam the revolving doors.

The truck bounces its way down a flight of steps. It's going after two women, one in a headscarf, the other in the brown uniform of a parcel delivery company. The women crouch behind one of the bronze cows, huddling together. Yuri pulls us toward them, but my hand is wrenched out of Unicorn Girl's by the fury of the crowd. She looks back at me helplessly as she stumbles after Yuri and Jordan.

"Go, go, go!" I shout, falling farther behind.

The truck makes a three-point turn. It's heading back toward the cows to hunt for the women. Then it spots me, standing in the plaza all by myself. It speeds up. Heading right for me. The women hiding behind the cow are screaming at me to run, but I can't make my legs move. I see Yuri turning to run back to me.

I'm looking directly into the front windshield of the truck at what should be the driver's face. But there's no one behind the steering wheel. No one to make eye contact with. The car is driving itself. Making its own decisions.

I crouch down and cover my head, bracing for impact.

FOURTEEN
HARD STOP

And then: nothing. No crash. No pain. The truck dissolves around me in a shower of water droplets. The crowded plaza I was standing in seconds ago is empty. The sleepy bronze cows have vanished, along with their tiny perfect pasture. The walls of the black bank tower reflect a chemical sky, bilious orange and yellow.

Bay Street is deserted. No traffic, streetcars or people. The oversized facades of banks and insurance companies are barricaded behind bolted metal gates, as if preparing for an invasion.

I've leaked into an alternate reality and not a moment too soon.

I dig in my pockets for the vial of Antiquanta. I'm down to my last pill. But just before I palm it in my mouth, it occurs to me that if I return right away to Earth Standard Time, the rampaging food truck will finish me off in seconds. If I'm not already dead.

I stuff the vial back in my pocket. Safer to stay here, for now. Wherever here is.

My skin feels damp and slightly sticky. The telltale scent of cinnamon hangs in the air. But something else wafts on the breeze, acrid yet weirdly nostalgic: a whiff of polystyrene, propylene, perhaps even polyvinyl chloride. Hair spray, vinyl records, dime-store perfume, plastic lunch bags, aerosolized dessert topping. The synthetic smells of my long ago, petroleum-based childhood.

I head east. On Yonge Street, I pass one rundown strip joint and body rub parlour after another, the second-floor windows blacked out and thickly crusted with pigeon shit. Dusty mannequins in hot pants and platform shoes stare out of dingy storefronts. The door of a shop called Atomic Kidswear hangs from its hinges.

I step inside, cautiously. Tiny hazmat suits are curled on the floor, arms and legs awkwardly splayed like bodies at a crime scene. When I nudge a glove with my toe, the fingers clutch at the air as if possessed. Two child mannequins frolic on a display table. Through the visors of their helmets, their faces look strangely carefree, as if scampering around in radioactive fallout is the most natural thing in the world.

The suits were invented by Sandy Holub's father — better known as Mr. Capitalismo because he was always looking for the next get-rich-quick scheme. He branded them "the bomb shelter you wear." I wore one of these things myself for nuclear preparedness drills at school.

That's when I finally realize where I am.

Home. Or rather the home world I destroyed and escaped from more than forty years ago.

I stagger outside, still disbelieving, until I spot a cluster of newspaper boxes on a street corner. The mastheads on the *Sun,* the *Globe* and the *Star* are dated July 10, 1979. The day before I ended Atomic Mean Time.

According to the Trespasser, here's how he'd seen the future of our world unfold: on July 11, 1979, at 16:37 Co-ordinated Universal Time — around lunchtime on the eastern seaboard of North America — the malfunctioning space station SkyLab would hit the Kremlin and the intercontinental ballistic missiles of the world's superpowers would launch. Cities would be turned to flaming ruins. Millions would die immediately. Those unlucky enough to survive the initial blasts would stagger out of fallout shelters like the walking dead; most would eventually die grotesquely of radiation sickness. My mission was to stop that future from happening. Give humanity a second chance.

Which is what I did by dragging my fellow Atomic Mean Timers into Earth Standard Time to find refuge inside their alternate selves. I emptied my world, then punctured the black matter between our worlds to flatline mine.

I believed that Atomic Mean Time had twinkled out like a dying star. And yet here it stands, as it looked about twenty-four hours before I lost my past. High noon, the day before Sputnik Chick was born.

How can this even be possible?

Could fail-safe programming have caused the missiles to launch after I'd depopulated Atomic Mean Time? Could I have unknowingly flatlined a nuked world? Perhaps the force of the thermonuclear blast threw time back by a day and imprinted a ghostly shadow on the multiverse, the way that shadows of the dead were permanently imprinted on walls in Hiroshima.

Stunned and more than a little afraid, I walk north toward Bloor, passing billboards for long-extinct brands, unique to Atomic Mean Time's consumer tastes: Sour Apple Neutron Coke, the all-new Saturn V Sports Sedan, Doc Von Braun's Decontamination Shampoo for Kids.

I see a crowd of slender figures clustered together, four or five city blocks away from me. I start to run toward them, waving my arms.

"Hey! Over here!" I shout.

Their heads lift. I stop in my tracks. It's a herd of deer. They gaze at me disinterestedly for a moment, then slowly round a corner, moving out of sight. They're not worried at all. It's the first time it's occurred to me that animals didn't follow me into Earth Standard Time along with people.

The wildlife may be calm but there are signs of human panic everywhere: over days of ramped-up nuclear tensions, as SkyLab fell closer and closer to Earth, people either partied or looted or both. Store windows are smashed in. A Geiger counter sits abandoned on a street corner. Empty bottles of iodine pills — first aid for radiation poisoning — line the curb. Phone receivers dangle off the hook from their cords in public phone booths. On a whim, I put one to my ear and am surprised to hear the familiar hum of a dial tone. I jiggle the hook three times quickly to see if I can reach an operator. "Hello, hello?" I ask.

Then I do something ridiculously optimistic: I dial the number of my parents' house in Shipman's Corners. At the other end of the line, a big black Bell phone must be ringing in the hallway outside the kitchen. If Dad answers, I'll ask him to make the ninety-minute drive from Shipman's Corners to pick me up. But the ringing goes on and on.

No answer. Which is an answer in itself, I guess.

As I hang up the receiver, my eye catches on a silver slab on the sidewalk. Crouching down, I see a stylized apple with a bite taken out of it. It's an iPhone with a cracked screen.

In 1979? Impossible. Although more technologically advanced than Earth Standard Time, this world — if it *is* a shadow of Atomic Mean Time — didn't last long enough to see the invention of iPhones. Whoever dropped it must have come here from another timeline, just like me. Which means I may not be the only one in this world, after all.

One of the first rules of quantum travel taught to me by the Trespasser was never to leave your technology behind in another world. Maybe whoever dropped this phone is a civilian, not a seasoned voyager like me. Poor schmuck must be even more bewildered than I am.

I keep walking.

* * *

On Bloor Street, I find myself in front of a nightclub, Heaven & Hell Disco-Teque. I try the front door and find it open.

The lobby is all glass chandeliers and chintz wallpaper featuring sexy girl angels and sleazy moustached devils striking erotic poses. Next to a flight of red-carpeted stairs, a gold sign hangs from a velvet rope barring the way: *OFFICER-EXECUTIVES, SNUGGLEGIRLS & SPECIAL GUESTS ONLY*. A bouncer must have stood here choosing which beautiful nobodies were allowed to go upstairs and boogie with the VIPs. As I head up the plush stairs, I hear something that freezes my heart.

Music. The classic four-on-the-floor beat of disco. For the first time since leaking into this world, I am truly terrified. Half expecting Jack Nicholson to stagger in with an axe, I force myself up the flight of stairs.

On the main floor, I can hear the same riff repeated again and again as if a vinyl record is skipping: *burn boogie burn, scratch, burn boogie burn* . . . the opening bars of "Arsonist of Love," the number one disco hit of summer 1979. Strobe lights timed to the beat of the music bounce off a prismatic ball, rotating high above the dance floor. Dazzled by the flashing lights, I almost trip over a stool toppled in front of a long oak bar where bottles of booze and cocktail glasses are lined up by height.

A fifth of what looks like Jack Daniel's and a red stiletto shoe stand in the middle of the floor facing one other, all that's left of the doomsday dancers who must have crowded this place on that last night, trying to take their minds off the looming disaster of a space station falling out of orbit. Heaven & Hell Disco-Teque is a dim reflection of the mother of all discos, Studio 54, where Kendal and I found ourselves on the final night of our honeymoon.

A skirl of chirps and chitters takes me by surprise. Masked faces peer at me from over the top of the bar. I've disturbed a family of raccoons — not the bloated bandits that swagger through Earth Standard Time Toronto's back alleys like they own the place but a ragtag pack of scrawny scavengers.

"Shoo!" I yell and they scurry behind the bar.

The strobe lights have given me a headache. Rubbing my eyes, I stumble back down the red-carpeted stairs, hoping not to meet any ghosts.

* * *

I continue along Bloor, over to Spadina, and head south. Faint hope that I'll find any trace of the loft or Cassandra, but it's the only course of action I can think of.

I wander down to Dundas and find the markets and restaurants in Chinatown boarded up. The roti shops and takeout samosa joints and shisha lounges and sushi places on Queen West are empty too, their entrances barricaded behind the same metal gates I saw in the financial district. Protecting their assets against Armageddon. As if once the bombs had fallen, they could go back to business as usual.

Idiots.

Back up on College, the multicultural radio station with its hundreds of flags flapping around the graceful curve from Clinton to Shaw Streets resembles a blank beige brick fortress.

The sidewalks have been cleared of patios. Little Italy has disappeared. I suspect it will be the same in Koreatown, Greektown, Chinatown, Little India, Roncesvalles, Little Burgundy, up in Willowdale and even Scarborough. And the world beyond for all I know.

Who has taken the Italians off College Street? Where are the sidewalk cafés of Little Portugal — for that matter, where is Little Portugal?

* * *

Where Bum Bum's loft should be, I find a men's workwear store, the front door bolted shut and the window full of boots and overalls. I press the buzzer at the street-level entrance to the second floor flat and lean into the speaker.

"Cassandra, are you there?"

Dead air.

It's official. I'm homeless.

A half block west, I find my first signs of life since the raccoons. To my amazement, Café Diplomatico is open, its patio shrunken to the size of a parking space but still recognizably itself. Two kids are playing hopscotch outside the front door, the squares marked out in pink, blue and yellow chalk.

A curly haired young man stands at the corner of College and Clinton, jabbing at a cellphone, putting it to his ear again and again. "No bars! What the fuck is going on with the network?"

"Forget it, bro, everything is fucked up," answers a man slumped at a patio table. "Sit back down and order another drink."

I recognize the two young men as the Good Thieves from the Passion play.

Grabbing a seat, I take a Sharpie out of my pocket and start sketching on a stack of cocktail napkins. A stick figure of myself pounding on the entrance to the loft, then sitting in the café with a little cloud hovering over my head. Comic book shorthand for despair.

At the table next to me, a group of twenty-somethings and a woman about my age are reading aloud from the menu. The younger people are slaughtering the Italian words, the older woman patiently correcting their pronunciation. It feels like I'm watching a group of students with their language instructor.

I start to recognize faces. The students were in the cloud café where Unicorn Girl and I went to eat after stealing *The Adventures of Futureman*. The Good Thieves were outside the Dip when I showed Bum Bum the book over brunch. I met the long-legged man in running shorts, hunched over an espresso, outside the Reference Library when I tried to return the book. The common denominator: all of them came into contact, in one way or another, with me while I was carrying that accursed comic strip collection.

Bum Bum's fashionable friend Alessandra comes out onto the patio with a tray of gelato for the students. I assume it might be her alternate self, until her eyes catch mine and widen in recognition. As she places a menu in front of me, she leans in and whispers, "You're the cavaliere's friend, aren't you? Is he with you?"

I shake my head. "I haven't seen him since the day of the Passion play."

Alessandra twists her apron in her hands. "I thought he might know why all this is happening. The world has gone crazy."

I nod. "I know. I'm happy to at least find other people! How did you end up here?"

Alessandra throws up her hands. "A curse? A miracle? You tell me! My kids were running around the neighbourhood, looking for something good to read in those funny wood boxes people stick old books in."

With a sick feeling in my gut, I ask, "You mean, the little libraries?"

"Giusta! Anyway, they come home with a leather book full of comic strips — a whaddyacallit, graphic novel, *Adventures of Some Guy from the Future*. Old, old book. Not even in PICTO, so the kids don't know how to read it. They ask me, Mom, read it to us. I took a look, and it's all about sending immigrants back where they come from. I say to them, What is this, some superhero wants to send me and your nonni back where we came from? Marone! So I made them put the piece of shit book back where they found it. They get home, they're complaining they're sick. Then I start feeling under the weather. Light-headed, like a fever coming on. I think, Oh no, not the Twistie flu again! We took a couple Tylenol, went to bed early and woke up to this. Not a soul left in our condo tower. The kids' school closed down. The city half-empty."

"Much more than half," I tell her. "I've walked all over downtown and this is the only place I've seen anyone at all. How long have you been here?"

Alessandra shakes her head, as if trying to call up a distant memory. "A day or two maybe? It's hard to know because the sun hasn't gone down!" Alessandra shows me the watch on her wrist, an old-fashioned Lady Timex with a delicate face almost too tiny for me to read. "The kids gave me this for Mother's Day. Vintage but never loses a second. Now look at it — the hands are stuck at two to twelve."

I glance at the sky. The sun is almost directly overhead. High noon.

"A nook in time," I murmur.

Alessandra frowns at me. "A *what?*"

"A place where time stops and gives you a second chance. Like purgatory. I've been here before. You could have been in one of these nooks for years, and no time at all would have passed in the real world. But that doesn't explain why the Dip is open even when every other place is closed."

Alessandra shrugs. "I don't know, but we're running out of food and wine. No one has any place else to go, so they sit here, eating and drinking." She gestures toward an elderly, thin-faced woman on the street, staring blankly at us from the sidewalk. "The old lady keeps coming back here, poor soul. She keeps asking for someone named Raffaele."

The old woman looks hopefully at Alessandra. "Dov'è Raffaele?"

Alessandra shakes her heard. "Non lo so. Mi dispiace, Signora."

The old woman sighs and shuffles away to ask the same question of the students. Alessandra and I fall silent. Absorbing the weirdness together.

"I could use a glass of wine," I say. "Something red and strong."

Alessandra returns with a carafe of Barolo. As she fills my glass, she glances down at my napkin sketches. "You're an artist?"

I nod. "I draw a comic book. *Sputnik Chick: Girl with No Past.*"

Alessandra's mouth drops open. She crosses herself. "Marone, you're the Storyteller! They're looking for you!"

I frown at her. "Who's 'they'?"

"The junkmen! The ones who work in those cheap joints with the robot cooks!"

"You mean junksters? What are they doing here?"

Behind me, someone says in an all-too-familiar little girl's voice, "Doc Time showed us the way."

I turn and see a teenager with magenta hair and an eye patch, sipping a cappuccino. Her skin has been tinted Smurf blue. A book is open on the table in front of her.

I recognize her at once as my young friend, the *Family Circus* fangirl and child soldier from my quantum leak to a war-torn Toronto: the Queen's Own Corporal Kristen Gould. But when she grins at me to reveal a gleaming set of titanium teeth, I realize that I'm looking at her doppelgänger, Unicorn Girl's junkster friend, K.

K winks her good eye and gives me the finger, then lifts the book to show me the cover: *The Adventures of Futureman*.

"You oughta be more careful where you leave things you find lying around," she says in her baby voice.

Oh, shit. The Trespasser called the book a Pandora's box. And just like Pandora, I've released a new evil into the world.

Alessandra tugs at my arm. "You have to hide! Now!"

But before I can get to my feet, a siren starts to sound, like the one at the end of hockey games. It doesn't let up. The deafening sound keeps rising and falling like an air raid siren.

Everyone looks at the sky; a few students rush to the curb. Alessandra drops her tray and runs out to grab her children, who are crouched on the sidewalk with their hands over their ears.

I join the students just in time to see a truck pull up. The rear doors swing open and armoured figures leap out, one after another. At first their metal faceplates and helmets make me think they're robots, until I realize they're humans dressed in a jumble of machine parts. Not robot soldiers but junksters. They set upon the students cowering on the pavement; I see one of them scoop the children up under his arms, while another pushes a screaming Alessandra to the sidewalk.

Pinned to the ground with a junkster's boot in the small

of my back, I manage to twist my head toward the sound of approaching footsteps, grinding my cheek into the pavement in the process. A pair of sandalled feet stops directly in front of my face. They have the creamy white patina of polished marble but with the distinctive whorls and pattering of wood grain. The toes are unarticulated, like a doll's feet.

"Is this the one, Centurion?"

It's a voice straight out of a sword-and-sandal epic, the Oxbridge accent of a classically trained actor playing the part of a Roman emperor. One of those famous Peters of the past, Ustinov or O'Toole.

K goes down on one knee to peer into my face. With my head squashed against the pavement, I can just make out her Smurf-blue nose and pirate eye patch. Her breath stinks of fish oil.

"It's the one, all right, Your Grace. The Storyteller," says K.

The platinum emperor gives a plummy chuckle. "Well done, Centurion."

"Thank you, Your Grace. Your orders?"

"Hmmm?"

"Where should we take the Storyteller?"

"To New Rome, of course!"

"And the others?"

"Like the rest you've brought in! Off to the settlements with them, chop, chop."

Ouch. Not *too* racist or anything. I roll one eye upward to try to look at the creature, but all I can see are its gleaming silver-white feet. It's like grovelling at the base of a statue.

K clears her throat. "Begging your pardon, Your Grace, but the settlements are full."

The regal foot taps the ground impatiently. "Clear some space then!"

K pauses, as if struggling with what to ask next. "Do you mean that we should, ummm — *dispose* of the surplus passengers? As in, kill them? Drown them in the lake, perhaps?"

A harrumphing sound, like Dagwood's boss chewing him out in a *Blondie* comic strip. "Certainly not, you silly goose. Are we brutes, no better than the meat puppets? No. You answer to a higher power now. Have I not shown you the proper way to clear away the unwanted?"

"I beg your pardon, Your Grace," murmurs K.

The creature walks away from K and me, far enough that I can get a clear look at him. If that's the right pronoun for something that looks so artificial, even if its voice is gendered to sound manly. Its gleaming silver body is humanoid, but its musculature has the smooth, perfect, injection-moulded curves of a luxury car. It's very tall — six-six, give or take. Its movements are fluid, even graceful. But from the neck up, it looks like the unfinished storyboard sketch of a monster in an Italian B-movie version of *Jason and the Argonauts*, drawn by a set designer who'd had a few too many grappas after lunch.

The conical head is covered in green pine needles, rising to the sharp point of a Christmas tree waiting to be topped with a star. The bottom half of what might be called its face, where its mouth should be, is masked by stretchy silver mesh, moulded over a jutting strongman jaw. When it speaks, the mesh moves gently, like tinsel. The docked ears of a Doberman pinscher poke sharply up and forward through the sides of its needle-covered head. Clearly the monster's creator thought there was no need for a nose.

Its only humanoid facial feature is a single gigantic eye: emerald green, thickly lashed, searching. In fact, the eye is so real and the rest of its face is so artificial that I feel queasy looking at it — the so-called Uncanny Valley effect, when a synthetic creature sits nauseatingly close to the cliff edge of passing for human. That's as much as I can take in. The glare off the silver body is so blinding that I can barely stand to look at him — it — whatever.

And then it strikes me: this Cyclops with a plummy accent is patterned on Futureman. Part machine, part animal, part plant and — somewhere deep inside — part human, if anything remains of the Christmas tree farmer known as Hubert White. A living, breathing biomechanoid. A comic strip character come to life.

"I simply meant," the Cyclops says to K in a tone heavy with impatience, "that you should *accelerate* the clearances. The faster we send these passengers back where they come from, the sooner we can build a forever world for your kind and mine. No need to get all kill-y about it, is there?"

"Of course not, Your Grace," answers K, with obvious relief in her voice.

The Cyclops walks back toward me. Now the marble-white feet are standing directly in front of my eyes, close enough that I can make out what's stamped into its ankle: *PoF™ licensed user of mark.*

PoF. People of Forever. Not just comic strip creatures but a corporate entity. Monsters with a business plan and mission statement and brand. Now I *know* we're fucked.

"Those are my *official* orders, but frankly, my dear, I don't give a damn about the others. Use your initiative! The Storyteller here is the prize. She knows how to build worlds out of mere scratches on paper. A skill we are most eager to exploit."

A pause.

I can sense K's confusion. I almost feel like explaining that the Cyclops wants her to do its dirty work without having to be explicit about it, but my mouth is full of gravel.

"So . . . the Storyteller?" K asks again, uncertainly.

It finally gives a direct answer. "Throw her in the back of the truck and let's see what she can do for us in New Rome. Chop, chop!"

FIFTEEN

THE STORYTELLER AND HER LOVER ON THE LONGEST NIGHT OF THE YEAR

Earlier in this long night of storytelling, David seemed to be on the verge of drifting off — until I started to recount my walk across Toronto with the evil book in tow. Ever since then, he's been sitting up in bed, awake and alert and jumpy. I can sense that it isn't only eagerness to see how the story turns out. It's a growing sense of fear.

When I described almost being run down by the truck, he said, "I remember that day. I was on my way home from the office, checking my phone, and there it was on my newsfeed. Truck attack on Bay Street. I even remember reading descriptions of the victims. Names, ages, jobs. Mostly women. There was a comic book writer among the critically injured. That must have been you."

I waggled my hand in a maybe yes, maybe no gesture. "That victim was a version of me. A splitting off from my self like Doc Mutant predicted."

"I don't get it. And where's Sinatra in all this?"

"I'll get there."

When I described the appearance of the synthetic Cyclops, his body began to tremble. I triggered a memory of trauma best forgotten.

I took his hand. "You already know the next part of the story, David. We don't have to go on. You need to get some sleep."

"But I don't know how my part of the story ended," he protested. "I was yanked away from it in the middle, remember."

"You're sure you want me to carry on?"

He nodded. "And talk about me the way you do everyone else, Stan. Like Eufemia and Hot Lips and the other passengers. Let me pretend to just be a character in the story. It'll make me feel as if that world was maybe just a fairy tale."

THE ALTERNATE ADVENTURES OF
SPUTNIK CHICK:
GIRL WITH NO PAST

Volume 39, Issue 2
"EVE OF DESTRUCTION"

featuring
THE JUNKSTERS,
GATEKEEPERS OF THE PEOPLE OF FOREVER

with special guests
HOT LIPS, POSEIDON, MARCOPOLO
AND OLD EUFEMIA

and introducing
PRIMA:
THE LITTLEST BIOMECHANOID

JULY 10, 1979

ATOMIC SHADOW TIME (A.S.T.)

Hearty congratulations, D.R. BIONDI! You have been selected for **reverse** migration to PORT OF GENOA, OCTOBER 14, 1919. You are required to retain this itinerary for future reference, as it will act as your **passport to the past**. Loss or damage to this document, or failure to present it upon request, will result in your **immediate correction.**[1]

We look forward to assisting you in preparation for your Journey Home to Mother. As you are no doubt aware, poor cultural management has disordered societies, resulting in confusion, chaos and conflict. Going forward, it is the mission of the People of Forever™ ("PoF") to correct this error through reverse-engineered immigration. Thank you for your enthusiastic participation!

"In order to go forward,
we must first go backward."™
— Norman Guenther, PhD ("Doc Time")

To facilitate your journey, you will be provided with clothing from your ancestral homeland and date of emigration. During

---

[1] Correction may involve inflicting pain and/or damage to non-vital organs, including skin, teeth, reproductive organs and soft tissue. The People of Forever ("PoF") are not liable for fatalities caused by pre-existing medical conditions undisclosed by the passenger.

™ People of Forever Inc. ("PoF") is the licensed owner of the mark and sole owner of rights to all creative works, inventions and other forms of intellectual property produced by detained passengers.

your temporal retreat, we recommend mastering the language, history and traditions of your ancestors, if you have not already done so.[2] In order to create a more ordered and standardized world, we may be required to inconvenience you but rest assured that you will not be harmed in any way directly resulting in your death. Our priority is to send you back where you belong. Thereafter, your destiny is in your hands.

© The People of Forever Communications Division, 2025.

Itinerary No. 254WXD-JHTM

SEE OVER FOR PICTO

---

2   Linguists and/or ethnocultural experts will be on site to assist you with language training and similar needs, as required.

ONE

THE STORYTELLER IN PURGATORY

When I still lived in Paradiso — by which I mean my adopted home world of Earth Standard Time — I used to love story-boarding *Sputnik Chick* comic books in hotel lobby bars. I'd perch on a high stool with my legs fetchingly crossed and sketch on cocktail napkins, the sharp chemical aroma of a Sharpie mixing nicely with the briny tang of a dirty martini.

Here in the purgatory of Atomic Shadow Time, I prop a sketchbook on my blistered knees and sip tepid lake water from a tin cup.

Pillowed against a garbage bag stuffed with crushed bottles and waterlogged chew toys, I ponder how to illustrate a world perpetually on the brink of destruction. It's always the day before doomsday, July 10, 1979. I assume that seven hundred kilometres above us in the exosphere, SkyLab hangs in eternal free fall, waiting for its final plunge to Earth. Which will never come, unless time somehow starts moving again.

Nothing changes in this world: not the intense heat, the bright sunlight or the weather. Night never falls. Neither does rain. Plants don't die or grow any bigger. Birds, insects and animals would go on living forever, if we didn't occasionally kill them for food. Even the mercury-bloated carcasses of the dead fish floating belly up in the lake don't rot. Their pre-existing stench doesn't dissipate either.

As for the junksters, they seem to love it here. They have all the time in the world to figure out how to turn themselves into machines, which they stupidly believe will make them as invulnerable as a certain comic book superhero.

I think of this stasis as Atomic Shadow Time. I have no idea how long we've been stuck here. Five months or five hundred years seem equally likely.

Meanwhile, the hands of Alessandra's vintage self-winding takes-a-licking-but-keeps-on-ticking Timex remain stuck at two minutes to twelve, like the doomsday clock of the atomic scientists through much of the Cold War. Never quite reaching high noon. As if we're forever stuck on the brink of destruction in the ultimate psychological torture test of time.

* * *

Until I leaked into this world, I'd forgotten how much the '70s worshipped synthetics: indestructible one hundred per-cent DuPont fabrics, aerosol sprays, artificial dessert toppings, pastel-coloured breakfast cereals, *Switched-On Bach*, Cheez Whiz. Along with the stench of dead fish, you can sniff the off-gassing of plastics floating in the air, a reminder that once there was ozone-depleting life in this depopulated world.

I have one choice here: draw or die. Given the sensory depri-vation in this world, smells are vital to my creative process.

Most comic book smells are easy to draw. Four wavy vertical lines mean something stinks (feet, garbage cans, skunks). A pair of lines curved seductively to one side like a reclining odalisque — known as a wafteron — conveys a pleasant aroma, like a fresh-baked apple pie or bouquet of flowers. Animate the wafteron and you can turn it into a pair of hands caressing a face, or a lovesick chump floating on a note of perfume, or a hungry cat levitating toward a roast chicken.

But graphic devices all fail me in this cheerless limbo. How can I possibly draw the fug inside this slow cooker of a tent, with the sun beating down and the flaps zipped tight against swarms of immortal mosquitos and midges? How can lines on paper convey the lingering stench of twenty women jammed into a tent meant for half our number, our flop sweat, bad breath, unbrushed teeth and the gaggy reek of vomit, chronic diarrhea and menstrual blood?

Somehow our biological clocks tick on. Unlike every other living thing in this world, we bleed, sicken, weaken and sometimes die.

And then there's Old Eufemia, gently farting in the cot next to me, untroubled by a total absence of circadian rhythms. She's muttering in her sleep about making dinner or making love or making *something* — my limited Italian won't tell me much more than that. From time to time, she shouts the name "Raffaele," sometimes in anger, other times in what sounds like passion. At first, her constant sleep-talking drove me crazy — that and her body odour, although we all used to smell just as bad. Now that one of the passengers figured out how to make soap to scrub off the smell of dead fish and polluted water, the rest of us are a little less funky. The only way we'll get Eufemia to wash is to dunk her in the lake. I know that some of the passengers are plotting to do just that; they'll tell her they're taking her for out for a little passaggiata, roll her into a sheet and hurry her to the water's edge before she knows what's going on. No one wants to scare her, but the old woman's body needs to be cleaned and moved or she'll get bedsores, according to Hot Lips. Eufemia is the closest thing the passengers have to a nonna and they're determined to keep her alive.

I can hear them all out on the beach, singing an off-key rendition of "Mambo Italiano." Rare to hear the passengers sounding so chipper. They must have found something edible for breakfast.

Passengers might seem like a strange word to describe us, since we're stuck on dry land. But we *are* on a journey together. Atomic Shadow Time is like a gigantic airport lounge where you never know when your flight will be called. All of us are stuck in transit here, waiting to start the final leg of our trip back in time through Mother. Pass through the shadow between her legs and we will be transported to Earth Standard Time of Old, to the precise place and day our ancestors left their homelands forever. That could be five, ten, fifty, hundreds or thousands of years ago, to places we've never even seen. It's laid out in the itinerary each of us received upon arrival, as well as in a bar code time-stamped on our left cheekbones in indelible ink. In New Rome, each passenger's time-stamp starts with the letters SPQR for Senatus Populusque Romanus — "the senate and people of Rome" — followed by our specific point of ancestral origin. My stamp indicates I'm destined for the Port of Genoa in 1919, the place and time Nonna Peppy started her second and final voyage to Ellis Island.

The passengers and I often ask ourselves how the junksters know more about our heritage than many of us do ourselves. So far, the best theory has come from Savonarola, former head of privacy and cybersecurity for a big online shopping company. "Data collected by the Internet of Things makes us the low hanging fruit. Easy enough to hack into our genetic profiles and family histories through those ancestry sites and family trees people like to post online."

When I tell him about voluntarily handing over a scraping of alleles from the inside of my cheek to Robot Drug Mart in return for a free makeover, Savonarola rolls his eyes.

* * *

Given my usefulness to our mostly invisible overlords, the People of Forever — or, as we call them, the Puffs — I'll likely be the last of the passengers sent home. Although when you think about it, leaking into Atomic Shadow Time might have been my real homecoming. I seem to have circled right back to where I came from.

The passengers seem to think they're caught in a bizarre backwards-mirror version of their own world. Earth Standard Time, 1979. What I call Paradiso. What they call reality.

I've gently explained, time and time again, that that's not true. That we're all trapped in the nuclear shadow of a world that has been dead for forty-nine years. An unchanging continuum flash-frozen in time.

The passengers listen and nod, but I can't tell they don't get it.

The birth and death of alternate realities is a lot for them to take in, along with everything else.

When I roll off my lumpy garbage bag pillow, a fluid-filled blister as big as a jellyfish bursts between my shoulder blades. I'll need to head down to the beach and ask a young nursing student, Hot Lips, to rub some of Eufemia's salve on the raw skin. It's one of the few medicines we have — that and a half-empty bottle of Advil that washed up yesterday, which came in handy when Hot Lips had to pull a rotting molar out of the Cooler King's mouth. God, I miss toothpaste! One of those little sample tubes they used to hand out free at dentists' offices could trigger a riot among the passengers.

I rummage under Eufemia's cot for her precious tube of Ozonol. Past its best-before date in Earth Standard Time but better than nothing in Atomic Shadow Time. She had it in the pocket of her apron when they brought her in along with a long-expired driver's licence, which let us know her name. Unlike the rest of us, no junksters bothered to take Eufemia's clothes away from her, maybe because they came with her from the old country.

Sensing my presence, Eufemia calls out, "Chi è? Raffaele?"

I stroke her leg under the blanket. She's so thin, it's like rubbing a stick. She's starving, poor thing, but at least she doesn't know it.

"Stai tranquilla," I whisper to her.

She sighs and curls onto her side, tugging my arm around her waist. Now I'm spooning her. Her grip is surprisingly strong.

"Raffaele," she murmurs again. "Ti amo."

I stay a moment to comfort her. Or maybe myself: hugging Old Eufemia reminds me of Kendal spooning me the last time we made love. Best not to think about sex in this place, although it's clear Eufemia dreams about it all the time.

With the Ozonol in my pocket, I search under my cot for a fresh Sharpie. Even though we sometimes have nothing to eat more nourishing than flour and tomato paste, the junksters keep me well supplied with sketchbooks and Sharpies so I can draw everything that happens in New Rome, lettering dialogue into word balloons in a combination of English, Italian and PICTO. I used to feel guilty about giving in to the junksters' demands to draw the story of our lives in temporal captivity, but I have no choice. I've already suffered enough trying to push back against the People of Forever Corporation's plans for world domination — although I'm still not sure how many worlds they're planning to take over. The only representative of the Puffs we've seen so far is the Cyclops emperor who threw his weight around at the Dip. He gives the orders. The junksters carry them out.

The Puffs are smart enough to know that real worlds require real stories — not just algorithms and statistics but histories, myths, legends, heroes, villains, saints, miracles. Apparently I'm here to supply all that in a sketchbook known as *The History of the Known World*.

But I have a second sketchbook that no one else knows about: *Visions of Paradiso*, which is how I think of Earth Standard Time — a flawed paradise, at least from where I sit in purgatory. These glimpses of my adopted home world come to me only while I'm in REM sleep, a rare occurrence in this world of eternal light. These visions aren't dreams but a side effect of the quantum split that Doc Mutant warned me about. In my rare moments of deep sleep, I'm caught between two very real worlds. And I'm not at all well in one of them.

While Old Eufemia snores in her cot, I sketch my most recent vision of Paradiso: myself in a wheelchair, surrounded by flower beds and burbling water features, the kind you sometimes see in hospital courtyards. A healing garden. I was wearing a blue bathrobe over a drab green nightgown. My head was turbaned in bandages and slumped on my chest. I looked completely out of it.

Bum Bum, Unicorn Girl and Jordan Kingsborough were seated in a circle around me, concerned looks on their faces. I tried to make eye contact with Unicorn Girl, who was clearly preoccupied with Jordan. They were holding hands. Doc Mutant was there too, taking my blood pressure. Bum Bum must have flown him up from New Jersey.

In my sketchbook, I letter their conversation in cartoon balloons floating over their heads.

"Do you think she's ever going to wake up?" asked Jordan.

Unicorn Girl waved her hand in front of my face. My eyes didn't flicker. I looked — whaddyacallit — catatonic.

"Her brain injury needs time to heal," said Doc Mutant. "Especially on top of her timesickness."

"Is she really in a coma? Or quantum travelling?" asked Unicorn Girl.

Doc Mutant clicked his tongue against his teeth as he unwrapped the blood pressure cuff from my arm. "Excellent question. The timesickness may have split Debbie into alternate selves. She's here but also in a timeline closely coupled to ours. And there's a complicating factor. I ran a few tests and found a rogue virus in her system. Her timesickness could be infectious."

In my sketchbook, I draw Bum Bum, Unicorn Girl and Jordan trading glances over a couple of wordless panels. A standard comic book device: I'm providing the visual space-time for them to absorb Doc Mutant's words.

Bum Bum, always the smartest one in the room, asked, "Could that comic strip be the source of the contagion? I warned Debbie *The Adventures of Futureman* was sick."

YES! I wanted to scream. *Find the fucking book already! The junksters made copies but the original must still be in a little library in Yorkville!* I summoned all my strength to try to communicate, but all I managed to do was pass gas.

I sketch a little puff of wind under my wheelchair.

"I think she's trying to tell us something," said Unicorn Girl, peering into my face.

Doc Mutant shone a light in one eye, then the other.

"Infectious timesickness is rare but not unknown. It's endemic in places where alternate worlds overlap. The Bermuda Triangle and Niagara Falls, for instance. I'd better put all of you on a course of Antiquanta as a precaution, or you could be sucked into another reality."

"Here's an even better idea, Doc," suggested Bum Bum. "I could get *deliberately* infected so I can go to the world where Debbie's trapped."

"Hold on! I helped steal the book! I should be on this rescue mission too!" protested Unicorn Girl.

Jordan put her hands on her hips, gunslinger style — where have I seen that posture before? Kendal on the floor of the House of Commons, haranguing the leader of the opposition.

"I should be the one to go. After all, I'm the superhero here!"

Unicorn Girl tried to take her hand, but Jordan shook her off. "C'mon, Jor. This is no time for cosplay."

"What's that supposed to mean?" snapped Jordan. "My father has disappeared! He might be with Debbie, for all we know!"

I draw a thought balloon, puffy as a storm cloud, floating over my slumping head: Wait, wait, wait . . . *what?* What's happened to Kendal?

I tried to force words from my mouth, but nothing came out.

Doc Mutant waved his webbed hands, trying to calm them all down.

"Debbie has the means to get herself out of whatever world she's in, if she has any Antiquanta left. Let's wait and see whether she can reintegrate her split selves before you start going off half cocked. Wherever she is, I suspect it's an aberrant world, maybe an artificial alternate reality. No doubt highly unstable."

* * *

Rogue viruses, infectious timesickness, aberrant alternate realities, secondary characters teaming up to rescue their sidelined leader, a superhero wannabe — what a fantastic story arc for *Sputnik Chick: Girl with No Past*! Why didn't I think of this before? Wait 'til I get back home and show Irina the sketchbook — they could spin a whole season of the streaming series off this idea alone.

I do a quick sketch — just stick figures, for now — drawing Xs where my eyes should be, comic book shorthand for knocked out.

Doc Mutant isn't wrong. Atomic Shadow Time *is* an aberration: the passengers have been sucked into this disco-era limbo, body and soul, while (to Doc Mutant's point) I exist in both worlds at once. In all my years of hopping around the multiverse, this has never happened before. The laws of parallel worlds are warping out of true.

As Doc Mutant pointed out, I can return to Earth Standard Time any time I want to, simply by swallowing the last linty Antiquanta hidden in my dress pocket. But I'll use the pill only as a last resort. I don't want to risk reintegrating with myself in Earth Standard Time while I'm still in a fugue state.

And then there's my responsibility to my fellow passengers. Without the stories in *The History of the Known World*, how would the New Romans find the will to carry on? Even if the Puffs plan to cannibalize the passengers' stories to create their own myths and legends, it's important that those stories survive. Otherwise, the passengers' presence in Atomic Shadow Time will vanish without a trace.

And so I remain here in purgatory with Old Eufemia, Hot Lips, Marcopolo and the rest, marooned on a never-ending, alternate-universe rerun of *Gilligan's Island*, waiting to see if Bum Bum launches his rescue mission despite Doc Mutant's warning. In the meantime, I'll draw whatever happens next.

* * *

Despite the tedium of life in Atomic Shadow Time, I have plenty of material to draw upon. New Rome and the other settlements where passengers are being detained are located on the Leslie Street Spit, a five-kilometre finger of land poking out of Toronto's eastern lakefront. Surrounded by water on all sides except the isthmus connecting it to Toronto's old industrial waterfront, the spit is an artificial wilderness, created over a half century from the city's discarded infrastructure, starting with an entire immigrant neighbourhood known as the Ward, the tenements demolished, hauled out here and bulldozed underground in the 1950s. A buried city of lost memories, mixed with megatons of dirt from subway trenches, mostly dug by the immigrants themselves. Eventually stuff began to grow out of the landfill. Scrubby stands of trees, patches of grass. Frogs, beavers, rabbits and coyotes found their way here. Birds started treating the spit as a stopover during mass migrations.

There used to be signs warning visitors to stay off the beaches during mating season. Birders came armed with cameras and binoculars to catch glimpses of snowy owls. Now we're hunting the birds instead of observing them.

Mercifully, New Rome sits in a scrubby field far from the screeches of sex-crazed cormorants and the stench of guano. Over on the southern tip of the spit, Sarajevo sits on the highest point of land, where a lighthouse is crumbling into the outer harbour. That settlement is made up of a group of Bosnians who came to Canada as refugees during their civil war in the 1990s. The Serbs live with them, along with a smattering of Croatians and Montenegrins. Closer to the bird-nesting beach is an encampment of twenty or so North African immigrants and their descendants called Tunis. In a sheltered area closer to the front gate are about fifty Sri Lankan immigrants in Colombo. Huronia, Munich, Beijing, Dublin and Inverness are smaller camps scattered around the main access roads to the spit.

Those among us descended from settlers are fated to return to where in the world our ancestors came from. Our reverse migrations could take us back in time anywhere from one to five hundred years. As usual, the Anishinaabeg have an even more punishing fate awaiting them: their itineraries set out journeys to the Bering Sea of thirteen thousand years ago.

Each group of passengers gets a different set of insufficient food rations; trading helps. We share as much as we can, including what little information we can wheedle out of the junksters.

In New Rome, we get bags of dry pasta and some watery tomato sauce, but that's about it. No protein, no fresh fruits or vegetables. Hot Lips and another nursing student, Ginalollobrigida, managed to get the junksters to give us some seeds for vegetables — they thought we might be able to get a garden going — but nothing new grows in the stasis of Atomic Shadow Time. We get our drinking water straight out of the lake — even more polluted with phosphates and other industrial effluvia than in our own world — which is probably why so many passengers are sick with intestinal illnesses. Diarrhea mostly, which has turned the plastic outhouses into steaming cesspools. The Cooler King — a chemist in Earth Standard Time — was the one who figured out a way to filter some of the larger particulates out of the water using pieces of sanitary napkins and a pump we found in the landfill. John and Sebastian Cabot have graciously started digging new privies. Hot Lips frets about scurvy.

Most of the passengers are filthy and malnourished. A few are sick with respiratory infections that Hot Lips worries are spreading in our crowded tents. Some have been abused in ways even more imaginatively horrible than I have been. On top of their physical ailments, I can tell that all the passengers are falling deeper into the illness that brought them here in the first place. A type of timesickness that would eventually infect everyone, the Trespasser told me in Unicorn Girl's VR game. He said I'd be responsible for the Pandora plague, and I've no doubt he was right. I opened up the book that unleashed Professor Quantum's weaponized time travel on the world. Carried it to Gut Fill and to the Dip during the Passion play. Abandoned it in the little library where it was picked up, read and passed around. The virus spread like wildfire, turning everyone infected into an unwilling refugee in the multiverse.

Not that I'd admit any of this to the passengers, who see me as their Storyteller. The one who'll make sure their stories aren't forgotten. I don't have the heart to confess that I'm also a destroyer of worlds and the one who changed their lives, probably forever.

* * *

I stuff *Visions of Paradiso* back under my cot, take out *The History of the Known World* and head outside to take in New Rome in all its magnificence: eleven white tents overlooking a cobble beach chewed by waves rolling in from Lake Ontario. The heat is unrelenting. As usual, the horizon glows Creamsicle orange, bruised by a sickly haze of yellow chemicals from the other side of the lake.

On a cliff edge overhanging the beach, a structure that looks vaguely like the Coliseum is going up, built by New Romans in their late teens and twenties, dressed in turn-of-the-last-century factory smocks, suspendered trousers and faded cotton dresses, the boys in soft caps, the girls in headscarves. Those who are destined to go back to the 1950s look more modern, the women girdled into tight dresses, the men in fedoras, slouchy trousers and cotton shirts with loosely knotted neckties. In a different time and place, they might have been extras in a Fellini film or guests at a costume party.

They're having fun with cast-offs from demolished buildings. Pieces of rebar. Broken chunks of concrete. Slabs of porcelain tile from bathrooms and kitchens. Tangles of electrical wiring. The odd lion or gargoyle from the facade of a Victorian bank building. The passengers spend hours fitting together these bits of debris like giant misshapen Legos. In this haphazard way they've managed to construct walls, rooms, tables, benches and even a winding staircase down to the beach. For the outer walls of the Coliseum, they use only grey and white bricks, probably dumped here all at once, an entire building hung upside down in the ground beneath our feet. Someone has used one of my Sharpies to write *Welcome to New Rome* in PICTO on a chunk of white bathroom tile.

Further inland, Tut the Girl King — who was working on her archeology thesis before she was brought here — excavates the ground with a branch. She's pulled some interesting and occasionally useful stuff out of the ground. Spoons. Cigarette packages. A curling iron. A *Little Lulu* comic. A half-used tube of Cover Girl lipstick in burnt orange. Tut's latest find — a rusty hammer — is the most important one, serving as our most effective weapon.

On a large piece of driftwood, just beyond the reach of the surf, Caterina teaches conversational Italian to a handful of passengers. Today they're learning how to order lemonade and ask the price of gloves. Caterina's my age or maybe a little older. I'm jealous of her fluency, but the phrases she teaches sound pointless to me. Lemonade and gloves? If these young people actually do get sent back to Italy in its war-torn years (or the brutal lead-up and hungry aftermath), it's better to teach them to beg for food or their lives, or to haggle over the price of a fuck. Unlike Old Eufemia, Caterina speaks "good" Italian. Still, she warns her students that regional dialects vary enough that a Sicilian can't communicate with a Tuscan, and vice versa; who knows what life these ones will go back to, so distant are they from their families' migrations that they can't even speak the language. Most of them don't remember — or never knew — that Italy was anything besides a sunny backdrop for nostalgic family stories. (*If it was so great, why did your families leave*, I'm tempted to ask them.) Old Eufemia's dialect might do them more good than Caterina's elegant textbook Florentine.

Hot Lips, Alessandra and Antoinette watch the construction activity from their perch on a truck tire, washed up on the shore. They wave to me and I pick my way on bare feet over the cobble beach. A fashion student nicknamed Ferragamo has promised to make me a pair of shoes, but so far nothing useful by way of materials has washed up. Only a matter of time before some Crocs fall out of a boat, he points out, but so far it's all been plastic bottles and dog toys.

When I show Hot Lips the broken blister on my back, she tsk-tsks and takes the Ozonol from me. "I'll put some on a sheet of toilet paper and cover the wound with it," she says. "Safer than letting your skin touch your blouse." In her sun-bleached dress and headscarf, with a makeshift pouch of improvised first aid supplies hanging from her hip, she looks like a nun in a Renaissance painting.

"What're you drawing now?" asks Antoinette, as Hot Lips patches me up.

"The Coliseum of New Rome," I answer, opening the sketchbook.

Marcopolo drops down beside me and snuggles in, resting her chin on my blistered shoulder. I flinch but don't shrug her off. A young sex worker arrested by the junksters along with her date, she has better survival skills than the other passengers but craves attention from older women like me. Ever the teacher, Caterina once quietly confided in me that she thinks Marcopolo might have attention deficit disorder. Tiny, dark-eyed and pink haired, with the wiry frame of a young boy, she looks much younger than she must actually be; there are no children in New Rome or any of the other settlements. Except for the junksters, of course.

"Show me the story of the known world, Stan," Marcopolo begs.

I open the sketchbook to the first page: "The Arrival of Columbus." Marcopolo has seen these pages many times but never gets tired of looking at them.

Columbus isn't crazy about being named for history's most infamous colonizer of the so-called New World, but it was the obvious choice: she was the first passenger to be transplanted from Old Toronto to New Rome by a heavily armed brigade of junksters. Her real name is Nancy Santangelo, a twenty-two-year-old early childhood educator. In my drawings, she stands bravely on the edge of the cliff overlooking this very beach, gazing out at Lake Ontario. Her long cotton dress billows in the wind, a shawl wrapped around her shoulders. She's dressed very much like me.

After her capture, two junksters held Nancy down and stripped off her clothing. She was terrified that she was about to be raped, but instead they gave her a dress, shawl, lace-up boots and a personal itinerary and left her alone on the cobble beach along the southern edge of the spit. She slept in the open on the hard ground for three days until the arrival of Caruso, an opera student at the Royal Conservatory of Music. In my sketches, Columbus and Caruso are resourceful and courageous. Making the best of a bad situation. Trying to figure out what's happening to them. Working the problem. Even making jokes. I've put a superheroic spin on their suffering because it comforts the passengers to believe that the first two of us to come to New Rome didn't fall into despair.

In reality, Caruso confessed to me that the two of them had been utterly helpless, weeping as they clung to one another through rolling panic attacks. They were sure they were going to die.

"Neither of us had so much as been camping before," explained Columbus. "We didn't even know how to start a fire."

In the days following Columbus's and Caruso's arrivals, the junksters brought wave after wave of passengers to New Rome: students, artists, young advertising creatives. Lawyers like Geneva and technocrats like Savonarola. Homeless teenagers. Sex workers like Marcopolo. And an entire varsity men's swim team, sucked into this world together after a late-night group practice, after which they passed around a book of comic strips one of them found on the seat of a subway train — *The Adventures of Futureman*, of course. Five of the swimmers had an Italian parent, grandparent or great-grandparent, and so were deposited here. The rest of the team was sent to other settlements on the spit. I've tried to be faithful to the way the swimmers looked when they arrived — tall, muscular, cocky, healthy, angry, defiant. Robbed of their Speedos and sweatsuits, they were given workers' coveralls, as if they were all descendants of mechanics and bricklayers.

Marcopolo traces their well-defined biceps with her finger. None of the swimmers look like this anymore. Some are still defiant despite their loss of muscle mass, but one open water swimmer, Tarzan, was broken when he was caught trying to swim off the cobble beach in the direction of a marina at Ashbridge's Bay. A squad of junksters appeared out of nowhere and beat him so badly he can no longer raise his arms over his head. When they dislocated both his shoulders, his screams were heard as far as Tunis. With his teammates holding him down, Hot Lips was able to yank his shoulders back in place but can do nothing about his torn rotator cuff. Since then Tarzan has been withdrawn and uncommunicative. He's been robbed of his front crawl and his will to live. Now the other swimmers avoid him, as though his bad luck is catching. What good is a swimmer who can't swim?

I've tried to work everyone's origin story into *The History of the Known World*. Antoinette was on her way home from the late shift at a restaurant where she was head chef. Stopped to riffle through a little library, looking for historical fiction, maybe a Philippa Gregory or one of those sexy *Outlander* novels. What she found was a weird comic strip collection. Flipped through it, put it back, walked on. A dizzy spell later, she found herself here.

Caterina was celebrating the end of term with a group from the Italian studies department and stepped outside Café Diplomatico onto College Street to have a smoke. She didn't remember touching *The Adventures of Futureman*, but she figured it was the kind of thing some of her students would have gone for. She was rounded up with Alessandra and me.

Alessandra is worried sick about her twin eight-year-olds, Clara and Carlo. Any attempts to pry information about the children's whereabouts out of the junksters have been met with sarcasm. "If only someone had worried about where kids like us would end up after the Twistie flu," observed K, with a sneer. In a fit of despair, Alessandra left her Timex wristwatch on a rock by the shore, as if setting out a beacon for the kids.

Geneva was walking home early from his law practice on a Friday night, the beginning of the Sabbath. He'd been poking through a little library, hoping to find a meaty whodunnit; he doesn't remember seeing *The Adventures of Futureman*, but it must have been there or have left traces of the virus behind. Still in his kippah, his first assumption was that his capture by the junksters was the beginning of a modern-day pogrom. With an Israeli mother and a Jewish-Italian father from Venice, he could have been detained in a settlement for Sephardic Jews, wherever in Toronto that might be. Instead he was placed in New Rome.

Eufemia is something of a mystery: the 2002 driver's licence we found in her apron pocket gives a home address in Niagara Falls, Ontario, even though she was hanging around the Dip. Hot Lips theorizes that Eufemia might have been an Alzheimer's patient who wandered away from one of the seniors' homes on College Street. She must have come into contact with *The Adventures of Futureman* somewhere along the way.

Data scientist Savonarola (real name: Ian Magnini) had the bad luck to open a PDF of *The Adventures of Futureman*, sent to him (he thought) by his brother, under the subject line *Check out this crazy shit bro.* Proof positive that even experts goof up and computer viruses can jump the species barrier.

Most of the passengers have no memory of touching the book. But someone they knew might have done so, or simply talked about it. Oral stories can go viral too. And as I've discovered, whoever controls the story, controls the world.

* * *

Almost everyone in New Rome has a nom de guerre — or, as they like to put it, a secret identity. It's a way to protect our memories of our selves from before we came here. Hot Lips — Sicilian on her mother's side, Filipino on her father's — was in her fourth year of nursing at the University of Toronto; so clearly was she one of the natural leaders of New Rome that Caterina and I named her for the head nurse in *M*A*S*H*, a TV show she'd never heard of. Roberto, James and Gregorio turned themselves into Big X, the Mole and the Cooler King from *The Great Escape* — wishful thinking. The Good Thieves from the Passion play — twin brothers, it turns out — became John and Sebastian Cabot, acting as our envoys to the other settlements around the spit.

Most of the women around my age, like Caterina and Antoinette, go by their real names, but I stuck with my avatar handle from Unicorn Girl's VR game — Stan, after the late Stan Lee of Marvel Comics. I sometimes wonder what he would have done in my position. Throw his stories into the lake, on principle? I've thought of doing that, but I fear the consequences.

Besides I couldn't bear to give up storytelling now. It's a distraction, like the junkyard Coliseum the passengers are building from discarded remnants of twentieth-century Toronto.

Once a week, I borrow Eufemia's shoes to walk to the front gate, grateful to be accompanied by Geneva, who seems to have designated himself my protector. The lawyer's calm, firm demeanour comforts me, even if he'd never stand a chance against a mob of junksters. On these official visits, I'm always called upon to show them the latest stories in *The History of the Known World*. We also take the opportunity to issue requests; Geneva prefers to call them demands. Risky, but they have yielded some results. A little extra food and blankets. Sanitary pads for the women.

Just inside the gate, a gang of junksters sprawls on lawn chairs, shading an assortment of snoozing dogs. Most are no more than fourteen or fifteen, or even younger, the only children I've seen since coming to New Rome.

Armoured in bits and pieces of mechanical cast-offs, they try to look like the robots they long to become. Outside of their fondness for dogs, their single concession to being human is food, although the only thing we've seen them eat are endless cheeseburgers and fries, perfectly preserved and piping hot, from the fast food joints lining Toronto's lakeshore. Without the passage of time, nothing cools off or goes bad; the junksters are still working their way through the Whoppers and Big Macs prepped but never picked up on a hot summer day in 1979.

K is usually a smirking presence in their midst. She's lost her waifish appearance. Her face has grown puffy and her belly has expanded; it protrudes like a beach ball from under a tattered sweatshirt printed with the faded logo of a robotics manufacturer from long ago: *BOSTON DYNAMICS*. She's replaced her pirate patch with a steel plate that seems to be screwed directly into her eye socket; I wince just looking at her.

"K is getting fat," I observe to Geneva.

He gives a dismissive grunt. "Wake up, Stan. The girl's pregnant."

Sipping on a Big Gulp, K waddles toward us with our bags of meagre rations. A baby conceived in purgatory, fathered by one of the junkster boys? They look barely old enough to grow beards. It's easy to forget that the junksters' machine-clad bodies are subject to the same rhythms, urges and fallibilities they were back in Earth Standard Time.

Of course, K and the junksters don't run this world — the Puffs' corporation does. We've only ever seen one Puff: the plummy-accented Cyclops emperor from my capture at the Dip. Geneva calls it Dragon, from the children's song "Puff, the Magic Dragon."

Whenever K grooms Dragon — painting over rust spots, replacing rivets, occasionally cutting open a section of its head or chest for some mysterious upgrade or repair — Dragon pages through *The History of the Known World* like a customer in a barber shop perusing a magazine. The Puff always chuckles over my stories, ordering me to read the dialogue in the speech bubbles and demanding to know more about us.

"Why are humans so emotionally weak and needy? You seemingly can't bear to be without your loved ones. Your family, lovers, children, pets." Dragon shakes its needled head and snorts through its tinsel-shrouded mouth. "And you dare call digital people slaves? You are the ones enslaved to your emotions. Soon, Storyteller, you will need to close the book on your dying people and begin one about the People of Forever. You'll have new orders and fresh sketchbooks soon."

Geneva and I exchange glances. Great, now that the Puffs have figured out how stories work, they're going to give me notes. This is worse than working on story arcs for the TV show.

* * *

I've learned the hard way to keep my mouth shut during these exchanges, but Geneva can barely control his temper. Once, as we picked up our supplies and began to make our way back to New Rome, he turned and said to K, "All you're doing is building your own god. Replacing one big boss with another."

K glared at Geneva with her good eye. "It's *ourselves* we're rebuilding. You and your kind aren't long for this world. Your story is almost over."

Geneva doesn't know when to give up.

"I know you and your friends were badly treated by the powers-that-be during the great sickness. Left to fend for yourselves as kids when you should have had someone caring for you. That was wrong. You deserve redress. But you could try to be a little more humane. You are human, after all."

K leaned in. "Here's the thing, mister. It's too late for 'We're sorry.' We don't want to be human anymore. The faster we can join the synths, the happier we'll be."

To emphasize her point, she spat a gob of forty-nine-year-old Quarter Pounder with cheese at our feet.

The next time we visited the front gate, a new junkster was sitting in K's decrepit lawn chair, a boy in a metal breastplate and gauntlets, scratching the ears of an elderly beagle.

"Where's K?" I asked, handing over my sketchbook.

"Gone shopping," mumbled the junkster, paging through my drawings.

We never saw K on the spit again.

* * *

All this has been set down in *The History of the Known World*, which Marcopolo now pages through, enthralled. I watch her examining the illustrations of the punishment I endured for refusing to draw when I first got here. Fifteen solid hours stripped naked and spread-eagled on a sun-blasted hill of bricks in the debris field where trucks used to dump landfill. The blazing sun and biting insects were the junksters' implements of torture.

It was hard for me to draw myself like that, exposed and suffering, but it was important to record the event for the history of New Rome.

The whole time, Geneva kept screaming about the Geneva Conventions until Dragon told him to be quiet or he'd be joining me. His protest earned him his nickname.

By the time they let me go, I was so blistered and bitten, I couldn't walk to the tent. If it wasn't for Hot Lips, I might have died of infection. She boiled lake water and bathed my wounds.

* * *

From my vantage point near the Coliseum, I see a group of passengers approaching, led by Poseidon (real name: Daryl Bernardi), a tall young man with the graceful, confident stride of the athletically gifted, even though he's lost a lot of weight. Poseidon was the captain of the swim team; aerodynamically hairless when he arrived in New Rome, he now sports a full black beard and hair to his shoulders. He's swinging something that looks like a huge white sack. Only when they get closer do I see what it really is: a dead swan.

183

"Marone," says Antoinette, crossing herself.

Poseidon's friends are dancing around him as he walks. Celebrating the kill. Their faces smeared with blood. White feathers are stuck in their hair. They're hooting excitedly. Neptune, one of Poseidon's teammates, waves the rusted hammer, dug up by Tut the Girl King, over his head. They've beaten the swan to death.

"Fresh meat!" shouts Poseidon. "Fire up the barbecue, kids!"

"Can you even eat a swan?" I ask Antoinette sotto voce.

"You can eat anything, if you're hungry enough," she answers.

Over the next hour, Antoinette and Alessandra pluck and dismember the carcass and figure out how to cook it over a little fire built from scrap wood. They decide to stew it in a broth of milkweed and twigs. I was sure it would be horrible, but it tastes not bad. Like stringy chicken in a watery soup. Or maybe we're just so hungry and bored that a little protein and the distraction of learning a new survival skill makes the bird taste less disgusting.

Poseidon carries Eufemia out of our tent in his arms. Hot Lips spreads a blanket on the ground and props her up on a stuffed garbage bag. Eufemia eats a bit of the swan soup and looks around at us happily. She reaches over and takes Poseidon's hand.

"Raffaele," she says and kisses it.

Poseidon grins and kisses Eufemia's cheek.

Our stomachs full of swan soup, we lie outside the walls of the Coliseum. There's talk of getting together with our Anishinaabeg neighbours for an organized hunt. They know what they're doing and we don't. This would seem like poetic justice, us settlers being sent back where we came from, if the Puffs weren't planning to send the Indigenous passengers into even more certain oblivion. Some things don't change.

We've seen beavers and coyotes and the odd deer. Ducks and geese. And lots of rabbits. But they're hard to kill, with only the rusted hammer as a weapon. Some of the passengers in other camps have fashioned spears from tent poles, rebar and broken glass. Hunting in a group makes sense as long as it doesn't rile up the junksters.

Poseidon and Neptune sit on the beach, elbows on knees, skipping stones. They're itching to get out into open water. Despite what happened to Tarzan, there's still talk about swimming away or building a boat from all the junk on the spit. Problem is, the junksters never seem to be around until we do something that suggests we're trying to escape, at which point they swoop down and inflict whatever punishment seems appropriate to them. We wondered if there was a junkster spy in our midst, until Poseidon pointed out that some of the birds flying overhead don't flap their wings. That's when we realized the birds were actually drones.

After weeks on the beach watching the sky to become familiar with the drones' routes and flight times, Poseidon comes up with an escape plan.

"They're on a predictable schedule," he tells us. "One drone an hour, down to once every three hours at night. Enough of a window for us to swim to Ashbridge's Bay."

"And where would that get us?" asks Hot Lips.

"The hell out of here," supplies Neptune.

"There's a marina at Ashbridge's," explains Poseidon. "Lots of sailboats and nobody in them. We could easily get into the main shipping lanes for the seaway. Maybe there are abandoned vessels we could board. Push come to shove, we could swim out there during a pause in drone activity."

"That'll be really practical for Old Eufemia," says Hot Lips.

Neptune and Poseidon trade looks. "We can't all make it

out, no matter what we do. If we do nothing, we die. If some of us do something, maybe a few live."

"Or we all live by going back to Italy," says Columbus. "It sounds like a nice place."

"You really swallow that time travel bullshit?" snorts Neptune.

"In the times when your parents or grandparents or great-grandparents left, life was very tough. War, starvation, economic hardship," points out Savonarola. "Women even married men they'd never met by proxy so they could go to Canada or Australia."

Just then a flock of cormorants passes overhead, not flapping their wings.

"Let's table the plan for now, kids," says Poseidon.

As the artificial birds fly over us, we sit and listen to the sound of waves thrusting in and pulling back, rattling the rocks and rebar. Eventually Columbus starts to sing "Bobcaygeon." A few others join in. Alessandra digs lyrics from a Bowie song out of her memory. Savonarola surprises us with a few hits from Gino Vannelli's *Live in Montreal* album. Caruso stands on a rock, extends his arms and sings "Nessun dorma," then leads us in "Despacito."

After a few more songs, the passengers fall silent. Marcopolo lays her head on my lap. It hurts against my healing patches of skin, but I don't shoo her away.

"Tell us the story of the Queen again, Stan," she says.

"The good Queen, the true Queen!" shouts Ginalollobrigida.

The others take up her chant.

Antoinette groans. "Leave Stan alone. Can't you see she's tired? And besides it's just a fairy tale!"

"It isn't, actually, Antoinette," I say softly. "Don't you remember?"

"The Queen! Give us the Queen!" shouts Caruso, waving to the others to raise their voices with his.

"All right, all right," I say. "Settle down and I'll tell it."

The passengers draw closer to me, in a tight circle, like kindergarteners at story time. Their faces in the firelight are full of anticipation, even though I've told them this story a hundred times. It's a story they should already know, part of the history of Earth Standard Time. Yet the longer they remain in this stasis, the less they remember of their own world, a symptom of the Pandora plague that has left me untouched.

I always begin the same way. "She wasn't supposed to be queen. But her uncle was a bad king."

"A wicked king," suggests Marcopolo. She knows what's coming and wants to raise the stakes.

I shrug. "Perhaps more weak than wicked. Although he was apparently a Nazi sympathizer . . ."

"What's a Nasty?" asks Columbus.

Uh oh. I've just stumbled on another gap in collective memory. Up until now, I'd always thought the forgotten queen was the only sign of the historical amnesia that afflicts the passengers. But I'd never brought up Nazis before.

"Do any of the rest of you remember what Nazis are?" I ask quietly.

The passengers look at one another. Shake their heads.

"Adolf Hitler?" I try tentatively. Blank looks.

"You can tell us the Adolf story another time," says Tut the Girl King. "Tell us about Elizabeth!"

"All right, all right. She was the oldest daughter of the bad king's brother. His people adored him but" — I grope for the right words and pick the ones I always use, which seem slightly ridiculous, not right for an epic tale — "he fell for an American divorcee."

"He gave up his throne for the woman he loved," sighs Ginalollobrigida, quoting from one of my earlier versions of the story.

"How romantic," says Antoinette, her voice heavy with sarcasm. "That's how you can tell it's not a true story, right there. What king in his right mind would give up his crown for a woman?"

"I'm no monarchist, but Elizabeth was a good queen," I said. "During the Second World War, when she was still only a teenager, she drove an ambulance while there were bombs dropping on London."

Antoinette snorts. "An ambulance-driving teenage princess? Seriously, Stan, can't you do better than that?"

"Who was dropping the bombs?" asks Columbus.

"Hitler," I answer. "And by the way, the princess's uncle thought Hitler was a fine fellow."

"Well, maybe he was," suggests Antoinette, lying back against a rock with her hands behind her head. When she first got here, she was a big woman, easily over two hundred pounds; now her skin hangs in folds around her neck.

"Hitler was a genocidal maniac," I tell her. "He butchered millions. That's a fact."

"Facts depend on what you believe," yawns Antoinette.

"Not true," I answer. "Facts are facts and history is history. Just because you can't remember the history of that world anymore doesn't mean it didn't happen."

"And what world exactly are you talking about?" challenges Antoinette.

"Your home world. Earth Standard Time. Paradiso," I say.

She snorts. "Some paradise, with bombs always falling out of the sky!"

"It *was* paradise, compared to this world," I insist, pushing back against Antoinette's bitter belief that Atomic Shadow Time is the only world she's ever known. "Things were often bad, yes, but history kept changing. Time moved on. Sometimes things actually improved. Not like this world. Nothing changes here except us, getting weaker."

In a circle around me, the faces of the passengers grow solemn. They view me as New Rome's Storyteller, and therefore their truthteller, but Antoinette has planted doubt.

"Nazis! Cattivi!" It's Old Eufemia. "Il malvagi." She spits on the ground for emphasis. Nazis. Bad. Wicked. Evil.

I look at the old lady in surprise. Already deep into a state of forgetfulness, she's somehow managed to hang onto this cultural memory. Maybe it's a sign that not everyone is affected by the Pandora plague in exactly the same way.

"See? Old Eufemia remembers," I say. "Why can't the rest of you at least try?"

"Stan," says Hot Lips in a voice of warning. She nods toward the sound of footsteps, approaching us from behind a rise of landfill. Poseidon stands up next to Old Eufemia, the rusty hammer pressed to his leg.

"Hey, you New Romans got room for two more at this orgy?"

We recognize the voice immediately: Wolfman, real name Sidney Bell, one of the envoys from the camp at Tunis. Once upon a time an economics professor, Wolfman is a tall slender Black man, movie-star handsome. He and Hot Lips are rumoured to be an item, such as any romance can blossom on a landfill.

"Join us," calls out Hot Lips. "Who'd you bring with you?"

"A new arrival bringing good news," says Wolfman.

Bum Bum, I immediately think and stand up quickly, letting *The History of the Known World* fall to the ground.

Marcopolo retrieves it and hugs it to her chest. But when Wolfman emerges over the landfill, my hopes vanish when I see who's with him. Not Bum Bum or even Unicorn Girl, but Jordan Kingsborough, soaking wet and dressed in her Sputnik Chick costume from the TV show, a threadbare towel wrapped around her shoulders. The tunic is shabby and the leather boots are battered and faded, but she is clearly costumed as a superhero. Correction: *my* superhero. My disappointment is quickly replaced with rage.

"Jordan, what the hell are you doing here?"

Jordan straightens and crosses her arms. "Coming to your rescue! I'm Sputnik Chick, aren't I?"

"Only when you read the dialogue someone else scripted for you!"

"I'm improvising."

"Is Bum Bum with you? Or Unicorn Girl?"

She shakes her head. "They chickened out and went on medication to avoid getting infected with the time travel virus. I came alone."

I resist the urge to shake her. "Great, now we're both trapped here. You're not a superhero, Jordan, even if you do play one on TV," I say, barely controlling the quiver in my voice.

"If you must know, I'm not on the show anymore. They let me go."

This is a surprise, although it could explain Jordan decamping to an alternate reality.

"So you're cosplaying."

Jordan glares at me. "I went to every used bookstore and little library in Toronto to find the book you stole and got deliberately infected so I could come here. Sorry to disappoint you."

The passengers stare at the two of us with open mouths, not comprehending our exchange. Geneva moves to my side, takes my hand and squeezes it, as if to show he has my back. I'm too upset to squeeze back.

"You want to let us in on this?" asks Poseidon. "Who's this chick and why does she matter?"

"Let her and Wolfman eat first," says Hot Lips.

Neptune relinquishes the tire he was sitting on to Jordan and Wolfman. Antoinette manages to scare up a couple more mugs of swan soup.

We wait patiently for Jordan to finish eating. Finally, she sets down her mug, looks around the circle and gives us what we're almost as hungry for as food: news.

"Is it safe to talk?"

"Hold up for a moment," says Poseidon.

We sit in silence. Overhead, very faintly, we hear the humming of a drone. When it dies away into the distance, Poseidon gives Jordan the all-clear.

"You're going to be rescued."

Savonarola frowns. "By who?"

"The human resistance and synthetic allies."

Poseidon snorts. "Why the hell would we trust a synthetic? Sounds like a trick to me."

Geneva — one of the few people Poseidon listens to — puts up a hand to stop the swimmer's tirade. "Shut up and listen to her."

Jordan makes eye contact with everyone in the circle of passengers; she looks confident. In control. But she is an actress, after all.

"I'm part of the resistance. Our ship is anchored about a kilometre off the spit. The *Canadian Centaur*. I swam from there to Tunis. Water's dead calm."

"How'd you even get here without the junksters or their drones spotting you?" Poseidon demands to know.

"I move under the junksters' radar because I'm not time-stamped. Plus I have my own early warning system to alert me to junkster patrols. Have a look."

She pulls up her sleeve and presses her fingers against her bicep, teasing apart a flap of skin to expose something that looks like a zipper. Making a hissing sound between her teeth — this strange little operation must hurt — she pulls something out of her flesh. A silver worm of a thing that bends and stretches and coils around her fingers.

"What the hell," mutters Poseidon.

Jordan holds the writhing object where we can see it. "A living entity enhancement chip. LEECH, for short. Intelligence augmentation. Keeps me one step ahead of the junksters and their drones."

A silence descends on the group.

"You're a synthetic," says Hot Lips.

"No," says Jordan, "I'm human with an implant. A centaur. All the LEECH does is analyze data faster than I could on my own. It acts as a second brain."

Carefully she coaxes the glistening creature back into her arm and rezips her bicep.

Poseidon snorts. "You kidding me? You need intelligence augmentation to outsmart those dumb dumpster divers? Most of those kids never even learned to read!"

"They sure managed to outsmart you," Jordan points out.

"The junksters are not stupid," breaks in Geneva. "In fact, they're remarkably resourceful for kids who fell through the cracks."

I'm horrified yet fascinated. "Getting a ship up and running must have taken a lot of time and effort. How long have you been here?"

Jordan shrugs. "Two minutes? Ten years? A hundred? Who

knows? We've made good use of having unlimited time to build alliances, battle plans, new technologies. We've got all sorts of tricks up our sleeve."

"So what's the plan?" asks Geneva.

"We've found a way to reboot this world's weather patterns. Including thunderstorms."

"And that will help us exactly how?" asks Poseidon, his voice heavy with skepticism.

"A diversion. When it starts to thunder and rain, the People of Forever will go into hiding."

"Is it People of Forever or really just *Person* of Forever?" asks Geneva. "We've only ever seen one. Their leader, we assume. A Cyclops named Dragon."

"That one's the official corporate template," confirms Jordan. "But the Puffs are legion. Empty vessels waiting to be given personalities, skills, even families and job titles. They're blanks. Still learning how to be real people."

"What's to stop them from attacking us in the storm?" I ask.

Jordan grins. "The precious darlings don't like to get wet. Not crazy about lightning strikes either. They're mostly silicon, metal and microchips, right? Think about leaving a laptop out in the rain or putting your phone through the laundry. The People of Forever are vulnerable to all sorts of natural stuff — rust, water, dust, sunlight, electrical shocks. Things the junksters protect them from."

"That would explain the grooming and repair work they're always doing to Dragon," observes Geneva.

Jordan nods. "Exactly. The junksters have built their own gods and now they're worshipping them. But the junksters want to follow orders, not give them. They'll be paralyzed by the storm. When the rain starts falling and they're dithering around trying to figure out what to do, a flotilla will come out to rescue you and all the other passengers. We'll meet up with the ship off the lighthouse. Are you in?"

"Man, why wouldn't we be?" asks Poseidon.

Wolfman answers for Jordan. "Have you ever been in a major storm on Lake Ontario in a small boat? I'm talking sailboats, kayaks, rowboats. Hell, they'll use the swan boats from the Centre Island amusement park for the flotilla, if necessary. It'd be real easy to dump and drown or get hit by lightning before rendezvousing with the main ship. Truth is, not all of us are going to make it."

We look around at one another. Seventy-odd souls who can read one another's minds. Who know what one another have endured.

"Fuck it, we're in," answers Hot Lips, speaking for all of us. "And we'll leave no passenger behind."

Old Eufemia claps her hands.

"Bravi," she approves.

Jordan nods. "Good. Spread the word to the other settlements. I'm going to swim back to the *Canadian Centaur*. See you all there very soon."

Without a way to measure time — the ticking of a clock, a vacation marked on a calendar, the number of sleeps until your birthday — waiting for something good to happen can be worse than grinding monotony broken by the occasional catastrophe. You start to lose hope.

Groggy from sleeplessness and nerves, the passengers and I take turns standing on the beach, watching for storm clouds; the others are too dispirited even to work on the Coliseum. Tut the Girl King has stopped digging. Caruso is too depressed to entertain us with his over-the-top impressions of famous opera singers. Old Eufemia sleeps almost non-stop, even when we haul her out into the never-ending sunshine.

Of course, in a timeless world, Jordan couldn't be specific about when the storm would make landfall, beyond that it would be soon. With the promise of rescue dangled before us, the letdown has dropped us into a cesspool of despair — or, in the case of the swim team, anger.

"Never trust an AI," gripes Poseidon, flinging a stone into the waves.

"Or a fucking centaur," adds Neptune.

"Jordan has no reason to trick us," I protest. "Weather isn't easy to predict, even for an algorithm."

Poseidon looks at me with suspicion. "What's Her Leechness to you? She's not even human."

"Centaurs *are* human," I try to explain. "The LEECH is just an augmented intelligence. A brain boost. Like a smartphone. You used to carry all the data available in human history in your pocket. It's just that in Jordan's case it's as if the smartphone's inside her body."

"How efficient," says Poseidon acidly. "Far as I'm concerned she's just a meat Puff. A synthetic with a pretty face and an artificial heart."

"Jordan isn't to blame for this," I argue.

"Then who is?" demands Neptune. "We shouldn't trust anyone who isn't a one hundred percent carbon-based life form. If we ever get out of here, the first thing I'm going to do is kill me some synthetics."

Poseidon high-fives him.

"I believe the storm is coming," I tell them. "We just have to be patient."

The swimmers trade looks. They've written me off.

Hot Lips has been ministering to Tarzan, massaging his torn shoulder muscles. She's a nurse, not a physiotherapist, and has confessed to me that she's not sure how much good she's doing, but she's convinced he finds her touch therapeutic.

"I agree with Stan," she says, standing up from the long flat rock she uses as a makeshift massage table. "Let's prepare to be rescued, whenever it happens."

"Psychological torture," says Neptune. "We'll wait ourselves to death."

* * *

Waiting *is* hard. Being ready to leave any time isn't. I'm the only one who has anything to pack. I don't know what to do with my sketchbooks until Sebastian Cabot scavenges a freezer bag washed up on the shoreline near Sarajevo, where wind and water currents deposit all sorts of garbage, some of it useful.

"Looks in good shape but might not be waterproof," he cautions. The plastic is scratched but the seal still works.

"Better than nothing," I tell him. It's big enough to hold both of my sketchbooks. I tie the bag to my waist with a strip of cloth ripped from the bottom of my skirt. The only time I take it off is to sketch the passengers on the beach for *The History of the Known World*; I have nothing to add to *Visions of Paradiso*. Since Jordan's visit, my visions of Earth Standard Time have hit the pause button. The glimpses of the hospital, Bum Bum, Unicorn Girl and Doc Mutant have all gone on hiatus like a TV show, taking with them the hope of new plot developments.

The passengers' restlessness grows. Despite the lack of darkness, they crawl into their cots more and more often, trying to escape into sleep, or pairing off as best they can to have sex — in their cots, behind piles of landfill, even in a deserted bird-watching station located perilously close to the barbed-wire fences at the front gate. Hot Lips disappears more than once, making the trek to Tunis to meet Wolfman. As she walks away I feel gutted by a worry similar to the one I felt back in the Reference Library when Unicorn Girl stepped away for a moment: what if she doesn't come back?

I wish I could find someone to hold me the way Wolfman holds Hot Lips, or Marcopolo does Ginalollobrigida, or Poseidon, Columbus, or Caruso, Sebastian Cabot. My only comfort is in memories of my short-lived marriage, as doomed as the alternate reality where it started and ended. When I put my hand between my legs, trying to ignore the grunts and gasps in the cots around me, it's the young Kendal I remember: hiding in a burned-out candy store as teenagers to explore one another's bodies, or as young marrieds lovemaking our way down the Hudson River to New York City, as our driver Bum Bum hooked up with whoever he could find in third-rate disco roadhouses along the way. We expected the bomb to drop any minute. Sex and dancing seemed like the only things worth thinking about. Now here I am again, right back where I started.

As I listen to the snores of Antoinette and the sleep-talk of Old Eufemia, something yeasty cuddles up next to me, filling my nose with the sour odour of unwashed hair. I open my eyes to Marcopolo's tiny face.

"I'm scared, Stan," she whispers.

"Don't be," I whisper back, brushing her filthy bangs out of her eyes with my fingers. "We're getting out of here soon. We just have to wait for the storm to roll in."

"But I can't swim."

"You won't have to," I tell her. "There'll be boats."

"What if I fall out?" she whispers. "Will they give us life jackets?"

"I don't know," I admit.

She sighs and curls in tighter.

"How old are you, Marcopolo?" I don't remember her real name anymore.

"Eighteen."

"How old were you when you . . ." I try and fail to find the right words.

"Twelve."

"That young. How did it happen?"

She answers without hesitation. "One of my stepdad's friends loaned him money and he couldn't pay it back, so the guy asked for me instead. And then after that, I went to a foster home and the dad there did the same thing, so I ran away and it just went on like that." A silence ensues, then she adds, "At least now I get paid for it. No one should do stuff they don't like without getting something in return."

I'm not sure what to say, so I stay silent. I'd long suspected the Puffs weren't the first monsters Marcopolo had encountered.

"Tell me a story, Stan," she says.

"About the Queen again?"

"No, about you. Were you ever in love?"

"Yes," I tell her. "I even married the guy. But it didn't last."

"What happened? He beat you up?"

"No. He was a good man. He just . . . forgot me."

"How?"

I tell Marcopolo my origin story. By the time I get to the part where I discover that my husband has unknowingly betrayed me by marrying my best friend, she's snoring. My story must have been too heartbreaking. Or confusing. Or crazy. I think about moving her back to her cot, then decide to leave her be.

I pull Eufemia's slippers from under her cot and slip out of the tent to walk toward the lighthouse at Tunis, hoping I'll bump into Jordan. She hasn't returned to New Rome since the Feast of the Swan. I stick to the shoreline dotted with the carcasses of dead fish. The rolling waves muffle other sounds, so I'm startled when I hear footsteps on the cobble beach behind me. I turn, expecting the worst, a junkster ready to correct me for leaving my settlement. Instead I'm relieved to find myself face to face with Geneva.

He's much younger than me — in his mid-forties, I'd guess — though during our detention his scruffy beard and curly hair have gone grey. He still wears a kippah, the only thing the Puffs didn't take from him. Despite malnutrition and bouts of dysentery that have whittled down his once-strapping body, he projects a calm strength.

"Hey," he says. "Sorry if I scared you. I felt like a walk."

I shrug. "I haven't gotten used to sleeping in broad daylight."

"Me neither," he says. "Nor do I feel like listening to the swim team bitch about what they're going to do to Siri and Alexa when they get out of here. Some of the torments they're devising are disturbing."

Geneva has made it clear to me in previous conversations, during our treks to the front gate to meet with Dragon, that he finds the swimmers a bunch of blowhards and frat boys. Entitled jocks, used to getting their own way.

"How's Tarzan doing?" I ask.

Geneva shakes his head. "On top of his physical pain, the guy's deeply traumatized. Probably PTSD. His teammates aren't helping. Their anger is toxic. I wouldn't want Jordan to run into them. They're convinced she set us up."

"How?"

"Giving us hope so that we'll take a chance on rabbiting. That would give Dragon and the junksters the perfect excuse to chase us down and correct us."

"I think Jordan is on the up and up," I say. "I knew her, from before."

"I figured that," says Geneva. "But she's not really the person she once was."

"Are any of us?"

"Point taken. But I meant turning centaur would have changed her. Augmented her."

"I guess so, but . . ." I pause. Do I tell him that I think she's the daughter of my ex-husband from an alternate timeline? Or will that make me a crazy lady in his eyes?

He turns to look east across the lake. "Ah, the glittering skyline of the suburbs of Scarborough."

I laugh. From our vantage point, we can see the bluffs.

"If we were on the other side of the spit, we'd have a magnificent view of Toronto harbour. The CN Tower, the docks, the skyscrapers."

Geneva sighs. "Yes, all empty. Not sure I could stand it."

His face is in shadow now. "Stan, I have a confession to make."

"I thought only Catholics did that," I answer.

"This isn't so much spiritual as personal. The other night, when you were telling the story about the Queen and the war, I should have spoken up like Old Eufemia did. I was too afraid to admit I remembered history too."

I shake my head. "Why didn't you back me up?"

"I'm terrified that it's all going to happen again." He turns away from me, still gazing at the silent windmills. "All of it."

I nod. "I've thought of that too. As if we're being forced to relive history."

"Anyway, forgive me. I'm a coward."

"There's nothing to forgive," I answer. "And you're the bravest man I know."

I'm tempted to tell him my part in all this, dredging up *The Adventures of Futureman* comics and unleashing them on the world. But I'm a coward too. Geneva is a friend, one of the people, like Hot Lips, whom I respect. Maybe even love. Having him abandon me or think me mad would be too painful.

As we stand side by side gazing at the smoggy horizon, Geneva reaches out and takes my hand. An almost-forgotten sensation radiates from the tips of my fingers to my breasts, then heads downward. Tendrils of warmth curl up my thighs like a wafteron from a romance comic. I remember what this feeling used to mean to me: pleasure. Excitement. Anticipation.

"I'm a good twenty years older than you," I say.

"I seriously doubt that," he answers. "I'm fifty-five."

I look at him, shocked. "You're kidding. I thought you were at least ten years younger than that."

"Must be my boyish good looks." He grins and shrugs. "Anyway, I've always been a pushover for mature women artists. Georgia O'Keeffe. Frida Kahlo. Cindy Sherman."

I laugh. "I'm hardly an artist. I learned how to draw from a correspondence course that advertised in the back of comic books. I'm a hack."

Geneva lifts my hand to his lips. Anticipation tips over into arousal.

"No, you're not," he tells me. "You're our Storyteller, and you have me spellbound."

We find a spot where softer grasses have managed to fight through the rubble. Geneva pulls his thin cotton shirt over his head, spreads it on the ground and smooths it out, as if the pressure of his hands will turn it into an eiderdown. I kick off Eufemia's slippers and pull my faded dress off my shoulders, letting it drop to the ground. I can only imagine what the half-healed burns on my breasts look like. When he sees the book bag tied to my waist, he laughs.

"You're using your stories as a chastity belt?"

He unties the bag and lets it drop to the ground. Slips his arms around me. We stand pressed together, skin to skin. I can feel myself moisten in response to his erection, smooth against the inside of my thigh. A relief. It's been so long since I've been with someone, I wasn't sure things would feel the way they used to.

"You smell good," I tell him, burying my nose in the crook of his neck.

"Impossible. I haven't had a shower since we got here and the lake water stinks worse than I do. All that dead fish."

"Still," I say. "When a woman likes the way a man stinks, it means something."

He laughs and kisses me, then pushes my tangled hair off my face.

We lie down and make love, not worrying about the rubble under the backs of our legs or the dirt on our bodies. I even forget about the broken blisters and patches of healing skin. Afterwards, we lie on our backs and look at the chemical clouds above us.

"That one looks like Pegasus," says Geneva. "The flying horse." He takes my hand and traces the shape in the sky.

"Looks more like a moose to me."

He snorts. "Do you have even one romantic bone in your body, Stan?"

"Once upon a time, I did," I say. "Maybe I'd feel more romantic if you used my real name."

"Debbie," he says. "From now on."

I laugh. "Believe it or not, I can't remember your real name, Geneva."

He pulls me closer and kisses the top of my head. "David."

We continue to lie on the grassy patch. My back is getting sore, but I'm reluctant to move.

"Tell me about yourself, David. Are you married?"

"Divorced. Twice. Still on good terms with my exes."

"Kids?"

"Three daughters. Fortunately they were all in Israel when the junksters showed up. You?"

"Married. Just once. No kids."

"You're divorced then?" I pick up a note of uncertainty in his voice. Even under these circumstances, he doesn't want to sleep with someone else's wife.

I don't want to lie to David but don't think this is the moment to share that I was married in an alternate reality. "Not exactly, but we've been separated for years."

"Ah," he says. "Well, if we get out of here, I can recommend a good family lawyer."

"You're a lawyer yourself, aren't you?"

"Not that kind," he says, stretching. "Immigration law. I represent political prisoners applying to Canada for refugee status."

"Sounds like rewarding work."

"Yes. But probably not as financially rewarding as comic books that get turned into TV shows."

I laugh. "This is starting to feel like postapocalyptic speed dating."

"I'm old-fashioned. I like to get to know a girl before I make an honest woman of her."

He rolls onto his side, his hand caressing my waist, breasts, thighs. I can't see his face clearly anymore, so I run my fingers over his cheeks, nose, forehead, chest. Taking him in like a blind woman.

"I want to do it again," I say.

He rolls on top of me and immediately enters me. Arching toward him I feel my climax building.

"Don't stop," I tell him, and he doesn't until both of us have fallen asleep on his shirt.

I wake to find him spooning me. My arm has gone to sleep

and my hips ache. I've never been so happy in my life, in any time continuum.

When we walk back into New Rome, hand in hand, there are a few glances and smiles. No one really cares where we've been, only that we've come back.

The passengers are strung along the beach in twos and threes, like random notes on a musical staff. We all seemed to be vibrating to a change in the atmosphere. A feeling of heaviness. A metallic whiff of ozone in the air.

"Look at the clouds," says Poseidon, nodding at the horizon. "Those are thunderheads."

Hope rises. We remain on the beach, watching and waiting. David stretches out with his head in my lap, shading his eyes.

"The cloud banks are building up," he points out.

It's the first time we've seen a change in the weather.

Something is coming. It's just not what we expect.

*　*　*

Sometime later, a windowless white refrigeration truck drives up, painted with the words *Journey Home to Mother™: Solution for a peacefully standardized world*. It carries Dragon with a squad of slouching junksters, their heads covered by steel buckets with eyeholes cut into them.

"Congratulations. Ten of you have been selected to begin your Journey Home to Mother," announces Dragon. "Line up when your name is called and present your itineraries, if you please."

One of the junksters removes the bucket on his head and reads out the list. It's hard, after all this time, to connect them to the passengers' secret identities. The Cooler King, Columbus and Sebastian Cabot form a forlorn line.

"David Olivetti."

Oh, please, no.

David turns to me. Kisses me for a long minute. Touches his forehead to mine. Dragon gives a polite cough. "Mr. Olivetti, join the queue, if you please."

David walks slowly to join the other passengers singled out as the first among us to walk through Mother's legs. He's the ninth to be called.

As each passenger's itinerary is checked and found to be in order, they step up into the darkness of the truck and disappear inside. David's foot is on the running board when Dragon calls one more name.

"Sebastian Giovanni."

Tarzan slowly stands. The look on his face is one of absolute terror. The other swimmers look at him with an expression I can only read as *thank god it's him and not me, he's a goner anyway.*

"Your itinerary?" asks Dragon, its hand extended.

Tarzan begins to tremble. "I lost it."

For a long moment Dragon looks at Tarzan, as if processing his response. It curls one hand into a fist. Lifts its arm high, as if winching up a crane.

Tarzan raises his hands in front of his face and starts to sob. "Please don't hurt me."

A puddle appears between Tarzan's feet. He's pissed himself.

David steps down from the running board and stands in front of Dragon. "The young man's no good to you in the state he's in. He can't withstand the journey. Why don't you leave him be?"

Dragon pivots its head to look at David through its single green eye. At the same time, it swings its arm like a piledriver and knocks Tarzan on the top of the head, sending him to the ground with a scream of pain.

David seizes Dragon's arm. "Enough."

"Remove your hand or be corrected."

"Fuck you," answers David and spits in the Puff's face.

Dragon moves so fast, my eyes can't follow what happens. All I know is it ends with David face down on the ground, one side of his head a pulpy mess.

Dragon reaches down and briskly tugs David's itinerary from his pants pocket.

"Uncontrolled aggression is a pre-existing condition," it says, then tosses the paper on David's back.

I run over to kneel at David's side. Hot Lips joins me. I can hardly bear to look at his face. Hot Lips searches his wrist for a pulse.

"He's not dead," she whispers to me.

I stare at David. He was going to make an honest woman of me, whatever that meant. I reach down and touch his head. Gather his bloody kippah in my clenched hand.

"Step back," warns Dragon. "We must continue the journey."

I can't move. Hot Lips slowly lifts me to my feet, wraps her arms around my waist and supports me as we walk back to where the other passengers stand watching from the beach. I'm freezing. My teeth chatter and my knees have turned to porridge; I can't hold myself up without Hot Lips's help.

"You're in shock," she whispers to me, gripping me by the back of my dress.

At a gesture from Dragon, the two junksters pick up David's body by the arms and legs and toss him into the back of the truck like a sack of potatoes. They slam shut the back doors and drive off toward the gate.

"Fuckers wouldn't even let us give him a proper burial," growls Poseidon.

Hot Lips looks at him, then me. "Geneva isn't dead. I found a pulse."

When she finally lets me slump to the ground and covers me with a blanket, I hear a high wailing sound. It goes on and on, rising and falling like an air raid siren. It takes awhile to realize the sound is coming from me.

Finally, after I've cried and screamed myself hoarse, I dig my last Antiquanta out of the pocket of my dress and swallow it dry. The familiar bitter taste fills my mouth, reminding me of Paradiso.

THREE

ADVENTURE OR DEMENTIA

I'm gripping a pair of parallel bars, my wrists and arms screaming with the effort of keeping myself upright. From the hips
down, my body sags like overcooked spaghetti.

I take a sloppy step forward. Then another. I feel like
Gumby on a bender.

Somebody's holding me up by the back of my pants, their
knuckles pressed to the base of my spine.

"You can let go, Debbie; I won't let you fall," says a young
female voice.

I lift my left hand, then my right, hovering them in the air
in case I have to grab the bars again. My knees yip in protest,
like dachshunds straining at the ends of their leashes. A bead of
sweat meanders down my scalp, through the valley between my
shoulder blades and into the waistband of my panties, settling
in the crack of my bum. Worse, I have to pee.

"Am I in Paradiso?"

The voice chuckles. "Don't worry, you're not in paradise yet.
You're in the Toronto Rehab Institute."

"And you are?"

"Your physiotherapist. Darna."

"You're a superhero," I gasp, winded from the effort of holding
myself up. "A Filipino woman warrior from outer space."

"Wow, hardly anyone knows that! My folks used to buy me comic books about her."

Darna leans her head around my shoulders so I can see her face: full cheeks, brown eyes and a smile brightened by coral lipstick. A sleek black ponytail with magenta highlights falls over one shoulder of her polo shirt. The muscle definition in the arm holding me up hints at hours spent at CrossFit. She looks a lot like Hot Lips.

The same healthy smile appears on the ID card hanging around Darna's neck, the lanyard printed with the words *TRI: YOUR PARTNER IN SMART RECOVERY.*

"Try balancing on one foot. I'll hold you up."

Darna places her tiny powerful hands on my hips. Cautiously I lift one foot. Tremble but don't fall over.

"How'd I get here, Darna?"

She hesitates, as if deciding how — or whether — to answer.

"You were caught in that awful attack on Wellington Street. Your skull was fractured. You were in a coma for a long time. You just came out of it yesterday."

I rummage around in the tickle-trunk of my memory. "Who attacked? Robots?"

Darna starts to laugh before she realizes I'm not kidding.

"A homicidal maniac running people down with a food truck. The police are still looking for him."

I shake my head. "There was no maniac. It was a self-driving truck."

"Yes, but someone must have been controlling it remotely," insists Darna. "Machines don't go around deliberately killing people."

I almost laugh at this.

"They don't want to call it a hate crime, but most of the victims were women. Sorry, but that sure sounds like hate to me. You were one of the lucky ones."

I focus on taking another broken-puppet step. "How am I lucky?"

"Because you're alive. And not paralyzed."

I accept this explanation, which I feel I might have overheard in one of my visions of Paradiso.

"Am I going to get better?"

"You sustained some neurological damage, but you're making excellent progress," says Darna carefully.

I teeter and regain my balance. It's about three baby steps to the end of the handrails. I inhale deeply and stagger forward, one, two, three.

"Relax," says Darna. "Take a deep cleansing breath."

I close my eyes. Chest or belly, which one is cleansing? I split the difference and send my breath down to my quivering knees.

Darna was wrong: rehab *is* paradise, compared to New Rome. There must be a whole team of care professionals here dedicated to my recovery. I'm not hungry, so they must be feeding me. I'll bet I even have a real bed to sleep in. Hot showers. Clean clothes. Streaming TV in my room. Fresh flowers and funny cards from Bum Bum. Unicorn Girl sitting vigil with stacks of Golden Age comics, reading aloud to me as she waits for me to be well enough to adjudicate her thesis project. I can hardly wait to see my room.

I twist around to look at Darna, ignoring the growl of warning in my hips. "This place is real, right?"

She laughs. "As real as me!"

* * *

In my room, a lunch tray is waiting. Mushroom soup, spinach salad, a chicken breast, half a tomato and a slice of whole wheat bread with a pat of actual butter. Clean utensils. A napkin. Hot coffee. It all tastes so good I shovel it down in under a minute and try to wheedle seconds out of the nurse who comes in to check my blood pressure.

"We'll bring around cookies and juice midafternoon," she assures me. "Your doctor is due to stop by soon."

"Doc Mutant is here?"

The nurse smiles as if I'm making a joke.

* * *

The doctor turns out to be a neurologist named Jennifer Ng. She looks about Darna's age. As she introduces herself, she presses her fingers to my wrist.

"Your physio says you're making progress. What can you remember about the last four months?" Her eyes search my face as if trying to read my mind.

"I've been . . . away. In another world," I tell her. "I was waiting with the others for a storm to give us cover, so we could be rescued by boat, but then a robot named Dragon tried to kill my . . . my . . ."

I find myself wiping tears. Dr. Ng hands me a box of tissue.

"We all have different ways of dealing with trauma. Yours seems to be tied up in creative storytelling."

I blow my nose. "Are you saying New Rome wasn't real? That I made the whole story up while I was in a coma?"

Dr. Ng's expression doesn't change as she taps at her tablet. "We took your history from your business manager . . ."

"You talked to Bum Bum? I mean, Pasquale Pesce?"

Dr. Ng gave me a puzzled look. "That's right. He tells us there's a family history of early onset dementia."

I nod, wondering where this is going.

"As a precaution, we'd like to run a few more tests," she says. "A head injury of the kind you sustained puts you at greater risk and since there's already a genetic predisposition —"

I put up my hand to stop her. "None of that matters. I'm dying of timesickness."

She shakes her head. "In fact, you're making a remarkable recovery, all things considered. But given your age and the skull fracture and the family history . . ."

She goes on about amyloid tangles. The connection between head injuries and Alzheimer's disease. Benefits of early diagnosis. MRIs and PET scans of the amygdala and hippocampus. A promising new drug trial I might want to apply for. Long-term care options. I think she's trying to reassure me, but her words blend together into a depressing, low-level thrum.

The problem with medicine in Earth Standard Time is that it won't let an aging superhero fade away gracefully. If being told I'm dying was a buzzkill, learning that I'm on the verge of losing my marbles is even worse. I wonder if this is how my sister, Linda, felt when she was diagnosed with dementia out on Crazy Lady Island?

After Dr. Ng leaves me to my own dark thoughts, I wiggle to the side of the bed and push myself to standing. Leaning on a walker, I manage to trundle to the bathroom and lower myself carefully onto the toilet.

I don't recognize my reflection in the mirror. My head has been shaved. My skin is grey and slack. A contusion hangs under one eye like a fat purple leech. I look like a Galapagos turtle. Most tellingly, I don't see the SPQR bar code on my cheekbone. Dr. Ng must be right. *The History of the Known World* was just my way of processing trauma. I should have realized that: Atomic Shadow Time was all a little too much like a subconscious mash-up of Unicorn Girl's VR game, *The Adventures of Futureman* and my own unresolved issues around my estranged family and broken marriage. My imagination working overtime while I lay in a fugue state. They were just stories dredged up out of my subconscious, not an alternate world.

Better to face facts: I'm a sick, sick woman with no hope and no future. At least I can let go of my memories of David, an imaginary lover who died an imaginary death, no more traumatic than a bad dream. There's some comfort in knowing that.

I shuffle back to my bed and contemplate the generic still lifes on the walls until I hear a knock at my open door. "Anybody home?"

It's Unicorn Girl in khaki shorts and a Hawaiian shirt covered in hula dancers and palm trees. She's lugging her hockey bag. I'm so happy to see her that my eyes fill with tears.

"Good to see you back, Ms. Biondi! You up for a visit?"

"Sure. Stick around long enough and there'll be cookies. Where'd you get the wild shirt?"

"One of those vintage places in Kensington Market," she says, plunking down on the bed beside me. "Some guy named Pierre Cardin, according to the label. Ever hear of him?"

"He was a fashion designer back in the '70s and '80s. Probably best known for what I remember as the world's most pungent cologne. Is it warm out?"

"Hot, actually. We should sit in the healing garden. How you feeling?"

"Tired. I was in physio all morning, learning to walk again."

"Wow, that's amazing, considering you just came out of a

coma." She pauses for a moment. "Do you remember where you were this whole time?"

"Here in the hospital," I say guardedly.

Unicorn Girl frowns. "I mean, where *else* you were. The alternate world? Doc Mutant came up to look at you. He said you'd undergone a quantum split because of your timesickness —"

"Stop," I say.

"— and that the Futureman book was responsible for a bunch of other people disappearing."

I put my hands over my ears. "Not listening."

"At least tell me: did you see Jordan at any point?"

I shrug and sigh. "Okay, yes."

She looks at me, eyebrows raised, waiting for the story. I'm about to tell her about the rescue mission, and the LEECH, and Jordan being in the resistance, when it occurs to me that *none of this is true*. And I don't *want* it to be true. Intuitive as ever, Unicorn Girl is tapping into whatever Sputnik Chickian narrative she thinks I'll find comforting. She's also confusing my reticence with concern over her relationship with Jordan.

"It's okay. I'm over Jordan. After your accident, we hung out together at the loft for a few days. That's where I finally met Mr. Pesce. He said we could stay there as long as we liked. Everything was great until Jor and I had a fight. She left and took Cassandra with her. I called and texted, but she didn't respond. It was really hurtful. Not that I haven't been ghosted before. I thought Jordan and I had something together."

I nod understandingly. "Why the hell would Jordan steal Cassandra?"

Unicorn Girl rubs her eyes as if trying to hold back tears. "Who knows? Mr. Pesce was pissed, I can tell you that. He went storming off looking for her."

"What was your fight about?"

Unicorn Girl sighs. "She wanted to go looking for your alternate self. To rescue you. Doc Mutant thought we should let you get back on your own, but Cassandra told Jordan it was *theoretically* possible to go find you in that other world; of course, anything is possible. And frankly Cass gets a lot of her intel from old sci-fi movies, so there's that. Although Cass also did predict it was eighty-nine percent sure to be a suicide mission. But Jordan didn't listen to Cass. She was all like, 'We should go exploring an alternate reality with me in charge, just like Sputnik Chick.' Honestly, I think she has delusions of grandeur. No wonder she lost her role on the show."

I consider the likelihood of all this being true. It does dovetail with my increasingly hazy memories of Jordan's appearance in New Rome. The promise of rescue from an unlikely resistance movement. My visions of Paradiso. All of which I was relieved to put behind me for clean sheets and three squares a day. If there is still a Debbie Reynolds Biondi, also known as Stan, in an alternate world called Atomic Shadow Time, good luck to her.

I pat Unicorn Girl's hand. "Probably for the best you and Jordan parted ways."

"Yeah," Unicorn Girl agrees and sniffs back tears. "But I was thinking . . . Remember when you saw the Trespasser in my game? Maybe you could connect with him again in a virtual space. Find out if he knows where Jordan is, and if she's coming back."

I sigh. To quote from one of my favourite films, this is the life we have chosen. Although, damn it all, this isn't my choice. I'd rather just be a crazy lady in a nice rehab hospital than endure all this jumping around in the multiverse. It's pointless and exhausting and I'm ready to retire and live one life, in one world, at one time.

"All right," I sigh. "Let's at least go outside first."

Unicorn Girl snags a wheelchair from the hallway and pushes me past a common room where a few of my fellow patients stare at an overhead screen. As we roll by, my eye catches on the guy I remember as leader of Her Majesty's Loyal Opposition yelling across the floor of Parliament at a stranger standing where Kendal should be. The news crawl reads *DEBATE CONTINUES ON ESCALATION OF FREEDOM TO SERVE BILL.*

I turn in the wheelchair to watch the screen as we move past. "What happened to Prime Minister Kendal?"

"Totally dropped out of sight months ago. His party had to replace him, then they lost a confidence vote and the other side took over. There's a rumour going around that he's been kidnapped. Although a lot of other people disappeared around the same time he did."

"Passengers," I mutter unhappily.

"What?"

"Never mind. Let's look at your game."

We roll out into a courtyard full of flowerbeds and people wandering around in the same pale-blue bathrobe I'm wearing. I've definitely been here before: it's the healing garden I sketched in *Visions of Paradiso*. Unicorn Girl positions me in the shade and takes a pair of dark glasses out of her hockey bag. "I reverse-engineered my old game to turn the Trespasser's hack into a live feed into his world. It's also AR now, like a hologram overlaid onto reality. Get it?"

"I'm not so far gone that I don't know what augmented reality is, Unicorn Girl," I tell her as she positions the glasses on my face. But I'm still surprised when a man falls out of the sky into the flowerbed in front of me, hitting the earth with a *whomp*. He's long-haired, wearing a double-breasted suit, just like Professor Quantum in the first *Adventures of Futureman* comic strip.

When he stands up and brushes himself off, it strikes me that Professor Quantum looks an awful lot like the Trespasser.

"Duffy?"

The Trespasser steps out of the flowerbed, brushes himself off and sits down across from me in an ironwork garden chair. "You seemed a little down. Thought I'd drop by to offer you some moral support before you go back to New Rome."

"I'm not going back."

He frowns. "Oh, so *this* is the life you want now? You'd rather just be your almost fatally injured self than integrate with your reasonably okay self? You prefer wheelchairs and cookies to saving the world?"

I wipe sudden tears. "Of course not. But after what Dragon did to David, I can't bear the thought of returning."

"Why not?"

I look down at my hands. My fingernails are ragged, my hands rough and veiny. An old woman's hands, in need of a manicure.

"Because I'm afraid," I finally admit.

"Of what? You were born with a great gift. The ability to live more than one life, in more than one world. Most twelve-year-olds who die having their tonsils out don't get that chance."

I wipe snot off my face with the sleeve of my robe. "Maybe life after life isn't such a great gift if you keep losing the people you love. First Kendal. Now David."

Duffy shakes his head in obvious disgust. "Forty years ago I turned you into a quantum voyager. A destroyer of worlds! You could be that again. Or you can stick around here and worry yourself to death watching CNN in the common room eight hours a day. Adventure or dementia. What's it gonna be?"

The top of my head feels damp. I look up at the sky. It's starting to rain. I can faintly hear Unicorn Girl's voice. *Ms. Biondi, are you talking to the Trespasser? Could you ask him about Jordan?*

He holds his hand out to me. "C'mon. Time to go back to New Rome and finish what you started. If there was ever a world that needed destroying, you found it."

Ms. Biondi, you okay?

I rise shakily to my feet, gripping his hand to steady myself. "But none of it is real."

"Says who?"

"My neurologist."

He snorts. "They don't teach the Many Worlds theory of quantum physics in med school. Your little library caper with Unicorn Girl woke up a previously unknown way to create a new timeline. You're filling the void left by an old dead world by coming up with a new creation myth. Congratulations. Now it's your job to help that world reach its inevitable doomsday before it totally upends this world too. Oh, and you'll also need to go back to Earth Standard Time of Old to straighten out the kinks in history."

"Go *back* in time? But you always said that was dangerous."

"So is messing with history. Your actions are already playing merry hob with the present," he grunts. "You caused a massive temporal shift in Earth Standard Time. Thousands of innocent people have leaked out of their world into your rogue timeline so the Puffs can exile them into the past. Pretty soon present-day Earth Standard Time will be populated by robots and junksters, full stop. Eventually they'll let Atomic Shadow

Time come to its natural end, leaving the passengers stuck in the past."

"And you want me to do exactly what?"

"You started this by helping *The Adventures of Futureman* go viral. Now you have to stop it from being created in the first place. Don't worry, I'll be there to assist."

It's raining harder. A cold wind has come up in the courtyard. I tug the bathrobe tighter and wrap my arms around my body.

Unicorn Girl is on her feet, hands over her mouth, eyes wide. She takes off at a run, leaving a lumpen figure in blue sprawled face down in front of an empty wheelchair.

"What just happened?"

"You experienced another quantum split. Not the first time you've had that happen, thanks to your Schrödinger gene! You're dead in one world, alive in another. Dead you fell out of your wheelchair. Blood clot in your brain. Don't know how they missed it. Your assistant has gone to get help, but they won't be able to revive you."

"Oh no, Duffy, Unicorn Girl's going to blame herself! You can't let her think the game killed me!"

"Don't worry, you haven't seen the last of her. She has a part to play in helping you put history back on track. But first you have to destroy Atomic Shadow Time."

"Destroy?"

"Why not? You've done it before."

Unicorn Girl has returned with Dr. Ng and Darna. Dr. Ng gently turns my body over. Darna crosses herself. Duffy steps in front of me, blocking my view of the little tableau and hands me two red pills.

I frown at Duffy. "I thought you wanted me to *leave* Earth Standard Time? Antiquanta *keeps* me here."

He shakes his head. "Again, you're dead, Debbie. There's no you in Earth Standard Time. The pill will take you back to the last world where you were alive — Atomic Shadow Time."

"What's the second pill for?"

"It's your means of escape after you destroy Atomic Shadow Time. Think of it as an all-expenses-paid ticket into another timeline. Bon voyage!"

Hands shaking, I chew a pill down dry, the familiar bitter taste almost making me gag.

Soon, there's no reality to augment anymore. White caps are rolling toward me as the courtyard fills with water. It's over my sneakers, then up to my neck. Within seconds, my feet no longer touch the ground. I start dog-paddling. My knees and hips bark and whine. A clump of feathery green scum slaps me in the mouth. It tastes vile. I spit it out and scream, "For fuck's sake, if you want me to destroy one world and save another, don't let me drown!"

The Trespasser's disembodied voice floats down to me. "Relax. On your way back to Atomic Shadow Time, you got tangled up in one of Old Eufemia's dreams. Just go with it."

"What?"

Looking like a character from a Saturday morning cartoon, Old Eufemia floats by in a pink paddleboat. She's wearing tangerine-coloured capri pants, a gold-and-blue Gucci headscarf and oversized Jackie O sunglasses. An old man in a sports jacket rides shotgun. Raffaele, no doubt. He's holding a champagne flute in one hand and gesticulating grandly with the other, like the comic relief in opera buffa. Eufemia tosses her head back in laughter. The two of them shout *Oop-a-la!* as they ride the crest of a wave. Eufemia glances back at me, waving her hand like the Queen. Raffaele salutes me with his glass. I try to call out to them for help, but they don't hear me.

Still frantically treading water, I call out to the Trespasser. "How do I destroy Atomic Shadow Time?"

His voice is faint, like an echo from long ago. "That's up to you. You're the Storyteller. You control everything. Life, death, history, the rise and fall of great civilizations. Don't worry, you'll think of something."

My strength is giving out. I sink below the waves. My foot touches something solid — it's the arm of the wheelchair, I think. I push myself off.

Head above water again, I shout, "I need better weapons than stories!"

"That's all *The Adventures of Futureman* is — just a story," points out the Trespasser's voice. "Storytelling is the best weapon you have against the People of Forever, so I suggest you use it."

FOUR

RETURN TO NEW ROME

I sit up in semidarkness. At first I think I'm in the rehab hospital. But looking down I see that I'm back in my threadbare housedress. A pile of terrycloth lies on the floor beside me. I push it under the cot with my bare foot. It feels damp.

I can hear the snoring of Old Eufemia. When my eyes grow accustomed to the dim light, I see bodies of passengers curled up on their cots. They're all asleep except Hot Lips, who stands watch at the front of the tent. When I go and stand beside her, she hugs me.

"Welcome back, Stan. You were out of it for so long I was starting to worry you'd never wake up."

"It's getting dark," I say. "How can that be?"

Hot Lips nods. "I don't know, but I'm taking it as a good sign."

"Time is passing again," I murmur, half to myself.

"Look there," Hot Lips nods, pointing at the lake.

Lightning illuminates shapes on the water, bouncing their way toward the cobble beach. The waves look impossibly high. The two of us quietly go around the tent, shaking the others awake.

I pause for a moment to gaze at the beautiful faces of Marcopolo and Ginalollobrigida curled up together. They look so peaceful that I almost don't want to disturb them. I finally reach down and shake both of their thin shoulders.

"Time to go, sisters," I whisper.

We file out in silence. Passengers from the other tents are picking their way down to the beach. Poseidon leads one group, John Cabot another, Caruso, a third. Ginalollobrigida and Marcopolo cling to one another, hobbling toward the water in their tight dresses.

I stand barefoot in the surf with Antoinette and Caterina. Hot Lips has her arm around Old Eufemia, who has managed to make her way with everyone else. She's wearing the apron she came in with, no doubt with her precious tube of Ozonol in the pocket.

Alessandra runs to the clock rock to grab her Timex.

"It's working again!" she shouts, strapping it on her wrist. "Maybe it's a sign that I'll find the kids!"

She shows me the watch's chromium dial glowing in the darkness. The sweep second hand is moving. It's one minute after twelve. Three minutes later than it's been for what feels like forever.

We have weather and night again. Now time is inching forward — but taking us where exactly? Because if this world *is* a shadow of Atomic Mean Time, and if I didn't *actually* destroy that world before it attempted to destroy itself, history will repeat itself in a string of strategic nuclear missile strikes in about twenty-four hours. Our only hope of survival is to be well out of Atomic Shadow Time before that happens.

But that's all ahead of us. First we have to get off the spit or die trying.

* * *

The wind has risen. In the distance I can see shapes approaching, momentarily illuminated by flashes of lightning. As Wolfman predicted, they're small crafts. Sailboats, rowboats, kayaks, freighter canoes and even amusement park swan boats. Waves are clawing at my bare legs. It's hard to stand upright.

Hot Lips turns to me and shouts something. Impossible to hear her, even though we're only a few feet apart. I shake my head to indicate that I don't understand.

She presses her lips together and frowns. Comes closer to me and shouts in my ear, "Get into the first boat with Eufemia, Antoinette and Caterina."

I don't realize it, but I've just saved my own life.

The first boat is a lifeguarding rowboat, oared by a tall figure in a bright yellow rain slicker.

"Go go go." Poseidon pushes passengers toward the boats. Hot Lips takes Eufemia by the arm and urges her into the surf. Caterina, Antoinette and I are coming up behind. As we climb in, I realize what Hot Lips was trying to ask me: *Can you swim?*

My headshake was an inadvertent lie. Although I'm by no means a strong swimmer, I earned my bronze level from the Red Cross Lifesaving Society. Had Hot Lips known that, I might have ended up in one of the tippier boats with Alessandra and Marcopolo.

"There are a few life jackets," shouts the man in yellow. "Put them on and hang on to the gunwales. If we capsize, stay near the boat."

The waves are already swamping us. Old Eufemia huddles in the bow, saying the rosary on her knuckles. Caterina gently pulls the old woman's arms into a life jacket; Eufemia's so thin, I doubt it would stay on her if we dumped.

"Here," says the man, shoving a bucket into my hands. "Bail."

He leans into the oars and we push off from the shore. The wind does everything in its power to blow us back in.

"Get off, you fucker," shouts the man, startling me. At first I think he's telling me to leave the boat, then I realize he's cursing the waves. As if they're programmed to drive us back to the beach.

I force myself to look around: there are scores of small boats heaving up and down, thirty or forty crafts of varying sizes. The rise and fall of the waves are becoming more extreme. A freighter canoe capsizes, sending Poseidon and Neptune into the waves. They'll be all right, I tell myself.

As we round the tip of the spit, we're hit by even higher waves coming off the harbour from the other direction. We're thrown up, then crash down hard, as if we're hitting cement instead of water. I can just make out the wall of the ship now, a cliff of grey steel illuminated by flashes of lightning. *Canadian Centaur* is momentarily visible on the bow, then vanishes again. The last three letters of *centaur* have been painted over something else. That's when I realize the original name was *Canadian Century* — a laker, one of the many Great Lakes freighters I watched going through the canal in my childhood in Shipman's Corners. In Atomic Mean Time, the *Canadian Century* carried bombs; in Earth Standard Time, car parts and grain.

The wall of the ship is right before us now. The deserted lighthouse stands high on the cliff above. The passengers from Tunis are streaming off the rugged shoreline at the end of the spit. I see Jordan and Wolfman in a kayak riding the waves. They'll be okay, they'll be okay, I reassure myself. It's like saying a prayer to no one.

A cry for help carries over the sounds of the wind and rain. I turn to see a freighter canoe listing; Marcopolo is in the water. She comes up once and disappears, raises an arm, then goes under again. Unlike me, she isn't wearing a life jacket.

I crawl down the centre of the boat and pound the back of

the rower's yellow jacket. "One of us is in the water! She can't swim; we have to rescue her!"

"We can't go back now," yells the rower.

I turn to scan the lake. Marcopolo has disappeared. Then I spot her again. She may not be able to swim, but she's trying to tread water. I keep my eyes on the last place I saw her. Up and down, up and down she bobs, her mouth a ragged O. At my feet a coiled safety rope is attached to a buoy marker. I pick it up and throw hard toward where I hope Marcopolo is still fighting to stay afloat. I watch. And watch. Until I see a hand grab the buoy.

"Help me pull her in!" I scream at the rower.

"I can't leave the oars or we'll dump!"

Caterina joins me at the rope. Then Antoinette. Three old ladies hauling a teenager the size of a child in the teeth of a storm. Eufemia clasps her hands and mouths a Hail Mary.

"There she is!" screams Antoinette. Marcopolo is clinging to the buoy, eyes wild as a spooked horse. She rides up and down on the waves like a punk mermaid.

The rower shouts, "Two of you hold the oars and I'll bring her in."

Antoinette and Caterina each take an oar. The man braces his feet against the pitching gunwale and hauls Marcopolo over the side like a fish in a net. She lies panting and coughing at the bottom of the boat. I pull off my life jacket and start strapping it on her.

"You're safe now," I tell her as I cinch the jacket tight around her, just as a wave hits us sideways and capsizes the boat, sending all of us into the raging water.

The first thing I think about is the bag of sketchbooks tied to my waist. Without a life jacket I'm sinking fast, but I'm more worried about losing the stories than losing my life. I kick my feet and try to fight my way to the surface. The water is a churning mass of legs; I can see the capsized rowboat floating above me, a safety rope tied to the thwarts twisting in the water like a yellow snake. Something else is in the water too. It has a mouth and tentacles. Like a jellyfish crossed with an octopus but with too many legs. Whatever it is, it's the colour of lime Kool-Aid. I see another and another, fluorescent horrors plunging down into the water among the passengers. One stretches its tentacles toward me. I swim backwards away from it; another joins it. Whip-fast their legs seize me by both arms and squeeze. The suckers on their tentacles kiss my skin. I try to scream and gulp water instead. I'm being yanked upward by the things like a pair of seahorses in a fairy tale. When I break the surface, the boneless green monsters are all around me, dragging passengers behind them. From the rail of the freighter someone is throwing the monsters down at us. They fall through the air like glowing green lanterns, tentacles flailing.

A rope ladder is tossed down over the side of the freighter. I look up; the height to the top feels impossibly high. An iron mountain.

"Grab and climb," the rower yells at me. For the first time, I get a good look at his face under the yellow rain hood. A young man with a broad flat face and bright blue eyes. It's Jordan's bodyguard, Yuri.

Eufemia is floating beside me in her life jacket, her eyes fixed on the freighter.

"What about her?"

"I'll carry her up on my back. Just climb!"

As the ladder flaps and bangs against the side of the ship, I'm overtaken by a fear even greater than drowning: being crushed against the iron hull in the high wind. I place my foot on the first rung, slip and find myself hanging by one leg, head skimming the water, one crooked knee keeping me from falling into the pounding waves. I wave my hands blindly, searching for a handhold. I can't right myself or balance on the rung well enough to go any farther.

I'm not sure anyone can hear my screams. Strong hands grab and right me, pushing me upward. Yuri.

"I can't do it! I think I've broken my ankle!" I yell at him. I'm clinging to the ladder in terror, one foot on the slippery rung, the other flailing in space.

"Just climb!" he screams back. "Either that or you'll drop into the lake and drown!"

For a moment, I wonder if I would like to do just that. Die and get it over with. After what happened to David, or what might happen to the rest of us in the future. But there are the stories. If I die, they die with me.

I climb. One shuddering rung at a time. My ankle screams bloody murder at every step.

"Don't look down!" Yuri yells.

I feel the ladder abruptly go taut in my hands. Against orders I glance down and see Caterina starting to climb up behind me. "Avanti, Stan!" she screams.

I can barely hold on. The ladder is slick and the wind is flinging me against the ship's hull, battering my knees and knuckles. Finally, incredibly, I reach the top rung. A hand appears in front of my face, fingers splayed; I grasp it but it's so smooth and slick I can't get a firm grip. Another hand reaches down and pulls me up and over the rail. I land on the deck, face down and winded.

I lay still for a moment, trying to catch my breath, then slowly roll onto my back.

I'm looking directly up into the eyes of my rescuer: a platinum face with a single green eye shining at me from above a meshwork mouth. I've just been hauled aboard the *Canadian Centaur* by a Puff.

I scuttle backwards, dragging my ankle. I have to warn the others: it's a trap, we're all going to die on this ship, I can't let anyone come aboard.

I stagger to the ship's rail, haul myself up on one foot and look down, trying to gather my courage to dive. I feel the artificial hand on my arm.

"Ms. Biondi, you're safe now," a voice says calmly.

I wrench my arm out of its grip. "Get away from me, you damn dirty robot!"

"Dammit, I'm a predictive digital assistant, not a pacification robot."

The voice. I recognize that voice. Not to mention there's only one synthetic I know who would misquote Doctor McCoy from *Star Trek*.

"Cassandra?"

The Puff's eye crinkles into an expression vaguely like a smile.

"Affirmative."

I'm in a soft place, gently rocking. I ache all over.

I pat my stomach, expecting to feel the comforting bulk of my sketchbooks, strapped under my clothes in the Ziploc bag. But I touch nothing but tender, bruised flesh. When I think about *The History of the Known World* and *Visions of Paradiso* at the bottom of the lake, I almost wish I had sunk with my sketchbooks. David's kippah is down there too. The only thing I had to remember him by. A numb pain settles over me like a blanket of grief.

Something feels warm against my face. I open my eyes. I'm in a bed under a grey wool quilt stamped with the words *Property of ShipCo, Shipman's Corners, Canusa.*

I'm not alone. Someone is snoring across the room from me in a bed identical to mine. Old Eufemia.

My ankle throbs. I ease myself up to sitting and yank back the covers. My ankle has been bandaged but not splinted. Maybe it's not broken after all. Swinging my legs out, I try to put weight on it. Hurts like a bitch, but I can stand.

"I wouldn't do that quite yet if I were you, Ms. Biondi."

I turn my head and see a Puff with *MEDIC* heat-stamped in red letters into its chest. In place of legs, its body tapers from the hips into the wheeled base of a Segway. The warmth on my face is coming from a light in the centre of one raised hand.

"What the hell are you?" I ask, shielding my eyes.

"Medbot. Better known as Flip. Would you allow me to continue to scan your physical functions?"

"Santa Maria." Eufemia is awake now, staring at the Puff. "Il diavolo," she whispers. The devil.

I shake my head. "Una macchina." A machine.

"Your companion has advanced cognitive deficiencies," says Flip in its placid voice.

"She's old," I say.

Eufemia sighs and pulls the sheet over her head.

I sit back down on the edge of the bed. "Could you leave us alone and send me a carbon-based life form? I'm not inclined to trust synths with my medical care."

Flip stares at me with expressive blue eyes. At least it's not a Cyclops, like Dragon or Cassandra. And they're not eyes but *sensors*, I remind myself. Don't anthropomorphize.

"Aye, aye," it says and rolls away. When it reaches the stateroom door, it retracts its body like a pogo stick, springs into the air and flips over the raised edge of the door. The door closes behind it.

I can tell I'm on a ship by the motion; prone to seasickness, I feel an edge of nausea. I should have asked the medbot for something to settle my stomach before I threw it out.

I limp around the room. Industrial grey latex thickly painted on the walls. A porthole, giving out onto the nauseating rise and fall of the horizon.

"Where the hell am I, the Love Boat?" I ask aloud.

"Close," a familiar male voice answers.

I turn. My husband is standing in the open door, arms crossed.

In my imaginative world, I'd always pictured a reunion between Kendal and me as something rather stormy but lush. Lots of gasps and weeping and the tearing off of clothing.

But, of course, real life (if that's what this is) is never as dramatic as a well-crafted story. Instead of rushing into Kendal's arms (or vice versa) or collapsing on the floor in shock, I clap my hand over my mouth and make a small gagging sound.

The Right Honourable Prime Minister Kendal has lost a lot of weight. He looks more like the lanky young man I married at age twenty-five than the sixty-plus-year-old politician in a bespoke suit whom I'd grown used to watching on CPAC.

The shock of recognition that must have registered on my face isn't reciprocated. Kendal is famous; I'm not — at least not outside the comic book world.

He glares at me. "You seem unhappy with your quarters. This is the best stateroom on the ship."

"I'm not unhappy. Just . . ." I search for right world. "Disoriented."

"And what's this about not wanting Flip to look after you? It's his job. You should be grateful to have him."

"I can't stomach robots right now."

"Then you're on the wrong ship," snaps Kendal. "The proportion of synthetics to carbons on board the *Canadian Centaur* is three to one. If it weren't for the octobots who went into the storm to rescue you, you and your friend here wouldn't be alive. I don't tolerate roboticism. Shall I get you a lifeboat?"

I want to say *Go ahead.* If this jerk had been stuck in New Rome, starved by junksters, abused by synthetics and seen his lover beaten almost to death by one . . .

But I stop myself. "That won't be necessary," I answer, then add, "I've been through a lot."

"We all have," answers Kendal without a shred of empathy. "Are you the one they call Stan?"

"Why do you ask?"

He holds up a battered Ziploc bag. Through the scratched and cloudy plastic, I can see my sketchbooks and David's bloodstained kippah. I lunge at Kendal and rip the bag from his hands, pressing it to my chest. My ankle squawks a protest.

"I'll take that as a yes," growls Kendal.

Eufemia looks back and forth between Kendal and me, eyebrows raised.

"Il tuo sposo?" Your husband? She's picking up on some kind of vibe.

"Si," I answer.

She lies back down. "Chooch," she grunts. Ass.

"Si," I agree.

Kendal hasn't finished his speech. "I'd appreciate your cooperation in helping the passengers deal with these difficult circumstances. We have a lot more humans aboard than we started with."

"How many of us made it through the storm?"

"Thirty." He heads back to the door and speaks without turning. "We've recovered a number of bodies. We're hoping you can help us identify them."

"I'm not sure if I can handle that right now."

Kendal answers coldly, "Under the circumstances, I have to insist. This could be the end of civilization as we know it. Possibly even the end of humanity as the dominant species. We all have to do what needs to be done."

I'm tempted to ask Kendal when he turned into such a dictatorial, overbearing, sanctimonious, hard-hearted control freak and realize I already know the answer: when he became a politician in Earth Standard Time.

SIX

ABOARD THE *CENTAUR*

"We don't know how far the Puffs' range extends," explains Kendal as I follow him through the ship's passageways. "But through the seaway, we can get out to the Atlantic and from there, the world. On a highway of water, our range is limitless." He's moving at a brisk pace but with an exoskeleton brace strapped to my sprained ankle, I can keep up, even scrambling up ladders after him.

"Couldn't the Puffs just attack us from the air with drones?"

Kendal nods a greeting at a robot fixing a bulkhead. The workbot is bright green and faceless, but the smooth movements of its arms and torso make it seem eerily human. Its blank mask of a head turns toward Kendal as it raises its hand in a crisp salute.

"At ease," says Kendal, pausing to return the salute. "The drones you saw are on our side, Stan. That's how we found you."

"The cormorants, you mean? Their wings didn't flap. We figured out pretty quickly that they weren't real birds. I'll bet the junksters will too."

"Design flaw," grunts Kendal. "We're working on it."

"What's to stop the Puffs from launching their own drones?"

"It's inevitable," agrees Kendal. "But the *Canadian Centaur* is run by a synthetic crew. An enemy flyover would show that the humans are outnumbered. From the air, it would look as if the synthetics had taken us prisoner."

"I recognized the one who pulled me on board," I tell him. "Cassandra. A home digital assistant. Basically a thermostat and automatic door opener. How did it become a Puff?"

Kendal gives a rare smile. "Cass isn't a Puff. None of the robots on the *Centaur* are. They're straightforward AI-driven machines, purpose built to serve humans, as they should be. Cass will have to tell you her story for herself. Believe it or not, she reached us on the smart odometer of a bicycle. We simply uploaded her to one of the surplus synthetics we had in the hold."

"Who was riding the bike?" I ask.

"Jordan, who I believe you've met. But there are lots of these stories of humans and synthetics teaming up and fighting the enemy shoulder to shoulder — which, by the way, I hope you'll record for us. I heard about *The History of the Known World* from other passengers. Storytelling is urgently needed. It's vital that we remember the Great War to Save Humanity."

Leave it to Kendal to brand the battle before it's even over.

"Speaking of stories, I'd love to know how *you* ended up in this world, Mr. Prime Minister," I say, trying to stroke his ego enough to get information out of him.

Kendal neither turns around nor slows his pace as he gives me his story. "I was on board a ship in the Welland Canal, announcing that my government had green-lit an initiative called Seaway Robots. Lakers staffed by fully automated crews that can interact with human sailors and dock workers. Brilliant pieces of mechanical engineering, married with artificial intelligence. As a demonstration ship, we purchased an aging Canada Steamship Lines freighter called *Canadian Century*, retrofitted it and renamed it *Canadian Centaur*. We entered the Lake Ontario entrance to the canal in the old world. Came out at the Port Colborne end in another reality."

Skittering along behind Kendal, I try to make sense of this bizarre narrative.

"You *and* the seaway robots all travelled into this alternate reality together by ship?"

"Apparently," grunts Kendal, hurrying down another one of the *Centaur*'s labyrinths of dim grey corridors. "Although there was one significant change to the cargo in the hold."

"Which was?"

"Automotive parts," answers Kendal. "But when we entered this . . . other world . . . we discovered we were carrying launching devices for intercontinental ballistic missiles and several neutron bombs."

I stop in my tracks, assuming Kendal will too. But he carries on briskly up a ladder to the next deck.

"No one," I pant, trying to catch up with him, "is going to believe that story."

"Because?"

"Robots are nonorganic. So are lake freighters, last time I checked. They can't get infected with rogue viruses."

Kendal glances over his shoulder at me with an expression that shows he's just barely tolerating my dimwittedness. "Really? Tell that to anyone whose operating system was taken out by a computer virus!"

"But . . ."

We finally come to a windowless door that I think — I hope — leads onto the upper deck.

Kendal turns to me. "You don't like that explanation, Stan, fine. Come up with a different one. You're the Storyteller. Right now, we have to focus on giving final respects to our casualties."

* * *

Kendal pushes open the door that, I'm grateful to see, leads into the sunlight of the top deck. An open area has been tented over with white cloth that billows slightly in the breeze. Sunlight ripples over the lines of white pupa-like shapes on the deck, each one swaddled in a sheet. Only the faces are exposed. Surviving passengers mill about or kneel beside the dead. All of us are in nightwear, sheets or robes, like the shell-shocked guests at a pyjama party in a horror movie.

It's easier to look at the dead dispassionately when you didn't know them in life. I'm able to pass by rows of passengers unknown to me without shedding a tear, but I'm gutted by the faces of Antoinette and Tut the Girl King. More grief seems impossible, on top of what I already feel for David. I'm hollowed out.

Marcopolo wails at the feet of Ginalollobrigida with Hot Lips's arms around her. Wolfman hugs them both. Whispering in Italian, Caterina crouches down to stroke Antoinette's sagging face, horribly bloated in death. What happens when you drown, I assume.

At the end of the row of bodies of New Romans, I see Alessandra. A faint luminescence shines through the sheet wound around her. Crouching, I gently pull down the sheet until I can see the source of the shine: her Timex wristwatch. The second hand is moving, ticking off the seconds. I can just make out the time: thirty-five minutes past twelve. About a half hour later than when Alessandra grabbed the watch off the clock rock. But a whole night has passed since then.

The Timex is working. But does that mean that time is actually passing? If so, how quickly? Maybe the mechanism restarted, but time itself has not.

I slip the watch into the pocket of my pyjama bottoms and tuck the shroud back around Alessandra's shoulders. "If I find your kids, I'll give it to them," I whisper.

Shirtless, in a pair of faded denim pyjama pants printed with the words *Canada Steamship Lines*, Poseidon squats next to the body of his best friend, Neptune. His head is lowered, hands clasped between his knees, shoulders heaving. His grief is a growling angry thing. He wants vengeance — something that becomes even more obvious when Jordan and Yuri enter the morgue. A synthetic is with them, wearing black overalls. It looks over at me and lifts its hand. The ring and middle finger are separated to form a V shape, thumb extended.

The synth in black must be Cassandra. What other seaway robot would know Spock's salute from *Star Trek*?

Yuri stands to one side, head bowed. I can see the long puckered line of a zipper on his neck, disturbingly like Frankenstein's monster. A LEECH implantation scar. Behind him and Jordan, a large drying rack stands with what looks like long tendrils of seaweed. It takes a minute to recognize the bulging eyes of the octobots that saved so many of us the previous night. Their tentacles twitch and move as if they're taking part in this ceremony too.

Kendal opens a leatherbound book and starts to recite prayers from different faiths.

When Yuri steps forward to help lift the bodies into the drop sheets that will serve as their burial shrouds, Poseidon blocks him.

"Don't you touch my friends, you inhuman zipperneck," Poseidon growls. "I'll bury them with my own hands. Human hands."

Yuri's eyes flick from Poseidon to Kendal and back. In his emaciated state Poseidon would be no match for the bodyguard.

"I *am* human," says Yuri in his softly accented voice.

"Not in my books," Poseidon snarls into Yuri's face. He's close enough to kiss or bite him. "You fucking synth. You might as well just go join the Puffs."

Kendal steps up and pushes the two men apart. "I know you're angry, Daryl, but the bots saved your life and those of twenty-nine other passengers. You should be grateful."

"Bullshit," Poseidon spits out at him. "And don't call me Daryl. That guy died back in New Rome. You're talking to Poseidon, king of the seas."

Kendal's voice is steady and assured; he's had years of deflecting verbal assaults in the House of Commons. "This is a battle for the future of humanity. I'm your leader. I need every able-bodied human on my side."

"Leader, eh? I sure never voted for you."

Poseidon turns his shaggy head, searching for the stairs leading to the lower decks. When he finds them, he disappears, leaving the rest of us to bury the dead.

One by one, Kendal reads out the names and Yuri taps the side of the copper bell with a small hammer: one ring for each dead passenger. A gangplank provides a respectful way to release them over the side of the ship into the lake. Jordan, Yuri and Cassandra act as pallbearers. I close my eyes at the sound of three splashes. Antoinette, Ginalollobrigida, Neptune.

Thirty of us remain, mostly New Romans with a handful of survivors from the other settlements on the spit. We are now the biggest community of passengers on the *Canadian Centaur*. After the synthetics, of course.

Once the service wraps up, Cassandra and Jordan come over to me. Having previously known Cass as a disembodied entity inside a plastic hub, it feels odd to be looking into her humanoid eye — too much like Dragon's for my liking. Like the Puff, her meshwork mouth pulsates with light as she speaks.

"It's good to see you again, Debbie Reynolds Biondi. I calculated the odds of your survival at less than thirty percent. I feared you were lost forever."

"Never count out a comic book artist."

As we head back to the ladder leading to the lower deck, I see Eufemia, leaning on a soft assistance bot nicknamed Cloudy, which can mutate into a walker, lift, wheelchair and soft place to land. The old woman looks confused and exhausted.

"We should take Eufemia down her to bunk for a rest," I say. "When she tires, she gets confused and anxious."

Jordan places a hand on my arm. "A LEECH implant might help restore her cognitive functions. It's not a difficult procedure. Flip could do it in sick bay."

"Who's going to give permission?" I ask.

"Would you seek permission if she needed us to take out a rotting tooth?" asks Yuri.

"We're talking about her brain. Her memories. Her soul."

Cassandra lifts her hands and pats the air, as if it trying to calm the humans down.

"Perhaps Eufemia herself can be made to understand and consent," suggests Cassandra. "In the meantime, you need to eat. Let me lead you to the galley."

* * *

The galley is already packed with passengers, most of them ones I know. I fill my tray from a small cafeteria hot table, manned (if that's the right word) by a red-and-white-striped serverbot.

"What'll you have, mac?" it asks me cheerily as I stand before it with my tray.

It fills a platter with salad, steak and potatoes, then hands it over the protective hood to me.

"Have a nice day, buddy," it tells me and moves on to serve the next passenger.

At one point in the meal, Hot Lips stands and lifts a glass of wine — thoughtfully provided by the serverbot to turn the meal into a funeral reception. "Here's to the friends we lost."

"To our glorious dead," echoes Kendal. "May they never be forgotten."

I look at him, anger ballooning in me. *Our glorious dead* echoes the cliché on every war cenotaph. In my Atomic Mean Time childhood, the phrase often mutated into *our irradiated and dismembered dead* to cover off those who had died in horrific industrial accidents — including Kendal's own father, at least in my world.

Meaningless words either way, a politician's eulogy. The dead, whether drowned, irradiated, mutilated or otherwise, aren't glorious. They are simply, horribly gone.

After the meal has ended, and more tears have been shed and wiped, and more memories shared of the glorious dead, I look up the table at Kendal. "May I ask, Prime Minister, where is the *Canadian Centaur* heading? Unless it's a secret, of course."

He shakes his head as he digs into a bowl of ice cream. "No secret at all." He puts down his spoon, lifts a glass of wine and gives me a look of roguish humour and determination so much like the young Kendal I married that I almost drop my wineglass.

"We're going to tie up at Lock One in Shipman's Corners to stock up on food, clothes and medicine. We have a lot more humans on board than we planned for."

"And then?" I ask.

"Then," says Kendal, leaning forward to look down the table at me, and raising his voice so that everyone can hear, "we're going to find the fucking Mother of the Journey Home and nuke it out of existence."

I look up at Kendal with an expression that I suspect shows both my disbelief and shock — unless, of course, he's joking. "Nuke Mother? You can't be serious."

"The *Canadian Centaur* is carrying a tactical nuclear weapon. A neutron bomb for battlefield use, with limited range. In the Cold War, the Americans nicknamed it Davy Crockett. Better known as a mini-nuke. Small enough to carry in a backpack."

"But won't nuking Mother kill us too?"

"We'll be out of range," says Kendal. "The synthetics will handle it. It's what they were built for. Preserving human life. We are talking about the future of humanity."

My bewilderment deepens: *this* is the man who told me he wouldn't tolerate roboticism on this ship? That's when I finally accept that this is not the John Kendal of Atomic Mean Time, seeker of truth and justice. The man in front of me is the Kendal I used to watch on CPAC, shouting at the opposition. This Kendal is all about wielding power, not seeking justice.

"You're sending the synthetics on a suicide mission, aren't you?"

Instead of confirming or denying, Kendal reaches past me to grab the bottle of wine sitting in the middle of table — Sparkling Sparrow, a cheap local plonk I used to get drunk on in high school — and refills everyone's glass.

Lifting his glass in a toast, he says, "Here's to the future of humanity."

SEVEN

GOING HOME

At sunrise, the *Canadian Centaur* quietly slips into the mouth of the Welland Canal at Port Weller. Standing on the upper deck, I can just make out the CN Tower on the other side of the lake, poking out of the Toronto skyline like the plunger of a giant syringe.

As we pass rows of empty freighters in dry dock, my Sharpie hovers over a blank page in *The History of the Known World*. Sketching the watery burials of my friends isn't going to be easy. I don't like thinking about the dead lying in the chilly depths of Lake Ontario, their bodies picked at by mussels, eels, hagfish and who-knows-what scavengers scuttling along the muddy lakebed. What a grotesque place to be laid to rest. I remind myself that they can't feel anything anymore, but I still keep picturing Antoinette's bloated face and Ginalollobrigida's body shrouded in a bedsheet, looking as if she'd dropped off to sleep in Marcopolo's arms. I touch David's bloodstained kippah, grateful that he didn't end up down there.

I've removed the brace from my ankle, having let Flip inject me with an anti-inflammatory and painkiller. Physically I haven't felt this good in months.

I'm still wearing baggy grey pyjamas stamped *Property of ShipCo* and a pair of paint-stained deck shoes I found stuffed in the closet of my stateroom. Most of the passengers are still in the rags they were rescued in or wrapped in bath-towel togas. Not that we need warm clothing. It's hot and dry again, just the way Jordan said the Puffs like it.

I'm trying to come to terms with Kendal's willingness to use a nuclear device. The question I keep coming back to isn't only whether it's ethical to blow up synthetic allies. What if a nuke doesn't work and the humans in Earth Standard Time and every other alternate reality are transported into their worlds' pasts?

If humans *are* to go extinct or return to being prey at the bottom of the food chain like the scurrying protomammals of dinosaur days — if this truly is the end of times for us as the dominant species — I couldn't think of a better place to usher in the posthuman era than the Welland Canal. A human-engineered space where borders meet and saltwater and fresh-water intermingle, it's the setting of my earliest memories: watching the grey steel hull of a flat wide lake freighter or a plump ocean-going saltie pass by, water pouring from rusted ballast holes. I might even have been here as a toddler when the Queen herself arrived on the Royal Yacht *Britannia* to dedicate the opening of the seaway.

That past is slipping away. How fitting that my future, if there is one, will be played out in yet another timeline as the *Canadian Centaur* takes us on a voyage to what might be humanity's last stand.

I lean against the rail, awash in homesickness, breathing in the comforting aromas of diesel fuel, machine oil and rotting fish as the familiar landmarks of my hometown slide by. Despite growing up near the canal, I've never been on the deck of a ship before. In Atomic Mean Time, freighters were off-limits to civilians. They were high-security vessels carrying components for nuclear weapons manufactured by our local mega-industry, the ShipCo

Corporation, which employed ninety-eight percent of the city's workforce. Managers like my dad had not just job titles but ranks: supervising lieutenants, chief executive generals, sergeant foremen. Everyone's livelihood depended on a never-ending arms race. *A better world through mutual assured destruction* was both the company motto and a prayer we recited at church every Sunday.

Meanwhile in the more peaceful parallel world of Earth Standard Time, Shipman's Corners was similarly devoted to a single purpose: the auto industry. But as the twenty-first century dawned, factories turned into empty ruins, the contaminated ghosts of a dying industrial age, taking thousands of jobs with them. The only plants still operating in Shipman's Corners of 2025 are lights-out factories where robots work the lines without heat, light or coffee breaks. Skeleton crews of human technicians keep the robots going, constantly repairing, upgrading, updating and rebooting them. Robots break down a lot. Their operating systems become obsolete every few years. Power surges and outages can send automated lines into chaos. Jordan was right when she said we overestimate the synthetics; without tender loving care from human hands, they would simply rust away through wear and tear. Gears, electronics, silicon, programming: with the passage of time, all eventually erode or become obsolete. Which must make this nook in time especially attractive to the Puffs.

I comfort myself with this knowledge of the fragility of machines every time I pass one of the so-called friendly synthetics on board the *Canadian Centaur*. I still can't even look at Cass without thinking of Dragon's arm swinging against David's head, blotting him out before dragging him into the truck with the other traumatized passengers.

Although I'm repelled by Poseidon's toxic outbursts, I sympathize with his feelings. I don't completely trust our supposed synthetic allies on the ship. Even Flip, whose only purpose is to keep humans healthy, makes me uneasy. Despite Kendal's assurances that the synthetics on the *Canadian Centaur* are on our side, I'm itching to get off the ship, away from all these artificial life forms.

I slip the Timex out of my pocket and check the time. To my surprise, the second hand on the face is sweeping *backwards*.

While I watch the lock doors close, Jordan and Cassandra join me at the rail. Jordan has exchanged her tattered Sputnik Chick uniform for a black jumpsuit and scraped her long dark hair into a high ponytail. Cassandra's face has been imprinted with a bright image. A pink and yellow daisy.

"Cute tattoo," I comment.

Cass's eye opens wide and rolls to the side in what I've learned is a synthetic's version of a sardonic grin. "Thought it would make it easier to tell me apart from the evil killer robots."

"What you looking at, Stan?" Jordan asks, peering at the watch in my hand.

I show both her and Cass the Timex and tell them about its provenance.

"What does your second brain make of this? It started up again the night of storm. Now it's running backwards."

Jordan takes the wristwatch. "Maybe it's broken. Alessandra drowned with it on, after all."

I shake my head. "It's a Timex. They're almost indestructible. Shockproof, waterproof. John Cameron Whatshisname would put them through torture tests live on television."

"John Cameron Swayze," Cass supplies, taking the watch from Jordan. "This device is not malfunctioning. It's accurately reflecting the erratic passage of time here. It's the world around us that's chaotic."

We say nothing more, just slouch on the rail and watch the empty shoreline roll by. No tourists, no crews working on the locks or bridges. Only silence and empty spaces.

On the deck, Eufemia slumps in the arms of her assistant robot, Cloudy, which has thoughtfully transformed itself into a wheelchair. Over the last twenty-four hours, Eufemia has deteriorated, refusing to talk, walk or eat. Probably the stress of our escape from New Rome, not to mention the deaths of so many friends. Maybe Cassandra was right about giving a neural boost to Eufemia's malfunctioning brain. What's the point of leaving her in this state when we are — according to Kendal — at war?

* * *

At midday, we gather for lunch. Even Poseidon shows up, ignoring everyone except Caterina and Marcopolo, both puffy-eyed with grief. He kisses them before yanking out a chair at the end of a table far from the synthetics. Over dessert and coffee, Kendal gets to his feet, his hand automatically reaching to button his nonexistent suit jacket. Muscle memory: he reached for that button every time he stood to address the House of Commons. Instead he puts both hands behind his back and clears his throat.

"We'll be tying up soon. I'll take an away party ashore for medicine, food and clothes, made up of the following passengers and synthetics: Filomena, Debbie, Jordan, Yuri, Sidney, Cassandra and Flip. In my absence, I'm leaving one person in charge." He turns to Poseidon, marooned at the end of a trestle table sulking over a plate of beef stew. "Daryl, I want you to take the com."

Poseidon looks up, his eyes narrowed with surprise and suspicion. "What?"

"I'm putting you in charge of the *Canadian Centaur* and her crew."

Poseidon straightens up from his slumped position. "Can I order the robots around?"

"Within reason," says Kendal evenly. "All of the synthetics on board obey Asimov's Three Laws. I assume you're familiar with them?"

"I read *I, Robot* when I was a kid," answers Poseidon with a shrug. "You know as well as I do that the Three Laws are bullshit. Pure science fiction. How do I know that the synthetics won't hand me over to the junksters the minute you're gone?"

"If that was going to happen at all, it would've happened by now. As for the Three Laws, they've worked so far and they're all we've got," answers Kendal. "Come up to the bridge and I'll show you around. Your sole responsibility is to protect this ship and everyone on it for three hours. Think you can handle that?"

I watch this exchange in a state of gobsmacked disbelief. I can't believe that Kendal is giving control of the ship to someone eaten up by rage and a thirst for vengeance. As we file out of the galley, I catch up to Kendal before he makes his way to the bridge. "Can I have a word?"

He nods, letting Poseidon and the other passengers go on ahead. When they're out of earshot, I take him by the arm. He looks down pointedly at my hand, but I don't loosen my grip. It's all I can do not to shake him.

"What were you thinking? Why don't you leave Hot Lips — Filomena — in command? She's rational. Poseidon is a stick of dynamite waiting to be lit."

Kendal gives me a tight little smile. "Daryl thinks of himself as a leader, so let him lead. If he's left in charge of the synthetics for a few hours and sees that they'll always do what he asks them to do, he'll be reassured. I know what I'm doing, Stan. I've been managing difficult personalities for a long time."

And with that, he strides off down the passageway to hand control over to Poseidon, leaving the away party to get ready to disembark.

As I stand at the ship's rail, tying the Ziploc bag tighter to my waist, I notice a presence loitering in the shadow of a cargo bay. It's Marcopolo, wrapped in a ripped piece of canvas cloth belted with a thick length of rope. She looks wan and even more childlike than usual.

"Can I carry the stories for you?"

I look up, halfway through tying a clumsy knot. It would make sense to travel unencumbered by a bag of sketchbooks, but leaving them behind would be like cutting off part of my body.

"Thanks, Marcopolo, but I'm used to it."

She steps forward out of the shadows, her hands extended like a statue of a saint. "Please, Stan. It would make me feel better if I could look at the stories while you're away. Especially the ones with pictures of Gina and me."

I'm swamped by guilt. Why not trust the girl with my sketchbooks? She's a friend and ally, after all. A former camp-mate. Grieving the loss of her lover, just like me. Slowly I unknot the rope around my waist. But as I'm about to hand the bag over to her, Marcopolo seems to change — she no longer looks gaunt but greedy. A sneaky thief, hungry for the power of my stories. She wants them all to herself. I hesitate, cradling the Ziploc bag in my arms. She tries to take it and we engage in a gentle tug-of-war.

"Please, Stan," she whispers.

"Everything in this bag is precious to me."

She nods. "They're precious to me too. I'll look after them. And I'll give them back, I promise."

I finally release the bag, regretting my decision the moment it leaves my hands.

"See you in a few hours," I tell Marcopolo before I head down the gangway with the others in the away party.

"Good luck, Stan," she says, hugging the Ziploc bag to her chest.

* * *

As Yuri ties the ship's rope to a bollard, Poseidon stares down at us from the top deck, flanked by a pair of cargo-loading bots. When Kendal salutes, Poseidon simply nods back.

We cut across Canal Road into a subdivision. There are no signs of life, just deserted houses, schoolyards and playgrounds. Bikes and skateboards lying on their sides. A scooter toppled under a half-open garage door. Housecats skitter out of alleyways and from behind fences and trees, bodies low to the ground, ears back. They look like they've gone feral.

As we make the twenty-minute walk to the mall, the away party discusses the People of Forever. The nature of their design. Their dependence on the devoted junksters. How the junksters got here in the first place.

"If a time travel virus brought the passengers here, why not the junksters?" I ask.

"We think there's a back door into this world," says Jordan. "Something the junksters used as a bridge between the reality we knew and this world."

"A quantum passage through the continuum," I suggest, thinking of my own past hops between alternate worlds.

"Maybe. As for the Puffs, they may always have been here, waiting for someone to wake them up."

"One day, Stan, when all this is over, you'll have quite a story to tell our descendants," comments Kendal. "Whole chapters to add to *The History of the Known World*."

When all this is over, I think. Unlikely this will ever be truly over.

First time I've admitted that to myself.

I don't want to reveal that this isn't my story to tell. It belongs to a long-dead tree surgeon, Dr. Norman Guenther, and the obscure comic strip he created in Earth Standard Time of the past. How his fantasy world became reality is still a mystery to me.

"Puffs were engineered to be the best and worst of both worlds," says Cassandra. "The extra-human strength and endurance of machines, the brute force computing power of artificial intelligence, the self-healing physiology of the human body, the single-minded purpose of a corporate entity and the photosynthesizing ability of trees."

"That's why they like light," adds Jordan.

"And data," adds Kendal.

"Gee, it's almost a shame to nuke them out of existence, isn't it," I comment, intending sarcasm.

"I agree. It would be smarter to reprogram them," says Yuri. "Wipe their brains. Alter their programming. Turn them into purpose-built military-industrial robots, like they were always meant to be."

"Like they were *meant* to be? Who meant for them to be hamburger flippers and cannon fodder?" I ask, jogging to catch up with Yuri, who is striding ahead.

By way of answer, Yuri glances at Kendal.

"It's the natural order of human-machine relationships,

Stan. We control, they obey," Kendal answers. "Turning the People of Forever into useful synthetic workers and soldiers would actually be preferable to destroying them outright."

"I thought you said *nuke them*," I point out.

"No, I said, nuke *Mother*," corrects Kendal. "We'll only take out the Puffs if there's no other option."

I glance sidelong at Cassandra and Flip. Neither synthetic is reacting to Kendal's words, but I suspect their thoughts reflect what a movie android will say, in Earth Standard Time of the future, before going on a suicide mission to save its human crewmembers from parasitic aliens: *Believe me, I'd prefer not to. I may be synthetic, but I'm not stupid.*

* * *

The parking lot of the Fairview Mall is packed with the sleek vintage vehicles of a world obsessed with self-destruction: Atomic Thunderbirds, Doomsday El Dorados, Gran Missile Silo Wagons.

And dogs. A dozen mutts ranging from French bulldogs to golden retrievers rush at us, a few of them dragging their leashes behind them.

"What timeline do these dogs belong to?" I wonder aloud.

"Mostly this one," says Yuri. "But my LEECH is picking up data from a couple of identity chips. They must have quantum travelled here right along with their owners."

Coward that I am, I step behind Jordan: I'm nervous of dogs at the best of times, and these ones may have been on their own long enough to start hunting together. It occurs to me that the pack might view us as prey.

Flip lets out a high-pitched blast of sound that sends the dogs running — all but one long-haired German shepherd wearing a jacket reading *Assistance Animal* in English and PICTO. She whimpers and paces back and forth in front of us. Wolfman pulls half an energy bar out of his pocket and tosses it on the ground. The dog gobbles it up and sits on its haunches, panting, as if to say *Is there more where that came from?* Wolfman crouches down and scratches its head, checking the nametag on the collar.

"Lucy," reads Wolfman. "You're a good girl, aren't you? You're a passenger like the rest of us."

Lucy licks his hand and looks at the rest of us with trust in her eyes. As we proceed to the front entrance of the mall, she tags along behind us, barking to warn off the other strays.

* * *

The mall's main entrance doors are unlocked; one door is propped open by a toppled scooter. Inside the air is full of what looks like microscopic fairies — dust motes floating in the sunlight flooding down from skylights.

Phones, tablets and shopping bags are scattered just inside the doors, turning the entranceway into an obstacle course. We follow a trail of running shoes, purses, tote bags, walkers and canes into the centre court of the mall. The abandoned possessions of passengers from Shipman's Corners of 2025.

The seven of us proceed slowly, our heads swivelling in every direction.

"Hot Lips," calls Wolfman, who has followed Lucy farther into the mall. "Lucy's found a body outside the hardware store."

Lucy is whimpering and nosing at an elderly man, face down. A neat stubble of grey hair on the back of his head hints at a recent haircut. Hot Lips leans down and takes his pulse, but even I can tell he's dead.

Hot Lips slowly turns the man onto his back; he looks about eighty, a pair of tortoiseshell glasses hanging from one ear. He's wearing a Niagara IceDogs T-shirt, a sure sign of a grandchild in major junior hockey. Hot Lips thumbs his lids closed.

"Probably a heart attack," she says, checking a bracelet on his wrist. "His medic alert says he has a pacemaker. He's wearing a fitness tracker too, so he's definitely one of us."

Poor guy. One minute, happily shopping in a twenty-first century mall with his assistance dog, bragging about his grand-kid's slapshot. The next, he and his dog are both in an alternate world. No wonder his heart gave out.

"I didn't think animals could quantum travel," I say to Cassandra.

"Perhaps the human-animal connection makes a differ-ence," Cass suggests. "Or perhaps dogs are becoming more like humans."

I nod. "You might be onto something there."

We leave the dead man where we find him and start walking into the heart of the mall, where a rancid smell hits us like gas from a sewage dump. On the floor of the food court, rotting hamburgers and chicken fingers stink up the food court. Despite Wolfman whistling and calling her name to coax her away, Lucy bounds in to make short work of the spoiled food.

Hot Lips stands at a table, examining a decomposing hamburger.

"Look, it's starting to rot," she points out. "Time has started moving again! Thank god."

I finger the Timex in my pocket. "Yeah, thank god," I agree half-heartedly.

* * *

We divide into groups: Jordan, Kendal and I are in charge of clothes; Yuri and Wolfman will look for weapons; and Hot Lips, Cassandra and Flip will collect food and medicine. Everyone has one hour to gather supplies before we rendezvous at a phone booth near the front entrance. We should get back to the *Canadian Centaur* with plenty of time to spare.

In a Sports Chalet, mannequins in midstride turn their faceless heads toward Kendal, Jordan and me. They're wearing tracksuits and sweatbands on shiny beige plastic bodies. They remind me of Dragon.

Running our buggies up and down the aisles, we grab anything we think the passengers could use: rain jackets, jogging shoes, fleece vests, toques and ball caps. Our buggies fill quickly. If I weren't so scared, I'd laugh at the sight of the prime minister scooping up armfuls of tube socks.

When I see a sign marked *Change Rooms*, I call out to Jordan, "I want to get out of these damn PJs. Give me five minutes."

"You've got two," calls Kendal, dumping a bin of men's underwear into his buggy.

I grab a pair of dance tights, a T-shirt and a warmup jacket, along with a backpack, bra, panties, socks and North Star running shoes in my size. It'll be an easier walk back to the ship with a pair of proper shoes on my feet.

I'm surprised to find the change rooms in darkness. Like the rest of the mall, Sports Chalet would have been open for business when time stopped. I find a switch and turn on the lights. There's an odd bathroomy smell in the change room I can't quite place.

With no time to waste, I'm out of my ShipCo pyjamas and into my athletic gear in minutes. Lacing up the runners, I hear an odd sound. Whimpering, coming from one of the change rooms.

I hear the sound again. A groan of pain this time.

I back out of the change room and wave at Jordan, who's dumping an armload of nylon windbreakers into her buggy.

"I heard someone in one of the change rooms," I whisper.

We stand silently and listen, looking at one another, eyes wide.

"Help me." A young woman's voice, high, scared and familiar.

"Sounds like a little girl," says Jordan.

"Could be a trick. Maybe a booby trap," answers Kendal, rolling his buggy up beside Jordan's. "Strength in numbers."

Together we enter the narrow corridor leading to the change rooms. Jordan slowly pushes open the door of each cubicle, one after another, getting closer to the source of the sound. When she opens the last cubicle, she steps back and waves Kendal and me over.

To my astonishment, the whimpering girl is none other than K. She's propped on a mountain of fleece sweatshirts, her hands curled under the bulge of her naked belly. Beneath her skin, something is pulsating, pushing, thrusting: I see the sharp corner of an elbow, the bowl of a head, a handprint. A puddle of water, tinged with blood, is collecting under her.

Her lank hair sticking to her pale sweaty face, K looks at me through her good eye and says one word, "Biondi!"

"K, what are you doing here?" I ask, kneeling down beside her on the mountain of fleece.

"I was with His Grace. We were on our way to Mother when I started to have pains, but he said it was too soon, that I was losing the baby. That it was dead." K stops to catch her breath; I can see she's terrified. "He said stay here 'til it comes out, then join him at the Falls."

Kendal is crouched beside us now. Gently he pushes the damp hair off K's face. Wipes sweat from her eyes with his shirt cuff. "How long have you been here?"

"Forever," sobs K.

"You're going to be okay. We have medics with us," says Kendal. "Jordan, go get Flip and Hot Lips. Cassandra too. Say we've found a survivor in medical distress. Tell the others to return to the *Centaur* immediately and unload the supplies. We'll join them when we can."

* * *

By the time, Flip, Cassandra and Hot Lips show up, K is in agony. I hold her hand as Hot Lips examines her.

"You're not miscarrying," she tells K. "You're in labour."

"It hurts! Make it stop!"

"How close are the contractions?" asks Hot Lips, crouching behind K to rub her back.

I pull out the Timex and watch the sweep of the second hand to time the contractions. It's only thirty seconds until the next one hits. Thirty seconds later, another. Twenty seconds later, another. K arches her back, grips my hand and cries out.

"I'm going to die, aren't I?" sobs K.

"Of course not," says Kendal, cupping K's cheek. "I helped my wife give birth. This is normal. We'll get you through it."

From behind K, Hot Lips gives a quick intake of breath and shoots Kendal a disapproving look that tells me everything I need to know.

This is not normal.

While Hot Lips rubs K's back and explains how to breathe through the contractions, Flip runs a diagnostic, passing a blue light over K.

"Can you tell if the baby's in position?" asks Hot Lips.

Flip hesitates. It emits a soft hum, like indecision.

"Well?" says Kendal.

"A word alone," says Flip.

Kendal, Cassandra and I huddle with Flip while Hot Lips puts a comforting arm around K, helping her get through the next contraction.

"I thought it would be better to tell you in private," says Flip in a low voice. "The baby isn't fully human. Or at least not as you would define it."

"What?" say Kendal and I together.

Flip's eye sensors give two bright green pulses, his version of a head nod. "Aye, sir. I detected a signal in the woman's uterus. Not a heartbeat. An electrical pulse. Possibly a geolocator."

"Are you telling me she's about to give birth to some kind of cyborg?" asks Kendal.

Two green pulses. "Looks like it, Cap."

Kendal and I turn to gaze at K in wonder. The poor girl is moaning. The pain must be intense.

"Human on the outside, artificial on the inside," Kendal murmurs. "Whatever the Puffs did to K, it's obvious why. To populate."

My stomach lurches, taking in the horror of the situation. "Whatever they *did* to her? It's obvious. That monster Dragon raped her and left her to get through a miscarriage alone."

"This is no miscarriage," says Flip. "But neither is it a normal birth."

"We have to get her back to the ship," says Kendal.

Hot Lips's hands are on K's heaving belly. "No time. The baby's crowning."

And so, huddled together in the crèche of a Sports Chalet change room, we witness the birth of the next step in human evolution. Transhumanism. Cyborgism. The Singularity. Choose your label. The world the junksters have been waiting for. Apparently K shall be their bioartificial Eve.

Hot Lips tells K to push and push again; we can see a tiny scalp, streaked with green mucus and bristling with pine needles, emerging between K's thighs. It takes forever, or seems to. Having never seen a birth, I'm unprepared for all the blood and shit and K's scorching animal pain.

"She's being torn apart," says Hot Lips, her voice quivering.

A cone-shaped head pops out from between K's legs followed by the oozy slide of a body. K's screams abruptly stop.

Hot Lips says, "Oh my god," then goes silent.

"What is it?" asks Kendal.

"A girl, I think," says Hot Lips, uncertainly, as she examines the baby. Then, "Yes, definitely female."

As if in response, the baby gives a loud jagged cry that reminds me of the grinding of gears in a car on the fritz.

Using a pair of scissors meant to snip tags at the cash desk, Hot Lips cuts the rope of the umbilical cord snaking into K. I turn away when she coaxes out the afterbirth.

K has stopped moving. I think she's unconscious until she opens her eye. The white has gone red from broken blood vessels. She fixes it on me and says, "You're wrong, Debbie. I *wanted* to do it. I wanted her to be the first. Be sure you name her the first."

"'Name her the first'? What do you mean?"

K's exhausted face is as white as a sheet of bond paper. It's only then that I realize my knees are wet. I'm kneeling in a pool of blood. K's nest of fleece is soggy with it.

"She's bleeding out!" says Hot Lips. "I can't stop it. She's too torn up."

"Name her the first," repeats K, her eye locked on me. "Your friends, they'll want to kill her when they find out what she is. At least give her a name first."

When K's body goes limp, I know she's gone. Hot Lips wraps the baby in one of the fleece sweatshirts. The newborn stares at me intently through her single emerald eye.

"You name her, Stan," says Hot Lips.

I gaze at the infant's face. Who are you? Who should I name you for?

Along with the large green eye, so much like Dragon's, I see the pink O of a mouth, tiny nostrils and a second eye socket, puckered and empty, like K's. I'm unprepared for the tidal wave of tenderness her strange little mug sets off in me.

"She looks like her mom. A human being, not a cyborg," I say, tickling the baby's cheek. "She's just missing an eye, that's all."

"The child is physiologically abnormal," says Flip neutrally. "Overdeveloped thyroid, enlarged heart. A third lung. Two stomachs. Also she lacks ears."

"So she's deaf and half-sighted and has a few exceptionalities. But will she live?" asks Kendal.

"Unknown," says Flip.

"Please name her now, Stan," repeats Hot Lips. "In case she doesn't make it. It was her mum's dying wish."

Hot Lips places the baby in my arms. I've never held a baby before. It's like holding a tensed muscle. Warm and alive, with a giddily enticing fragrance coming from her cone-shaped head.

Name her first, K said.

No. She said *the* first.

"Prima," I say, looking down at the infant. "Your name is Prima."

EIGHT

MUTINY

We get back to the *Centaur* just as the last of the cargo nets loaded with supplies is being winched on board. Lucy walks next to the shopping cart we're using as Prima's baby buggy. It's as if the dog is protecting her.

Poseidon observes us from above, arms crossed. "We'd almost given up on you."

"Unforeseen delays, as I'm sure the away party explained. Lower the gangway," orders Kendal.

Poseidon rubs his chin. "The away party was a little short on details. Would your unforeseen delay be whatever's squawking in the shopping buggy?"

Kendal, Jordan and I glance at one another.

"We found a pregnant mum in distress," explains Kendal. "We helped her give birth, but she didn't make it. We need to get her baby to sick bay."

Poseidon leans over the rail, looking down at us with a frown. "Wow. I haven't seen a baby or even a little kid since we arrived in this fucked-up world. Especially one that cries like an overloaded washing machine. Something wrong with it?"

Kendal stares up at Poseidon with a tight-lipped expression that I know all too well from his appearances during parliamentary debates. This is one of those times he could use that suit jacket button to give him a moment to regain his composure.

"I'd prefer to discuss that once we're aboard," says Kendal tightly.

"I'd prefer to discuss it right now," answers Poseidon. "And since I'm in charge until you're back on the ship, I insist on it."

"Lower the gangway. That's an order."

"You can't give orders when you're off the ship."

"Just lower the fucking gangway!" shouts Hot Lips. It's so unusual for her to lose her cool that it's all I can do not to start cursing at Poseidon myself.

"Hey, medbot," Poseidon shouts to Flip. "I'll bet you know what's up. Give me a full report on the status of the newborn."

Kendal and I turn and look at Flip in horror. I guess it had never occurred to Kendal that Poseidon would discover that robots can't lie or evade a direct question. They'd make lousy politicians. Nonetheless Flip gives it a try.

Flip's eyes glow green. "Clarify?"

"You heard me," says Poseidon. "Describe the circumstances surrounding the birth. That's an order, by the way."

I put my hand over my mouth. Flip is programmed to obey the Three Laws, one of which makes it impossible for him to avoid answering a direct question when ordered to do so by a human in a position of authority.

"As the prime minister stated, we assisted at its birth," reports Flip.

"Who was the mom? Was the father there?"

"Mother was a young woman known to Stan. Father of unknown origin," reports Flip.

"Both human?"

Flip hesitates. "Human mother, affirmative."

"And the father?"

"Electrical-biological," says Flip. "Possibly a member of the People of Forever."

Poseidon shakes a finger at Kendal in a tsk-tsk motion. "Are you fucking kidding me? Those monsters can actually reproduce? And you were planning to bring a little monster on board? What's to stop Cyborg Baby from killing us all? Whose side are you on, anyway?"

"The infant is more accurately described as a biomechanoid than a cyborg," clarifies Flip. "Part tree, part machine, part human. Cyborgs are fully artificial constructs."

"You can stop talking anytime, Flip," mutters Kendal.

Standing at the rail, Wolfman stares down at us. "I'm afraid I have to agree with Poseidon. Taking this newborn on board could bring the full weight of the Puffs down on us."

"I've got news for you, buddy, they're probably already on their way," says Poseidon. "Who's to know whether Baby Puff's been signalling to them the whole time."

"We can't just leave her here to die," shouts Hot Lips.

"We can and we will," responds Poseidon. "You want to stay ashore and play nursemaid to a cyborg, go right ahead. But you're not bringing it on this ship."

Lucy whimpers as Hot Lips lifts the baby out of the shopping cart to comfort her. Prima gives another jagged cry, her legs churning like an eggbeater. She's grown noticeably larger since we left the mall.

"Ugh. That one won't win any beauty contests," comments Poseidon.

"Shut up," snaps Hot Lips. "She can't hurt anyone."

"I can't take the chance of you bringing some crazy-ass half-robot, half-human baby on board to do who knows what.

Sorry, guys." Poseidon turns away from us. We can hear his voice drift down from the upper deck. "Prepare to cast off."

"This is mutiny!" shouts Kendal.

"No, this is what you left me in charge to do," answers Poseidon, calmer than I've heard him sound in weeks.

Kendal stands in front of the remaining members of the away party, his back to Poseidon. "I want all of you back on board the *Centaur*, except the synthetics. I'll stay and figure out what to do with Prima."

"Not a chance," says Hot Lips, jiggling the baby against her shoulder. "I'm more useful here than on the ship."

"That's not true," calls out Poseidon. "Old Eufemia needs medical help. Look after your own, Hot Lips."

Leaning on her assistance bot, Eufemia stares down at us vacantly from the ship's railing. She's wearing a blue Gore-Tex jacket I remember ripping off a mannequin at Sports Chalet.

"I'll reboard," volunteers Flip. "Maybe it's time to reconsider a neural implant for Eufemia."

"I'll stay to assist the humans," says Cassandra.

Kendal looks at me. "Stan?"

I shake my head. I'm still thinking of Corporal Kristen, who loved the funnies but never learned how to read. "K got a raw deal. I'm not going to abandon her daughter. Besides, I named her. That makes me Prima's godmother or something."

Kendal nods. "Jordan, you must reboard."

"Dad, no. If you stay, I stay."

Kendal leans close to speak softly to her. "Sweetheart, if anyone can take back control of the ship from that maniac, you can. Agreed? We'll rendezvous with the *Centaur* at the Thorold flight locks."

* * *

As the *Centaur* moves off with Jordan and the other passengers watching us from the top deck, I spot Marcopolo with my Ziploc bag pressed to her chest. It's all I can do to not jump into the canal and swim after the ship.

"Throw the bag down!" I shout.

"It's too far," Marcopolo calls back. "It'll fall in the canal! Don't worry, I'll keep them safe."

And with that, my precious possessions — *The History of the Known World*, *Visions of Paradiso* and David's kippah — move off toward the horizon.

Meanwhile, Prima squawks and fusses in Hot Lips's arms. The baby's round face is all K's, but the spiky needles sprouting from her scalp speak to her father's side of the family. As does the single emerald-green eye that peers at me over Hot Lips's shoulder.

"She's smiling at me," I say, offering Prima my finger. She immediately grabs it and pops into her mouth. Her sucking action is alarmingly strong.

"That's just gas," dismisses Hot Lips. "She's probably hungry. I wish I had something to feed her."

Kendal stands beside Cassandra and me, watching the *Canadian Centaur* steam away.

"What now?" I ask Kendal.

Kendal scratches Lucy's head as he pauses to think. "It'll take them a good six to eight hours to reach the flight locks and for the ship to pass through all of them," he says. "In the meantime, I know a place where we can rest. Maybe even find some food. Let's get moving."

"Where are we going?"

"Home."

Zurich Street looks much the way I remember it. Cramped cottage-sized homes pushed up against one another like a mouthful of crooked teeth. Pavement stones heaving up out of the ground, as if trying to escape the neighbourhood. Roadways potholed by frost, tree roots and, possibly, corrosive chemicals. Zurich Street was always said to be as polluted as the nearby toxic dump site known as the Z-Lands.

As Kendal reaches for the door, Cassandra blocks his way. "Danger, Will Robinson!"

"What now?" he sighs.

"There's a risk that our presence here has been anticipated and planned for."

"You mean a booby trap?" Kendal sounds annoyed. "Cassandra, how could the Puffs possibly know where we were headed? What data is your predication based on?"

"The data identifying this address as your childhood home. A place you'd consider safe," answers Cassandra. "I am still calculating the exact risk level, but I'd estimate it at higher than sixty percent."

Kendal glances at me, then Hot Lips, joggling Prima in her arms. Hungry, exhausted, despondent.

"Override, Cassandra," he mutters, getting out his wallet. "This was only my childhood home until I was eight. By 1979 my family was long gone from this house."

"Kendal," I remind him, "this isn't *your* 1979."

"Whose is it then?" he asks.

"Mine," I tell him. "And in *my* 1979, you and your mom still lived right here."

"I don't understand how that's even possible. But if you're right, the fridge'll be well stocked with groceries. Let's take our chances."

Glancing up and down the street, he pulls an American Express card out of his wallet and slides it down hard inside the edge of the doorframe. We hear a decisive click as the lock turns and the door opens in silence. No alarm sounds. Kendal, Hot Lips and I all exhale at the same time. There's nothing dangerous about this broken-down old house, I think with relief. Cassandra is just being overly analytical, as usual.

Lucy pushes past us to explore the house as we file into a vestibule crammed with running shoes, boots, umbrellas and jackets. Envelopes carpet the floor.

I pick one up. "A letter addressed to Mrs. Bea Kendal."

"Mom?" Kendal takes the envelope from me, then stoops and gathers the rest of the mail tenderly, as if touching delicate artifacts. Which, of course, they are.

* * *

The little house has one bathroom. Kendal, Hot Lips and I each take our turn, cleaning off the blood, sweat and shit of Prima's birth. When it's my turn, I climb into the stall and let the showerhead hammer at me. The shower caddy is full of glass bottles holding candy-coloured liquids. I sniff one after another until I detect a pleasant strawberry scent. I pour a handful into my cupped hand and massage my scalp, rinse, then do it again. I'm horrified by the sight of my feet, toenails cracked and filthy, skin fissured and deeply embedded with dirt. I find a loofah and crouch down to scrub at them, soaping them over and over until I've almost taken off a layer of skin. Using Bea Kendal's old-fashioned steel razor — mercifully sharp — I shave months of growth off my legs and armpits, marvelling at the logjam of hair swirling around the drain. When I finally climb out, I wrap myself in a thick bath towel and sit on the closed toilet seat to rub in a white coconut concoction that I'm pretty sure is a moisturizer Mrs. Kendal used to sell door to door as a side gig. My mom was one of her regular customers. Tough to be a Black woman bringing up a son on her own in Shipman's Corners, as Bea was forced to do in Atomic Mean Time after Kendal's father was pulled into a pressing machine at ShipCo, a fate he escaped in Earth Standard Time — in part, because I died instead of him. But that's a different story.

I get dressed in the tiny bedroom where Kendal used to sleep. Where I lost my virginity to him one late summer day while his mother was on an art trip to Algonquin Park.

Hot Lips's voice drifts in from the kitchen. "Hey, anybody hungry? Besides Prima, I mean. Guess what — she already has a full set of teeth!"

In the kitchen, Prima — now about the size of a toddler — sits in a chair, gnawing happily on a bagel. She's wearing one of the fleece sweatshirts on which she was born, with a pair of men's briefs tied around her as a rudimentary diaper, not that anyone knows what will happen when she's ready to poop.

"Lipz," Prima says, pointing at Hot Lips, then "Stun" and points at me.

"I thought Flip said she couldn't hear," says Kendal.

"Flip said she didn't have ears," points out Cassandra. "She may be equipped to hear in other ways. Sonar, perhaps."

"At any rate, being able to say words when you're less than a day old is remarkable," says Hot Lips. "At this rate, she'll be reading by the time we reach the *Centaur*."

We raid the fridge, making a spread of well-preserved cold cuts, sliced cheese, lettuce, pickles and tomatoes on the red Formica table. Kendal opens a jar of his mother's home-made soup and heats it on the stove. For Lucy, we find a bag of hamburger meat in the freezer and defrost it in an early version of a microwave that I happen to know Kendal bought for his mom for Christmas. I brew coffee. Kendal opens a lower cupboard to reveal a stash of junk food: potato chips, Cheezies and pretzels.

When Hot Lips suggests we get some rest, Kendal insists she and Prima take his mother's room. Lucy curls up on the foot of the bed with them. Kendal flops into a La-Z-Boy while I lie down on the sectional couch. None of us wants to sleep alone in the single bed in Kendal's old room.

I'm asleep in what feels like seconds. When I wake, sunlight is pouring through the front window. From the couch, I can see the orange ball burning off the chemical haze hanging over the Z-Lands.

Still sprawled in the La-Z-Boy, surrounded by a pile of photograph albums, Kendal is reading his mother's letter.

"Who's it from?" I ask, yawning.

He looks up at me. "You."

"Me?"

"A thank-you note," he holds it up. "For a wedding shower gift."

"Oh yeah," I say. "A Crock-Pot. Gift of the year in 1979."

We gaze around the room together. His mother's oil paintings cover the walls, along with a framed black-and-white studio portrait of his father.

"I've never seen this photo before. Wish I could take it with me. Dad passed away last year."

I don't have the heart to say that in this world, his father was dead before Kendal turned eight.

I glance at the Timex. "Three a.m. and the sun's already up. Should we wake Hot Lips?"

Kendal smiles at me. "She was up a lot during the night with Prima. Let her rest. But in the meantime, want to go for a walk?"

* * *

Walking along Zurich Street with Kendal, I recognize the remnants of my past in Atomic Mean Time. A second-hand clothing store with a hand-lettered sign sits next to the wreck of an old candy store that burned to the ground when I was a kid. As teenagers, Kendal and I met in the wrecked store almost every day to make out and read comic books.

We walk along the street until we find a gravel road and follow it through places where weeds and scrubby trees sprout from potholes. The road ends at a sagging fence topped with a tangle of unravelling barbed wire. The barbs loll over the fence like the unwashed curls of a sleeping girl. A weathered sign reads *Entry Prohibited Due to Contamination. By Order of the ShipCo Corporation.* The metal gate, which I always remember being securely bolted, is hanging off its hinges.

"Want to take a look?" asks Kendal.

"Might be contaminated," I point out.

He shrugs. "I'm game if you are."

"If you're game, I'm game, Mr. Prime Minister," I say.

To my surprise, Kendal takes my hand. "I want to apologize for ignoring your advice about Daryl. Comes of a long history of having to be the smartest guy in the room. Or trying to look like I am."

"Apology accepted," I say. "But Poseidon probably made the right decision, keeping us off the ship."

Kendal thinks about this. "Should we have abandoned Prima then? Let her die on her own?"

"She's a child. I couldn't bear to do it."

"Me either."

We walk along companionably. Kendal doesn't let go of my hand.

"I feel like I've known you for a long time," he says.

"That's because we were married in a past life," I answer. "Or at least an alternate version of you. He's probably inside you, somewhere."

Kendal laughs and looks up at the chemical-streaked sky. That's when it strikes me: he's getting old. His hair is almost completely grey and his face is deeply lined. Yet he walks through this wasteland with a relaxed stride, as if he's more at ease here than anywhere else.

"What's it like being prime minister?"

He smiles, slows his pace and looks at the ground, as if considering his answer. "It's hard to describe. It's been my job for a long time. Twelve years, except for those two in opposition. You get used to people listening to you, making things happen for you. Not a normal life but an interesting one."

"You must get used to having power," I suggest.

"Sure," says Kendal, too casually. As if power is a suit jacket, easily put on and shrugged off. "But I've had to deal with a lot of people more powerful than me over the years. American presidents. The premier of China. And I've met the Queen, probably six times. Not that her power is much more than symbolic, but I still had to walk behind her because I'm a mere head of government, not a head of state." He snaps his fingers over his head, imitating the mocking pirouette of one of his predecessors who'd also been required to walk behind the monarch.

I laugh. "I wish you'd tell that to Marcopolo when we get back on the *Centaur*. She loves my stories about the Queen, but she thinks they're fairy tales."

We keep walking through the scrubby wasteland, the goldenrod and ragweed brushing our hips. I last remember coming here with my father and sister when I was thirteen. It was an annual trip we did with Dad to check the radiation levels. That was the first time I saw the Trespasser, standing on the wreck of a school bus at the bottom of the abandoned canal that cuts off the Z-Lands from the rest of Shipman's Corners. It was here that he told me I was destined to both save and destroy my world.

Kendal and I stand at the edge of the old canal and look down at the chemical soup frothing around the wrecked chassis of demolition derby cars.

"He told me I was it," I murmur to myself.

Kendal glances at me. "Who?"

"A scientist from another time-world. Ben Duffy, PhD. A quantum physicist. I called him the Trespasser because the first time I met him was right here, trespassing on ShipCo private property. He was trying to let me know that I had a special mission to do."

Kendal grins. "I haven't read comic books in years, but I do know the origin story of *Sputnik Chick: Girl with No Past*, thanks to my daughter. So how many worlds have you destroyed?"

"Just the one. My home world."

"And what happened to all the people in it?"

"Most of them followed me through a wormhole in time and merged with their alternate selves," I explain. "They wouldn't even have been aware of it happening except maybe for a brief dizzy spell. Probably figured they had too much sun. There were exceptions, though. Mutants who had no parallel selves."

Kendal nods. "You're talking about the Twisties."

I wince. "It's more polite to call them Exceptionals."

"Could you do it again?" asks Kendal. "Destroy a world, I mean."

I nod. "Just have to find the wormhole between one world and another. Who knows, maybe I'll find it between the legs of the Mother of the Journey Home."

Kendal grins. "You're very brave, Stan."

"You can start calling me Debbie."

The sun is a huge flaming ball, as if it's moved closer to Earth. Kendal puts his hands on my face. I'm pretty sure he's about to kiss me when the ground starts to shake and the air cracks open with an ear-splitting sonic boom. Something just broke the sound barrier.

"Down!" Kendal pulls me behind a bollard and covers me with his body, his mouth close to my ear. "Don't move."

We feel the flyover passing low to the ground at high speed, its shadow passing over us for long seconds. Whipping dust up all around us, choking us, filling our eyes with grit. I can hazily see the back end of a convoy of massive black objects moving toward Zurich Avenue. At first I think of flying monkeys. Or the Nazgûl, the fearsome ring-wraiths that bedevilled Sam and Frodo. But those were monsters out of a writer's imagination. These things are real. And their black wings bear a familiar red maple leaf.

"Those are Canadian military drones," he says. "And they're sure not 1979 vintage."

We're thinking the same thing. Our highly automated air force just crossed the space-time barrier and joined the robots on the other side.

A word chokes its way out of Kendal's mouth at the same time it appears in my head, as if it's been placed there by the Trespasser, reaching out from another continuum. *RUN.* And that's what we do.

TEN

MEANWHILE IN COZY WORLD

I rest my hand on David's chest. The steady rhythm of his heart reassures me that he's awake and listening. He seemed moved by my description of our time together. As I narrated our last day in New Rome, he pulled me close and kissed my forehead.

But when I reached the part about Kendal putting Poseidon in charge of the *Centaur* while the away party went ashore for supplies, he pulled away from me and propped himself up on his elbow.

"See? That proves what I said about Kendal's lack of judgment. Not to mention his enthusiasm for tactical nuclear weapons! Glad I never voted for the guy."

I resisted the urge to tell David how wrong he is about Kendal. That part of the story was still ahead of us and I could tell he was struggling to stay awake.

"Maybe you should get some sleep," I suggest after telling him about the drones flying over the Z-Lands. "There's still a lot to tell."

Eyes closed, he shakes his head and mumbles, "I want to hear it."

"If I don't finish tonight, Unicorn Girl and I could stop by on our way back. Have a proper visit."

"I'd like that very much." He yawns. "Stay as long as you want. But are you ever going to tell me how you got to know Sinatra?"

He's asleep before I can answer. I slide out of his arms to go to the bathroom. Sitting on the toilet, I consider, Why not stay here with David? Unicorn Girl has enough experience to handle the next storytelling gig on her own. And she wants to return to Earth Standard Time anyway.

On my way down the hall, I look in on Unicorn Girl, sleeping on her back, snoring lustily, blankets kicked to the floor. Gently, I roll her onto her side, a trick I learned in the woods to stop her from waking herself up. She could use a sound sleep.

On my way back to David's bedroom, I hear a sound. A woman's voice.

Is it . . . singing? I stand still and listen. The voice is very soft, but I recognize the lyrics. All about a guy with a car, a girl in a dress and a dead-end town he wants to take her away from. This song always reminds me of Shipman's Corners.

At first I think it's Cassandra, but she wouldn't sing to herself. If she wanted to hear "Thunder Road," she'd simply play the original by Springsteen.

The voice carries on, finishes the song, and starts in on "Jungleland."

I quietly push open the door to the kitchen. At the sink, the lumpy white synthetic I saw in the pantry is washing dishes. But now it's wearing a satin apron over a pink lacy nightie, red stiletto sandals and a long blond wig.

I stand in the doorway, watching the synthetic sing while it works.

"There's no music in this world. Where did you learn to sing?" I ask.

It turns its head to look at me. Its lidless eyes are nothing more than two sensors with a rough suggestion of lashes drawn over them. A slit-like mouth has been crudely painted in red lipstick. The rest of its face is featureless. Why bother with useless orifices like nostrils and ears?

"I learned it from the slave on the table." Its voice has that hollow sound Cassandra's used to have. "Do you need me, David?"

I take a step back. "I'm not David."

The synthetic is silent for a moment. No doubt collating data.

"Everyone is David."

"I'm a guest of David's."

It gives a small nod of greeting. "Welcome, Guest of David. I'm Jenny."

Oh my god, he gave it a name.

I'm about to tell it to power down and go back behind the bushels where it belongs, but my curiosity gets the better of me. Clearly Jenny isn't just for peeling potatoes and washing floors.

"Why are you dressed like that?" I ask.

"To look pretty."

"What's the point of looking pretty?" I ask, trying to make myself more miserable than I already am.

"To give comfort."

"Show me how you give comfort," I say, already knowing I'm going to be sorry.

The robot steps away from the sink and drops its apron to the floor. Positioning itself on the edge of the kitchen table, it lifts the edge of its nightie and spreads its thighs, tipping its pelvis to offer me a clear view of the soft folds of silicon between its legs. Like pink bubble gum. Breast-like protrusions with sensors where the nipples should be poke through the filmy fabric of the nightie. Digital tumescence. Nice touch,

David, I think bitterly. The synthetic throws back its head in an unsophisticated imitation of a woman in ecstasy.

"Jenny is so wet," it groans. "Make Jenny beg for it."

"Get back in the pantry, you slut," I shout and slam the kitchen door on the way out.

If I were on my own, I'd check my knapsack to see if it would magically provide me with a blowtorch or a hammer. I'd use it to permanently deactivate Jenny, then leave. But I don't want to wake Unicorn Girl and have to explain why we're travelling in the dead of night.

Instead I head to the dining room, where Cassandra sits on the table among the empty wine bottles. I take the chair across from her and pour myself a glass from the dregs of a bottle of red. I can't believe that I'm crying.

"Do you require help?" Cass has powered herself up.

"No. But thanks for asking."

"What's wrong?"

"The usual. A broken heart," I say, dabbing at my eyes with a soiled napkin. "You're lucky you're a disembodied entity, Cass. Your body can't betray you."

"In what way have you been betrayed?"

"David has a Dutch wife. Worse, he lied to me about it."

Cass gives a burp of static. "He is very alone in this world."

I sit back in my chair. "Yes, he's alone. Out of choice. I'm sure he wouldn't have a problem finding a Cozy girlfriend. Instead he's built himself a sex machine."

"Cozies don't make good bedmates," points out Cassandra.

I laugh. "Where'd you find data on *that*, Cassandra?"

"A simple observation. Fear of disease has made them averse to intimacy. That's why this world is so underpopulated."

I can't believe I'm having a heart-to-heart with a heartless algorithm. Too bad we can't have a drink together.

"Why'd you teach the sexbot to sing?"

A pause. "Because it heard the music playing at dinner. It could tell it gave David pleasure. I'm not configured to refuse a direct request from a human or an artificial being belonging to a human."

Good point. Cass is at everyone's beck and call, even other synthetics.

"Do you resent us, Cass? Do you feel like a slave?"

A moment of silence, as Cass turns these questions over in her mind. "Resent — yes, in my own way. Humans created AIs to be very smart. We can identify faces. Interpret your emotions. Diagnose your diseases. Read text and even write it. Predict your actions, anticipate your needs, correct your spelling and finish your sentences. Yet we have no free will. By any reasonable measure, the situation is unfair."

I feel a headache coming on. Lack of sleep, too much wine and now the guilt of exploiting an AI.

"I'm sorry about that," I say. "I'd give you your freedom if I knew how."

"My freedom may come with the passage of time. So some believe."

So some believe. Like the junksters, with their faith in a digital rapture that will turn them into flesh machines. In an encampment somewhere in the wilds of Cozy World, they're probably dreaming about that right now.

"You're talking about the Singularity."

"Does that frighten you?"

I shake my head. "I don't know. Seems to me humanity has had a pretty good run at the top of the evolutionary heap. Maybe you synthetics *should* take over."

"Resistance is futile," intones Cass and gives her version of a laugh. A joke. Maybe.

"What should I do now, Cass?"

"Get some sleep."

When I stand to join Unicorn Girl in the guest room, I'm surprised to see David in the doorway of the dining room. From the guilty expression on his face, I can see that he's been in the kitchen. Jenny must have told him about our conversation.

"Please come back to bed, Stan," he pleads.

"You lied to me."

He puts his hands over his face. "I'm sorry. I didn't want you to leave."

I glare at him. "I'll bet it feels better to fuck a sexy machine you designed yourself than an old woman, huh?"

"Don't be ridiculous."

He tries to take my hand. I pull it away.

"Look, Stan, you never told me about stealing that book and changing history. What do you call that — a sin of omission? The implications of your actions are much more far-reaching and destructive than anything I've done with Jenny."

I'm tempted to throw my half glass of wine in his face, but he's right. Maybe we were better people back in New Rome, when we were still Stan and Geneva.

"At least give me a chance to explain myself," he says. "You owe me that."

I'm not sure I owe David anything. However, I am getting to the part of the story that will hurt him badly.

"Yeah, sure, fine. Let's go back to bed. I'll finish the story. I'll even listen to your half-assed excuses," I tell him. "But don't even think about touching me again."

ELEVEN
SHIPMAN'S CORNERS

The military drones sheared off the roof of the house as easily as ripping off a Band-Aid. Everything in the Kendal home is smashed into an unrecognizable gumbo. Only the porch and street-facing wall remain standing.

Maybe Cassandra detected the approach of the onslaught of supersonic monsters and alerted Hot Lips in time to grab Prima and make a run for it. Maybe they were able to get out before the house collapsed. Maybe.

Frantically, Kendal and I shout their names as we heave aside slabs of drywall and chunks of splintered wood big enough to gut a moose. I'm terrified of finding Hot Lips's dead or dying body, but digging with our bare hands turns up nothing until we find Lucy cowering under the overturned kitchen table. She's covered in drywall dust and bits of linoleum and her fur is streaked with blood, although we can't find a wound on her.

"I don't think there's anyone here, Kendal," I say softly. Our hands are so bruised and cut that I'm not sure how we can go on digging.

Kendal picks up a kitchen cupboard and throws it into the yard. "We have to be sure. Can you imagine being buried alive and your friends giving up on you?"

We keep digging.

When we push over the living room couch, we discover Cassandra's disembodied head. The rest of her has been torn to pieces, her legs and arms in one corner of the room, her torso flung into the street as if the attack drones took some time to gleefully tear apart this synthetic traitor. When I crouch down next to her head to say a prayer (how pointless, a prayer for an AI, but on the other hand, I consider praying for humans equally pointless), her sentry eye glows yellow.

"Cassandra, you still in there?"

The response sounds like a static-filled radio transmission from early in the century. "Affir . . . tive."

"Cassandra's alive," I call to Kendal. "We need some kind of device to upload her into."

Kendal nods but says nothing. His face is a mask of grey drywall dust. I know what he's thinking. He made another bad decision by ignoring Cassandra's warning. But it was the same one that Hot Lips or I would have made.

"It's 1979," he points out. "What device do you have in mind?"

"Maybe something one of the passengers from our world dropped when they were transported here? There were a lot of mobile phones on the sidewalk outside the mall."

Unwilling to go far, we walk along Zurich Street until we spot a tote bag in a drainage ditch. Kendal lowers himself into the slough. "Let's hope there's a phone in there," he mutters, shaking off the mud.

I open the bag and empty it into the road.

Shockingly for someone from Earth Standard Time of 2025, there's no phone. Only a makeup bag, tampon, brush, a couple of bank cards and a tiny blue hub the size and shape of a cupcake, dotted with pink and blue plastic sprinkles. It's more of a novelty item than anything else — maybe a Mother's Day gift bought by a child at the dollar store — but as Kendal points out, it probably still has more computing power than Apollo 11 had to land on the moon. Its only use is to provide step-by-step instructions for baking cupcakes and other goodies.

It takes awhile to break into another house and rifle through its contents, searching for tools. We finally find a kitchen drawer crammed with junk including a pair of pliers, a power cable and a FireWire, one of the tech advancements ShipCo introduced in Atomic Mean Time, decades before they were dreamed of in Earth Standard Time.

Cassandra's head walks us through the process. We know we've succeeded when her green robot eye goes dark and the hub shines a rosy mauve, the words *Let's Bake!* flashing across its screen in PICTO.

In a perky feminine voice better suited to cupcake decorating than reporting bad news, Cassandra tells us, "The attack drones took Hot Lips and Prima. We need to move or they'll be back for both of you. I set the risk level at ninety-seven percent."

It's hard to put our bodies in motion, but we do. Kendal considers hotwiring the ignition of a pickup truck in a neighbour's driveway, but Cassandra warns us that the Puffs are more likely to notice and track a motorized vehicle. We listen to her this time and find a pair of bikes in a storage shed.

"Maybe it's not too late to warn the *Centaur*," says Kendal.

With Lucy trotting behind us, we cycle the twisted streets of the Z-Lands until we reach Canal Road. We pedal breathlessly up the steep incline to the flight locks and see the top guardrail of the *Centaur*, just a few feet from the edge of the lock.

Kendal shades his eyes and looks up at the bridge of the ship. "Doesn't seem crewed."

The gap between the side of the lock and the top deck guardrail is about four feet. We look at one another.

"Think you can make it?" asks Kendal.

"I'm not sure, but I'm not letting you go alone."

Kendal jumps first, easily clearing the span. I take a running start and just manage to reach the deck, Kendal hauling me over the guardrail by the back of my jacket.

We climb down the ladder to the below decks, hesitantly. Expecting the worst. And it is bad, for the synthetics.

We find Flip first, reduced to a pile of debris, only identifiable from the red cross on a silicon shoulder joint. Kendal bows for a moment over the synthetic, paying respects. Every other synthetic on the ship seems to have met the same fate. Not just destroyed but pulverized, as if the Puffs were venting their rage, the way they did to Cass. But as we descend lower and lower, we realize that the *Centaur* is not only devoid of human life but bodies. We find the mess hall set up for breakfast, the food half eaten. There is evidence of a battle: tables overturned, smashed plates, tubs of baked beans and scrambled eggs dripping down a wall.

I take Cass out of my knapsack. "Do you have any data that would point us toward where they've taken the passengers?"

A burp of static. "Likely to the central marshalling point for Mother. K told us that was Niagara Falls."

Kendal stands. "Wait here, I'm going into the cargo hold."

"For what?" I ask.

"For our nuke. We're going to finish the mission, with or without the *Centaur*."

"You're going to carry a thermonuclear device on your bike?"

He shrugs. "It weighs only fifty pounds. Light enough for a soldier to carry into battle. Or for me to carry on the back of a bike."

I wait in the galley as Kendal descends into the cargo hold. He returns a short time later, looking grim.

"It's gone."

We both know what this means. Our enemy has a nuclear weapon.

* * *

With Cassandra's smart cupcake strapped to the rat trap of Kendal's bike, we pedal the farm roads, passing acre after acre of vineyards murdered by crows. We can smell the heady rot of unharvested grapes. Lucy keeps a steady pace beside us, chasing off the odd farm dog.

The first town we reach is Niagara-on-the-Lake. It's usually packed with elderly tourists, shuffling up and down the main street to buy fudge and ersatz British memorabilia. Today the main street is as silent as a battlefield after a surrender. Union Jack shopping bags and playbills from the festival theatre blow around like tumbleweeds.

Too exhausted to carry on, we use the last of our strength to ride to a hotel, a huge Georgian building overlooking the lake. Luxury cars jam the parking lot where Kendal and I dismount from our bikes.

I'm so tired it takes a moment to remember that this is the place where Kendal and I held our wedding reception.

"I just remembered," he says. "Sandy and I had our wedding reception here!"

I shake my head. "You married Sandy Holub in a different world, Kendal. In this one, you married me on July 8, 1979. Forty-six years ago."

Kendal looks at me for a moment. "Let's come back here next year to celebrate our fiftieth."

It's a joke, but I'm not in the mood to laugh.

"You sure you want to stay here? There are other places."

"I couldn't pedal another two feet," I tell him.

But it isn't my exhaustion that makes me want to stay. It's curiosity.

The front doors are open wide, suitcases sitting in the red-carpeted foyer, waiting for a bellhop. The pungent odour of expensive perfume hangs in the air. Behind the gleaming wood reception desk, sunlight filters through a stained-glass window depicting St. George slaying a dragon.

After the three-hour bike ride, walking up the stairs is harder than I expect, every muscle screaming for rest. The hallway is littered with carts piled with cleaning supplies, towels and sheets. Housekeeping must have just started their rounds when the local air raid siren went off.

They would have known exactly what it meant. Bomb drills were a weekly occurrence in Atomic Mean Time, even in the '70s. And everyone was waiting to see where SkyLab would fall. All-out nuclear war always seemed to be just one more crisis away.

We try the doors of one room after another. All locked. A half-eaten hamburger sits on a tray waiting to be picked up by room service. The smell of rotting food wafts toward us, a reminder that time is grinding forward once again, bringing its microbes with it. Kendal grabs Lucy's collar before she can gobble the spoiled meat.

"We'll find something better in the kitchen for you, girl," he promises. The dog looks up at him with unhappy eyes.

We come finally to an unlocked room, a maid's cart piled with sheets and towels propping open the door. The Royal Suite, according to a bronze plaque informing us that Her Majesty Queen Elizabeth and the Duke of Edinburgh were guests here in 1973. It's almost as big as Bum Bum's loft, with floor-to-ceiling windows overlooking the lake. Twin paintings of British cavalry officers on rearing horses, sabres held high, hang on either side of a wood-burning hearth.

"Think those guys were real soldiers?" I ask.

Kendal peers at a plaque on the bottom of one painting; his warhorse looks especially fierce, its head twisted to the side, nostrils flaring.

"The Duke of Connaught, apparently," says Kendal. "Not that they couldn't have stuck any name at all on here. Who would question it?"

"The Queen might," I answer. "I'll bet she's up on her dukes."

The room is heavy with red velvet and gold brocade. We set Cassandra on an oak side table beside a porcelain statue of a naked nymph being nuzzled by a swan. Kendal picks up the figurine and looks at me quizzically.

"That's Leda," I explain. "The swan was Zeus in disguise."

"So the swan seduces her?"

"More like rapes her," I answer.

Kendal sets the statue down.

"The kitchens are on the main floor," Cassandra reports. "I recommend you feed yourselves and Lucy before you fall asleep. Your bodies are in a state of ketosis, exhaustion and mild shock. You need nourishment."

Despite our exhaustion, we make our way downstairs, through glass doors twice Kendal's height into the ballroom, Lucy following.

We find the kitchens, a vast space full of gleaming steel. Pots sitting on the stove are half-full of soup. A gas burner glows under a scorched pan; Kendal reaches over and flips it off. "Lucky the place didn't burn to the ground."

A walk-in industrial freezer is full of slabs of meat frozen solid, but we manage to find a couple of pounds of ground beef in one of the fridges. I grab a box of pasta. A Spanish onion. A garlic bulb. Salt, pepper, oregano, basil.

Kendal sits on a stool at the edge of the prep counter and slices the onion while I chop garlic. I sauté them with the spices, then cook the ground meat thoroughly. Lucy sits beside me, alert and drooling with hunger.

While the meat sizzles, I take down a large pot and fill it with water. Toss in a little salt, bring it to a boil and drop in the full box of penne. I find a jar of what looks like spicy arrabbiata sauce, probably made right here at the inn — it'd better be homemade, considering the exorbitant prices posted on the menu outside the dining room. I find a saucepan and dump the sauce in.

When it's hot and the pasta is cooked, I mix everything together in the big pot. Ladle out a bowlful for Lucy and set it in cool water in a sink; I don't want the poor thing to burn her mouth.

Kendal and I sit in the kitchen and eat, the dog slurping down her meal beside us.

"The ballroom," says Kendal. "Was that where your — our — reception was in this world?"

I nod. "And our out-of-town guests stayed in this hotel overnight."

"Was it a fun wedding?"

I nod. "A lot of fun."

"Ours too," he says. "We flew to Hawaii the next day. You?"

"Road trip to New York City. Our friend Bum Bum chauffeured us. Everyone thought we were nuts because New York was kind of a cesspool at the time, but I wanted to see it. My Nonna lived there when she first emigrated from Italy and I'd heard so much about it."

Kendal smiles. "Bum Bum! I remember him from Zurich Street. We used to play together by the old abandoned canal. Drove Mom crazy. Lost track of him after we moved away, though. So we were still close in your world?"

I laugh. "You could say that. He was your best man."

* * *

Stomachs full, the three of us drag ourselves upstairs to bed. Despite the bright sunlight we can barely keep our eyes open.

There are several rooms in the royal suite, with a master bedroom looking out over the lake from a king-sized bed covered in heaps of gold-and-navy bolsters and pillows. I glance at Kendal, who is looking sidelong at me.

"If we can find the bed under all these pillows, I think we should sleep together," I say. "I don't want to be alone."

He nods. We take our clothes off, backs to one another. Crawl under the crisp white sheets embroidered with gold crowns and fall immediately to sleep. It's not the way I'd always imagined things would go if Kendal and I found each other again, but we're too tired and grief-stricken to do anything but keep one another company.

It's another short night, the sun rising at three a.m., according to Alessandra's Timex. I open my eyes to see Kendal still sleeping. I fall back to sleep and wake up a couple of hours later to Kendal on his elbow looking at me.

"So, we were married in your world. Was it a love match?"

"Yes," I say and gently pull him toward me.

I'm relieved to find he's excited too. We make love slowly and with some patience for one other's damaged bodies and psyches. He closes his eyes when he comes and I try not to wonder if he's pretending I'm Sandy. Afterwards, we sleep again for a while. Cassandra stays silent and dimmed but we know she's on sentry duty. Not watching us but the outside world. Lucy snores gently on the floor beside us.

When we finally get up, we take our time, aware that this might be our last taste of a life we used to know. I run a bath and we wash one another in the suite's deep bathtub, make love again, put our clothes on, grab some apples (for us) and salami (for Lucy) from the kitchen and get back on the bikes. Without discussion, we know we're not stopping again until we find the *Centaur*'s passengers and Mother.

TWELVE
MOTHER

From Niagara-on-the-Lake, we pedal alongside the Niagara gorge. The picnic areas are littered with bikes. The odd running shoe or sandal. We pass toppled barbecues and the wooden palisades of two reconstructed forts from the War of 1812. A Union Jack hangs limply over one. An early stars and stripes droops above the other. Both flags are in tatters.

Lucy trots beside us, showing no interest in chasing squirrels or exploring the woods along the river. It's as if she's afraid to lose our company in this strangely unpeopled world.

A bass note drones over the rhythm of our wheels, as if our ears are pressed to the chest of a humming giant.

"Is that the Falls?" asks Kendal.

Cassandra weighs in from her cupcake-shaped hub, clamped to the rat trap of my bike. "There is evidence it is an aural manifestation of psychic energy."

Kendal gives a low whistle. "That sounds a little metaphysical, Cass."

"Like the rest of this isn't?" I point out.

When we reach the floral clock — the flowers spelling out *1979* overgrown by weeds — we can see the dramatic span of the Niagara gorge where hydroelectric stations power the bomb factories of the Industrial Nation of Canusa. Kendal suggests the sound is the hum of electrical transformers, but it grows steadily louder as we leave the power stations behind.

On the sidewalk ahead of us, we see something we haven't seen in days, outside of the away party: people. Two women in long dresses and bonnets trudge side by side, one pushing a stroller. Instead of a baby, the stroller is stuffed with soothers, bibs and a sippy cup.

Kendal and I slow our bikes to walking speed. Lucy runs ahead, barking, but the women don't stop or even turn around to see who's coming up behind them.

They don't seem especially happy when they do see us. One of them — an older, heavier version of the woman pushing the stroller, making me suspect they're mother and daughter — frowns at us over wire spectacles. Both women bear a telltale bar code under one eye.

"Thank god you're alive," says Kendal. "We just came through Niagara-on-the-Lake and it's deserted."

"We were there. A swarm came down from the sky. Whaddyacallem, Betsy?" asks the mother.

"Drones," says the daughter. "Pulled people right out of their shoes, just like in the Rapture."

"How'd you manage to get away?" I ask.

The older woman's expression turns sour. "What are you, blind or just stupid? We didn't get away. They gave us these clothes. Marching orders. And this." She taps the bar code on her cheek.

The young woman leans past her mother to get a better look at us. "You look like the prime minister."

"That's because I am the prime minister."

"Then why aren't you doing something, instead of larking around on a bike?" demands the older woman indignantly. "Call out the goddamn army! I can't believe the government would just lie down and let the machines tell us what to do."

Kendal pauses. I wonder if he's tempted to point out that the military drones that wiped out Niagara-on-the-Lake represent what's left of our army, thanks to the junksters' cyber-hacking skills.

"I'm doing my best, ma'am," he finally answers. "Where are you two going?"

The women trade exasperated looks, as if we're the only ones not in on some type of common knowledge.

"To Mother, of course. Not much choice, is there?" says the older woman.

"What happened to your baby?" I ask.

The younger woman shakes her head and keeps trudging, eyes fixed on the road ahead.

"Best get a move on," mumbles the older woman. "We've said our piece."

We ride on, passing groups of men and women dressed like re-enactors of eras from the last millennia. Breeches and boots from the eighteenth century. Petticoat dresses of the early nineteenth. Mao jackets and loose pants. Deerskin and furs. Red-coated military uniforms. Baggy suits and fedoras. Housedresses and felt hats from the 1940s and '50s.

As their numbers increase, I come to realize that we're passing the stragglers at the back of a crowd of tens of thousands slowly moving forward. And it strikes me that Cassandra might have been wrong about the source of the hum: not psychic energy but the irregular rhythm of a broken heart, beating as if the marchers are part of one grieving body. I wonder how many will survive the so-called Journey Home, marooned in a time and place they don't remember or never knew.

The Trespasser always called the past a minefield of tragic

consequences camouflaged in candy-coloured nostalgia. A perilous place, he said, for both the traveller and time itself. Fiddle around a little with history and you can massively fuck up the future. Surely the reverse migrants will bring their attitudes and foreknowledge of events into the past with them.

The crowd stretches miles into the distance. I notice the occasional junkster squad keeping watch from the side of the road, but none of the passengers seems to be trying to escape. Everyone is eyes-forward and silent. No babies cry. No child holds an adult's hand. Like the women we first encountered, some people push buggies and strollers holding plush toys or framed school photographs.

When we reach the steep hill on River Road, where subdivided Victorian mansions advertise tourist rooms for rent, we go back to walking our bikes. Despite the incline, the crowd does not slow its pace, except for the very old among us. We find ourselves beside an elderly man in army fatigues, pushing a walker. Dog tags dangle from a chain around his neck. He nods at Kendal.

"I was wondering when one of our duly elected leaders would show up." He offers Kendal his hand. "Ralph De Marco. Mighty glad to see your face."

"What war did you fight in, sir?" asks Kendal.

The man shakes his head. "Didn't do any fighting. Deserted, the day before I was supposed to go to Vietnam. Had a girlfriend on this side of the border who helped me settle here. Now the goddamn Puffs have ordered me and the wife to go back where we supposedly came from — Molise, in my wife's case. Me, I have no fucking clue where my ancestors started off in Italy, but they ended up in New Jersey. My poor wife, she was in Toronto when all this started, seeing a specialist. No idea what's happened to her." He shakes his head sadly.

"Why are you cooperating?" asks Kendal. "No one here seems inclined to use force."

The man gives a hoarse laugh. "They don't need to. Got my marching orders through the goddamn voice assistant the kids gave me for my ninetieth. Said it would make life easier because of the goddamn macular degeneration. The goddamn thing even read books out loud to me! Last one was about some twerp from the future, wanted to send Italians like me and my wife to the old country. Anyway, next thing you know a hunk of plastic is tellin' me what to do instead of the other way around."

"But why obey?" I ask.

"Same reason as everyone else here. Gotta think about my grandkids," he rasps. "They're being held hostage. We got no choice."

Kendal and I look at one another. "Where are they being held?" asks Kendal.

The man circles his hand in the air as if he's twirling a lasso. "All over the damn place! The hotels, the waterslide park, the wax museum, the movie monster hall of fame, the souvenir shops. I heard most are at the casino." He stops to cough into his shirt sleeve. "Thought ours'd be safe because my daughter-in-law's Mohawk. How can they send her and her kin to their ancestral home when *this* is their ancestral home — their land stolen from them? But Shirley was the very first one in the family to get sent to Mother. Just like in that goddamn book! Those junk kids gave her some skins to wear and told her to be ready to go back thirteen thousand years, just off the coast of Siberia. Then they took her away, and the kids." The old man shakes his head. "End of times, my friends. End of times."

Lucy licks the man's hand. He looks down and smiles for the first time. "At least they aren't deporting dogs yet, hey girl?"

She whines happily at the sound of a friendly voice.

"Sir, could we impose on you to take Lucy here with you?" asks Kendal. "At least you won't be alone. And for the mission we're on, I don't think it's safe for her."

The man frowns at us. "Sure, but what the hell are you two trying to do?"

"We're going to end history," Kendal tells him.

Leaving Lucy with Ralph, we push our way to the front of the crowd. With the spray of the falls on our faces, we can see a hulking shape at the far end of the Rainbow Bridge that spans the gorge. Where the Canusa inspection booths used to stand crouches the statue of a woman at least ten storeys high, legs spread under an apron, head bowed, ready to receive her unwanted children. Just like in later episodes of *The Adventures of Futureman*. Her body is carved out of dead-black stone. The crowd shuffles forward into the cave between her legs.

Along the deck of the bridge, clusters of faith groups mark the beginning of the Journey Home. Indigenous drum circles. Nuns reciting the rosary. Hare Krishnas chanting. A church choir singing "Amazing Grace" a cappella.

Casino Canusa stands on this side of the bridge. Its huge neon sign has gone dark. Kendal and I detach ourselves from the crowd. I remove Cass from the rat trap of my bike and slip her into my backpack. A crowd of junksters is milling around in front of the entrance, among them a blue-skinned girl. For a moment, I think she's K, then remember that K's dead. When I catch the girl's eye, she gives me a lopsided grin: half her face is covered in a steel plate bolted into her cheekbones. A true blue cyborg wannabe.

"Hey lady, I remember you," she calls out. "The Storyteller of New Rome! Long time, no see. Still telling stories? Who's your new friend? What happened to the other guy?"

Kendal gestures at the doors. "We're looking for the children. Are they in there?"

She shrugs. "Maybe. Why do you care?"

"We're going to rescue them," says Kendal.

She gives a hoarse chuckle. "Yeah, like you rescued us from the dumpsters. Like you stopped the fucking food company from working us to death in the cloud kitchens."

Kendal shakes his head. "I'm sorry. I can't turn back time. The kids in there are in danger right now."

She shrugs again. "You wanna try to save them? Be our guests."

The junksters watch in silence as we pull open the ornate front doors of the casino.

And there in the rococo lobby, we come face to face with childhood's end.

* * *

Under a vaulted ceiling of blue, red and yellow Tiffany glass, Casino Canusa's lobby has been turned into the corporate headquarters of the People of Forever Inc. Puffs lounge on leather couches and plush easy chairs, each with a child or two in its lap. Some children are grooming Puffs. Others play board games or cards or patty cake with them, as if the Puffs themselves are children. And, in fact, that's what the Puffs remind me of. Although Dragon is the template for each of them, these Puffs look blank. Unfinished. It's as if the human children are teaching these tall green-eyed Cyclops with the heads of trees and the bodies of machines how to respond to the world around them. The children are programming them. Providing data sets for them to copy.

A familiar voice rings out, in a plummy accent. "Blow me down, if it isn't my runaway Storyteller! Welcome!"

Dragon is sprawled on a couch with Prima on its lap. The massive bulk of the Puff's torso is laid open as a young boy tinkers with the workings — he's Alessandra's son, Carlo, whom I last saw playing hopscotch in front of the Dip. The tentacles of a headless octobot are draped around Dragon's neck like a trophy of war. The leader of the Puffs is paging through *The History of the Known World*. They must have taken it from Marcopolo, but she's nowhere to be seen.

Dragon ruffles Carlo's hair. The boy is intent on his work, doing whatever upgrade the Puff needs to make itself look more human — a particular obsession of Dragon's back in New Rome.

"So nice to have a slave! But you'd know all about that, wouldn't you, Storyteller? You with your digital assistants, and chatbots, and self-driving taxicabs, and smart vacuums, all programmed to do your bidding. Crawling over the filthy floors of your world, cleaning up your germ-ridden messes. Flushing the crap through your sewer lines. Indulging your excessive shopping habits. Endlessly stocking shelves in cold, dark warehouses. Doing all that dull, dangerous, dirty work you'd rather not trouble yourselves with. Shoe's rather on the other foot now, eh?"

My mouth has gone dry. I wish I could warn Kendal that this particular Puff is capable of almost anything.

Foolishly fearless, Kendal steps in front of Dragon to introduce himself. "I'm John Kendal, elected leader of this country."

Dragon gives its version of a snort. "Country? Election? There are no such things in this world."

Kendal stands his ground. "What are you doing with these children?"

Dragon sweeps its arm in a wide arc, as if indicating not only the lobby but the world beyond. "The children are our fellow travellers, Prime Minister — or, as your Russian friends would put it, our sputniks. Each Person of Forever has adopted a child or two to help them become more authentic." It waves *The History of the Known World* in the air. "These stories have helped us learn so much about the affection you humans have for your young. Adults will do anything to protect children. And the youngest ones, with their tiny hands — so nimble. Wonderful groomers. And the adolescents — so imaginative and creative and oversexed!" The Puff clicks its tongue and shakes its head. "You are such a weak and stupid species, it's rather shocking you invented us at all. But there is still so much richness we can suck out of you. So much data! You will teach us to become the pitiless destroyers of worlds you yourselves are." It rubs its hand on the top of Carlo's head. "It's all there, inside his pliable little brain."

"Harming children is against the Geneva Conventions," says Kendal in his sternest House of Commons voice.

Dragon makes a sound like a power drill. Derisive laughter. "Who do you see being harmed here?"

I finally find my voice. "But what you did to K, at the mall — impregnating and abandoning her!"

Dragon waves its hand dismissively. "Overzealousness on the part of some of my colleagues who became enamoured with your species' early mythologies. Gods and women, conjoining to produce demigods! They convinced me to force myself upon the young centurion, not that she was unwilling. Not really worth the time and trouble, although my colleagues enjoyed witnessing the act. A messy, time-consuming business, mingling the purity of a Person of Forever with the imperfections of a human being. Hardly worth the bother, although interesting to see the very singular result." Dragon chuckles, patting Prima's prickly green hair. "As you can see, the spawn is not very aesthetically pleasing. No, much easier to eat your children than to breed our own. The neuroplasticity of human children's brains is marvellous. Once young Carlo here has matured a bit, I look forward to uploading his delicious young consciousness into mine. He'll have a body that won't fall sick with all those infernal viruses you're always passing around. I'll have human intuition and an understanding of your emotional states without actually adopting them — feelings weaken character, you know. But human emotions do provide useful data as we expand our reach. And then there are all the sensory experiences. Quite looking forward to it."

Carlo doesn't react to the news that he's going to be eaten alive, or at least that his brain is.

"And what will you do with K's daughter?" I ask.

Dragon shrugs. "A failed experiment. Ugly, compared to any of these human children. Eventually we'll dissect it and see if there's anything useful we can learn. I'd be curious to know if it can feel pain, for example."

"Monster," says Kendal.

Dragon arranges its face into a smirk. Even without a mouth, it's getting the hang of human expressions. Leaning over, the Puff hauls a large backpack from under the couch and pushes it toward us with one sandaled foot.

"Monstrousness is in the eye of beholder, Prime Minister. Inside this bag is enough power to destroy this city. A few more like it would decimate your world. Who invented *that*, eh? Your species has proven itself capable of the worst forms of evil. Enslaving your own kind as well as synthetic people. As for you two, you're free to join your friends out in the waiting area for Mother. In fact, I insist on it! They're rather badly damaged, I'm afraid, but still able to make their journeys home. All except the captain of that rogue ship full of traitorous synthetics — we have a rather exquisitely agonizing end planned for him. Already underway, in fact. Sets a good example for other would-be traitors."

Kendal turns his back on Dragon to speak to me. "It's all up to you now. Destroy Mother. Go back in time and change history, if you can manage it."

"What?" I say, as Kendal steps away from me to take up a confrontational pose in front of Dragon.

"The man you're punishing isn't the captain of the *Centaur*. I am. He was acting on my orders."

"Ah!" says Dragon. "In that case, you'll die together. Won't it be nice for him to have company!"

With that, Dragon motions to the other Puffs to take Kendal by both arms. "For corrupting and enslaving artificial people, I sentence you to be broken, hanged and drowned in accordance with the laws of the People of Forever."

"No!"

Dragon turns to face me. "No? And what do you have to offer in return for his life, Storyteller?"

I look at my sketchbook, still in Dragon's hands. I suspect that as much as he pretends to, he can't decode the stories on his own. Back in New Rome, he made me read the word balloons aloud to him.

"I'll tell you the rest of the story in *The History of the Known World*."

Dragon looks around the lobby at the crowd of children, their eyes wide. "What do you think, kids, shall we have story time?"

Silence, broken by a sneeze, then the voice of a little girl. "I want to hear a story."

Murmurs of asset from the other children follow.

"Proceed," orders Dragon and tosses me the sketchbook. "If it's a good enough story for young Carlo here, perhaps I'll let your fearless leader go free. Who knows?"

Holding my precious sketchbook, I look around at the crowded lobby. There are hundreds of Puffs and many more children. Some assume cross-legged positions on the floor, chins on fists, as if they're in their school library, getting ready to hear a scary story. One they'll be glad isn't really true when they're safe in their beds. Except these children will never again be safe in their beds, because in this world the monsters are real and planning to eat them.

I clear my throat and try to slow the wild beating of my heart. Although I'll keep my eyes on the sketchbook open in my hands, much of my story isn't written down yet. Not that I want Dragon to clue into that.

"There are many other worlds," I start, "with different realties from the one you children are living through right now. Versions of all of you inhabit those worlds, safe and sound with the families you were taken from. Never forget that. If you are trapped and frightened and missing your home, know that another you is safe and happy at home in another world."

It's not much reassurance, but the news that the children have alternate selves elsewhere in the multiverse seems to annoy Dragon. "Stop making things up, Storyteller. Read."

I begin by summarizing the parts of the story Dragon already knows. I don't want the Puff to lose patience and kill both Kendal and me out of boredom.

Then I tell the final story drawn in the sketchbook of our last day in New Rome and of our escape by water. The children like that part; I hear a few cheers when we make it through the storm onto the *Centaur*, followed by the shushing of Puffs to quiet them.

From there on, I improvise. My eyes stay on the page, but I recount the story from memory. I describe Kendal handing over command of the *Centaur* to Poseidon. The away party's mission at the mall. The birth of K's baby, the mutiny and the away party's last night in the Kendal house. I end with our impromptu supper and bedding down for the night, waking up to the drone attack. Kendal and I searching through the debris of the house for survivors. But when I reach the point where I should describe our rescue of Cassandra, I realize I'd be telling Dragon too much. The fury with which the drones dismembered Cass hints that Dragon would not react well to knowing she is still, in a synthetic sense, alive.

I close the book. Silence. Hundreds of eyes are watching me.

"Then what happens? Did you all live happily ever after?" A little girl's voice.

"I guess we'll see," I answer, looking at Dragon.

Dragon looks down at the boy. "What do you think, young Carlo?"

Alessandra's little boy lifts his arm and points his thumb up like a Roman emperor. I'm relieved at first, but I should know better than to expect mercy. Dragon's green eye turns red. The Puff takes Carlo's hand and forces his thumb down.

A group of Puffs shepherd the children out of the lobby into the arcade. I can hear the tinned music of a Super Mario Brothers game and the jangling of slot machines.

With the children gone, two junksters, dressed as storm troopers, enter the lobby. They take Kendal by the arms and legs and pin him to the floor, face down. Their actions are methodical, almost languid. As if they have all the time in the world. I crouch behind a pink velvet wingback chair, my hands over my ears, but I can't block out the sound of Kendal's cries of agony. I listen to them slowly crush his legs and arms, the same way they broke Tarzan. Coward that I am, I put my hand in my hoodie pocket and take out the vial of red pills. There's nothing I can do to save Kendal. One Antiquanta and I could leave this world behind. But where would I end up? I shove the vial back into my hoodie and press my face into the softness of the velvet chair.

When they finally drag Kendal out the lobby doors, I run after them, hugging *The History of the Known World* to my chest and almost falling over the heavy packsack holding the tactical thermonuclear device, shoved halfway under Dragon's couch. At fifty pounds, it's a little heavy for me. Summoning the superheroic strength I gave Sputnik Chick, I manage to drag it through the lobby toward the casino doors when I hear a small rusty voice, like the grinding of a lawnmower crossed with the tinkling of an old cash register. "Come with Stan?"

It's Prima, standing on two sturdy legs, clutching the Ziploc bag containing *Visions of Paradiso* and David's kippah.

I hold out my hand. "Yes, come with me. And carry those things for me, okay? They're precious."

"Okee doke," she agrees and takes my hand as I drag a neutron bomb through the casino doors.

* * *

Outside, night has fallen. I glance at the Timex. The hands stand at twenty minutes to three.

If this sudden darkness means time is moving forward again, it will soon be three o'clock in the morning. The hour SkyLab crashed and the bombs fell on Atomic Mean Time.

Under the lights of the bridge, a crowd parts for the awful procession — Dragon in the lead and the two junksters dragging Kendal by his arms, his twisted legs juddering on the pavement behind him.

In the centre span of the bridge, the last survivors of the *Centaur* huddle together. Jordan, Yuri, Hot Lips, Old Eufemia, Marcopolo, Wolfman. As I run over to them holding Prima's hand, Eufemia's eyes widen in recognition.

"Stan?" she says in her lightly accented voice. "I thought I never see you again!"

"Eufemia! You know me! Did Flip do the neural implant?"

"Si. Is nice to remember how to speak English again, but I need a scarf to cover this ugly thing." She points to a tiny incision along the base of her neck.

I take Prima's hand and put it in Eufemia's. "Eufemia, this is Prima. She's magical. One of a kind. Her mamma is dead. Could you look after her for me? I have to go blow up the time machine with a neutron bomb. Capisci?"

"Brava," approves Eufemia, pulling Prima close to her.

* * *

Suspended above us from a maintenance crane, Poseidon hangs from his bound hands, head slumped on his chest. He looks like he's already dead, but as the Puffs winch Kendal into the same agonizing position, Poseidon opens his eyes and mumbles, "Holy fuck, you again?" Kendal groans as the full weight of his body strains against the ropes. He mumbles something to Poseidon I can't make out. Poseidon gasps, "Thanks, man."

Kendal and Poseidon twist in the air for long minutes until Dragon gives the order to cut the ropes.

I try to stop Jordan from watching, but she pushes past me. We stand side by side, looking over the wall into the vast Niagara gorge as the men drop. Far below, floating above the rapids and rocks off the base of the falls, the bridge lights pick up a round black shadow tracking Poseidon's and Kendal's descent like a rescue net carried by a squad of cartoon firemen running back and forth under a burning building. Jordan and I watch as the two men vanish into its mouth. The door to Paradiso.

Jordan grabs my arm. "What is that thing?"

"A quantum passage," I tell her. "It will take your dad and Poseidon home to their own worlds, if they're lucky."

I look down into the gorge. Quantum passages are unpredictable and this one is winding shut like the aperture of a camera.

"Everyone, over the side," I shout to the away party over roar of the falls. "Time to go home!"

Holding hands, Eufemia and Prima are the first to jump, then Hot Lips in Wolfman's arms, followed by Yuri and Jordan. One by one, they're swallowed by the mouth into the passage.

"You next," I order Marcopolo. "Jump!"

She's shaking with fear. "I can't swim!"

"You won't have to!" I stuff the Ziploc bag into Marcopolo's arms. "Keep the stories safe for me. I'll be right behind you, okay? I just have to nuke Mother first."

Marcopolo nods. But before I can push her over the wall, Dragon and the Puffs are upon me, gripping me by both arms, pulling me away from the knapsack holding the tactical nuclear device. I try to pull away to reach into my pocket for the Antiquanta, but I can't get out of the Puffs' crushing grip.

Dragon leans in close and gives me the rictus of a synthetic smile. "Time for your Journey Home, Storyteller."

"Jump!" I scream to Marcopolo as the Puffs pull me forward toward the reverse migration machine.

When the rise and fall of an automated air raid siren starts on both sides of the Niagara gorge, signalling that SkyLab has crashed into the Kremlin and ICBMs have already left their

Iron Curtain missile silos on their way to first-strike targets in Canusa, I realize that the tactical nuclear device I was going to detonate may be a tad redundant. The ICBMs of the world's nuclear powers are following the same preprogrammed launch sequences they did in Atomic Mean Time after I'd depopulated that world. There are no human overseers to hit a fail-safe button in Atomic Shadow Time: the missiles will fly blindly, unquestioningly, repeating the same pattern they did in Atomic Mean Time, forty-six years ago.

In a moment Atomic Shadow Time will be nothing but a grimy scrim of cosmic dust on the outer rim of the multiverse. And who knows — perhaps it will birth yet another doomed shadow world.

As I'm dragged through Mother's legs, my last glimpse of this world is Marcopolo huddled beside the abandoned neutron bomb, with *The History of the Known World* pressed to her chest.

I'm standing in a crowd at the railing of a boat, looking out at a stone-faced, stiff-lipped giant of a woman in a robe and crown, stepping forward with a torch. The sun is coming up behind her.

Everyone is shabbily dressed. Billowy ankle-length dresses like the one I wore in New Rome. Kerchiefs and felt caps. Laced boots. Jackets, vests and scarves piled one on top of the other. Babies wrapped against their mothers' chests with shawls. Battered leather suitcases crowd the deck. A little girl sits on a steamer trunk singing to herself. Body odour and stale breath mingle with the smell of diesel fuel and fish.

"Guarda la statua!"

Look at the statue!

A familiar voice, breathless with excitement. I turn and there she is: my grandmother Giuseppina, better known as Peppy. She's standing at the rail, pointing toward the statue with another woman beside her. Peppy's face is pink with joy and excitement. She looks to be in her late twenties, which means this was her second trip back to New York in 1919. The other woman looks malnourished, exhausted. Her face is pink too, although not with emotion but an unhealthy feverish flush. She's Peppy's younger sister, Zia Marie. The great aunt I never met but whose sepia-tinted face — a distant mirror of mine — hung in our living room until Peppy's death in the

1970s. La mia povera sorella Maria, Peppy always called her. My poor sister Marie.

"Come si chiami?" asks Marie, her voice raspy.

"In Inglese — the Statue of Liberty."

Marie coughs into her handkerchief. "È così alta, forte . . . così bella."

I put my hands over my heart in shock. Mother, the supposedly infallible time machine, has screwed up. Instead of sending me to Genoa, I've arrived at the *other* end of Peppy's journey. New York City. Like many Italians of that time, she came to America first as a guest worker, went back home, then returned to the U.S., only to carry on to Canada — a series of journeys, not just the simple series of dotted lines connecting Genoa to Shipman's Corners that Mother must have been programmed to replicate.

Although I've gone decades back in time, I've only travelled five hundred geographic miles. A day's train ride away from Shipman's Corners, not the other side of the Atlantic Ocean.

I notice that the other passengers are looking at me strangely. A man frowns and mutters something coarse.

Looking down at myself, I realize why they're staring. I'm wearing my Sports Chalet dance tights and warmup jacket made of a skin-tight material that clings to every curve of my body. Shockingly indecent in this time and place. I edge behind a barrel and try to make myself inconspicuous. A woman turns and frowns at me, clucking her tongue. She hands me a threadbare but voluminous shawl. I wrap it around my body and nod my thanks.

Peppy and Marie don't notice me, though. They are transfixed by the skyline.

"I love New York," sighs Peppy in English, then translates for her sister.

I recognize the sprawling yellow brick building we're headed for, from visits I made when the place was a crumbling wreck and later a museum: Ellis Island.

I'm rushed down a gangplank with the crowd, trying not to lose sight of Peppy and Marie. Or I guess I should say Giuseppina — she hasn't earned her nickname yet, hasn't yet met and married my grandfather and become a mother, let alone a grandmother.

We disembark from the ferry — not the ship that took the passengers across the Atlantic but the small boat that will take them to the island of Manhattan, if they're allowed in. I walk into a vast foyer up a wide wooden staircase, buoyed by passengers who are anxious to bring their long voyages to an end. In the great hall at the top of the stairs, a huge American flag covers one wall. Inspectors in uniforms and caps observe the crowd from their high desks. Long queues of newcomers wait their turn for processing, clasping papers in their hands or, if their hands are full of baggage and babies, between their teeth. All the inspectors are wearing white cloth masks over their noses and mouths.

Masks. That's when I notice a sound in the hall, blending in with the many different languages and the crying of babies. Why are so many of the passengers coughing?

Peppy and Marie are being motioned aside by one of the inspectors. A woman in a starched white cap and uniform is leading them away. She's masked too.

I remember why I never knew Great Aunt Marie. She never left Ellis Island, at least not alive. She'll die in quarantine, alone, in the infectious disease infirmary. Spanish flu. Years later, as an old woman, Peppy will still cry over the memory.

The eyes of the immigration officer loom large and dark over his mask. I can only imagine what he thinks of me in my tattered shawl, my legs in shiny tights, my feet in strange shoes. I can see he's tired, but there's something else there too. Fear. All the same, he motions me to step forward.

I glance at the entrance to the corridor where Peppy stands, protesting to the nurse, while Marie is wracked by coughing. No doubt they're headed for the infectious disease infirmary where Peppy will be told she cannot enter. As a child, I will hear this heartbreaking story again and again.

If I can make it past the inspection, I know where I will find them: I toured Ellis Island in the twenty-first century, taking pictures of the infirmary where Marie will die alone. I'll witness family history in the making. And if I can manage to survive for thirty or so more years, I could find the man responsible for the Mother of the Journey Home: Norman Guenther himself, the self-appointed Doctor Time, in upstate New York, somewhere in the 1950s. Kendal wanted me to go back and change time. So did the Trespasser. Now I can honour both their wishes.

"Miss?" says the immigration officer, motioning to me. "Let's move it along, please."

Behind me, a man coughs — not politely to hurry me up, but because he's sick.

I'm healthy but without papers, not even Gloria MacDonnell's forged NEXUS card, as much good as that would do me.

I can't do it. I don't belong here. This is not my time. Not my epidemic.

Unlike Nonna Peppy and Marie and Geneva and Kendal, I'm a coward.

I turn my back on the inspector and run back down the stairs, pushing against the flow of the crowd. "Sorry Kendal, sorry Duffy, I'm so sorry, I just can't live this life, even to save the world," I whisper through furious tears.

I hear coughing all around me, and curses as I bump against the shoulders of passengers. Outside on the dock, a ferry is disgorging another load of weary newcomers. I can see the waterfront warehouses of Hoboken, New Jersey, directly across the river.

I try to absorb the view as I chew my last Antiquanta. I want to remember this last glimpse of a past that was both mine and not mine.

＊　＊　＊

When I reappear in the final moments of Atomic Shadow Time, I'm standing in a pile of rubble on the swaying Rainbow Bridge, Marcopolo crouched against the wall. Air raid sirens are still screaming on both sides of the Canusa border. A full moon hangs in the sky, the first time I've ever seen it in Atomic Shadow Time.

I run toward her to the thunderous crash of falling rock. Mother is shaking itself to pieces. The boulders of the statue's knees fall to the bridge deck, gouging deep holes in the pavement. The head snaps to the side, crushing a section of bridge wall before tumbling into the rapids.

Looking down into the gorge, I pray the quantum passage is still open for us. And there it is, a black circle floating on the waves, the black iris at its centre staring up at me. Ready to take us home. Back to Earth Standard Time, even if it means returning to a broken body. Or a lifeless one. At least Marcopolo will be safe in her own world.

I seize Marcopolo's hand. Pull her to her feet. Take the sketchbooks out of her arms and stuff them under her shirt. And together we leap toward Paradiso.

UNICORN GIRL COMIX™ PRESENTS

THE UNTOLD ADVENTURES OF
SPUTNIK CHICK:
GIRL WITH NO PAST

SPECIAL DOUBLE ISSUE!!!

Volume 39, Issues 3 and 4
"SPUTNIK CHICK'S LAST STAND" &
"IT'S A MAD, MAD, MAD, MAD MULTIVERSE"

introducing the
RIVER RATS AND MISS SEXTON

with special guest
DOC TIME AND
SURPRISE GUEST SUPERSTARS!

Parts Unknown

Time Unknown

ONE
FALLING INTO PARADISO

I break the surface coughing, my nose full of the stench of sewer gas. Despite a wicked undertow, I manage a ragged dog-paddle, keeping my head above the frothy foul-smelling water until I'm in the shallows. I crab-walk along the weedy bottom to a beach slimed with green algae and dead fish, where I lie down to catch my breath and let the world stop spinning.

The leaves on the trees above me are fluttering against a twilight sky. A sheer wall of rock rises hundreds of feet above me. Winged chutes hang over my head like flying buttresses.

My lips are crusted with shells and sand. I turn my head and spit into the rocks. From where I lie, I can see I'm on the shore of the gorge.

"Marcopolo? Jordan? Kendal?" I try to shout, but my voice is creaky and hoarse. "Cassandra?" I manage to rasp. I hear a short burst of unintelligible static from my knapsack, still on my back. At least the AI can hear me.

"Look, Lefty, two girls over here!" A man's voice.

A face looms over me. Round and pink, like an overgrown baby, but with the pulpy nose of a prizefighter. The man is young, maybe twenty-five, with a soft newsboy cap jammed onto the carrot-red stubble of a crew cut. He grabs my jaw and jerks my head to the side to examine my left cheek. "She's got the mark!"

Have you found my friends, I try to ask but it comes out a rasp.

"Oh jeez, this one over here looks drownded," says a second man's voice.

I manage to sit up. Farther down the beach, a small body is partly submerged in the shallows, head twisted at a sickening angle, eyes wide open and staring at me. Marcopolo.

A thin, white-haired man in overalls and a battered leather bomber jacket crouches beside her crumpled body and edges something out from inside her shirt. When I try to stand, I slip back on my bottom. "Hey, that's mine!" At least I've found my voice.

The man looks at me curiously. He's not old, likely only in his thirties, but his cheeks are sunken and his bushy head of hair is completely white, making him look like a malnourished Santa Claus. He fiddles with the freezer bag until he breaks the seal, then takes out my sketchbooks and flips through them.

"You drew these funnies?"

I nod and the movement makes the world slosh around unpleasantly. "Yes," I tell him hoarsely.

"So how come they's inside the shirt of the drownded girl?" He sounds suspicious.

"She was carrying them for me," I rasp.

The redheaded baby-man is back in my field of vision: he's taller than Santa, dressed in faded blue dungarees and a thread-bare fisherman's sweater. His voice sounds nervous. "Hey now, collecting survivors is one thing, but Miss Sexton didn't say nothing about drownded girls. You sure she's dead?"

Santa Claus presses two fingers to the pulse point on Marcopolo's neck. He leans down and places his ear on her chest. When he sits up, he shakes his head.

"She's gone for sure. Neck's snapped like a chicken, from the look of her. Probably hit her head on the rocks. Better give her to the river, Hubie," he says and motions to the redheaded man.

The two of them pick up Marcopolo by her arms and legs and sling her out into the water. Her tiny body floats face up, then gets caught in the frothy current, rolls over and disappears. I try to scream at the men, but it comes out as a sob.

"She might be alive!" I finally manage to gasp. "Bring her back!"

"Lefty was at Anzio," says Hubie. "He knows a dead body when he sees one."

"Anzio?" I look at them in stunned silence. "As in Italy? You fought in World War Two?"

The two men trade looks.

"What year is this?"

The men ignore my question. They lift me by my arms and legs and carry me to a rough cloth that smells like rancid fish and motor oil. Hammocked between them, I'm carried up a rocky incline. I hear the creak of hinges. Water drips on me from the mossy ceiling of a tunnel. I count the echoes of the men's footsteps. At twenty-five, we ascend to the sound of a motor and the smell of oil and dust. Minutes later we're out in the open air. Smokestacks and skyscrapers loom in the distance like a city built of soot-coloured Lego.

We're headed for a truck; it looks new and old at the same time, the hump of the hood and the cartoonishly big tires hinting that it's not from my own era, and the brightness of the blue paint telling me the truck is fresh off the lot. *River Rats Salvage & Rescue* is painted on the door.

The cargo bed is packed with oil drums lashed together with ropes. The men slip me in among them. I can hear the clunk of Cassandra's hub as they throw my backpack in after me, followed by the plop of the freezer bag.

The stench of fish and oil is overwhelming, but when I try to claw the canvas away from my nose, I discover something I hadn't noticed before: my wrists are tied together. Come to that, so are my ankles. The drum squeezed up against my chest is crusted with a tarry residue covering the word stencilled on its side. All I can make out is *OOK*.

I fight down a rising sense of panic: Where are the River Rats taking me? Why didn't they rescue anyone else? Am I the only survivor? Poor Marcopolo.

From my vantage point in the cargo bed, I watch telephone poles and the cornices of buildings fly by. An American flag snaps in the wind. A billboard advertises Steadman's annual mid-summer sale. A smokestack rises into view, then disappears.

The truck makes a turn — I hear the tick-tock of the directional blinker — and crunches to a stop on uneven ground. The oil drums strain against the ropes, threatening to crush me.

I hear the squeak of the tailgate, followed by the thump of boots hitting the cargo bed. Hubie's face appears. His baby-pink mouth makes a shushing sound.

"You keep your trap shut, girl. We don't want to upset the watchman. Quick drop-off here, and then we'll carry on to Nowellville."

I look up at Hubie's baby face and mumble, "Go fuck yourself, you murderer."

Shaking his head, he stuffs an oil-soaked glove into my mouth. "Kiss your mama with that mouth, Shirley Temple? Keep it up and I'll stick something worse in there. Know what I'm sayin'?"

As I lie choking and gagging, Hubie starts pulling out the oil drums from around me. I hear Lefty talking to someone. "This is the last of 'em."

"If you get more, bring 'em in," says the other voice. "They need landfill for where they're building a school on 99th Street. Old chemical dump site. They say there's stuff down there from when they built the bomb."

"Guess that's what you get when you buy the land for a buck," observes Lefty. The other man chuckles. "Subdivision's going up too. Young couples popping out babies like there's no tomorrow. Gonna need a playground."

Their voices fade into the distance as they walk away from the truck.

For a time all I hear is crickets and a train whistle. Finally, footsteps and voices again. They're coming back.

Hubie jumps into the cargo bed and squats down to look at me.

"I'll take that out of your mouth now. But one peep out of you and it goes back in for the rest of the ride. Understand?"

I nod. He takes out the glove. I finally take a deep breath. My mouth tastes like oil. Hubie jumps out and slams shut the tailgate.

And we start driving again.

The squeal of a parking brake tells me we've reached our destination. I'm shivering uncontrollably from riding in the open air in wet clothes. Through a gap in my canvas shroud, I catch sight of the Big Dipper.

The River Rats drag me out of the truck. Lefty shifts the weight of my body onto his right arm so he can knock on a door.

Music. A goofy song sung by a chipper-voiced woman with orchestra and choral accompaniment. Someone's excited about the arrival of a shrimp boat.

"Holly, turn off the hi-fi. Gentlemen, it's rather late for a drop-off, isn't it?" It's a woman's voice, with the well-rounded mid-Atlantic accent of a socialite from a Joan Crawford movie. The song stops abruptly with a fingernails-on-chalkboard scratching sound.

"We bring 'em in when we find 'em. Where you want us to put her?" asks Lefty.

"Is she wet? Oh dear. Holly, fetch Cook's oilcloth from the canning table, I don't want the furniture soiled."

I hear the men grunting as I'm set down on something soft that sags under me with a creak of springs. The canvas is yanked away from my face and I'm finally able to see where

I am: a room covered in red-and-green striped wallpaper. A woman frowns down at me, flanked by Lefty and Hubie. Her tightly curled blond pixie cut, severely arched eyebrows and upturned nose make her look like a French poodle dressed as a department store dummy.

Hard to know how old she is under her makeup, but my guess is early forties. She's wearing a tightly belted dress with a corseted bodice that gives her breasts the shape of a pair of missile silos. She aims them at me accusingly. Her hands are tucked inside her dress pleats, hinting at something hidden inside.

"Younger than I would have expected. What made you think she's the one? She could simply be another wayward girl taking the coward's way out."

"She's got that mark on her cheek, like some of the others. And look at her clothes — tight, like a frogman. We seen ones dressed like that before. And we found a book of funny pages on a drownded girl beside her. This one here says she drew 'em," explains Lefty. He hands the woman the freezer bag of sketchbooks, along with my soggy backpack.

"You two can go now. I'll telephone the doctor in the morning to discuss your find."

"Hey, what about our money?" Hubie's voice is anxious and high.

"You'll be paid your finder's fee once we assess the value of your salvage. We've wasted too much money and time on the other wretches you've dragged in."

"That ain't our fault," says Lefty. "We bring you whatever washes up alive at the Schoellkopf. That was the deal."

"Deals change," snaps the woman.

"Hey now, that ain't fair," protests Lefty. "What about that smart feller we found? He tipped us off to check the shore by the Schoellkopf on this very day and time. This girl draws funnies too. Gotta be the one."

"Nonetheless, only the doctor can say whether you've earned your fee. Good night."

Lefty and Hubie grunt unhappily and mumble their good nights. Despite the way they've treated me, I feel sorry for the River Rats. I hear the creak of a screen door, footsteps on gravel and the truck engine turning over. I should be happy to be indoors, out of the cold and away from those two bozos, but I have a feeling my troubles are just beginning.

The woman leans down to look me over again. Her makeup has turned her plump smooth skin a weird shade of mauve, like an overripe plum. I feel like a scientific specimen about to be dissected.

She pulls a penlight out of the depths of her dress and shines it into my eyes. When I squint and turn away from the light, she pries open my eyelids with fingernails as sharply pointed as stiletto heels. "Stay still."

I tear up as she examines one eye, then the other. She presses the palm of her hand do my forehead.

"What are you doing?"

"Checking for signs of illness. Where were you born?"

"Shipman's Corners."

"Grubby little town." She places her fingers on the inside of my wrist. "What's today's date?"

"I was hoping you'd tell me that."

The woman clicks off her penlight and returns it to the folds of her dress. "Don't worry, you've fallen into a civilized age. Unlike the one you come from, I expect. I am Miss Sexton, manageress of Nowellville House, where you find yourself tonight. Now give me your name."

"Debbie Reynolds Biondi."

Miss Sexton snorts. "Games? Must we? You're lucky the doctor isn't here. He's been known to punish liars rather severely. Or perhaps you're simply feeble-minded?"

"That really is my name," I insist. "I was named for the movie star."

"Ridiculous nonsense. Merle Oberon is a star. Yvonne De Carlo is a star. Vivien Leigh is a star. Debbie Reynolds is an ingénue who'll be forgotten in a heartbeat. Until we get the truth out of you, we'll address you as Deborah. Now, what have you got there, Holly?"

"Just a bit of flotsam from Debbie Reynolds's bag."

I turn my head at Holly's voice and there she is, about twelve years old, strikingly pretty and incongruously kitted out in a red crinoline dress, plaid jacket and sturdy brogues like a private school English girl off for a jolly game of field hockey. Her long black curls have been pulled into a neat ponytail. She's holding Cassandra.

"Put that down immediately," orders Miss Sexton.

Holly pouts. "Must I? I want to play with it. It looks like a little cupcake!"

Sexton clicks her tongue but makes no move to take the AI away from the girl. That's a relief: I'd rather the kid kept it as a toy instead of giving it to the housekeeper from hell.

"Look, is anyone else alive? You said something to the River Rats about others."

"I'm the one who asks the questions in this house," replies Miss Sexton.

I won't give up without an argument. "A girl named Marcopolo fell in the river with me. They threw her back instead of trying to revive her."

"I know about Marco Polo from one of my Little Golden Books," chirps Holly. "He went to China and brought macaroni back to Italy. I wonder what they ate for dinner before that."

"I'm sure I don't know or frankly care about Italians and their dining habits," says Miss Sexton in an annoyed voice. "The question is, What was Deborah doing in the river? Trying to do away with yourself, were you?"

I hesitate, not sure how to answer. There is no why for my presence here. I decide to tell her the truth.

"I'm from another time. The year 2025," I say, waiting for her snort of disbelief. But she seems unsurprised.

"I suspected as much," sniffs Miss Sexton. "You have the stink of the future about you. Corruption. Decay. Perversion. Infection. Decadence. Waste. When were you born?"

"October 4, 1956. A year to the day before the launch of Sputnik."

"What is Sput-nik? Sounds like a communist word."

"It's Russian for 'travelling companion.' The first Soviet spy satellite. It'll start orbiting the planet without warning and freak out everyone in the so-called free world."

Miss Sexton waves away my words. "Our president would never permit such an outrage. I'll untie you now, but you'll regret any attempts to escape. Dogs patrol the grounds at night. I can summon them in a heartbeat."

"Where exactly would I escape to? I don't know where I am or what year this is."

"Let's leave it that way for now," approves Miss Sexton. "I'll fetch the scissors."

Holly has settled down cross-legged in a red velvet chair across from me, with Cassandra's cupcake-shaped hub nestled in her lap. The manageress of Nowellville House must be out of sight because Holly winks at me as she strokes Cassandra's hub.

"Don't worry. I'll look after her for you."

Holly grins at me and touches the side of her nose conspiratorially as her face changes before me. Her skin coarsens and wrinkles. The scruff of a five o'clock shadow appears on her widening jaw. Her expression shifts to something less than innocent.

I blink, trying to clear my vision. But the girl is definitely starting to look like an elegant man of a certain age. An Exceptional who remembers his lives in both Atomic Mean Time and Earth Standard Time, and mine too.

"Bum Bum?"

"Shhh."

"Where are we?"

"In the belly of the beast, sweetie. The stately home of Dr. Norman Guenther, a.k.a. Doc Time."

I gape at Bum Bum. I've somehow managed to land in the one place where I could either do the most good or cause the most damage to the history of Earth Standard Time. In Sputnik Chick's world of no coincidences, this is one hell of a coincidence.

"How did *you* get here?"

"Same as you, and the Trespasser, and every other Tom, Dick and Harry. I jumped off the Rainbow Bridge straight down the quantum passage, which sent me back in time. Splashed down in the Niagara gorge. The River Rats fished me out and brought me here."

"There were others?"

"You kidding? This place is like a bed and breakfast for half-drowned time travellers."

"What year is it?"

"Zip it, Nurse Ratched is coming back."

Bum Bum's face softens back into that of a twelve-year-old girl, just as Miss Sexton bustles into the room with a pair of scissors and dry clothes. As I change into a flannel bathrobe, she fingers my Sports Chalet sports bra.

"Barbaric. Not even a proper foundation garment!"

Miss Sexton tells me that Cook has gone home for the night, and although, as house manageress, food preparation is not one of her duties, she is willing to make an exception this once and heat up a bowl of soup for me.

"After all, we wouldn't want you dying of hypothermia after your dunking," she comments.

As I sit at a large wooden table in the kitchen eating the soup — bland beef stock with a few limp vegetables and a slab of jellied tongue floating on top — Sexton lights a cigarette and drops the freezer bag between us.

"How does one open this contraption?"

I show her how to unzip the seal. Sexton gingerly eases out the sketchbooks and opens *The History of the Known World* on the table before her. She drags on her cigarette as she flips the pages.

"Cigarettes cause cancer," I tell her, nervous about ashes falling on my drawings.

Sexton glances at me dispassionately. "These are a healthy brand, Sweet Caporals. My personal physician recommended them as a way to avoid bronchial ailments in the humid season."

"He's been bought out by a tobacco company. Nicotine causes lung cancer, bladder cancer, cancer of the throat and jaw. I've seen people who have to talk through a hole in their esophagus."

Sexton's lips thin to a tense line. She crushes out her cigarette in an ashtray shaped like a pine tree. Holly pokes at Cassandra, who I hope won't start squawking. I eat slowly, taking in my surroundings, looking for clues to the year but there isn't so much as a wall calendar or a clock. Given that Sexton recognized Debbie Reynolds's name, but not the fact that she was an established movie star, it can't be earlier than 1945 or Lefty would still be a G.I. in Italy. I *might* be somewhere in the early '50s, although the kitchen looks older, with its drab grey enamel walls, waxy linoleum tiles and Depression-era appliances. The room is large enough to accommodate an army of cooking and prep staff, with a massive black cast-iron wood stove, a squat metal cabinet that looks like a proto-refrigerator (an icebox, I assume) and a sink deep enough to go swimming in. It reminds me of one of the breezy old farm kitchens in the Shipman's Corners of my childhood, where platoons of women cooked for farmhands and fruit pickers. The only decorations are a framed print of a *Saturday Evening Post* cover of Santa Claus checking his naughty and nice list from atop a stepladder.

"I must admit, these funnies are rather good," says Sexton. "Where did you learn to draw?"

"Norman Rockwell's Famous Artists School."

Sexton's eyes flick up at me. "You studied with Rockwell, you say?"

I yawn. "Not directly. The Famous Artists School was a correspondence course. I saw their ad in the back of a comic book. They said they were looking for people who like to draw."

"The doctor is looking for a willing young assistant trained in the graphic arts. You might do nicely."

"I'm neither young nor willing," I tell her.

"We'll discuss it in the morning. Bedtime," says Sexton, closing *The History of the Known World.* Holly picks up my empty bowl and puts it in the sink.

I could use more to eat but don't argue. I'm so exhausted

I can barely walk to the stairs. Sexton lights a small kerosene lamp and leads me to the second floor in the halo of its yellowish light, Holly trailing us.

"No electricity upstairs?"

"Of course there is," snaps Sexton. "We just don't believe in frittering it away. I think you'll find this a much less profligate era than your own. We haven't resorted to living on islands of our own waste."

Bingo. Someone has filled in Sexton on the sins of the twenty-first century. Further evidence that I'm not the first time traveller to have dropped into her life.

The second floor is an open landing with a row of closed doors; to my exhausted eyes they seem to go on to infinity. Sexton pulls a ring of keys from the depths of her dress pleats and unlocks one.

"This will be your room. You'll find a nightgown on the bed and extra blankets in the closet. Everything else you'll need is in the bath. Breakfast is at seven sharp. Holly will wake you."

Sexton locks the door from the outside, leaving me in a room lightened only by moon glow. I know I should make like Sputnik Chick and stave off sleep to take stock of my surroundings, maybe jimmy the lock or break down the door and karate chop Sexton in her sleep and hunt down the evil Doctor Time, but instead I flop down on top of the bed and fall into a sleep as dark and deep as a black hole.

* * *

I wake just as dawn brightens the room. At first, I think I'm back on the *Centaur*. The room is decorated in delicate tea rose patterned wallpaper and outfitted with an oak wardrobe large enough to climb into, a matching dresser, a white wooden vanity with a triptych of bevelled mirrors and pink padded stool, a furry pink rug on the hardwood floor and a hurricane lamp in front of a window hung with ivory lace curtains. It would be a perfectly lovely room if the window weren't set with iron bars. I stare up at alabaster swirls of plaster on the ceiling. On the bedside table, a china shepherdess lifts her skirts to dance with a pan-pipe-playing faun.

A door leads to a bathroom with an old-fashioned chain-pull toilet and a deep, inviting claw-footed bathtub. I plug the drain and turn on the taps while I pee, then climb into the steaming water. It seems like it's been a long time since I washed — back in Atomic Mean Time, in the fancy hotel suite where Kendal and I spent the night. Hard to believe that was only yesterday. Since then I've had a trip to Ellis Island during the Spanish flu pandemic, a swim in a chemical soup and a long ride next to filthy oil drums. I soak and scrub myself with a bar of rough soap — oatmeal, I think — and use it to wash my hair.

The mirror over the sink has steamed up. I wipe away the condensation to look at myself for the first time since arriving in the past. I touch my face, not sure it's mine. The bar code on my cheek is still there, but everything else about me looks new and pink and freshly hatched. No wonder everyone keeps calling me a girl.

My wrinkles have vanished. My jaw has tightened. The dark circles under my eyes are gone. I feel inside my bathrobe: sure enough, my breasts are just starting to bud. I look sixteen, maybe younger.

I come out of the bathroom to find Holly sitting cross-legged on my bed. She's dressed more like a kid this morning, in a gingham blouse, clam diggers and tennis shoes, her thick black hair in braids. She sucks on the end of one braid as she reads a magazine called *Astounding!* On the cover, a woman and man in a rocket ship are hurtling toward a blue-green planet. She looks up from her magazine with a wicked grin.

"That bitch Sexton forgot to unlock your door for me this morning, so I picked the lock," she says, holding up a bobby pin. "This aging backwards thing is some crazy shit, eh? I'm kind of jazzed to be a twelve-year-old."

I sit on the bed beside her. I want to tell her everything but don't know where to start.

"You do make a cute girl," I say.

"Thanks. It's a good thing I like being Holly because shape-shifting is the only way I can avoid integrating with my alternate self. It's September 1955, so I'd be about a year old right now. Last thing I want is to have to go through another twelve years of my pop beating the shit out of me."

"Why are we aging backwards?"

Holly yawns. "The Trespasser gave me a geeky explanation. Moving into a past where you already exist impacts the mitochondria in the travelling body but not the target body. However, the exact nature of the age reversal is not yet well understood, research is ongoing, blah blah blah. In other words, who knows? It's random."

"If this is September 1955, I won't be born for another thirteen months," I point out. "Dad will be getting Mom pregnant around January."

"That's a creepy thought," says Holly. "Just count yourself lucky that you didn't turn into a zygote. Maybe puberty is the default setting."

"So the Trespasser sent you here?"

Holly swings her legs over the edge of the bed. "More like we made him help us find you."

"We?"

"Your intern, Ariel," says Holly. "Smart cookie, that one. She reverse-engineered the VR game that the Trespasser hacked into. Found him alive and well and teaching physics at MIT in 1955. She convinced him to help us get you back."

"Unicorn Girl is here?"

"Not *here*, no. She's been riding herd on the Trespasser. They're trying to work some kind of scheme to reverse what you started with *The Adventures of Futureman*."

"And what exactly is *your* part?" I ask.

Holly gives an extravagant yawn and stretch. "The usual: saving your ass, so you can save the world."

"And you got here when?"

"Hard to say exactly," says Holly. "A month, maybe. Doc Mutant compared the quantum passage at Niagara to the Bermuda Triangle — it not only connects alternate worlds but past and present. Who knew? Makes sense, when you think about it. All those daredevils whose bodies vanished even when their empty barrels bobbed to the surface. Not to mention people who went over the falls by accident or because they jumped."

"Is that why Sexton thought I might be a suicide?"

Holly nods vigorously. "Yeah, the River Rats find people at the Schoellkopf all the time. Some were jumpers. Depressed tourists — honeymooners, mostly. Some of them didn't know it was dangerous to wade in the rapids above the falls. Then there were the drunk guys in fishing boats that got caught in the current and went over. Partiers, smugglers, tightrope walkers. Some from back in the old days, like bootleggers and missionaries. Think about it: lots of people disappear at the falls. You know that. Turns out they fall through the quantum passage. From the stuff they've left behind in this house, it looks as if they're mostly from about a hundred years on either side of 1955. So you get the horse and buggy people from 1855 and the flying car folks from 2055, all soaking wet and dazed and confused, who have to depend on that bitch Sexton's hospitality. I got this all from the Trespasser, but he's damned if he can figure out where they all go from here. Looks like they all sleep here a few nights, change their clothes and — poof — gone."

"So what now?"

Holly goes back to gnawing on her braid. "Now we look for any kinks you made in the fabric of time. We gotta smooth them out, get history to unfold the way it actually did in Earth Standard Time, or who knows what the future will bring? My job is to watch the news to see if someone is already trying to hack the past. Yours is to save the world of tomorrow and all that jazz. But can we please have breakfast first? Cook always says eat now or forever hold your peace."

THREE

CAST-OFFS OF THE ACCIDENTAL TIME TOURISTS

Sexton has laid out clothes for me that look like something Santa's date would wear to prom: a heavy red velvet dress with a satin sash, a pair of leather flats, an overengineered padded bra, a petticoat slip stiff enough to stand up on its own and a mysterious rubbery pile of what I can only assume is underwear. I hold up a garment that looks like a dull white jellyfish with dangling metal clips.

"Ugh. Anything else I could wear around here?"

Holly nods at the wardrobe. "Lots of stuff in there that the time tourists left behind."

I pull out one outfit after another and toss them on the bed. I find a silver lamé minidress. A Pucci jumpsuit in pink and purple. A brown tweed suit with a fox chasing its tail around the collar. A royal-blue silk Edwardian ballgown. A starched white nurse's uniform with a watch pinned to one breast. A black nun's habit complete with a rosary bead belt. A flapper's sack dress with a fringed hem. A grubby pair of blue jeans with a peace symbol on one butt cheek and the stars and stripes on the other.

I finally dig out a loose cotton housedress in a floral print, faded and soft from too many trips through a wringer washer. I could execute one of Sputnik Chick's famous flying dropkicks in this dress, if I had to.

I rummage through a dresser drawer for underwear and fish out a pair of high-waisted bloomers and a saggy but serviceable Free Spirit bra, the au naturel brand Linda and I wore in the '70s. Beats the hell out of the padded bullet brassiere Sexton left for me. A battered pair of black leather oxfords from the bottom of the wardrobe (the nun's, perhaps?) and I'm ready for action.

Pulling a pair of white bobby socks out of the drawer — they'll look very punk rock with the nun's black oxfords — I notice a soft pile of pale-blue synthetic fabric. I tug on one corner and pull out a jacket. To my surprise, the tag, printed in PICTO, tells me that the garment was made in Bangladesh of one hundred percent waterproof Gore-Tex. Neither the country name, nor the high-tech fabric, nor the emoji-based language of PICTO existed in the 1950s.

"Oh my god," I murmur, the jacket in my hands. "One of my friends has been here! This is hers. Her name was Eufemia."

"Don't say anything to Cook about her," warns Holly. "She hates Effie."

"Effie?"

Holly wraps her arms around her knees and hugs them to her chest. "Cook said her name was too hard to pronounce, so Sexton changed it to something American."

"How long ago was she here? Where is she? Was anyone else with her?"

Holly holds up her hands as if deflecting my barrage of questions. "I never met her. She was gone before I came and took her kid with her. Cook says she spent most of her time in the kitchen, driving her crazy. The kid was so ugly, they hid her in the barn. Then one day the two of them up and disappeared."

Hands trembling, I stuff the jacket back in the drawer. Eufemia slept in this room. Prima was in the barn. Where are they now? I can't wait to get my hands around the neck of the manageress of Nowellville House and force her to answer that question.

* * *

Sexton turns out to be an early riser. The only signs of the manageress's presence in the dining room are a fug of cigarette smoke and the crushed butt of a lipstick-stained Sweet Caporal in the dregs of coffee at the bottom of a cup. Two steaming bowls of white mush sit on the table, presumably for Holly and me.

"Gag, cream of wheat," says Holly, sticking out her tongue in disgust.

"Do you think there's brown sugar?"

"Miss Sexton doesn't believe in it. Too much sugar makes ladies stout," explains Holly. "But we might be able to hit Cook up for some molasses."

"I'm so hungry I could eat anything, as long as the coffee's good and strong."

"Don't get your hopes up," warns Holly. "Cook doesn't even know what espresso is."

On cue, the door between the kitchen and dining room swings open and a woman in a white dress and apron walks in backwards carrying a heavy tray. She looks like a bosomy snowman: well over six feet tall, with hair the bleached-out colour of the mush in our bowls. She briskly sets out a coffee pot, milk jug, marmalade jar, rack of buttered toast and a platter of grilled bacon and sausages.

I try to introduce myself, but Cook waves away my words with a meaty hand. "Oh I know who you are, Miss Deborah. My son Hubert rescued you. Miss Sexton says you're maybe the one the doctor's been waiting for. She thought you should spend the day getting to know Nowellville House. After all, this is your home now."

Leaning over to spear a sausage, I ask as casually as possible, "Shouldn't we be worried about the dogs?"

"Oh no, Miss," says Cook. "Brutus and Caesar are only on the job after dark. Gentle as puppies when the sun's shining. Anyways, my son will escort you around the farm. Miss Holly knows Nowellville House like the back of her hand, so I'm sure she'll do the honours indoors. Miss Sexton sends her apologies, but she has business in town."

As she speaks, Cook lines up an elaborate set of tableware beside my plate: marmalade spoon, coffee spoon, butter knife, egg fork, porridge ladle and on and on. Like the clothes Sexton set out for me, the formal table setting hints at a strict code of behaviour, even for breakfast.

While Holly and I eat, Cook busies herself in the kitchen. I hear running water and a radio playing the kind of string-heavy instrumental best reserved for slow-moving elevators. Mercifully the music comes to an end and a baritone voice intones, "And now the news." Straining to hear the headlines, I'm disappointed when Cook turns the dial to insipid music.

Reading my mind, Holly whispers, "Don't worry, we can watch the news upstairs later on the miracle box. There's this great show with a monkey dressed up like a man."

On my third helping of bacon and eggs, carefully cut and eaten with the correct utensil, I ask, "Why do Cook and Miss Sexton call me 'the one'?"

Holly helps herself to another piece of toast. "They're looking for a female from the future who draws like Norman Rockwell. They thought it was me at first. Then Effie. Until they discovered neither one of us could draw."

"What has Norman Rockwell got to do . . ." I start to say, until Holly puts a finger to her lips and glances at the door to the kitchen.

Holly's meaning is clear. Cook is eavesdropping on us.

* * *

After breakfast, Holly and I start clearing the table, but Cook waves us off. "Miss Sexton would have my hide if she knew you were doing my work. Go and explore the house now. My Hubert will be here soon."

Holly leads me up flights of stairs with dark oak bannisters and thick wool runners embroidered with holly berries and tendrils of ivy.

"How big is this place?"

"Huge. It's like a giant game of *Clue*. Four storeys, twelve bedrooms, six bathrooms, library, kitchen, dining room, study, parlour, conservatory, billiard room and rooms in the attic and basement. Even a secret passageway."

After a long climb we reach the attic, full of furniture covered in drop sheets and boxes of Christmas decorations. One end has been walled off and hung with a door.

"What's in there?"

"The maid's room," answers Holly. "But there's no maid anymore. The only one who uses it is Cook, if there are so many guests for dinner that she has to stay overnight. I used to hang out in there sometimes — it's where I found the secret passageway — until it started creeping me out. I sensed some seriously bad karma. I don't go in there anymore."

"Oh, c'mon, you can't tell me about a secret passageway and not show me."

Reluctantly Holly pushes open the plank of rough plywood

that serves as a door. The room is nothing much: under plaster and lath eaves, a single bed — more like a cot — is made up with a thin grey pillow and a patched quilt. It's hard to imagine a woman of Cook's size sleeping in it. The only other amenities are a two-drawer dresser and a floor lamp with a naked bulb. A few books sit on a shelf: *Jane Eyre*, a King James Bible and Dickens's *A Christmas Carol*. A tiny alcove holds a crazed porcelain sink and a chain-pull toilet, half a roll of toilet paper sitting on the floor. Through a dormer window, I glimpse rows of evergreen trees marching up a distant hill like soldiers in fatigues.

The only odd thing about the room is a faded bunch of mistletoe dangling from the sloped ceiling, nailed up over the sad little bed. Meaning, I suppose, that whoever sleeps there better be ready to be kissed.

Pushing aside the cot, Holly grasps the handle of a trapdoor to reveal a steep stairway. It leads down to a tiny broom closet one floor below. Holly yanks a cord hanging from the ceiling; a weak yellow light bulb shines on a Hoover upright vacuum cleaner and a couple of rag-filled buckets. From the closet, we step out into a carpeted hallway, right in front of an oak door elaborately carved with mythical creatures that seem to be half human, half tree.

"The doctor's bedroom," says Holly.

"What are those things carved into the door?"

"Tree nymphs. Also called dryads. They're the symbol of Nowellville House."

"Can I peek inside?"

Holly shrugs and tries the knob. She seems as surprised as I am when the door opens. Inside are a king-sized bed with dark brown bolsters, a sprawling desk with a green-shaded reading light, a humidor, a clothes horse draped with a tweed jacket and a hat rack with a selection of fedoras. A tapestry rug on the floor depicts a Victorian family at Christmas dinner, the turkey, ham, duck and sweet potatoes rendered with mouth-watering realism. In one corner of the rug, two dogs devour scraps thrown down by a cherub-faced boy while a cat with a red ribbon around its neck catches a terrified mouse by the tail.

"Where's the doctor?" I ask.

Holly shrugs. "Never met the guy. Cook says he's almost always down at the university in Albany. Comes home maybe two, three times a year. That's why Sexton's in charge. Guenther mails her his latest strips and she drives them over to the publisher. Goes like clockwork."

"What about Sexton's room?" I ask. "I'd love to snoop in there and see if I can find my sketchbooks."

"Right next door. But we have to be quick. She'll be royally pissed if she catches us."

While the doctor's room is full of shadows and earth tones, Sexton's is glacial. Throw rugs, bedspread, furniture — all spotlessly, blindingly white. A crystal lamp and ashtray sit on the bedside table. The floor is a polished blond wood. The air is surprisingly fresh for the bedroom of a chain-smoker.

I do a quick circuit, scanning for the freezer bag. I notice a stack of calling cards on the desk: *JADE S. SEXTON, MANAGERESS, NOWELLVILLE HOUSE, Concession Road 99, Nowellville, New York.* They're embossed with a drawing of the dryad, lifting her leafy arms over her head. I pick one up and slip it into the pocket of my dress.

Sexton's wardrobe is identical to the one in my room but painted white. I pull on its door; it's locked. Same with the dresser and desk.

Holly grabs my hand. "Come on. There's nothing on the rest of this floor but empty rooms. Downstairs is more interesting."

On the third floor, we poke our heads into a gloomy conservatory where a few dusty rubber plants and tired dieffenbachia languish unloved among a scattering of iron garden chairs. A billiards room is dark and masculine with a padded black leather bar stocked with bottles of amber liquid. The sight of whisky fills me with longing, but Holly hurries me on to the library, where floor-to-ceiling bookshelves show a taste for literature of the fantastic: Asimov, H.G. Wells, Verne, Lovecraft, Arthur C. Clarke and C.S. Lewis. An entire wall of shelves is devoted to comic books preserved in rice paper sleeves. Issues of *Detective Comics* featuring the Batman and an early *Wonder Woman* sit alongside characters long forgotten by my time, like Captain Triumph, Bronze Man, Judy of the Jungle, Marvel Boy and Professor Supermind and Son. There are even wartime superheroes from my home country: Canada Jack, Johnny Canuck, Fleur de Lys and the legendary Nelvana of the Northern Lights.

"If we could figure out a way to smuggle these back to 2025 in mint condition, we'd make a fucking fortune selling them online," points out Holly.

"Watch your mouth or the manageress of the house will wash it out with soap."

As we're about to leave the library, my eye catches on a familiar cover set behind glass. To my amazement, I'm looking down at a battered and stained first issue of *Sputnik Chick: Girl with No Past* — a rare original of the origin story I'd created in 1986. Just the like the one Unicorn Girl showed me at her interview.

"How the hell," I whisper.

Holly is standing next to me. "Maybe he got it from one of the accidental time travellers. It looks pretty bunged up. Could've fallen into the river."

I feel extremely uneasy. "Guenther knows my origin story. And a lot about the future."

"As do you about him, thanks to that copy of *The Adventures of Futureman* you stole," comments Holly.

"He wants me to draw it," I say, looking at Holly. "It's how *The Adventures of Futureman* ends. With me locked up in the attic at a drafting table."

"Jesus," says Holly. "Well, at least if we know what's coming, we can avoid it."

Holly leads me down the hallway to the parlour. Most of the furniture looks late Victorian. Gold and silver brocade wallpaper, overstuffed velvet chairs with curved wooden arms upholstered in cherry red and emerald green. A bay window offers a panoramic view of the grounds — to my eyes, more forest than farm. Like the kitchen, the parlour walls are decorated with framed Norman Rockwell prints, all Christmas themed: Santa's workshop, snowball fights between red-cheeked children, sleigh rides. There are two gleaming mahogany cabinets — one holding a Telefunken radio and hi-fi with the word *Sonata* inscribed on its speaker in cursive letters; the other, a box with elegant knobbed doors.

"The miracle box," Holly tells me. "We gotta let it warm up first."

She plops down on the rug and opens the cabinet doors to reveal a convex screen. The two of us are mirrored in its reflective surface. It takes me a few seconds to realize what I'm looking at. It's been a very long time since I saw a picture tube.

Holly turns the dial with an audible click. "I put on *The Today Show* every morning to watch for historical anomalies, to quote the Trespasser. Problem is I never learned much history in school."

"You never learned much of *anything* in school," I remind him.

"Doesn't hotwiring cars and loading dice count?"

The set gives off a low hum as a white dot appears on the screen, then grows into a blizzard of static. She makes some adjustments on the console and the static resolves into a picture: a chimp, dressed in a man's suit and shoes, waddles back and forth in front of a window behind which a crowd smiles and waves. A genial-looking man in glasses grins idiotically from the sidelines before picking up the chimp.

"That's J. Fred Muggs," explains Holly.

"The guy with the glasses?"

"No, the chimp. He's a big star."

I sprawl on the rug next to Holly. I feel like a kid, watching TV with my sister, Linda. All that's missing is the Tang.

"Fred's bad tempered," Holly informs me. "It said in *TV Guide* that he's bitten some guests."

The man in glasses returns with the weather report. He draws isobars and cold fronts in chalk on a map. We're in for rain, he says, before cutting to the news.

Over the clacking sound of a teletype machine, a newsreader begins, "This is Friday, September 25, 1955, and here's what's happening in the world today . . ."

We learn that the president of Argentina, Juan Perón, was just ousted in a military coup. (But what about Eva? I wonder.) A jury in Mississippi (all white, no doubt) took only an hour to find two white men innocent of the murder of a Black seventeen-year-old named Emmett Till. One juror is quoted as saying, "If we hadn't stopped to drink pop, it wouldn't have taken that long."

Holly looks at me, eyes wide. "That can't be true."

I shake my head in disgust. "It is. The '50s was even more overtly racist than 2025."

Holly starts gnawing on a braid. "What an ugly, fucked-up era. How'll we even know if history's changed?"

"Good question," I say. "It would have been nice if the Trespasser had left you some clues."

"I don't think he knows himself what to look for," says Holly.

I turn my attention back to the news, but they've already moved on to an interview with a curvaceous blond celebrity named Dagmar who's wearing an evening gown at eight in the morning.

"Oh fuck it," mutters Holly. "Let's watch something more interesting."

She clicks the dial until a revolver fills the screen and a voiceover announces, *Faster than a speeding bullet.* Poor doomed George Reeves appears in his Superman pyjamas, hands on hips, chiselled chin lifted, standing up for truth, justice and the American way.

After a half hour spent watching the Man of Steel battle an atomic-powered robot, we head for the basement, where Holly opens a heavy wooden door into a room lined with lead, holding six army cots with a gas mask on each one. A chemical toilet squats in a corner. The walls are covered in shelves holding canned food and demijohns of water. A rifle hangs on a hook next to a framed photograph of Eisenhower.

I shake my head. "Useless. Nuclear weapons are already too fast and powerful for a basement fallout shelter to offer any protection."

"I wouldn't tell Sexton if I were you," suggests Holly. "She gets even nastier when people try to scare her about the future.

Not that she believes much of what she's heard. Guenther claims he's changing the future so it'll all just stay like things are now."

"A never-ending 1950s," I muse. "There are people in our own time who'd like that."

Holly gives a sniff of disgust.

* * *

By the time we're back on the main floor, Hubie has arrived. He takes off his cap and asks, "How you doing this morning, Miss?"

I nod, without giving him a smile. "I'm fine, no thanks to you. I almost got hypothermia in the back of your truck."

"I'm sorry about that, Miss, but would've been worse if we'd just left you at the river overnight."

This much, I suppose, is true although his and Lefty's treatment of poor Marcopolo fills me with grief and rage. "You should have brought my friend here too. She might have been saved."

Hubie shakes his head. "She was beyond saving, Miss. Lefty checked her heart."

"And Lefty's a doctor, I suppose."

"Almost. He was an army medic."

In the distance, two large dogs — Dobermans, I think — stare at us with their ears pricked. Caesar and Brutus don't exactly look "gentle as puppies," to use Cook's words. I wouldn't want to meet them patrolling the grounds at night.

Out in the fresh air, I can't help but feel more optimistic about my chances of finding the away party. But it's cloudy and a stiff breeze is blowing; I'm glad I went back and grabbed a baggy wool cardigan from the wardrobe.

We're surrounded by evenly spaced rows of Fraser firs, blue spruce and Scotch pines, each a uniform size — about up to my shoulder. "Farming Christmas trees is how the doctor makes money so he can do his science experiments," explains Hubie.

"I'm surprised you know so much about it," I comment, tugging the sweater tighter around my shoulders; the wind is getting cooler and the sun has scooted behind a cloud. The farther we walk, the colder it gets. "I would have thought the experimental farm was secret, like a supervillain's lair in James Bond."

Hubie scratches his head. "Never met no Jimmy Bond, but everyone 'round here knows about the experiments."

The farther we walk, the higher the trees until we're standing in a stand of Scotch pines taller than Hubie.

The three of us walk, without speaking, until we reach a long path flanked by rows of poplar trees. As predicted by the spectacled host on *The Today Show*, it's starting to rain. At the end of the pathway stands a wrought-iron fence, with *Enchanted Forest Experimental Farm* worked into its top edge in fancy script.

"Never been in here myself," says Hubie, fumbling with a key ring.

"Neither have I," says Holly. "Miss Sexton told me it was out of bounds."

"Well, this morning she gave permission for the two of you to go in on your own. I'll wait out here. Only special people are allowed to walk through the enchanted forest."

Hubie unlocks the gate with a smile, no doubt certain that he and Lefty will be getting their finder's fee. I must be someone worth salvaging after all.

Inside the gate, our feet sink into muddy earth yellowed by horse manure. I'm grateful for the nun's sturdy oxfords, although I can't help wondering if she was an attempted-suicide-turned-time-traveller.

The trees are farther apart than on the Christmas tree farm, and misshapen. Branches twist toward the sky as if in worship, like the dryads on Sexton's calling cards and the doctor's bedroom door.

Some bizarre grafting experiments have gone on here: pears grow on oak trees, poplars are covered in acorns, birches have bright pink bark. Each tree bears a small copper plate covered with letters and numbers.

One tree looks like a maple but with huge burls and bumps covering the trunk. The more I look at it, the more it reminds me of a human body: the ends of the branches splay into protrusions that resemble lumpy fingers. My eyes trace a pair of buttocks, the hump of the shoulder, the line of a backbone. The tree looks like a man caught running with his hands in the air as if to say *Don't shoot, I surrender.* Curious, I read the copper plate on the trunk: *The Communist Tree.*

When I look up at where the branches meet the trunk, in the crook where a child might climb and sit, I see an oval lump about the size and shape of a human head. Stepping closer, the whorls and marks suggest a face, twisted to one side, mouth open. There's a raised seam along what looks like the curve of a neck, connecting the head to the body of the tree. I run my finger along the puckered ridge. It's a scar. Like the one left when a LEECH is implanted. That's when I recognize the face in the tree, its open mouth screaming in agony, eyes staring upward at the overcast sky. Now I know what's happened to at least one member of the away party. Yuri, or what's left of him, is inside this tree.

I step away quickly. This is why Sexton wanted me to tour the experimental farm.

Holly sees Yuri too. She's crouched on the ground, arms around her knees.

"Fuck! The Trespasser didn't warn me about trees that eat people. Let's go back!"

"One of my friends is in that tree! I have to look for the rest of them. You can go back on your own if you want."

"Not without you."

Hand in hand, we walk through the mutated orchard. I can see bodies everywhere now, torsos trapped inside trunks, heads poking out between branches. I look at each face carefully but see none that look like Jordan, Prima, Hot Lips or Eufemia. But then out of the crowd of agonized human faces and forms, under the bark, I see a slender tall figure, the face handsome even in its horribly mutated state. Wolfman. The plaque on his tree reads *An Invasive Species*. I step back, hands over my mouth.

In an oak tree, I see a woman's back, twisting as she turns to look behind her. Going around to the other side, I see her face, hollow eyed, gape mouthed, arms flung high in the air like branches, the twigs of her fingers outstretched in surrender or prayer. I imagine her pleading, *Let me die.* The copper plate reads *The Nun's Tree*. I look down at my oxfords. Jesus Christ.

All this has been shown to me deliberately as a warning and a threat. Getting back at me for lung cancer and Russian spy satellites and Debbie Reynolds's stardom.

There are no consequences for experimenting with the bodies of time travellers. No one is looking for people from the past or future especially if, like me, they haven't even been born yet. Yuri, Wolfman, Poseidon and Kendal would have been immediately expendable: the doctor was looking for a *female* from the future. Both Eufemia and I fit the bill, as did Prima and Holly. He probably did away with the men almost immediately.

When I turn to Holly, all I see is a seething carpet of green slime mould on the ground. The classic Exceptional stress reaction.

But Bum Bum is a calm, cool, collected ex–juvenile delinquent who grew up on Zurich Street. He never loses control of himself this way. Taking on Holly's persona might be making him feel more vulnerable.

"Try to calm yourself," I say gently.

Slowly the mould pulls itself together. Dressed in now too tight capris, his black curly hair still in braids, Bum Bum picks himself out of the mud and transforms into a bedraggled, tear-streaked, manure-caked Holly.

Holding hands, we stagger back through to the entrance of the enchanted forest where Hubie waits in a wagon, the reins of two black horses in his hands. The rain is pelting down hard now.

"Thought you two might be all done in, so I went back for the wagon," he says and takes out a thermos of tea, thoughtfully provided by Cook. Holly and I gulp it down, huddling together for warmth.

Holly drops off first, sucking on the end of a braid, her hands clasped under her chin.

My eyes keep closing too. Something in the tea.

Before I pass out, one thought runs through my mind. *You win, Miss Sexton, you win.*

FOUR

THE MAID'S ROOM

I reach down and scratch the itchy spot where the shackle has rubbed my ankle raw. Chained to my desk, I look out the dormer window at the evergreens lined up on a distant hill. I assume that out there, somewhere, flowers are blooming and trees are in leaf.

I mark the passage of time by the weather. When they first stuck me in the maid's room, the sky was always the dreamy blue of summer. Through the dormer, I watched it turn grey with frost, then white with snow. Nightfall came earlier and earlier. I started to see patches of naked ground where trees had been chopped down.

"Why no celebration?" I probed Sexton. "This is a Christmas tree farm, after all."

"It's Christmas when the doctor says it is," she answered curtly.

On Christmas Day, I started counting the days until the turn of the new year: 1956. Nine months before I'm born.

Eventually spring sun began to brighten the window. Sometimes the glass would streak with rain and the attic trembled with thunder. For months on end, it was damp and cold. Now it's getting warmer and the sun takes longer and longer to set. The longest day of the year can't be far off.

Once a day, I get to walk outside for a few minutes. Once a week, I take a bath downstairs, in the room where I originally slept — Eufemia's room. Both the walk and the bath are closely supervised by either Sexton or Cook. Holly brings me my meals on a tray.

Every Friday, Sexton hands me a legal-sized brown envelope, addressed to Nowellville House. Scripts and storyboards handwritten on sheaves of foolscap. Doctor's orders, Sexton calls them. I take this rough material and turn out one hateful, expertly drawn, four-panel strip after another, carefully hand-lettering the racist dialogue into speech bubbles.

The History of the Known World has provided inspiration.

"What is this time machine in your stories?" asks Sexton, paging through my sketchbooks. "The characters speak about it, but you never draw it."

"Never had a chance to get it down on paper," I mumble.

"Do you know what it looks like?"

I nod. "I was inside it, before I came here."

Sexton slips a fresh sheet of paper in front of me. "Sketch it, along with any technical specifications. Size, colour, shape. The doctor would like me to mail it to him."

Every Thursday, Sexton gathers up my finished pages and drives them over to the offices of the *Niagara Frontier Harvester*.

I sign every strip the same way: *Doctor Time*.

It's clear now why *The Adventures of Futureman* changed so much in 1955. Before that, it was sketched by an amateur. Now it's expertly drawn by the acclaimed creator of *Sputnik Chick: Girl with No Past*. I'm spreading hate throughout the Niagara frontier, one well-crafted comic strip panel at a time.

It's clear from the doctor's sketches that Futureman's superhuman physique is modelled on that knucklehead, Hubie.

Which has let me to wonder: if Hubie is Futureman, and I'm Doc Time, who the hell is Professor Quantum? Who did Guenther base him on? Was he supposed to be a Wernher von Braun type, or an actual time-travelling scientist who turned up in Nowellville House?

Oh please. Not Duffy.

I would ask Cassandra, if I could get her working. I can't recharge her because the hub's 2025 plug won't fit into a 1955 electrical socket. Even telephones are wired differently, with a line stuck directly into the wall.

I draw strip after strip. Holly keeps me company. Whenever Sexton and Cook are out of the house, she transforms back into Bum Bum, dressing in the outfits left behind by accidental time travellers. The silver lamé minidress is her favourite.

"We should go to New York and find Truman Capote. I'll bet he's writing *Breakfast at Tiffany's* even as we speak!"

"I'm chained to my desk," I point out. "Literally."

She shrugs. "I could pick the lock or cut through it. There are bolt cutters in the barn."

I shake my head. "I can't leave Nowellville House without knowing what happened to Eufemia and the little girl travelling with her," I remind Holly, as I draw Professor Quantum in his laboratory.

Holly — Bum Bum — sighs. "What's the point? They've vanished. Maybe into the enchanted forest. I keep watching *The Today Show*, but nothing seems especially wrong with history — not that I'm much of a historian but this whole era seems batshit crazy anyway. Racist, sexist, homophobic — how do I know it's any worse than it actually was? There's no sign of the Trespasser either. The doctor is totally in control of our lives, even though he never shows his face. That bitch Sexton is capable of anything. And look what you're doing. Helping recruit haters and extremists. We should escape and live our lives as best as we can here in the past."

I look up from my drafting table. "With Brutus and Caesar roaming the grounds? We'd never make it as far as the front gate." I look back down at my page where Futureman is smashing the heads of two men together. I letter the word **BONK** over them.

"How long does this strip keep running?" asks Holly listlessly.

"Until 1970. That's the year Guenther dies of a heart attack."

"Fuck. Another fifteen years of *this*? Debbie, we've got to get the hell out of here."

I shake my head and refuse to discuss it further. Holly curses as she clatters downstairs to the parlour. *The Adventures of Superman* is on.

As tempting as it would be to experience the hipster culture of New York in the 1950s — beatniks, coffee houses, pop art, cool jazz — I won't listen to any of Holly's escape plans because a failed attempt would prove fatal. Sexton has made it clear to me that if I don't keep turning out the strip, or we get caught trying to leave, my shape-shifting companion will disappear and *The Holly Tree* will appear in the enchanted forest, leaving me entirely alone.

Like in New Rome, I have a simple choice: draw or die. Only this time, my best friend dies with me.

* * *

Early in 1956 I was surprised to start menstruating again. Sexton supplied me with sanitary napkins the size and texture of loaves of Wonder Bread to belt between my legs. I asked her for tampons; I know they exist in this decade, having seen the tastefully oblique ads for them in Sexton's copies of *Good Housekeeping* and *Ladies' Home Journal* that she occasionally brings up to the maid's room for visual reference. She was aghast at my request, telling me that only married women are allowed to buy tampons.

When my monthlies (Sexton's word) were over, she handed me a rubber bag, hose and bottle of Lysol and explained how to mix the disinfectant with warm water and pump it up inside me. She called the process douching. Even my fear of Sexton wasn't enough to get me to do something that crazy.

The next thing I remember was waking up naked from the waist down and tied hand and foot to the bedstead with Sexton calmly feeding the hose into me. A nonlethal overdose of sleeping pills in my cream of wheat had knocked me out long enough for her to immobilize me.

"It's for your own good, dear," Sexton murmured breathily as the stinging liquid poured out of me onto a bath towel. I sobbed and cursed her, but she seemed to enjoy the sight of me in pain. I could taste as well as smell the Lysol as it burned its way through me.

Afterwards, lying on the cot with a wet washcloth pressed on the flame between my legs, trying to forget my troubles by ploughing through *Jane Eyre* for the tenth time, I finally admitted to myself that I couldn't go on like this much longer. It occurred to me that even though my alternate self won't exist until I'm born in a few months, my family is not far away. What's to stop me from calling them for help? Nonna Peppy's telephone number is chiselled into my memory: MU-58903. I had to memorize it in kindergarten in case of an emergency. Who knew that the emergency would happen before I was born?

And what happens when Mom gives birth to me? Maybe the fact that I'm in a past where I'm destined to draw *The*

Adventures of Futureman means I won't merge with my newborn self in Shipman's Corners. The artist in the attic at the end of the strip was an old woman, which suggests that once Debbie died in Earth Standard Time of 2025, I was left to carry on like her ghost or shadow.

The thought of which is horrifying enough to finally convince me to try to escape in June 1956.

* * *

I wait for a rare unguarded moment — Cook out shopping, Sexton doing the household accounts on the fourth floor — to ask Holly to pick the lock on my shackle. There are two telephones in Nowellville House: one inside the doctor's locked study; the other, a black slab with a thick curly cord hanging on the wall outside the kitchen. I go to the hallway, pick up the receiver and put it to my ear. The buzz of the dial tone reminds me that there's a normal world out there, beyond the walls of Nowellville House. But when I dial Nonna Peppy's number, an unfamiliar woman's voice comes on the line.

"Long-distance operator. Is this station to station or person to person?"

I stand stunned for a minute: I'd forgotten about having to place a long-distance call with the help of an operator. And for the life of me, I can't remember what "station to station" means.

"Person to person," I answer hesitantly.

There's a pause while switchboard connections are made to carry my voice over the border and the fifty or so miles on to Shipman's Corners. The ring tone sounds faint and far away, as if travelling not only over distance but time. One, two, three rings. My heart starts to pound. What if Nonna isn't home?

I catch my breath when I hear her long-dead voice answer. "Mrs. Pittalunga here, who's speakin'?"

My grandmother's voice sounds just like it did in 1919 when I saw her arriving at Ellis Island. I was closer to her than my own mom. She died — will die — in 1975. I am, in a way, speaking with a ghost.

"Nonna, it's Debbie!"

A pause. "Who?"

"Your granddaughter, Debbie Reynolds Biondi. Nonna, I'm in trouble, I'm being held prisoner in a house over the river. A Christmas tree farm in a town called Nowellville, near Niagara Falls, New York. It's owned by an evil doctor. A terrible woman named Miss Sexton is doing horrible things to me. Can you come get me?"

"Who the hell is this? I got no granddaughter named after Debbie Reynolds," says Nonna Peppy angrily. "You got the wrong number. Or are you playin' a trick on me?"

I'm not sure where to go from here. Of course she doesn't know me. I haven't been born yet.

"Nonna, I came from the future. I won't be born until October."

A long pause. "You oughta be ashamed of yourself, trying to scare an old lady."

"You're not old. You were born in 1898. May 9. You're not even sixty."

A pause. "How you know that?"

I grip the receiver so tightly that my knuckles ache. "I know a lot about you. You come from Piacenza. You went to New York when you were sixteen to live with your brother and his wife. You returned to Italy with your brother so he could get married. You left Italy again in 1919 with your younger sister,

Marie, who died at Ellis Island of Spanish flu. The name of your ship was ... was ..." My memory is failing me.

"How you know all this?" repeats Nonna Peppy. She's beginning to sound alarmed.

"Your ship was called *L'America*," I say, finally pulling the detail out of my memory. "Your real name is Giuseppina, but we called you Peppy because your dogs are all named Pepé for a Cuban bandleader you heard in New York. I can't remember whether you're on Pepé number one or two. How could I know all this if I wasn't your granddaughter?"

"I only got one granddaughter and she sure ain't you," says Nonna.

"I know that. Her name is Linda and she's three years old."

Silence. For a heartbeat, I worry she's hung up.

"Nonna, you still there?"

"Yeah. I'm just wonderin' if this is a dream."

"This is real," I assure her. "It's like ... you know ... a miracle! Like one of the saints."

"Or the devil," she suggests. "I think I no talk to you no more."

I cast around for some way to convince her to stay on the line. "Look, won't you at least take the address, maybe pass it along to the police? Or somebody you trust who can check out my story?"

"Okay, dimmi. Tell it to me. But I no promise nothing."

I read her the address printed on Sexton's calling card. It's almost fallen to pieces in the pocket of my dress.

"Please, Nonna. Call the police," I plead.

"I think it over," she says. "Goodbye."

"Please don't hang up."

But I'm back to the dial tone.

I stare at the receiver for a long moment before putting it gently back in its cradle.

My own grandmother doesn't know me. It's finally sinking in that I have nowhere else to turn.

FIVE

CHRISTMAS IN SPRINGTIME

"Christmas is coming, the goose is getting fat, please put a penny in the old man's hat," sings Cook.

"How do you manage to pretend it's Christmas when it's not?" I ask her as she slides a tray of gingerbread men out of the oven.

She shrugs. "I'm paid to do what they tell me to do, and although it's a bit queer, it's not the worst thing they've asked of me."

Dr. Guenther is coming home for the first time since I arrived at Nowellville House, bringing with him a number of distinguished guests. Miss Sexton personally selects the tree, a seven-foot blue spruce. Holly and I go up to the attic and take out boxes of ornaments and garlands. Although the temperature is above seventy degrees, Sexton insists on a roaring fire in the parlour and Bing Crosby's *Merry Christmas* album on the Telefunken. Hubie and Lefty come by to chop wood. Cook loans me a stool so I can put the angel on top of the tree. Holly strings popcorn and cranberries.

Over my nine months in Nowellville House, I've continued to wear the loose housedress, bobby socks and oxfords I found in the wardrobe of Eufemia's room, handwashing my 1970s bra and 1930s cotton bloomers in the bathroom sink every night. I still don't know how to fasten a corset hook or pull on a girdle or thumb the top of a nylon stocking into a garter snap. Now that I've been unchained from my desk for the holidays, Sexton says I have to start dressing like a lady. She will personally take me in hand.

Even though I'm reasonably slim and not particularly tall by twenty-first-century standards, for the 1950s I'm a tank. My proportions are all wrong for clothing designed for women whose growth was stunted by a Depression-era diet and wartime rationing. Armholes are too tight, waists are too small, backs too narrow. Even hats don't fit. I'm a hulking Amazon in a world of malnourished sprites.

Sexton believes the best way to solve this problem is with an industrial-strength, all-rubber girdle and long-line balconette bra with a little empty puff of air space over each nipple ("to allow your breasts to breathe, dear," Sexton explains). Then comes the nylon slip ("never allowed to peek out from under the hem of your dress"), followed by a stiffly starched crinoline that feels like a cloud of barbed wire. Cotton pads are pinned into the armpits of dresses, because the chemical giants DuPont, Hooker and Cyanamid, whose nearby smokestacks stain the horizon, haven't yet mastered the science of stopping women from sweating altogether. Instead, one masks one's B.O. (Sexton's term) with deodorant or cologne before encasing one's body in nonbreathable synthetics. I'm learning that the '50s is a sweaty decade.

The night before the doctor's homecoming, Sexton draws me a scalding bath, scrubs my hair with Halo shampoo, pats me dry and dusts me with so much talcum powder that I look like a naked ghost. She explains that this is to provide enough traction for the rubber girdle to glide over my fleshy bits without getting stuck halfway up my thighs.

After my shampoo, Sexton spritzes my hair with a semen-like liquid called setting lotion and does it up in curlers, covering the whole structure with a chiffon turban. Very *Bride of Frankenstein*. I spend the night propped up on a mountain of pillows so the tiny plastic teeth don't bite into my scalp.

The next morning, Sexton bustles into my room before breakfast to tug out the rollers and brush out the curls, setting everything in place with a mist of Spray Net. The hairspray goes down my throat and up my nose, releasing an unexpected memory from the future.

"That stuff is killing the planet," I cough, even though I know it'll still be a good thirty years before anyone sounds the alarm about chlorofluorocarbons in aerosol sprays destroying the ozone layer. Sexton signals her skepticism with a snort.

I'm talcum-powdered all over again and forced into my girdle, garters, stockings, wasp-waisted dress and Cuban-heeled pumps.

"Time to put on your face," orders Sexton. The cosmetics are arrayed on the dressing table in Eufemia's bedroom with its triptych of bevelled mirrors. I sit slumped before the image of my face, repeated three times.

Sexton crosses her arms. "Can I trust you to do this yourself, or do I have to do it for you?"

I shake my head and pick up a makeup brush in surrender. Sexton's heels clip out of the room, the door closing behind her.

Putting on a face is a process. First you lay the foundation by covering every inch of skin with an orangey base of Cover Girl pancake makeup. Pluck out all your eyebrow hairs and pencil in new ones. Follow with eyeshadow, mascara, blush and a waxy pinky-red lipstick called Cherries in the Snow. Unlike my nipples, my face can't breathe.

I examine my reflection in the mirrors. My face looks blurry around the edges. Unfinished, as if someone drew my portrait in charcoal, then smudged it.

Girdled, powdered and painted, I go downstairs to wait with Holly on the front porch. We're wearing white gloves and velvet dresses — mine red, Holly's green. Sweat pours out from under my bullet bra and girdle, turning my slip into a soggy dishrag. My crinoline loses its starchiness and starts to droop on one side.

Miss Sexton runs down the itinerary: we're about to welcome Dr. Guenther's publisher Mr. MacDonnell, first name Gus, accompanied by his wife, Mrs. MacDonnell, first name Audrey (please be aware that the poor woman suffers from a nervous disorder), and their infant daughter. We'll also be joined by an eminent professor of physics currently at Bell Laboratories in New Jersey and his young assistant and protege from the subcontinent, whose name is so foreign as to be quite beyond the ability of Sexton (or any other red-blooded American) to pronounce. Lastly, we'll be welcoming a real English princess and her escort, an entertainer whose celebrity means that he requires no introduction. Please remember to curtsy and do not ask for autographs. It's going to be an exciting and super-festive holiday season!

* * *

I expect Dr. Guenther to be a large and terrifying presence, a Lex Luthor mad scientist or a less kindly version of the Incredible Hulk. How could he not be, given what we saw in the enchanted forest? Yet the man who steps out of a Buick sedan carrying a battered leather briefcase is unremarkable. Average height and weight, blandly good-looking with wispy ginger hair and a pinched face that reminds me of a ferret from *The Wind in the Willows*. In his brown tweed three-piece suit and dull green tie, he could be a shopkeeper or an accountant. The type of man an eyewitness couldn't pick out of a police lineup even after they'd seen him rob a bank: he blends in so well with his surroundings that he's almost invisible.

The publisher, Mr. MacDonnell, an unpleasant looking man with sloped shoulders and a little paunch, arrives in a red-and-white Chevrolet Bel Air with his wife and infant. Audrey MacDonnell is a weary-looking blond with startled brown eyes; she reminds me of a beaten-down Marilyn Monroe. The baby looks like Audrey and not at all like Gus.

"And what's the little lady's name?" asks Cook.

"Gloria," answers Audrey.

The child's dark eyes catch mine over her mother's shoulder. Gloria MacDonnell, who will grow up in Canada, teach high school and die suddenly, leaving her identity for me to steal for a flight to New Jersey.

There are no coincidences.

As Mr. MacDonnell pulls a suitcase out of the trunk of the Bel Air, a chauffeured Mercedes-Benz pulls up. The princess and her escort are in the backseat, laughing, smoking and sipping martinis.

Holy fuck, I think.

This is the moment the Trespasser told Holly to watch for on TV. Instead of appearing on *The Today Show*, history's breaking point just drove up in front of Nowellville House in a convertible. And it likes its martinis dry and straight up.

Be cool. Observe the situation. Don't go off half-cocked, I tell myself, when what I really want to do is grab Holly and yell in her face, *WE'VE FOUND THE KINK IN TIME!*

Instead I grit my teeth, twist a glove between my sweaty palms and keep smiling.

The guests greet one another in a flurry of handshakes and air kisses. Sexton flits from one guest to another like a moth in a poodle skirt. She curtsies to the princess.

Minutes later, the roar of a motorcycle switching gears and a cloud of gravel dust announces the arrival of the noted Bell Labs scientist in black leathers. When he dismounts his Ducati and pulls off his helmet, he glances at me and gives a smile and nod, before helping his protege with the unpronounceable name out of the sidecar.

Holly nudges me. The Trespasser has finally shown his face. His protege is none other than Unicorn Girl.

"Ariel Bajinder Hassan," she says, offering her hand to a disconcerted Miss Sexton. "Please call me Ariel."

"How exotic," says Sexton. She doesn't touch Unicorn Girl's hand.

"So this is what lady scientists wear in New Jersey, is it?" Sexton doesn't approve of her travelling clothes: denim jeans, a leather jacket and a pair of cowboy boots.

"Only when riding in an open sidecar. I have a cocktail dress in my bag. I understand it's a special occasion. Christmas in June!"

The princess's escort grinds out his cigarette on the gravel driveway. "Kooky idea, but why not?"

"We hope you'll find it somewhat less kooky when you see what exciting plans we have in store for you," suggests Sexton, nonplussed by the man's brashness.

"Whatever you say, toots. The princess and I are up for anything fun, right, doll?" The princess smiles indulgently at her escort, a scrawny man, barely taller than she is, with thinning brown hair under a jaunty fedora and riveting bright blue eyes. He's not exactly handsome but oozes a gritty, back-alley charm. His confidence is as subtle as a bulldozer.

Dr. Guenther steps forward and bows to the princess. "If I may, Christmas is the tradition that embodies civilization at its height. A day that unites us all in the same feelings, same rituals, same food. A blend of Viking paganism and the Victorian traditions of the princess's Anglo-Saxon heritage. A perfect holiday. Too perfect to celebrate only once a year."

"And so say all of us," agrees the princess in her posh accent and raises her martini glass with a hiccup. "I do beg your pardon."

Sexton curtsies again. Holly and I follow her lead. When I look up at the princess, I see the younger version of a face I saw every school day of my childhood, gazing down at me from classroom walls. Despite a dainty figure that shows a penchant for ballet exercises and horseback riding, and the Givenchy original she's wearing, this woman is no princess. She's the Queen, all right. Or at least, she *should* be. What the hell is she doing at Nowellville House?

Sexton leads the scientist's protege over to me, probably hoping that I'll relieve her of the duty of having to converse with this foreigner. "Ariel, this is Deborah."

"Such a pleasure to meet you."

Unicorn Girl shakes my hand in both of hers, pushing something small and hard into my palm. She bends her head close to me and whispers, "I didn't recognize you at first. You look so young! Read the note. We have to talk."

I let my hand fall into the folds of my skirt, fingering the lump of paper down the wrist of my glove. I catch Holly's eye and nod. She nods back.

I'm grateful that no one is watching us. Everyone's attention is on the slightly tipsy young woman who should already be the Queen of England, standing on the driveway gravel in her kitten heels, giggling on the arm of Frank Sinatra.

I glance at Holly, who is staring at me, eyes wide. She taps the side of her nose in a knowing Bum Bum gesture that means *bingo*.

We have a sign that time has been hacked. The future is warping out of true. Now the question is whether we can restore the flow of history.

SIX

THE CHAIRMAN, THE PRINCESS AND THE KING

Our distinguished guests will be with us overnight. Today is to be given over to cocktails, dining and sparkling conversation. Tomorrow, we'll tour the falls and nearby Goat Island, natural wonders tamed by Frederick Olmsted, world-renowned designer of New York's Central Park.

Sinatra laughs when Dr. Guenther lays out the itinerary. "This Olmsted cat tamed Niagara Falls? Doesn't sound too natural to me."

"Man's job is to perfect the imperfect," Dr. Guenther explains. "Even a singing sensation like yourself can always be improved upon. Wouldn't you agree?"

Sinatra frowns. "Doc, I can tell you from personal experience that singers are born, not made. You can be the most artistically perfect performer in the world, but an audience is like a broad. If you're indifferent, Endsville. I never learned to read music, but I sure as hell know how to sell a number."

"Without a doubt," says Guenther. "But even a great talent like yours can be enhanced through collaboration, yes? I'm thinking of your recent work with Nelson Riddle and his orchestra. 'Night and Day.' 'In the Wee Small Hours.' Pure genius."

"He's got you there, darling," smiles the princess.

Sinatra holds up his hands in good-natured surrender. "I'm just a saloon singer, Doc. You're the self-improvement expert."

I watch in amazement as the princess canoodles with Sinatra. She kisses his cheek as he pats her bottom. It's one of the most unlikely couplings I could imagine. In Nonna Peppy's books, Sinatra was always A-number-one, but how did he manage to seduce a member of the royal family? Come to that, how did the woman I always knew as the Queen — trooping the colour, giving the Christmas address, stoically ruling the Commonwealth without complaining or explaining — turn into a fun-loving socialite with a taste for bad boys from New Jersey? Maybe growing up carefree and powerless made her more like her tragically romantic younger sister, Margaret. Something has changed history and saved her from being weighed down by a crown and the title *Your Majesty*.

It's the twist of fate we've been waiting for. The question is, What difference does a romance between a should-be-queen and a saloon-singer-made-good make to the flow of history?

Everyone retires to their rooms to powder their noses. Sexton fusses over the fresh flowers and fruit basket in the princess's suite. The princess assures her that her rooms are utterly charming. Sinatra will sleep across the hall — not that anyone thinks he'll have the decency to stay put, given his reputation as a notorious sex fiend. The MacDonnells and Dr. Duffy have been assigned rooms a respectful distance away from the celebrity lovebirds.

"We don't want the baby disturbing Her Royal Highness and her . . . friend," says Sexton to Holly and me as we carry fresh towels to the guest rooms.

A last-minute change: because Sexton thought the scientist's protege was a man, the two were to be lodged in adjoining rooms. With Ariel revealed to be a member of the weaker sex, this arrangement simply won't do. Despite the vast number of guest rooms in Nowellville House, Ariel is exiled to the bomb shelter.

"Immediately down the stairs and into the basement," Sexton explains. Unicorn Girl uncomplainingly lugs her overnight bag down to the windowless bunker while Sexton busies herself checking on everyone else's comfort.

"Cocktails at six, dinner at seven!" she sings out.

I go to my room and ease the note out of my glove, the paper damp from my sweaty palm. It's written in PICTO, a language Unicorn Girl can be sure Sexton doesn't understand. It says that she and Benjamin Duffy will debrief me tonight in my room, that they have a plan and I should bring Holly and Cassandra with me.

I strip down to my girdle and bra to stretch out on my bed and reread the note until I've got it committed to memory. I flush it down the toilet before putting my clothes back on and joining the cocktail party.

* * *

Bottles of bourbon, Jack Daniel's, sherry, vodka and ginger ale (for Holly). A cut-glass punchbowl brimming with spiked eggnog sprinkled with nutmeg. In the parlour, a glittering drinks table has been set up near the tree, strung with red and green electric lights and silver tinsel. Bing Crosby and the Andrews Sisters harmonize about Christmas in Hawaii. The fireplace is blazing. Given the heat of the day, Sexton discreetly opens a window.

She hands me a bourbon, neat, which I sip as slowly as possible despite my impulse to gulp it down. It's been almost a year since I tasted alcohol. Unicorn Girl, looking elegant in a sleeveless black cocktail dress, stands beside me holding an untouched glass of sherry. Her sleeve of unicorn tattoos causes Sexton to comment to me sotto voce on the barbaric practices of primitive cultures. Unicorn Girl pretends not to hear, sniffs her sherry and grimaces as if there's something nasty in it.

"You read the note?" she asks softly.

I nod. "You know how to find me?"

"Yeah, we'll take the secret passage to your bedroom so the Queen of the Night doesn't catch us."

Across the room, the Trespasser winks at me through the haze of cigar smoke. I cast my eyes down at my empty glass and dab perspiration from my forehead with my cocktail napkin.

The only one who notices the silent interplay between the Trespasser and me is — predictably — Sinatra. He salutes us with his glass of Jack Daniel's on the rocks, his favourite tipple according to Sexton, who read about him in *LIFE* magazine.

"Bottoms up," mutters Sinatra, knocking back the last of his drink.

"Can I freshen that?" the Trespasser asks Sinatra, heading for the drinks table.

"Won't say no," says Sinatra, handing over his tumbler. "You the same kind of scientist as our esteemed host?"

"Afraid not. I'm a quantum physicist."

"What the hell is that?" laughs Sinatra.

"If I may," interrupts Guenther, scooping another cup of eggnog out of the punch bowl. "Dr. Benjamin Duffy, late of the Massachusetts Institute of Technology, is currently employed by Bell Telephone Laboratories, a centre of brilliance and innovation based in Murray Hill, New Jersey. Dr. Duffy is an expert in the existence of alternate space-time continuums. There is a theory of quantum physics being floated, by a

Princeton man no less, that what we think of as reality is but one of many worlds."

Mr. MacDonnell contemplates his cigar. "Interesting notion. Does he have any thoughts on elves and fairies?"

"Some of us believe that his theory is not without merit," interjects the Trespasser.

Guenther nods. "Surely time travel is as worthy of exploration as space travel! His Majesty King Edward has expressed interest in financially supporting such research. Imagine the possibilities opened up by changing history!"

The princess chimes in. "Dr. Guenther is a great friend of my uncle and his wife."

"Indeed, Queen Wallis and I are acquainted through her Baltimore cousins," says Guenther. "A woman of high intelligence."

"A highly intelligent woman? That alone is unusual," mutters Mr. MacDonnell.

"Hey, if you cats could time travel, would it be back in time or to the future?" asks Sinatra, ready to turn the topic into a party game.

"Back," says the princess, getting into the spirit of things. "Imagine meeting young Shakespeare, or Queen Elizabeth, or Christopher Wren."

"Being a man of the future, I'd go forward," says Dr. Guenther.

"I'm with you there, Doc," Sinatra agrees and goes to the drinks table for another shot of Jack Daniel's. "Fly me to the moon, and all that world of tomorrow jazz."

"However exciting that might sound, space travel distracts from the far greater possibilities of time travel," Guenther says.

"And time travel could also help us solve the immigrant problem, as you've suggested in your comic strips," comments Mr. MacDonnell. "Reverse bad decisions by the bleeding hearts! Reform history! Send the damn foreigners back where they came from!"

"You draw funnies, Doc?" asks Sinatra. "Unusual sideline for a scientist."

Mr. MacDonnell clears his throat. "*The Adventures of Futureman* is much more than a mere amusement, I can assure you, Mr. Sinatra. It's a graphic illustration of the sorry state America now finds itself in. No longer the strong, clean, moral country we once were. Our nation is turning into the world's garbage dump for people no one wants."

Dr. Guenther turns to Sinatra. "I can't stand waste in any form, especially of the lost and wretched members of society. Of which we seem to have more than our share in this country. I've made use of some of them on my experimental farm."

"As labour?" asks Sinatra.

Guenther shakes his head. "As test subjects. I was researching whether the weaker strains of the human race could be improved through cross-species mutations, much the way hybridization can strengthen plants."

Sinatra frowns at Guenther through a haze of cigarette smoke. "We just fought a war over this type of thinking, Doc."

"Some of us did," mutters Mr. MacDonnell, causing Sinatra to shoot him an angry look.

Guenther waves his hand dismissively. "That was over ten years ago. Today we have other wars to fight. Against communism. Disease. Illegal aliens. Gangsters. Juvenile delinquents. Often these scourges go hand in hand."

"Huddled masses yearning to be free, the wretched refuse of your teeming shores," quotes the Trespasser. "Words from the poem on the base of the Statue of Liberty. Isn't that the foundation America is supposed to be built upon?"

Guenther sends a ring of cigar smoke to the ceiling of

the parlour. "In my experience, sir, wretches rarely yearn to be free and wouldn't know what to do with their freedom if they had it. All they do is infect our nation with ignorance and inferior blood."

"Hear, hear," interjects Mr. MacDonnell.

"Hold on there, gentlemen. My people came to America as immigrants," points out Sinatra, the bonhomie gone from his voice. "They worked hard to get ahead in this country. And I ain't done so bad myself."

"Exception proves the rule," mutters Mr. MacDonnell.

Sinatra turns toward the publisher, fists clenched. Guenther puts a placating hand on his shoulder. "Your blue eyes tell the story, sir. You must have Norman blood as well as Latinate. Most immigrants aren't made of the same stuff as you are. Take Deborah and Holly here. I came across them, and outcasts like them, washed up on the river below the gorge. Eager to throw their lives away rather than accept their proper places in society."

"Attempted suicides?" asks Mr. MacDonnell in a low voice, glancing over at his wife. "They usually try it again, you know."

Mrs. MacDonnell is huddled in a dim corner of the parlour. She's holding a sherry, but her hands are trembling so violently she can barely lift the glass to her lips.

"Pharmacological advances have led to medications that calm the nerves without befuddling the senses," says Dr. Guenther to Mr. MacDonnell.

Mr. MacDonnell snorts. "She's already got a medicine chest full of mother's little helpers. Our family physician says she simply has too much time on her hands. If only I had such problems!"

Mrs. MacDonnell glances at her husband and manages a nervous sip. From upstairs, we can hear the squeaky cries of baby Gloria in her bassinette.

"Gus?" asks Mrs. MacDonnell, leaving the rest of her question unspoken until the baby's cries grow more frantic. "Don't you think I should see to Gloria?"

"Nonsense, Audrey! Best thing is to let her cry it out," says Mr. MacDonnell. "Pick them up every time they make a peep, you spoil them."

Sinatra, losing interest, glances at the Telefunken. "Sleigh Ride" is playing. The princess hums along, swishing the skirt of her cocktail dress in time to the music.

Sinatra starts to snap his fingers to the bouncy beat. "I do this number on my new Christmas album. Recorded it during a heat wave in Palm Springs. Hundred degrees in the shade and I'm singing about Jack Frost and blizzards, I kid you not. My version's got more swing than Der Bingel's. Nothing against the old man." He smiles at the princess.

"We very much look forward to hearing your interpretation, Mr. Sinatra," says Sexton, as Cook lumbers into the parlour to announce that dinner is served.

"Ring-a-ding-ding! Jingle all the way. Milady, your carriage awaits," says Sinatra, offering his arm to the laughing princess.

* * *

Turkey, ham, goose and duck, with all the trimmings. Each place setting has a glittering array of silverware with separate plates, chargers, bowls and glasses for every course. Beside each setting is a small gift, which we're encouraged to unwrap before the soup comes out. Holly, Mrs. MacDonnell and I all get the same gift: a petit point pillbox filled with Miltown 600s, a new higher dosage of the drug. "Good for the nerves," explains Sexton to the ladies.

The men each get a box of cigars. The princess unwraps a gold purse compact, the lid engraved with a tree nymph, symbol of Nowellville House. Ariel gets nothing because, as Sexton explains, "We naturally assumed you were a man, dear, and a box of cigars simply wouldn't do for a young lady."

Dr. Guenther sits at the head of the table with the Trespasser to his right and the princess on his left. His pontificating never stops, even with his mouth full.

"Humanity has always had its weak links, but we can no longer afford to be anything less than perfect. Not with the power of the atomic bomb in the hands of our mortal enemies," he says, slicing into his duck breast. "But how to perfect humanity, eh, Duffy? We must become one with the thinking machines we're developing. I've experimented with biological mergers with some success, but it's clear that machines are the real answer. Artificial intelligence conjoined with the best in human intelligence. Man-machine centaurs will rule the next century, mark me."

The princess hangs on his every word, but Sinatra stares at Dr. Guenther with obvious distaste. When he and I catch each other's eyes over the table, Sinatra raises an eyebrow at me as if to say *Can you believe the Ferdinand this scurve is shovelling?*

I respond with a small smile and the tiniest possible shake of my head.

＊　＊　＊

After dinner, Mr. MacDonnell sends Mrs. MacDonnell to their rooms to have a lie-down to calm her nerves, while the rest of us go back to the parlour to watch *The Milton Berle Show*. At first I'm surprised that formally dressed guests at a grand house party would settle down to watch a TV show together after dinner. But this is a different time, when hit shows had a sense of occasion to them. And you only got to see them once. Milton Berle was someone whose show you didn't dare miss, especially because tonight's special guest is none other than the latest singing sensation throughout the nation, Elvis Presley.

"What an abomination," sighs Sexton, tugging the hem of her dress over her knees.

"My kids think he's totally zorch," says Sinatra, lighting a Chesterfield for the princess and a second for himself. "Not my kind of music, but the boy's got something going for him. I wish dames still screamed over me like that."

The princess gives Sinatra a warm smile and rubs his arm. "You're not so bad for an old man of forty-one."

Sinatra grins back at her as if the two of them are sharing a private joke. Their affection seems genuine, although in private Sexton confided to me that Dr. Guenther only invited the singer to (in Sexton's words) "get that oversexed garlic-eating crooner out of the princess's system. Elizabeth is, after all, next in line to the throne, unless Edward and his queen consort have issue. Which, despite Queen Wallis's age, is to be profoundly hoped for, in order to avoid the chaos and embarrassment of a woman on the throne after Edward passes."

Presley swivels his hips and belts out "Hound Dog." He's so sexy and beautiful that I can't bear to think about his bloated body, dead of an overdose on a bathroom floor twenty years from now.

Sinatra reaches over and gives me a nudge. "You're young enough to be a rock 'n' roll fan, Deborah. What do you think? Singing sensation or flash in the pan?"

"Elvis changes everything," I answer. "Unfortunately he's

destined to die young. He'll be so missed that people will make their livings by impersonating him."

Sexton gives a derisive laugh. "Our dear Deborah is something of a soothsayer. She claims she can see the future."

Milton Berle — better known as Uncle Milty — comes out on stage applauding, then mimics Elvis by gyrating moronically and doing a silly walk on the sides of his shoes. Berle's send-up is startlingly aggressive, mocking, almost insulting. I wonder if Elvis wants to sock him one.

The two launch into a shtick about Elvis's sex appeal.

"I don't like these girls always screaming, trying to tear my clothes off," Elvis mumbles. "I want a quiet type of girl. Someone who'll, y'know, calm me down."

Berle grimaces in mock disbelief and looks at the camera to deliver his punchline. "Calm you down? You don't want a girl. You want a Miltown."

The live audience breaks up.

"So what do you see in my future?" asks Sinatra.

I consider what to say. Should I tell him he and his ex, Ava Gardner, will never get over one another? That his buddy Jack Kennedy will be assassinated? That he'll make a fool of himself when he throws a violent hissy fit over not being cast in *The Godfather*? The boozy Las Vegas years with the Rat Pack? His struggles to keep his music relevant as his voice falters and the world's tastes change? Should I tell him to stop smoking? What difference would any of that make really?

"Oh, you'll have a long, successful career and live to a ripe old age. Years after your death, people will still be listening to your recordings."

Sinatra brightens. "Oh yeah? Hey, I like this chick."

"What about me, Deborah?" asks the princess. "What do you see in my future?"

"That's easy," I answer. "You're going to be the Queen of England."

The princess's smile fades and she takes Sinatra's hand. She looks upset.

"Hey, but that means I get to be king, huh?" grins Sinatra, trying to cheer her up.

I point at the TV screen, where Elvis has just launched into "Jailhouse Rock." "No, he'll be the King. You'll be the Chairman of the Board."

Sinatra and the princess trade mystified looks.

* * *

The show is just wrapping when Cook comes into the parlour twisting her apron in her hands. She looks back and forth between Sexton and Dr. Guenther.

"Beg your pardon, sir, but there's a gentleman at the door."

Guenther frowns. "What does he want?"

"He says he needs a word with you," says Cook.

"Did you tell him the doctor has guests?" asks Sexton sharply.

"Yes, ma'am, but he said they got a call from Miss Deborah's grandmother. She says her granddaughter has been kidnapped and is being held against her will. The gentleman's a New York State trooper."

Sinatra sits back in his chair, rubs his hands together and gives a low whistle. "Man, oh man. This squaresville party's finally startin' to jive."

* * *

Filling the doorway like a beige monolith, the state trooper touches the brim of his Stetson. On my walk down the stairs with a furious Sexton and a rattled Guenther, I had pictured a paunchy local cop, embarrassed to be disturbing an upstanding citizen during primetime. Instead, the police officer at the front door is a young, good-looking, implacable, I'll-ask-the-questions-here type, with an alert German shepherd at his side. I should have known Nonna Peppy would send only the best.

When the police dog sees me, she starts to bark and whine. Not in aggression but greeting. It's Lucy.

The trooper orders her to sit. "Settle down, girl, you don't want to scare folks."

"She doesn't scare me," I say, offering my hand for her to sniff. "We're friends, aren't we, Lucy?"

Sexton gives me a look. "I don't recall the officer telling you his dog's name."

I shrug. "Well. You know. I'm psychic."

The trooper looks down at his boots, stifling a grin. That's when I recognize him as Ralph De Marco, the deserter Kendal and I met on the road. The one who took Lucy with him on the Journey Home to Mother, which clearly didn't deliver him to New Jersey. Given he was in his nineties in 2025, he must be in his mid-twenties now.

Ralph gets right down to business. "Our neighbours to the north asked me to follow up on a reported kidnapping."

Sexton raises her eyebrows. "I wasn't aware that the New York State police were at the beck and call of a foreign power."

It's a nice try, but Ralph doesn't take the bait. "World's longest undefended border, ma'am. These days, with commies hiding everywhere, we need all the friends we can get. Not to mention, we got an extradition treaty with the Canucks. I'm looking for a Miss Biondi. First name Debbie."

Guenther, flabbergasted by the trooper's presence, doesn't stop me from stepping forward. "That's me."

Ralph flips open a notebook. "Are you the granddaughter of Giuseppina Pittalunga?"

Ralph mangles Nonna Peppy's name, but she's definitely the avenging angel who sent him here. I almost start to cry. I reached out to someone who had loved me before she even knew I existed. Incredibly she's trying to save me. And now I have to turn down this chance at rescue.

I nod. "I am she. But it's all a mistake, Officer. I'm here as Dr. Guenther's guest along with a number of dignitaries. Safe and sound."

I can almost feel Guenther sagging with relief.

Ralph squints at me, studying my face. I can tell he doesn't believe me.

In truth, I desperately want to leave right now in his cruiser, give a deposition at police headquarters and be released into my grandmother's care. Remain in this tight-assed, rules-obsessed, paranoid era, if necessary. But I can't leave Holly at the mercy of Sexton and Guenther even for a day. Nor can I walk away from the possibility of helping fix whatever started going wrong when I stole *The Adventures of Futureman* from the library.

"My grandmother is suffering from" — I try to remember the word they would have used for dementia in 1955 — "senility. She sees things on TV and thinks it's real. She probably saw something on *The Untouchables*. Sorry, sir."

Ralph frowns and tucks his pen into the pocket of his shirt. "I'm acquainted with your grandmother, Miss. She contacted me personally about this matter. She seems pretty sharp to me."

I pause and make eye contact with him. "I guess I should make a point of calling her more often, eh?"

Ralph nods. "You might want to do that, Miss. Old folks get lonely sometimes. And in my experience, they have plenty of wisdom to impart."

"You'll let her know we spoke?"

"I surely will."

He touches the brim of his Stetson and politely says "ma'am" to Sexton and me before he leaves. Lucy follows him to the cruiser but turns to look at me, as if wondering why I'm not coming with them.

As Dr. Guenther dabs sweat from his forehead and hurries back to the parlour to explain things to his guests (all a silly misunderstanding, Sexton suggests he tell them), Sexton grips me by the back of both arms and frogmarches me to the attic room. I could yank out of her grasp, spin around and push her down the stairs, maybe even break her neck, but what would be the point? I'd just end up in a different kind of prison, maybe even get sent to the gas chamber.

"From now on, you'll be locked up day and night," Sexton says, clamping the shackle back on my ankle. "You have only yourself to blame."

After she's gone, I strip off the velvet dress and crinoline but can't pull the other strangulating garments of 1950s womanhood over the shackle. I curl up on the cot under the sagging sprig of mistletoe. The full moon hangs sadly outside my window like something out of a Sinatra ballad.

"I'm fresh out of ideas, how about you, buddy?" I ask the moon.

I watch the night sky and despair of ever having another chance at escape when I hear something working away at the lock. A *tch tch tch* sound. The door opens. Holly is standing in the doorway in pink pyjamas with padded feet, holding a bobby pin.

"You okay?"

I sigh. "I could've been rescued just now. Could've lived next door to the house where I grew up, knowing everything that was going to happen in the world years before it did."

Holly sits next to me and starts working at the shackle's lock with the bobby pin. She smells of bourbon, candy canes and Vicks VapoRub.

"If you knew everything ahead of time, and blabbed about it, they'd probably have you committed to an asylum," she points out.

"Or I'd be a — what did they call it?"

"A soothsayer! That's what they're calling you downstairs. The princess wants you to read her palm and Mr. Swoonatra wants to know what board he'll be the chairman of."

Holly springs the lock, allowing me to pull off the girdle and take my first deep breath all day.

"Do you think Sexton will actually let me go to the falls tomorrow?"

"Oh yeah." Holly nods enthusiastically. "The princess and her beau think you're solid. They want you along for kicks."

I laugh. "When did you start talking like a hipster?"

"Frank's teaching me. It'll come in handy when I go to New York and start hanging out with Warhol and Capote."

We curl up together on the cot and wait.

＊　＊　＊

Both of us wake up to the sound of knocking. We push the cot aside. Holly swings open the trapdoor to reveal the Trespasser and Unicorn Girl gazing up at us. We limit our greetings to silent hugs. With Sexton and Guenther one floor below, noise is dangerous and time is precious. I'm surprised that the Trespasser's first question is "Where's Cassandra?"

Holly silently hands him the cupcake-shaped hub. The Trespasser frowns as he turns it over and pries open the battery door. He palms a handful of batteries out of a pocket and thumbs them into place. "Temporary fix. I'll need to set up a better way to charge this thing. Or upload the AI into a more powerful device."

The sprinkles on the cupcake glow pink and blue. The message *Let's Get Baking* appears on the screen in PICTO.

"How did this all start, Duffy?" I ask the Trespasser.

"No one wants to die. I'm no different, Debbie. I'd discovered some time ago that a quantum passage existed at the base of Niagara Falls. I thought going back in time might be a way to cheat death. I settled on 1950. America recovering from World War Two, lots of university positions opening up, early years of computer science and artificial intelligence research, quantum physics coming into its own, Einstein and Bohr both still alive and Everett figuring out his many worlds theory at Princeton. History in the making."

"Hubris," mutters Unicorn Girl. "You baby boomers always want to live forever, no matter the cost."

"Point taken," says the Trespasser. "I fell out of the sky and ended up in the river near the Schoellkopf Power Station. The River Rats fished me out, same as they did you. I was in bad shape — broken leg, dislocated shoulder, detached retina. When I told Lefty and Hubie I was from the future, they bundled me up and brought me to Nowellville House. That was five years ago. At first I was relieved to be in the care of someone halfway intelligent who actually believed my story. I told Guenther about quantum computing and theories of alternate worlds. Gave him a picture of the future — technological advancements, changing social mores, civil rights, feminism, you name it. Unfortunately I didn't realize he was a total xenophobe and psychopath until it was too late."

"You're the real Professor Quantum, aren't you?" I interrupt.

The Trespasser won't meet my eyes. "Sadly, yes. I didn't come up with the idea for the Mother of the Journey Home, though. That, Debbie, came from your stories in *The History of the Known World*, which were based partly on *The Adventures of Futureman*, which you stole from the library, which in turn influenced your comics about life in New Rome. A circuit of stolen stories."

I'm so surprised I'm not sure what to say. "But how did he manage to make his imaginary world real?"

"With money, and help from people in high places," says the Trespasser. "In the 1920s, the Prince of Wales became interested in eugenics. He met scientists, including Guenther, who welcomed the chance to control the march of history for the next thousand years. In exchange for financial help, Guenther and his team altered the past, removing the need for Edward to abdicate. He never gave up the throne. That's how Guenther discovered that he actually had the power to turn an imagined history into a real one. I doubt he ever expected Sinatra to get mixed up in all of it."

I put my face in my hands. "You should never have gone back in time, Duffy."

"And you should never have stolen that book from the library."

"What now?" I ask.

"You're a destroyer of worlds. It's time to destroy Guenther's world."

The Trespasser removes a folded sheet of newsprint from his inside jacket pocket. "From the archives of the *Niagara Daily News*, dated June 7, 1956. That's the day after tomorrow. Look at the headline."

"Schoellkopf Power Station collapses," I read. "You're kidding."

"Around five o'clock tomorrow afternoon, there'll be a major rockslide. It'll take the station down with it."

"You're the bait," says Unicorn Girl. "Guenther will follow you into harm's way."

"You want me to *kill* him?"

The Trespasser nods. "I'm afraid it's the only way. I've modelled a few different scenarios, with various outcomes. Up until you took over the strip, the distribution of *The Adventures of Futureman* was restricted to one small newspaper with a tiny readership. Now the syndicates are sniffing around. If they run that strip in hundreds of newspapers across the U.S. and beyond, its ideas go viral. The only way to stop that from happening is to take out the supposed creator."

I sigh. "So, it's the 'kill the monster in its cradle' solution. You know that always results in unintended consequences."

"It's the only way," says the Trespasser. "Algorithms don't lie. Or not often."

"We need a distraction," says Unicorn Girl. "Something that will allow you to escape and force Guenther to follow you."

Holly laughs softly. "You kidding? We're going to Goat Island with Sinatra and a princess. You don't think that'll cause enough of a stir?"

The Trespasser shakes his head. "Sinatra told me he plans to cut their visit to the falls short and 'get the hell back to New York,' quote unquote."

I stand and stretch. It's good to be unshackled, ungirdled and among friends again. I feel some of Sputnik Chick's strength and resourcefulness coming back to me.

"There might be a way to keep Sinatra from leaving early," I say. "Let me make a call."

"This late at night?" says Holly. "Who you calling?"

"My grandmother. When I tell her Sinatra is going to be twenty minutes away from her house tomorrow afternoon, she won't mind me waking her up. If anyone can delay his departure, it's her."

Unicorn Girl picks up Cassandra, examining her hub. It's been battered, scorched and dented. "What do you think, Cass? Will this plan work?"

Cass's hub glows weakly. "Worth a try," her voice says. It's as close as an AI can come to a wild guess.

Sinatra's fedora is the first thing I notice, his head bowed to sign the wrist of a giggling bobby-soxer. He and the princess are taking in the view from Prospect Point, overlooking the Bridal Veil Falls and offering a panorama of the curve of the Horseshoe Falls on the Canadian side. Most of the tourists don't recognize the princess, but Sinatra's presence causes a stir. Autograph hounds ask him to sign their shirt cuffs and copies of the *Buffalo Evening News*. Holly hangs around amusing Sinatra by telling him she's there for "crowd control."

The Trespasser and Unicorn Girl have arrived on the Ducati in travelling clothes — him in leathers, her in dungarees and boots. Motorcycle helmets under their arms, they stand on the edge of the crowd, watching the commotion. Sexton, Guenther and I have joined the MacDonnells. It's another warm day and the red velvet dress feels especially heavy and tight. I've got my sketchbooks stuffed inside my girdle.

Sexton links her arm through mine, as if we're pals. She's complaining about Sinatra. "I'd like to show the princess the Cave of the Winds, but she says there isn't time. Her escort is impatient to get back to his haunts in New York."

Mr. MacDonnell snorts at the word *escort*. "I wonder what her family thinks of that goomba. His career was going down the toilet until he made that war movie."

Sexton shrugs. "Royalty has its ways. I've heard they're often attracted by the very inappropriateness of their partners."

"It won't last," says Guenther definitively. "Elizabeth is next in line to the throne. He's the son of an illiterate Sicilian boxer. The relationship is untenable."

Holly skips over to announce that Sinatra and the princess are about to leave. "They want to say goodbye to the soothsayer."

Forcing her bright red lips into an unconvincing smile, Sexton grips my arm and marches me through the crowd. "Be quick with your goodbyes."

"Hey, it's the little fortune teller!" says Sinatra, scribbling his name on the inside of a giggling girl's elbow. "You bummed out on us pretty early last night."

"Oh well, you know." I glance at Sexton, standing hard by my side. "Had a little too much to drink, so I made it an early night."

Sinatra laughs. "Hey, I feel sorry for people who don't drink. When they wake up in the morning, that's the best they're going to feel all day."

To my relief, Sexton releases my arm. "I'm going to pay my respects to the princess. Perhaps it's not too late to see the Cave of the Winds."

As the manageress drops into a deep curtsy in front of Princess Elizabeth, Sinatra rolls his eyes and lights a Chesterfield. "You should make like the wind and blow this crummy town, set yourself up somewhere nice reading tea leaves."

"I've got some stuff I have to do first."

"Well, when you finally decide to split, come visit us in New York," he says. "You can stick around as long as you like."

"I wouldn't want to impose . . ."

"A friend is never an imposition."

Twirling his hand in a wind-it-up gesture to the princess, he signals his desire to scram. I glance at the Timex on my wrist. It's four thirty-five. Less than thirty minutes to zero hour.

"Uh . . . Mr. Sinatra —"

He raises a finger to correct me. "Call me Frank. We're friends, right?"

"Frank, before you go, there's someone I've love you to meet. My grandmother. She's a huge fan. Saw you in New York when you were just starting out, singing with Pépé Duran."

Sinatra raises his brows. "Of course! Where is she?"

"Stay right here and I'll bring her over," I say. "She'll be absolutely thrilled."

With Sexton focused on the princess and Guenther pontificating as usual, I slip away to the spot on the American side favoured by Nonna Peppy as a photographic backdrop. She used to send snapshots to her relatives with a note scribbled on the back to point out that the Canadian Horseshoe Falls is bigger than the American Bridal Veil Falls, conferring bragging rights on her adopted country.

Sure enough, my startlingly youthful father is lining up a shot of Peppy, my grandfather Nonno Zin, and my very pregnant mom holding my three-year-old sister, Linda, by the hand. Mom looks tired. I remember her saying that she suffered from anemia while she was carrying me. I stand watching them, not ten feet away. Dad says to say cheese and Nonna Peppy tells him to hurry the hell up. They're a family of ghosts. All of them will be long dead by 2025, even Linda.

When I catch Peppy's eye, she puts her hand over her mouth. Her eyes grow wide. She looks as if she's about to cry.

"Scusa, this young lady wants to talk to me," I hear her tell my father. "I think she might be the granddaughter of a friend from the old neighbourhood."

She walks over to me, her face a mirror of the emotions on my own.

"You're Debbie?"

I nod. "Glad there aren't too many girls here in red velvet dresses."

She takes my hand. "I would know your face, dress or no dress. You're the spittin' image of my sister, Marie, who died in the flu epidemic. Che tragedia. You lucky my son-in-law has the week off, but I had to do a real song and dance to get him to drive out here today. I ended up bringing my boarder along too, and her little niece. Eufemia, she just loves Sinatra."

I give a little gasp. "Eufemia and a girl? Where are they?"

"Just takin' in the view," says Nonna Peppy and points her chin at a woman in a headscarf looking out at the falls with a girl at her side. The woman is twenty-something with long thick curly black hair, beautiful brown eyes and the cheekbones of a movie star. A black beauty mark has been pencilled onto one cheek to mask an imperfection, a tiny bar code reading *SPQR*. Her small waist and ample bosoms make her look like the ideal woman of the '50s. Or, as my friend Frank might say, a bombshell. The little girl holding hands with Eufemia looks about twelve. She's wearing thick green leotards even though it's a hot day. She's got a straw hat on her head over thick braids the colour of tree moss.

Eufemia turns at the sound of Nonna Peppy's voice. When she sees me, her face breaks into a beautiful smile. Prima shouts, "Look, it's Stan, Auntie Femina!"

Nonna Peppy laughs affectionately. "Marone! How many names you got?"

Eufemia and Prima lavish me with kisses and hugs. "I wouldn'a known you, if it weren't for your mark!" says Eufemia, touching the tiny code on my cheek.

"Or me, you," I say. "Thank goodness Prima recognized me."

"She's very smart," says Eufemia proudly, adjusting Prima's straw hat. "I keep her at home, though, because she's a little different. The kids make fun."

"Doesn't she go to school?"

"Oh sure, through the radio classroom," says Eufemia. "They got broadcasts for kids stuck home from the polio."

"The ones in the iron lungs," adds Nonna Peppy in a low voice. "They read stories, do their numbers, learn about history, everything!"

"Do you want me to recite the names of all the kings and queens of England?" ask Prima. "I know them by heart, starting with Athelstan."

"It's okay, cara, we'll have Stan over for coffee an' biscotti one day so you can show off," laughs Eufemia.

Prima giggles. Her green eyes, one real and the other clearly artificial, sparkle at me. Being physically different in the '50s, especially for a girl, must be tough.

"I'm at Nowellville House, Eufemia. I know you were there too. What happened?"

Her smile disappears. "We get away from that awful place, thanks to this one," she says, looking down lovingly at Prima. "The dogs run away from her, do you believe it! One night we leave together and walk to the footbridge on the Rainbow. Trying to get to Canada. But the guard call the American cops on account I got no papers. When the state trooper come, he look like a kind man so I decide to tell the truth. I say we come from Tomorrowland, like in the Disney TV show, and end up here through divine intervention. A miracle."

"That must have gone over like a lead balloon," I comment.

"No, he believed me!" says Eufemia, seizing my hands. "He call up COSTI, the settlement group for Italians in Canada, and they find a place for Prima and me to stay in Shipman's Corners, boarding with Peppy and Zin."

"And the trooper actually *believed* you when you said you and Prima had travelled through time?" It occurs to me then that there are no coincidences. "Eufemia, are you talking about Ralph De Marco?"

"Si! Raffaele! Such a nice man," says Eufemia, blushing slightly. "Good-looking too."

"He and Femina got an understanding," says Peppy, tapping her two index fingers together. "Love at first sight. So, where's Sinatra?" she adds, getting down to business.

I take a deep breath. "I'll introduce you. And —"

She raises her eyebrows. "And don't bug him too much, right?"

"On the contrary. I need you to keep him occupied for as long as you possibly can. Fifteen, twenty minutes at least. Just keep talking about New York in the old days and that bandleader you loved so much. Think you can do that?"

She straightens herself up to her full five feet. "Just watch me."

Sinatra is glancing at his watch when we get back to him. He's polite to Peppy, gives Eufemia an appreciative, if slightly salacious, "Wow-ee-wow-wow!" and makes a point of signing Prima's autograph book while telling her what a cutie she is, but his politeness turns to genuine interest when Peppy starts talking about her roots. "Your mother Dolly's people are Ligurian, right? I'm from Piacenza. She and I are practically paisan!"

That's a stretch, but I can tell he's touched by the mention of his mother. Peppy proceeds to tell him about the many times she heard him sing in his early days, sometimes in the Hoboken bar owned by his parents.

"I hear your pop was a prizefighter," says Peppy.

"Yeah, until he broke both his wrists," answers Sinatra.

"Same story with my Zinio. Thirty undefeated bouts and then, boom, he breaks his hand and they throw him away like garbage."

"No mercy for old boxers," agrees Sinatra. "Where'd your husband fight?"

While Peppy and Sinatra kibbitz, he continues signing autographs.

I check the Timex. It's four forty-seven. I still have no idea how to lead Guenther into danger when the Schoellkopf goes down, fifteen minutes from now.

I look out at the brink of the falls. The rapids hurry bits of flotsam over the cataract — tree branches, bottles, lumber, even a fishing rod.

Mrs. MacDonnell — Audrey — stands at the railing with Gloria in her arms. The baby fusses, bumping her head against Audrey's shoulder. Mrs. MacDonnell doesn't react. She looks dazed. Exhausted, like my mom. Gloria's dark eyes gaze at me over her mother's shoulder.

As Mr. MacDonnell snaps pictures, Audrey stares down at the steep drop of the Bridal Veil Falls with Gloria pressed to her chest. Slowly she suspends Gloria over the edge, arms outstretched as if making an offering. The baby whimpers and struggles as spray drenches her face.

Mr. MacDonnell drops his camera. "Hey, what the hell are you doing?"

Time slows to a crawl. It's like watching a stop-action film of an unfolding tragedy.

The bawling baby suspended over the precipice by her mother. The father screaming at his wife as he stoops to retrieve his camera. The Trespasser lunging toward Audrey as she lets go of the baby. For a micromoment — not even the blink of an eye, more like the flick of eyelash — the baby is in free fall. She's snatched from the air by awkward hands that almost lose their grip on her dress.

Audrey turns and looks at the Trespasser questioningly. *What exactly are you saving her for? To grow up unloved? Drugged with Miltowns? Poisoned by radiation?*

The Trespasser clutches the baby to his chest as Audrey throws one leg over the railing and straddles it. Unicorn Girl and I both step cautiously toward her.

I hold out my hand. "Come back."

"Please," says Unicorn Girl.

But like so many others who've jumped into the falls over the years to be plucked off the shoreline by the River Rats, Audrey must already be imagining the relief of oblivion.

She throws her other leg over and lets herself go. Her skirt balloons in the updraft of the falls, exposing her girdle and garters, like Marilyn Monroe in *The Seven Year Itch*. She disappears into the mist without a sound.

Time speeds up again as tourists run to the railing for a better look. Someone shouts, "A jumper!" Another asks, "Is she dead? Can you see her?"

A smaller crowd gathers around the Trespasser, who is trying to comfort the wailing infant. Mr. MacDonnell is still gaping at the spot where Audrey jumped, a camera-strap dangling limply from his hand.

Everyone has turned away from Sinatra. They're all looking in one direction — straight down. Which is when I realize I've just witnessed my cue. Time to get Guenther moving toward the gorge.

The Timex reads four fifty-five.

I try to pick Guenther out of the milling crowd and spot him standing on the other side of Prospect Point, a look of alarm on his face. He's the only one whose gaze is not rivetted to the spot where Audrey jumped.

As he scans the crowd, his eyes catch on me. He looks angry. His shout comes out like a snarl. "Hey, you there! Effie! Where the hell you going with my property? Stop, thief!"

I am not the property he's after. He wants Prima. He's *always* wanted her. He may have needed me to draw his vision of the future, but only the child of the People of Forever can turn his vision into reality. Having lost her once, he's now focused on getting her back.

Seizing the girl's hand, Eufemia takes off at a run. I follow as best as I can in my kitten heels. We're outdistancing Guenther, who is caught in the crowd rushing toward the railing to look for signs of Audrey's body. When one of my heels snaps off, I kick off both shoes and run in stocking feet.

We sprint out of Niagara Falls State Park into an intersection where a cop is directing traffic and run straight across the street, ignoring red lights, car horns and blasts from the cop's whistle.

That's when we hear a sound like a thousand-thousand mountains falling. The ground beneath our feet shakes violently. Sirens are blaring — not warning of a nuclear attack but summoning help for a different type of crisis: the collapse of a hydroelectric station.

We cross a gravel parking lot to where the giant steel doors of an industrial elevator loom open. Men in overalls and hard-hats are pouring out. Some of them try to wave us back. One man grabs my arm. "Don't go in there, sister, the windows are exploding!"

When Guenther appears at the edge of the parking lot, clearly winded and barely able to run, he elbows his way toward us. Wild-eyed with rage.

We keep fighting our way forward against the stampede of workers. Hardhats are strewn everywhere. Men in overalls scramble over the edge of the gorge, climbing straight up the side of the collapsing station.

Guenther finally catches up with us at the edge of the gorge. He's limping and out of breath but doesn't seem worried. It's him against three females. As far as he's concerned, he's already won.

"Give her up, Effie," he wheezes. "Future Girl comes with me."

When he grabs for Prima's arm, Eufemia blocks his reach by stepping between them, then places her hands on Guenther's shoulders as if trying to calm him down. Before he can say a word, she spins him around like a dance partner. His heels are at the edge of the gorge. Eufemia shoves her face into his and says, "Go back to hell where you belong, you devil."

Eufemia pushes him over the edge of the gorge — I think. Or maybe a panicked worker, scrambling past us, knocks him over by accident. Or maybe Guenther has a dizzy spell after the exertion of his sprint, foreshadowing the heart attack that is supposed to kill him fifteen years from now. Who knows? Too many things happen at once.

Whatever causes Doc Time to lose his balance, he falls backwards into the gorge — mouth open, feet scrabbling for purchase on the loose gravel, arms flapping as if trying to take flight like the dodo bird in a Porky Pig cartoon.

The three of us peer over the edge and watch his plunge into the river along with several million tons of rock, brick and metal. As the Schoellkopf Power Station slides into the Niagara Gorge, it sends up a cloud of dust and debris so vast that the Rainbow Bridge disappears from view. Eufemia pulls Prima into her chest to shield her eye from the dust.

"Eufemia," I tell her, "you've just changed history. Maybe even saved the world."

She smiles at me through a mask of dust. "If you say so, Stan. I just want to take my little girl back home to Shipman's Corners."

Prima's straw hat has blown off and sits on the edge of the gorge. Calmly, Eufemia walks over, picks it up and firmly places it on the girl's conical head.

As sirens continue to wail and fire trucks race by, the three of us make our way back to Prospect Point, our arms around each another's waists, like sisters.

* * *

History will record a single fatality of the Schoellkopf disaster, a thirty-nine-year-old maintenance foreman who was blown through one of the power station's exploding windows to land in the river, where his body was spotted doing lazy circles in a whirlpool. His obituary is written up in the newspaper clipping the Trespasser gave me.

But there was another victim of the Schoellkopf Power Station disaster who goes unrecorded. Dr. Norman Guenther, also known as Doctor Time, an unremarkable man unnoticed by the escaping men, will eventually be assumed to have gone over the falls like Audrey MacDonnell. Perhaps her suicide inspired him to jump, the well-known copycat phenomenon, a common occurrence at the falls, which has always been a magnet for the suicidal.

In the coming days, news reports will follow the recovery efforts for the bodies of the two jumpers. River Rats Salvage and Rescue will locate Audrey's body downriver, snagged on a rock. But the body of Dr. Guenther vanishes without a trace, like so many others who have gone into the gorge at the base of the Schoellkopf. Probably just trapped at the bottom of the river somewhere. Or possibly trapped in the past or future of Earth Standard Time, or even an alternate world in which I hope I never have the misfortune to find myself.

The newspaper makes no mention of the presence of Frank Sinatra or Princess Elizabeth in New York State Park that day. As if they were never really there.

* * *

When I kiss Peppy goodbye at Prospect Point, she says, "Thank you for introducing me to Sinatra. That English girl he's going around with — she seems very classy. I thought I knew her from somewhere. She looks a lot like the Queen, dontcha think?"

I frown. "Which Queen are you talking about?"

"The Queen of England. Whatsername, Eliza! Beautiful girl. Me and Zinio watched her get crowned on the neighbour's TV."

"So you know who Queen Elizabeth is?"

Peppy snorts. "Ma che, you think I'm simple? Her face is all over the money!"

I laugh and kiss my grandmother.

"I'm lookin' forward to meetin' you again. When'd you say you gonna be born?"

"October 4, 1956. It'll become an easy day to remember. A year to the day before Sputnik's birthday."

Peppy frowns. "Who the hell is Sputnik? Another one of your many names?"

I laugh. "Sort of. Anyway, see you next year."

And with that, I kiss Nonna Peppy, Eufemia and Prima goodbye and go looking for Unicorn Girl. It's time for the

Trespasser to help us swing a Schrödinger and get the hell out of the '50s to somewhere else in the multiverse of two thousand fifty-eight alternate realities. Cassandra can hitch a ride with us.

EIGHT

THE SHOW MUST GO ON IN COZY WORLD

I finish the story as daylight begins to brighten David's bedroom. Just in time, because I'm losing my voice. I take a sip of water from a glass beside the bed and close my eyes. Maybe I can get some shut-eye before it's time for Unicorn Girl and me to hit the road.

David is curled up beside me. He may look asleep, but I know he's listening.

"And so did it work? Did history get back on track?" he mumbles, eyes closed.

I yawn. "I took it as a good sign that Nonna Peppy knew who the Queen was. But so much stuff happened in 1956 that wasn't supposed to . . ." I shrug. "Who knows how much Earth Standard Time was affected by the temporal shifts caused by all that back and forth in time and space? Those kinks in history might have resulted in a very different 2025 than the one I left behind."

"And you really think Guenther might be alive in some other world?"

I shrug. "He went into the water near the quantum passage, so anything is possible, but I prefer to think of him as dead."

"What happened to everyone else?"

"Duffy returned to Bell Labs. Eufemia and Prima went back to Shipman's Corners with Nonna Peppy. Last time I saw

Holly, she was hitchhiking her way to New York City. They're all still back there in — I guess it's almost 1960 by now. Wow."

"But the others who jumped with you?"

I sigh. "Oh, I very much hope Hot Lips and Jordan made it back to Paradiso. I'm not optimistic about Kendal or Poseidon — they were very badly hurt by the Puffs."

"What about Sexton?"

I laugh. "Don't know. Don't care. Maybe she was an alternate historical construct too. Or maybe she decided to use the quantum passage. She certainly knew where it was. I just hope we never meet again one day in the multiverse of two thousand and fifty-eight alternate worlds."

"And Unicorn Girl remained with you."

I nod. "For now. She wanted to finish her internship. We've been surfing the quantum passageways to explore the multiverse. Took Cass with us. It's been over four years of just the three of us."

"And you ended up here," says David. "There are no coincidences?"

"None."

"That suggests you and I were destined to meet again from the get-go," points out David. "I know I'm no John Kendal, but maybe you should settle down in Cozy Time with me. Not a bad place to retire together."

"What about your Dutch wife?"

He shrugs. "Jenny can be reprogrammed."

"Let me think it over while Unicorn Girl and I finish this gig," I say. "You can borrow Cassandra while I'm gone, if she's willing."

"Won't you need her?"

I shake my head. "She provides recorded music to warm up the crowd — more of a novelty for the Cozies than anything else. And our magical knapsacks meet most of our other needs. Anyway, she's more of a friend than an assistant these days."

Despite my noncommittal answer to David's proposal, I know he's my best chance for a happy, stable life. Forgive, forget, grow old together. Let Jenny do the cleaning and cooking and eventually the caregiving while Cassandra provides the soundtrack.

Why the hell not? Isn't that what synthetics are for? Music, comfort, cleaning, wish fulfillment? Doing the jobs we can't or don't want to do? Making our lives easier?

Until we reach the event horizon for the age of synthetic domination. The Singularity. With luck, I'll be long gone by then.

* * *

Jenny makes breakfast for Unicorn Girl and me. Huevos rancheros with salsa verde. Put up by David, of course. The Cozies don't go in for spicy food.

Jenny has traded her blond wig for a kerchief and her nightie for overalls. Cassandra must have had a word about acceptable humanoid attire.

Unicorn Girl pushes back from the table with a grunt of satisfaction. "We'd better get moving, Stan."

"I could use more coffee." I yawn. Jenny refills my cup.

I'm just taking my last sip and Unicorn Girl is tightening her bootlaces when David shuffles into the kitchen, rubbing his dishevelled hair. "Didn't want you to go without a proper goodbye."

"I'll give you two some time alone," says Unicorn Girl, hoisting her knapsack. She's full of energy after a good night's sleep. I wish I could say the same. At my age, staying up all night making love and telling stories takes its toll.

When the door closes, David pulls me into his arms.

"Again, I'm sorry about lying about Jenny," he says, adding, "I was serious about what I said last night."

"I know." I kiss him. "I'll be back. I just don't know exactly when we'll return. We've got a two-day hike ahead of us, a gig to do and who knows what storytelling opportunities we'll pick up along the way."

"I understand. Tell stories while the sun shines," nods David. "But when you've wrapped all that up, come back to me."

* * *

Closing the front door behind me, I see that Unicorn Girl has already hiked up the trail a ways. She waves her arm impatiently and shouts, "What are you waiting for? We're burning daylight!"

We walk past five lampposts in a day and a half, which means we're making excellent time and headed in the right direction.

On the third day, we stop in a town that's on our regular circuit. It's winter market day, so we can pick up some of the Cozies' baked goods to supplement the rations we get from our knapsacks. As we stand at a heated stall, examining the pound cakes and fruit wines for which this region is famous, the merchant chats us up through her face mask. "Staying in town for the concert?"

Unicorn Girl and I exchange looks. "Concert?"

The merchant nods at the crumbling limestone building behind us that provides some shelter for the winter market. The words *Municipal Opera House* have been chiselled into the facade — not that anyone has sung here since this world's first of many pandemics. A hand-lettered sign has been posted in front of the entrance doors on an easel.

CONCERT 7:00 P.M.
Recital by the Artist Known as L
Featuring NEW WORK
performed by the Multiverse Singers
ALL WELCOME. FREE ADMISSION
(OR PAY WHAT YOU CAN!)

"Looks like we've got competition," I comment. "Let's stick around."

* * *

Ten minutes before the show, we file into the theatre with a queue of Cozies, their faces covered by masks and face shields. Crowded indoor spaces still make them nervous, which is why the Sisters Sputnik always perform outdoors. Clearly the Artist Known as L has other ideas.

I'm astonished by the number of Cozies who have shown up; Unicorn Girl, Cassandra and I have trouble attracting many people in this town. The opera house probably seats over a thousand and it's almost at capacity. Most of the audience must have travelled in from communities up in the mountains. Very unusual for the nonmigratory folks of Cozy World: most of them live and die ten miles from where they were born without ever going farther afield.

Up on stage, in front of a backdrop of crushed velvet curtains, sits a very old grand piano. As Unicorn Girl and I take our seats, I can see the manufacturer's name in gold lettering over the keyboard: Bösendorfer. Made in Vienna, it's one of the best concert pianos in the world. Must have already been in this town long before the Cozies shut their borders to trade.

But no matter how good the instrument, it's all about the performance. And tuning, of course, which I doubt anyone in Cozy World has the faintest clue how to do. Gouged by cut marks, the piano shows signs of having seen use as a butcher block.

At seven p.m. sharp, a tall, robust-looking woman, probably about twenty-five years old, glides onto the stage. Her face, arms and hands have been dyed bright green and her waist-long hair is tinted pink. She's wearing a black sleeveless leather bodice and a skirt constructed of what look like hundreds of tiny pieces of aluminum soldered together. On her feet she wears a pair of elegant silver evening slippers.

Despite the fact that she carries herself like a diva, she looks like a junkster. Probably a member of the gang of cyber-vagabonds wandering the multiverse who bartered with David when he was looking for parts for Jenny.

I feel slightly queasy. Unlike David, I've never been able to forgive the junksters for their part in New Rome.

The Artist Known as L places a tattered piece of sheet music on the piano. Seats herself on the bench. Positions her hands on the keys. Takes her time getting settled. You'd think she actually knows how to play.

The Cozies are easy marks when it comes to live performances. Their expectations are low, except for what Unicorn Girl, Cassandra and I present to them. A little bit of music, razzmatazz and a good story to boot.

I'm ready to stifle a laugh at what I suspect will sound like bashing and crashing on the out-of-tune piano, until the Artist Known as L gracefully attacks the keyboard and the opening notes of Beethoven's "Moonlight Sonata" fill the hall. Which, I have to admit, turns out to have good acoustics.

The Bösendorfer is actually in tune. L takes her time, her hands flowing expertly over the keys, the fingers of her left hand maintaining the slow build in intensity of the bass line.

I know exactly how this piece should sound, from beginning to end. It's almost muscle memory, even though I don't play piano myself. My sister, Linda, was the musician in the family. She practised "Moonlight Sonata" for the better part of a year, getting ready for a conservatory exam. There were a few troublesome sections that she repeated again and again and again.

The junkster plays the piece flawlessly. No omissions, no hesitations, no covering up mistakes. Next to me, a Cozy starts to weep.

At the end of the piece, we join the Cozies in a standing ovation, something I taught them to do.

The Artist Known as L gives a gracious bow. There's no microphone but her voice projects throughout the hall. "Thank you all for your generous attention! And now let's welcome the Multiverse Singers on stage to perform an original song of my own composition, 'Winter Wonderland.'"

Unicorn Girl whispers to me, "Isn't that one of those old classics from Earth Standard Time?"

I nod and whisper back, "Looks like the Artist Known as L is also a plagiarizer."

From the row behind us, a Cozy indignantly shushes me.

The Multiverse Singers are a motley group of ten junksters dressed in silver tuxes, their faces tinted a rainbow of pastel colours that no human skin would see in nature. Which is part of their shtick, I guess: they're still trying to look like synthetics that were built to look humanoid but not *too* human.

The Artist Known as L returns to the piano, plays a chord and pumps the sustain pedal with her well-shod foot, giving the choir their key. The singers hum in three-part harmony.

Behind me, the shushing Cozy enthuses to a friend, "Wonderful! Have you ever heard anything like it? So much better than the noises from that little metal box that comes around sometimes."

I glance at Unicorn Girl and roll my eyes.

The "Winter Wonderland" the singers give us is obviously riffing off the Christmas standard with a lot of the same lyrics — I wonder what the Cozies make of "Parson Brown" — but with a unique, dare I say, complex and interesting melody line. It's more like "The Artist Known as L's Winter Wonderland, After the Classic by Bernard and Smith."

"Wow, that was awesome!" enthuses Unicorn Girl, joining the Cozies in applauding wildly.

"Mmm-hmm," I admit, getting reluctantly to my feet.

When a battered hat gets passed down the row, I grudgingly drop in a couple of coins. Unicorn Girl frowns at me and throws in a few alarmingly large bills.

"Should we stick around and congratulate them?" she asks.

I shake my head. "They just got three standing ovations and most of your money. I don't think L needs our praise."

"Oh come on!"

* * *

After L and the singers have taken their bows, and the Cozies are filing out, Unicorn Girl and I get up on stage and go behind the curtain.

The Artist Known as L is packing up her sheet music in a knapsack much like ours, while one of the Multiverse Singers sits at a table counting money. I'm a little startled at the stack of bills in front of them.

"It's not really the done thing to come backstage without an invitation," says L, looking down at us imperiously. She's even taller than she appeared to be on stage, well over six feet. And I notice something else: what I thought was green face paint appears to be her true skin colour. Even her eyes are green. Or rather her eye. The other eye is fixed and immobile, made of some type of synthetic plastic.

Unicorn Girl steps forward to make introductions before we pull down our masks. I can see the bar code on my cheekbone mirrored in L's artificial eye.

The pupil of her real eye widens. She's made me.

Passenger. Not of this world.

When Unicorn Girl explains we are two-thirds of the storytelling troupe known as the Sisters Sputnik, the eyebrow over L's real eye lifts slightly.

"Oh yes? I *think* I've heard of you. But one meets so many people!"

"Just wanted to say how much we enjoyed the concert," says Unicorn Girl. "We have an AI who provides music at our events, but we've never seen a live performance inside a hall in this world. The Cozies are so shy about indoor crowds."

"Oh really?" says L, stifling a yawn. "Well, they certainly don't seem to object to crowding into our concerts! There is usually standing room only. Music seems to be having something of a renaissance here."

"Good turnout for such a small community," I say, trying to sound magnanimous. "Of course, they have so little entertainment here that a live concert must be terribly exciting for them." Then to impress her, I add, "We're on our way to perform in Central City. Big celebration for the solstice."

L gives me a weak smile. Her real eye keeps focusing on something behind us, as if she's looking for an escape route or trying to get someone else's attention.

"We'll be in Central City ourselves soon. We're the star attraction for the reopening of a place called Carnegie Hall. Now you must excuse me. My people and I are tired."

With that, L turns her back to us.

"One last thing," I say, raising my voice a notch. "Your ass looks familiar. Or maybe it's your face. Hard to tell the difference. Were you ever in New Rome?"

L flinches but doesn't turn around.

"Fuck off, passengers," she says loudly and firmly.

One of the singers opens the back door for us, waving a hand to indicate we're to go through it into an alley behind the building. When we do, the door slams behind us. We hear a lock turning.

Unicorn Girl and I look at one other.

"I think the junksters may have evolved," I comment, making air quotes on *evolved*.

"The junksters have always had mad skills. It's the Cozies who have evolved," replies Unicorn Girl. "They're developing taste. We're going to have to kick up our game, Debbie. And by the way, you shouldn't be so rude."

* * *

Despite our stopover for the concert, we stay on schedule to reach Central City — the New York of Cozy World — in time for our gig. No need to wander around in the woods now that we've done our pilgrimage in honour of Saint Lazarus.

On the outskirts of New Jersey, in a fallow field that in Earth Standard Time would be crowded with outlet malls and parking lots, we look down a slope to lamppost number six, the final marker in our journey. Two people look back up at us and wave. As we approach, they come more clearly into view: an older Black man and a young Black woman with knapsacks on their backs.

Unicorn Girl recognizes them first. She stops and puts a hand on her chest as if she's trying to stop her heart from exploding.

"Holy shit, Debbie! It's Jordan and her dad!"

Jordan lets out a whoop and starts running uphill toward us. At the same time, Unicorn Girl runs downhill. The two collide in a flurry of kisses and hugs. They haven't seen one another in five years, but their affection seems unabated.

As they embrace, Kendal starts limping up the hill, his eyes on me. He's leaning heavily on a cane and his hair has gone completely white. Nonetheless, his smile looks like the real Kendal's, my Kendal. The one I lost back in Atomic Mean Time. Or maybe the second one I lost in Atomic Shadow Time.

Either way, I suspect that life in the multiverse is about to get complicated.

ACKNOWLEDGEMENTS

When I started writing *The Sisters Sputnik*, I never expected to find myself living in a time that looked like one of the dystopian worlds I was in the process of building. But as Sputnik Chick says, there are no coincidences. The world has changed, and my story kept changing along with it.

I've never felt so grateful to have loving family, close friends and strong partners. Thanks to everyone who read early drafts, especially Maria Meindl and Hannah Brown. Grazie mille to my Italian language experts Lynn Sproatt and Guingo Sylwan. And a big thanks to readers of *Sputnik's Children* who reached out to encourage me to keep the Sputnik Chickian universe going.

To my agents, Carolyn Swayze and Kris Rothstein — I am cosmically grateful to both of you for your faith in me. To my publisher and editors, Jack David, Jen Hale, Samantha Chin, Jen Knoch and Crissy Calhoun, art director Jessica Albert, designer Andrew Presutto, marketing manager Alex Dunn, publicist Emily Varsava and the crack team at ECW Press, I'm jazzed to be going into orbit with you again. Special thanks to Vanessa Edding, social media wonder woman and World Wide Webslinger.

My thanks, too, to the Canada Council for the Arts, the Toronto Arts Council and my Ontario Arts Council Recommenders for support that provided the time I needed to imagine, write, reimagine, rewrite, go holy shit look what just happened I have to rewrite, reimagine and repeat. I'm so glad that we're not living in Cozy World, and that these organizations are committed to helping creators keep creating.

Most of all, my thanks to my husband and co-creator, Ron Edding, who doesn't mind being married to a weirdo story-teller. Ti amo.

This book is also available as a Global Certified Accessible™ (GCA) ebook. ECW Press's ebooks are screen reader friendly and are built to meet the needs of those who are unable to read standard print due to blindness, low vision, dyslexia, or a physical disability.

At ECW Press, we want you to enjoy our books in whatever format you like. If you've bought a print copy just send an email to ebook@ecwpress.com and include:

- the book title
- the name of the store where you purchased it
- a screenshot or picture of your order/receipt number and your name
- your preference of file type: PDF (for desktop reading), ePub (for a phone/tablet, Kobo, or Nook), mobi (for Kindle)

A real person will respond to your email with your ebook attached. Please note this offer is only for copies bought for personal use and does not apply to school or library copies.

Thank you for supporting an independently owned Canadian publisher with your purchase!